A
DANGEROUS
EDUCATION

A DANGEROUS EDUCATION

A Novel

MEGAN CHANCE

LAKE UNION
PUBLISHING

Published by Lake Union Publishing, Seattle

www.apub.com

Amazon, the Amazon logo, and Lake Union Publishing are trademarks of Amazon.com, Inc., or its affiliates.

ISBN-13: 9781542039024 (paperback)
ISBN-13: 9781542039031 (digital)

Cover design by Adrienne Krogh

Cover image: ©plainpicture/Agnès Deschamps / plainpicture

Printed in the United States of America

For Victoria Bruno
Te amo amica mea
Dis Manibus Sacrum Victoriae

Chapter 1

Rosemary's waking thoughts of her mother were so strong that when she opened her eyes, she expected to see Dorothy Chivers smoking at the kitchen table and staring out the window at the backyard rhododendrons, muttering about how the purple ones always bloomed so late— *"Why is that?"*

Rosemary had not thought of home, or her mother, in months. Besides, her parents didn't even live in that house anymore. There were no rhodies in their backyard now.

The pale light of dawn peered in through the crack in the curtains; next to her, someone breathed slowly and deeply. She looked over her shoulder, her head pounding, to see dark curly hair poking from a tangle of blankets, and it came back to her: the Chinook Hotel and the Blossom Room with its lush carpet patterned with blooming fronds and flowers, the salesman with the crooked front tooth, too much gin.

Everything her mother would hate. That must be why she was thinking about her. It was guilt she felt, not apprehension.

But Rosemary had long since stopped feeling guilty for this behavior, if she ever really had. She tried to shrug the anxiety away, but like her mother, it was stubborn, and it remained lodged, like her mother's disdain, an uncomfortable splinter she couldn't quite get to.

What had she forgotten? An anniversary? Mother's Day? Some other special occasion? What bothered her so?

She climbed from bed as quietly as she could, picking up her clothes in the opposite order of how she'd abandoned them last night, the panty girdle and stockings, the brassiere, the dress, then the gloves and hat on the dresser and the shoes at the door, the path of their encounter laid out piece by piece.

She glanced at the bathroom. She was hot and sticky but there was no time even to bathe. Her uneasiness nagged relentlessly. As she pulled on her clothes—she should have left last night; this dress would look ridiculous on the bus home—she heard him stir in the bed behind her.

"You're not staying for breakfast?"

"I have to get back."

"I thought they fired you."

"They didn't renew my contract for next year. That's different. There are still three days left." Three days of sideways looks and smug expressions. Three more days of pretending the gossip hadn't caught up with her. Three days of teaching unengaged students how to finish seams in the increasing late-spring heat. She'd thought the principal would at least wait until the school year ended to let her go, but it wasn't a surprise. Everything had been pressing so close lately; it was a small town, and she'd been here too long. What had Gerald said? *You've been seen in compromising situations. Very inappropriate for a teacher of young and impressionable minds.*

Well, she was constitutionally unable to do what she was told. Which must be why she was thinking about her mother.

"So don't show up. They can get along without you. Stay here with me." The fumble of a cigarette package, the strike of a match. "We'll set the world on fire. Or this room, anyway."

She shook her head. "I have to go. I have to call my mom."

He paused; she heard his surprise when he said, "I thought you hated your mom."

She slipped into her heels and wondered just when she had revealed that nasty little secret. She must have been even drunker than she'd thought last night. She went to the door. "I do."

The bus ride home was as uncomfortable as she'd imagined; who knew so many people rode the bus around sunrise? The moment she was inside her own door and had dumped her purse on the ugly blue floral couch that had come with the house—everything furnished, the only things that were hers were the guitar and the pile of records and the books—she saw the calendar on the wall, yesterday's date circled, and remembered with a groan what she'd forgotten. Mom's birthday. *Yesterday.* Rosemary sighed. One more thing she wouldn't be forgiven for.

For a moment she considered not calling. After the recriminations, it would only be another exchange of uncomfortable silences and pauses where no one could think of anything to say because there were so many topics that could not be spoken about. Then Mom would ask about her job, and Rosemary would have to decide whether to lie or tell the truth and either way it was just so complicated . . . Rosemary tapped the beige receiver. *Call. Don't call.*

She lit a cigarette and glanced at her watch. If she called now, she could use the excuse of having to go to work to get off the phone quickly. She dialed before she could think better of it. They would be awake. Dad woke with the sun, still on his professor schedule, even though he'd been retired for two years. The phone rang and rang. *Come on,* Rosemary thought impatiently. *Let's get this over with.* Though it was possible her parents might die of shock when they heard her voice. She couldn't remember the last time she'd called. Usually they phoned her, and she did her best to end the conversation in short order.

It rang.

Come on. Answer.

Rosemary looked again at her watch. She began counting the rings. Fifteen, sixteen . . . twenty . . .

Still ringing.

Where the hell would they be at six in the morning?

Her anxiety pinched.

She let it ring a few more times and hung up. Maybe they hadn't heard it. Mom was probably in the bathroom. Or out in the yard. But both of them? *At six a.m.?*

Rosemary put out her cigarette and went to take a shower. Then she tried again. She let it ring twenty-five times before she hung up. She eyed the clock. It was time to leave for school. She called once more.

Again, no one picked up.

Now she knew something was wrong. There was no reason for them not to be home at six forty-five in the morning. They were retired. Dad would be fastened to the radio listening to the Army-McCarthy hearings now that continuous coverage was no longer on television. Mom worked on the civil defense committee in Seattle as a volunteer, but she wouldn't be there so early.

Rosemary went to school. At every break, she called. All morning, the phone went unanswered.

At lunch, Marilyn Johnson, the English teacher who had not so long ago been Rosemary's friend, caught her in the staff room. "I'm so very sorry, Rosemary. Our Friday-night social hour won't be the same without you."

For a moment Rosemary thought Marilyn was talking about her parents, and then she realized that of course Marilyn had heard that Rosemary would not be returning to North Yakima High School next year. She thought of the Friday-night social hour, Marilyn's cluttered living room, her famous Gourmet Foie Gras of liverwurst and cream cheese spread on crackers, and her husband's watery Manhattans. Rosemary thought of the way the other women eyed her because she was always the only single woman there, and how she hadn't been invited since the Johnsons had seen Rosemary stepping from the Commercial Hotel three weeks ago. She thought of Yakima's hills rolling and rolling, rolling right over her, boxing her in its tight little dark rooms, curtained all summer to keep out the blasting sun.

Let them find someone else to finish seams and teach how to make economic, time-saving casseroles.

Rosemary walked out of the staff room and out of the school and into the bright June sunlight. Then she bought a bus ticket for Seattle.

Chapter 2

Seattle, WA

The bungalow-style house in the Wallingford neighborhood of Seattle was dark and quiet. Not even the porch light was on, and Dad's car was nowhere to be seen when Rosemary arrived. It was nearly ten p.m., and the streetlights were lit, though night had not fallen completely; the world was still blue with twilight. The *Seattle Daily Times* was on the porch. Clearly, no one was home.

Rosemary had managed to put her anxiety to rest on the journey here. She'd had no doubt that she would arrive to find her parents in front of the television watching today's highlights of the McCarthy hearings, Dad enjoying his nightly scotch while Mom smoked her final pack of the day. They would look at her in surprise, and she would feel stupid for coming all this way, and Mom would say, *What are you doing here, Rosemary? Don't you have a job to be at in the morning?* and Rosemary would wish she were back in her drab little rental, listening to the Weavers or playing her guitar or maybe finding her way back to the Blossom Room and hoping the salesman was staying in Yakima another night.

But no, they weren't here, and that was somehow worse. Had they scheduled a vacation she didn't know about? Absurd. Her parents never took vacations.

The door was locked, which only happened when they were gone. She'd never had a key to this house; the house where she'd grown up, in the Mount Baker district, had been sold long ago, and this one didn't belong to her. Nor, fortunately, did it have the same memories. But habits didn't change; she felt along the edge of the silver mailbox fixed to the white siding and found the key lodged behind it, as she expected. She grabbed the mail while she was at it—only a few bills; wherever they'd gone, they hadn't been gone long—and the newspaper, and went inside.

The house looked the same but for the mahogany cabinet of the big twenty-one-inch Philco Golden Grid TV. The last time they'd talked was on her father's birthday, and he'd told her he was buying it just for the hearings that started in April. Like the old television, it was already piled with books and pamphlets, including Dad's well-read copy of *How to Survive an Atomic Bomb*. Mickey Spillane's latest novel was on the yellow davenport next to the folded-over newspaper TV listings. An ashtray full of cigarette butts and a half-empty cup of coffee were on the coffee table.

Rosemary frowned and wandered into the kitchen, which was pristine but for the pot of cold coffee on the stove and Mom's ridged green jadeite creamer full of milk still on the counter. The window over the sink was open, the damp, chill air barely nudging the red-checked broadcloth curtains. Rosemary closed it. They'd left in a hurry, then. The refrigerator was full. A casserole of half-eaten Johnny Marzetti covered with foil sat on the top shelf. In bewilderment, Rosemary sank onto the bench at the kitchen nook. Yesterday's newspaper was opened to the Sports section. Peeking from beneath it was a government pamphlet on how to build an outdoor bomb shelter. *For Family Protection in an Atomic Attack*. Put out by the Federal Civil Defense Administration, so probably something Mom had brought home. Rosemary pulled it toward herself—

And heard the front door open.

She sprang from the nook and hurried into the living room to see her parents coming inside, Dad helping her pale, weary-looking mother through the door. He started at the sight of Rosemary: "What the hell!" And Mom made a screech of a sound, pressed her hand to her heart, and fell back against the still-open door.

"Oh, Christ. Christ! Dorothy! Sweetheart—" Dad bustled Mom quickly onto the couch. "Are you all right?"

"I'm fine." Mom spoke breathlessly. She waved Dad away. "I'm fine. Just surprised."

Dad straightened. His hazel eyes blazed behind his thick-framed glasses. "Look what you've done!"

"I'm . . . sorry?" Rosemary said, puzzled at his anger. "Where have you been? I've been calling for hours."

"Calling?" Mom frowned. She took off her hat and set it carefully on the coffee table. "Whatever for? That's not like you."

"Your birthday." Rosemary finessed. If Mom didn't know she'd missed it, she wasn't going to confess. "But no one answered."

"Well, of course we didn't. Do you think we sit around waiting for you? We'd never go anywhere."

"I was worried when no one answered."

"*You* were worried?" Her mother rolled her eyes.

"For God's sake, Mom."

"So you just hopped on a train—or was it a bus—and hurried on home."

"Yes," Rosemary said. "Why is that so hard to believe?"

Her mother just looked at her, and Rosemary felt exactly as stupid as she had imagined she might. She was thirty-four years old; how was it that her mother could so easily make her feel like an inconsiderate kid again?

Tightly she said, "I'm sorry to be so inconvenient."

"Inconvenient." Mom made a little laugh. "Now you sound like the Rosemary I know."

"Can the two of you just stop." Dad sighed.

"Could you hand me my cigarettes, George, please?"

"You're not supposed to be smoking," he said. He turned to Rosemary. "She's not supposed to be smoking. We were at the hospital."

"The hospital?"

Mom joked weakly, "Happy birthday to me."

Mom rubbed her brown eyes. There were pouches beneath them and it dawned on Rosemary then that her mother looked more than tired. She looked pasty, even fragile, and that was something that Dorothy Chivers had never been. Her honey-colored hair, the same color as Rosemary's, was graying now, and she'd had it shortened into a cap cut, which was not becoming to her once pretty but now slightly bloated face.

"Why?" Rosemary asked. "What's wrong?"

"It's nothing," Mom said.

Rosemary looked to her father.

"Her heart is enlarged."

"I'll be fine," her mother said. "There's no need for all this fuss. I wasn't even going to tell you. You'll have plenty of other things to worry about, what with your new job."

It was all Rosemary could do not to sigh in exasperation. She'd taught at North Yakima High School for two years now. It was hardly new. In fact, it was *past*. But she wasn't about to tell her mother that. "What does that mean?" she asked her father. "What does she have to do?"

"Take care of herself," Dad said, folding his arms. "No more smoking, for one thing. No exertion."

"I hardly do any exertion now," Mom protested.

"No more volunteer work."

Mom sat up straight. "George, that's impossible. I'm needed at the FCDA. You *know* that. Geraldine is hopeless, and Stella hasn't the time."

Trust Mom to make herself sound indispensable. The group she volunteered for at the Federal Civil Defense Administration resembled a women's social club more than a civil defense committee.

Dad pressed his lips together. "I think it best. You're no help to them if you're dead."

"It's crucial work. Women have the skills we need to survive a nuclear attack. *I* have the skills—"

Rosemary laughed.

Her mother spun toward her furiously. "You don't know anything about it, young lady."

"Really, Mom? Have you suddenly become crucial to our nation's defense?"

"All women are. We're on the brink of war, which you might know if you spent one moment listening to the McCarthy hearings—"

"Yes, yes, I understand. Communism lurks in every corner."

"You are the *last* person who should be mocking this, Rosemary."

There was sudden silence.

It was there now, again. Rosemary was never so aware of the past as when she was around her parents.

Dad glanced away.

Mom said quietly, "I'm sorry, but I won't stop volunteering for the committee."

Rosemary started toward the kitchen. Had she seen beer in the refrigerator? She couldn't remember. Nor did she know if her mother was still drinking that Paul Masson Chablis. Either would be good right now.

"Rosemary will be here to help anyway, at least for a while. She has her new job to consider."

Rosemary stopped and looked over her shoulder to see her mother smiling smugly. "What are you talking about?"

"The job at Mercer Rocks School," Mom elucidated. "They're very excited to have you for next year."

To her father, Rosemary said, "What's she talking about? Is she on medication?"

Dad threw up his hands in exasperation.

"You need a new job, don't you?" Mom asked.

That her mother knew was a surprise, and it was the last thing Rosemary wanted to admit, especially to her parents, but it had been a long day, and she couldn't help herself. "How do you know that?"

"You always need a new job," Mom said. "And honestly, Rosie, I could use your help, just for a bit. Until I have a little rest. You'll live here for now, and then when you start in September, I'll be right as rain."

There were so many shocking things in her mother's words that Rosemary had no idea which to address first. She ended up going for the most ridiculous. "You want me to stay here? To help you?"

"Just for a short while, until I have my strength back," Mom said casually, as if she had not just said something as ludicrous as *Oh, yes, the Rosenbergs were close personal friends of mine.*

Rosemary glanced at her father, whose obvious worry changed the tenor of her own. She'd been ready to dismiss her concern. Mom was so *Mom* that Rosemary had begun to think there wasn't much to worry about. But there was that new exhaustion, that paleness, and now, Mom's admission that she wanted help, that she wanted Rosemary to stay. It was not only astonishing, but frightening.

"All right," Rosemary surprised herself by saying. "For a little while, I'll stay."

"Good." Mom sagged into the davenport and closed her eyes, and again Rosemary saw that exhaustion, along with relief, and mixed with that was something else—a strange satisfaction that told Rosemary there was something more here—and she remembered uneasily what she shouldn't have forgotten: her mother had never stopped trying to mold and shape and control Rosemary's life. Though of course it was absurd and impossible, there was a part of Rosemary that wouldn't have put it past her mother to conjure a heart condition just to bring Rosemary home and put her in this position.

As for this job at Mercer Rocks School . . . she had no idea what it was or what purpose her mother had in getting it for her now, but whatever it was, Rosemary didn't trust it. Mom kept too many secrets, including too many of Rosemary's own.

The Past

Rosemary smoothed the skirt of her mustard-yellow print dress and approached the door of the blocky, towered ballroom. *Trianon* stretched in script just below the roofline. The arches of the windowed arcade lined the street; the crowd at the door of the ballroom swayed to the music leaking from the building, women rocking on their heels and men jogging their knees in time to the bombastic blare of the horns and the pounding drums of the orchestra. The very shadow of the place cast a spell of locomotion.

She loved it. If her parents found out she was here, they would go bananas—worse than that—but she'd managed to sneak out at least twice already this month, and she had no intention of stopping. Let them lock her in her room all they wanted. Mom could moan about how she was ruining her future and Dad could warn her about the crazies in the city, but Rosemary was sixteen now and there was enough gloom and doom in the world already; no jobs and the scourge of Hooverville down on the mudflats and the homeless and the unionists and communists and oh my God, it was enough to make a person want to run away to . . . to . . . well, to here, her own sweetest thing. What could be better than the Trianon on a July night during Fleet Week?

Inside was screaming, the orchestra swinging. Tonight was crazy! There were enough dress whites in the place to practically blind her. Maybe she would meet a sailor and run off with him to Manila or something. Wouldn't *that* send her mother reeling? At least it might give Mom something more to do than nag when she wasn't smoking cigarettes and staring moodily into space.

Rosemary hadn't been able to convince any of her friends to break out with her tonight, but that was fine; they were missing the fun. She leaped onto the springy maple floor, gazing up at the billowing rainbow of the ceiling fabric. Rosemary laughed at the sheer joy of movement, legs and arms pumping, spinning, shouting. Her hair came loose from its pins, strands of it slapping into her face. At the far end, a silver clamshell hood sheltered the orchestra; tropical murals decorated the walls; everything was bright and sunny. Here it was easy to forget the Depression, though to be honest it hadn't touched Rosemary all that much. Her dad's job at the University of Washington was secure.

Rosemary bounced and danced until she was dizzy. It was hot, and the sweat and breath of the dancers made the place humid and close, and when she finally paused, she saw him: tall and making a show of himself, his long arms and legs an enthusiastic blur, his dishwater-blond curls flopping as he spun. His brown shirt stuck to his back in patches of sweat, and the girl he danced with was bent nearly in half laughing at him, and he grinned right back as if he knew how ridiculous he looked and didn't care, and people around him backed up to avoid getting tagged by his flailing limbs, but in a good-humored way, no one wanting to spoil his fun.

Rosemary danced her way toward him—she didn't know really why she was doing it, except she wanted to get a good look at his face—and then she was right next to him and she, too, was trying to avoid his wild spinning.

Then—she never knew whether it had been deliberate or accidental—his arm caught her back, and the whomp of it sent her flying.

She reached instinctively for the girl next to her, missed, and went sprawling, and he was there instantly, helping her up, apologizing in a deep voice, "Miss, I'm sorry. I'm so sorry. Are you all right? Please tell me you're all right." His hand on her bare arm was moist with sweat, and his curls, too, were wet with it where they fell over his forehead. His face was angular, high-cheekboned. His previously grinning mouth was serious now.

She may have fallen in love with him at that moment. It was a possibility.

"I'm fine," she told him, brushing herself off. A streak of dirt marred the deep yellow of her skirt.

"You're not hurt?"

"I don't think so."

"I dance like a maniac."

"Yes, you do."

"I never mean to. It's just"—a shrug—"the music . . . I get carried away."

"Someone's going to end up in the hospital."

"Well, I'm glad it's not you. It isn't, is it? You mean it—you're not hurt?"

He was so intent that Rosemary laughed. "I'm really not hurt."

The music went on around them. Beyond that she was aware of nothing but his face, his light brown eyes staring into hers. His hand was still around her arm. "Hey," he said, as if a brilliant idea had just occurred to him. "You want to get a lemonade?"

Rosemary said, "I can't think of anything I'd like better."

∼

His name was David Tapper, and he was eighteen, and his father was a custodian at the university.

"My dad works there too. I wonder if they know each other?"

"What's your dad do?"

"He's a professor."

David shrugged. "Maybe. It's a big place. I do odd jobs there when I can get them. Lately I've been building stuff for plays. My dad got me the job."

They stood at one of the windows of the arcade, drinking lemonade and looking down on the street, the many-globed streetlamps making shadows of the stretching electric and telephone wires. A warm night, and beautiful, and he stood close enough that she could feel the damp heat of him against her shoulder, and she did not move away. The girl he'd been dancing with was no one he knew; he was here with one of his friends, whom he'd lost in the crowd.

"I've been working for the Federal Theatre Project—well, sort of," he said.

"What's that?"

"Part of the WPA."

The Works Progress Administration. She'd heard of it because her parents had talked of it, though she couldn't have said exactly what it was, except that it was one of the president's plans. "Roosevelt." She made a face.

"You don't like Roosevelt?" David's expression stiffened.

Quickly Rosemary said, "I don't know. My parents don't. But I guess . . . I never thought about it."

"He's changing everything for the better," he said earnestly. "Like the Federal Theatre Project. The government is paying actors and playwrights to work, and the Jameses—they run the Seattle Repertory Playhouse—they're putting on plays about real problems. They've got an entire Negro unit. They're not just talking about changing the world; they're doing it."

"That's what Roosevelt wants?" Rosemary was confused.

"Like I said, it's part of the WPA. But it doesn't go far enough. If you ask me, we should be in Spain right now. All these sailors dancing down there; that's where they should be."

Rosemary frowned. "Why Spain?"

"Don't you know what's happening in the world? Don't you know about Franco or what's going on in Europe?"

Rosemary felt embarrassingly stupid, when she was not that at all—God knew her mother was always saying, *"You've got such a fine mind, Rosemary, I wish you would use it."* She felt as if she had been locked in a tower, and here was this boy with a key, and she was suddenly desperate for him to use it. "I know about communists, and how they're trying to take over the world."

"Trying to *change* the world," he told her. "Trying to make it better. The old ways don't work anymore, Rosemary. Look around you—all this poverty and homelessness, the rich taking advantage of the poor—we need something different."

"You're . . . a communist?"

He straightened, lifting his chin. "A socialist. I'm a proud member of the Young People's Socialist League."

Dad would kill her. "Oh."

He eyed her equally carefully. "Does that bother you?"

"No. I mean . . . my dad doesn't think we should be supporting men who are too lazy to support themselves."

"What do you think?"

Such an intense stare. Rosemary felt as if what she said next mattered greatly to him, yet she had no opinion but those she'd heard her parents voice, and the two of them were of a piece, and she knew instinctively that it was not what David Tapper wanted her to say.

"I don't know what I think," she said quietly, hoping it was right. "I don't know anything about the world, really. Maybe you could tell me?"

Chapter 3

"At Mercer Rocks we keep a low profile and expect the same from our teachers. Our patrons trust us to do so." Stella Bullard, the principal of Mercer Rocks School, peered at Rosemary through blue-framed cat-eye glasses. "Beyond teaching duties, you'll be one of two housemothers for the older girls in the main dormitory. Your mother said you had experience with unruly girls?"

"Unruly girls?" Rosemary asked, puzzled and annoyed at the mention of her mother and the strangeness of the question. It didn't help that she was too hot. She had walked four blocks from the bus stop for this interview. Her hands were sweating in her white gloves, and her light brown flannel suit was too warm for the summer day.

"Troubled girls," Mrs. Bullard explained unhelpfully. "This *is* Mercer Rocks School for Wayward Girls, after all."

There had been no name on the school building. No signage at all. The two-story Georgian brick school with its attached wing and separate building had been almost hidden at the end of a narrow neighborhood street on Lake Washington, surrounded by maple trees that shielded the grounds from the street on either side. But for the few cars in the drive, Rosemary would have thought the place abandoned. Maybe *"Wayward Girls"* was the reason why. This was a reform school.

Mom had said nothing of that either. She hadn't even given Rosemary the entire name of the school. Again, Rosemary had the sense of being not-so-subtly manipulated. But she fought her irritation. Until she knew what this was all about, she didn't want to throw away an opportunity. After all, there was nothing in Yakima to return to. "I've been a teacher for several years. I've never had any trouble handling unruly students."

Mrs. Bullard nodded with satisfaction. "That's what your mother said. I serve with her on the civil defense committee. She's a marvel at organization. Simply a marvel. When she recommended you, well . . . I admit I am very hopeful, Miss Chivers. Our last home-ec teacher was a bit scattered."

"What happened to her?"

"She ran off with some musician." The principal patted her graying poodle-cut hair. "She left before the school year ended. Very inconvenient, as you must imagine. Your mother's timing was impeccable when she contacted me about you. She said you were reliable."

Rosemary stifled a laugh. Her mother certainly had never thought such a thing. "I confess I don't know much about Mercer Rocks. It's a reform school?"

Mrs. Bullard tsked. "We're a bit more than that. Mercer Rocks has a long history of serving Seattle's most-favored daughters. Those who belong to rich and consequential families. We have a storied reputation for turning out women of the highest caliber. Mercer Rocks girls enter as problems, but they leave biddable again, ready to be mothers and wives. To contribute positively to society. After all, our best hope against the scourge of communism is great American women who raise great American families, don't you agree? Our goal is to make these girls the patriots our country needs. Upon graduation, their pasts are erased. They start in the world anew."

"I see," Rosemary said.

"The job is yours, Miss Chivers, if you want it. Your mother gave me your résumé—"

How did Mom get her résumé?

"—and your references are very good."

Rosemary wondered what alchemy her mother had performed. Clearly Mom badly wanted Rosemary to have this job. Which made her wonder why she should take it.

"But you should know, there is one other thing. There have been some financial difficulties. The board is dealing with them—" Mrs. Bullard cleared her throat. "I can promise you the school will stay open at least through December."

"You mean . . . this is only a job for four months?" This was not an unwelcome revelation. "Does my mother know this?"

Stella Bullard looked chagrined. "I'm afraid not. You understand, it's not for public knowledge."

This also delighted Rosemary. Something her mother didn't know. Four months and gone. No time for things to close in. A limited time in Seattle with her family. Whatever her mother's motivations, this would surely thwart them somewhat. Mom could hardly win whatever it was she intended in four months; it was reason enough to sign on.

Mrs. Bullard continued, "I hope we're open the full school year, of course. I'm confident the board will work everything out. But I hope that doesn't change your mind about taking the job."

"No, not at all. I'm happy to accept."

The principal led Rosemary into the outer office, where a young, plump woman conservatively dressed in a blue business suit, her long brown hair swirled into a neat updo, sat typing before an open window. "Irene has all the paperwork ready for you. Irene, this is our new teacher, Miss Rosemary Chivers."

The secretary smiled a hello and held out a packet of papers, which Stella handed to Rosemary.

"It's all quite standard, you'll find. The contract, the informational form, and the loyalty oath."

Rosemary stilled. "'The loyalty oath'?"

"You have no objection, I hope? It is required. The father of one of our students is on both the board and the House Un-American Activities Committee. It's just the usual. You swear that you haven't belonged to any organization advocating subversion of the government, or taught such things, nor will you, et cetera . . ."

Rosemary had not expected it, although she should have. So many schools were requiring them now, but honestly, what was one more lie?

"Where is Lois?" Mrs. Bullard asked Irene. "I'd like her to show Miss Chivers around."

"In the staff room at the curriculum meeting," the secretary told her, handing Rosemary a pen, watching as Rosemary signed her name.

Stella offered a hand and a tight but obviously relieved smile. "Welcome to Mercer Rocks, Rosemary. I know you will be a wonderful addition. Before I introduce you to the vice principal, I want to show you the texts you'll be using. The curriculum this year has been approved by our board of directors. They have gone through a very rigorous process to choose the right materials for these girls. You are not to deviate. I trust you understand? These matters are very delicate, and the board and the parents expect our teachers to be exemplary and dutiful. We do have a reputation to uphold, especially now."

She brought Rosemary to a nearby table and indicated a stack of books. A booklet on top caught Rosemary's eye. *Operation Atomic Vision.* "What's this?"

"The atomic bomb unit."

Rosemary stared at her, not understanding, or, more accurately, hoping that her understanding was wrong.

"Women are our first defense against nuclear attack," Stella said— almost the same words Rosemary's mother had used. Well, of course, Stella and Mom were both at the FCDA. "Women's domestic and maternal skills will be urgently needed to help our nation cope with disaster."

"I'm teaching teenage girls how to help our nation cope with an atomic bomb?" Rosemary asked incredulously.

"Among other things, yes."

Rosemary laughed.

Obviously it wasn't a joke. Stella Bullard stared at her as if she'd just declared treason.

"Mothers naturally have the domestic skills we will need. That's why it's so important to teach these girls the importance of marriage and family." Stella tapped her sharpened fingernail on one book, and when Rosemary saw the title, her heart sank. *Facts of Life and Love for Teenagers*, as well as *Teen Days*, along with a reprinted article from *Reader's Digest* titled "The Case for Chastity." The books were ancient and out of touch.

"These are my family-planning texts? There are newer books, and of course Kinsey's report on female sexuality—"

"You must be joking." Stella's voice flattened in shock. "You will not be teaching these girls that . . . that *publication*. Surely you weren't teaching that in Yakima?"

"Well, no." Rosemary had lobbied for it, certainly, but at least it hadn't been disastrous when the school board there denied her. Even Yakima had more current textbooks than these dinosaurs before her now. "Don't you think young people should have the most current information?"

"This is what the board has approved," Stella said firmly. "We are *not* teaching promiscuity. We are teaching that the appropriate time to learn about the marriage act is when they are married."

The same old curriculum fight. Rosemary suppressed a sigh. "Of course."

"Is this a problem?" Stella Bullard's gaze was shrewd and assessing.

Rosemary smiled. "Not at all."

~

"You didn't tell me it was a reform school," Rosemary said to her mother as she pulled off the wretched gloves, which were damp with sweat. "Was there a reason you left that out? Does Dad know you're smoking?"

She'd gone directly to the backyard, where Mom sat in one of the green metal patio chairs looking through the *Outdoor Shelters* pamphlet Rosemary had seen in the kitchen.

"Does it matter?"

"He said the doctor told you to stop smoking."

"I meant the reform school. Does it matter? You have experience with troubled girls."

Rosemary gave her mother an incredulous look. "First, I do not, and second, how would you know that?"

Her mother took another drag on the cigarette. "Because you were one."

The words yanked Rosemary's protest away. *Troubled.* Her mother's word, her mother's memory. It did not match her own, but it disconcerted her anyway. "What does 'troubled' mean, Mom? That a girl doesn't do what everyone else wants her to do?"

Mom ignored that. "I hope you took the job."

The rush of irritation. The balk. The urge to do anything but what her mother wanted. *Rosemary, quite contrary.* The old rhyme her mother used to sing to her swam into Rosemary's head, the peril of being around Mom again. She hadn't thought of that rhyme in a long time. *Rosemary, quite contrary, how does your garden grow?*

Rosemary couldn't hide her annoyance. "Why are you so anxious for me to take it?"

"Because it seems a good position for you, since you insist on continuing with this home-economics nonsense. Isn't it? The pay is excellent, and I thought it would be good for you to experience what I went through with you." Mom smiled thinly.

"That's funny," Rosemary said.

"I thought so too."

"Really, Mom, maybe tell me the truth. What do you have up your sleeve here? Is there a teacher at the school you want me to marry? Or . . . maybe . . . what? I admit I can't think of anything else."

"Rosemary, you are too old for me to be directing your life, don't you think?"

Rosemary laughed. "That's never stopped you before."

Mom stubbed out the cigarette and reached for the glass of iced tea settled in the grass beside her. "It just seems to me that you're aimless. I thought perhaps dealing with girls like yourself might give your life . . . purpose."

"I hardly think teaching wayward girls how to help our nation cope with an atomic bomb can give my life purpose."

Mom twisted in her chair to look at Rosemary fully. "Really? Stella said something about there being a civil defense unit, but . . ."

"Really. *Operation Atomic Vision* is part of a new curriculum."

Rosemary's mother clapped her hands. "Well! We recommended that schools teach the program, but this is the first I've heard about it."

"I'm so glad to hear you had a hand in this. It's bad enough that I'm stuck with ancient textbooks and old ideas about sex—"

"You can't argue with them about this, Rosemary." Mom suddenly looked alarmed. "Don't fight them."

"—*Facts of Life and Love for Teenagers*, which is ridiculous, and a reprinted article from *Reader's Digest* called 'The Case for Chastity.' I can't believe they're still using it—"

"Rosemary, you cannot get yourself fired. Not yet."

The urgency in her mother's voice stopped Rosemary. "Why?"

"You just can't." Mom turned back to her tea. "I'm certain you can manage to endure an article on chastity. It might even be good for you."

Rosemary bit back a retort and reminded herself that she was no longer sixteen and Mom's comment was meant to hurt and she was a fool for letting it, and anyway, the job was only for four months. She doubted she would even get to "family planning," as they called it, in four months, especially if she had to teach an atomic bomb unit first. But she wasn't telling her mother that. The four months was her own secret. "Not that it has anything to do with you, but for now I've promised to follow the lesson plan developed by the school's board. They were adamant about my not deviating. They have a reputation to uphold, apparently."

"It's a very well-regarded school," Mom said, calmer now.

"I've never heard of it."

"That's the point. You're not meant to. They're very discreet. The parents are politicians and diplomats. Important people. They have high hopes for the futures of these girls. They can't afford for those futures to be derailed." Her mother gave Rosemary a steady, undecipherable look. "You should not forget that."

Rosemary frowned. She could not figure out her mother's relationship with this school; that there was one was obvious, and she didn't think it was only Stella Bullard. "Are you on the board or something, Mom?"

Her mother shook her head. "No. It's just . . . remember that there are watching eyes everywhere these days, Rosie. Be careful."

The Past

A month later, David took Rosemary to her first hootenanny. The room was crowded with actors and actresses from the Seattle Repertory Playhouse, as well as backstage workers like David. A bar sold beer and whiskey, and a Negro band played a kind of music Rosemary had never heard before, but which set her feet tapping. People mixed and danced with a fluidity that was both exciting and disconcerting. Rosemary had never seen a Negro man and a white woman dance together before. She was shocked, but no one else seemed to mind or even notice.

"They don't seem worried," she whispered to David.

"About what?"

"The police."

He followed her gaze to the couple spinning across the floor. "That's Jim and Beth. Why would they be worried about the police?"

"Well . . . you know."

David gave her a half smile. "Those things don't matter here, Rosemary. That's what this party's for. Raising money for the plays and the cause."

She leaned to kiss him. "It's the first time in months I've felt—I don't know . . . happy, I guess. Everything here is so new and different."

"Because it's how the world should be." He cupped his hand at the back of her neck and drew her closer, and then his tongue was in her mouth and she tasted the beer he'd drunk and the popcorn they'd eaten a little while ago, and the music jangled and jammed in her head, all these strange chord progressions and times that caught her up, and she lost herself the way she always did with him.

Someone whistled as they passed. She drew away with an embarrassed laugh—oh, that look in David's eyes; it burrowed inside her, something wild and blossoming.

"I love you, Rosie," he said.

"I love you." They'd said it dozens of times already, but each time it felt new. Everything had happened so quickly, yet she knew it was as true for him as for her. She was bursting when she was with David. At home, nothing seemed enough. She was so restless all the time. Life was racing by without her; she couldn't sleep or stay still.

But when she was with David, she felt alive. All these new ideas, so many possibilities. The world was so much bigger with him. She could no longer stand the thought of living the life her parents had mapped out for her. More school. College . . .

"Come on." He grabbed her hand, pulling her to her feet so quickly her beer sloshed over her fingers.

"Where are we going?"

He pulled her out back into the warm summer night air. The sounds of the street, shouting, wagon wheels, a car horn now and again, horses, all familiar and comforting. It smelled of nearby trash cans and the beer on her fingers and that heat-evaporating summer-night smell and cigarette smoke from inside the hall. The music from the band drifted out—jazz and blues, David had called it. She didn't know if she loved it, but she could not stop leaning to hear it. It never went precisely where she thought it would go; it had no melody she could follow, and yet the melody was there the moment it arrived, and you could say well, yes of course, that's where it was going all the time. Unexpected yet strangely inevitable.

"Look at that sky," he said.

There was a piece of it visible between the buildings and the trees, but it was dark gray and hazy from the streetlamps. The moon hadn't risen, nor were there many stars.

"This is just a tiny bit of it. Just like Seattle is a tiny bit of the world. You're looking at a corner—not even a corner, Rosie. You're looking at a dot of sky. If I stay here, that's all it'll ever be. Just a dot. Just this same bit of sky, just these same stars. I can't stay here forever. I'm going where what I do matters. Spain, as soon as I can, and then wherever the world needs me." He squeezed her hand. "Come with me."

"David—"

"I mean it. We could change the world together. You and me. I love you, Rosemary. We belong together. As soon as I have enough money for Spain, we'll go. We'll fight Franco together."

"Do they allow women revolutionaries in Spain?"

"They're not even allowing me," he said with a grin. "At least not legally. But I know how to do it. I'll take care of it."

"Yes! Let's do it. Let's go now." She turned to go.

He pulled her back with a chuckle. "Did you not hear me say I need to make enough money first? We need time to make plans anyway. And there are things we can do here in the meantime. The newspaper workers' strike will need protesters. I might join them."

In the darkness, she felt the change in him, the sudden heat, an intensity that nearly overwhelmed her. "Then I'll join too."

~

When she snuck back into the house that night—very late—she stared at the ceiling and thought about the sky outside the Polish hall, David's words about what a small part it was. She missed him already. She imagined the feel of his mouth on hers and the music that spoke to her of other worlds, that seemed to embody everything she and David dreamed about. It was easy to believe in those dreams at night, when that music filled her ears, when it was all around her. When she heard that music, she believed everything they spoke of was possible.

But in the daytime, stuck at school, buffeted by her parents' wishes, by her mother's desires, it was harder to keep hold of them. Now, in her own bed, she wondered if she could be the person David thought her, if she had the courage to just leave, to join him. She stared at her childhood awards pinned to the walls, which seemed not to be her own, but to simply mirror her parents' expectations: Six "Best" science-fair ribbons. Three second places. *"You take after your father, Miss Chivers."*

It all seemed as small as that tiny piece of sky. How could that girl join a revolution? How could the girl who'd built a worm farm and evaluated frosty crystal growth and made vegetable dyes fight against Franco and join the Young People's Socialist League?

She closed her eyes tight. The songs were the key. If she could only hold those songs in her head, if her fingers could only map them out on the strings. If she could play them at will, she knew she would never lose her courage. She would never lose the person she was with David, the person she wanted to be. By the time dawn showed pink and blue through her window, she could stay in bed no longer. She got up, pulled her guitar from its case, and ran her fingers over the strings, trying to imitate the sounds. She could not come close; she could not figure out the notes or the way the man had somehow changed them. She needed to hear it again. Were there records of that kind of music? What had David called it? Jazz? Blues?

In frustration, she ended up playing something she knew; a song she'd heard only a few days before, backstage at the Playhouse theater. One of the white actors, Jonny Marsh, had been singing a song to the tune of the "Battle Hymn of the Republic," but with words she'd never heard before.

She played it quietly now. "Solidarity Forever," singing about the inspiration of the union and the workers' power.

"Rosemary?" Mom's voice, sharp. "Rosemary? What are you playing?"

Rosemary flattened her palm over the strings to silence them. "Nothing, Mom. Just a song."

The door cracked open. Mom peeked inside. Her hair was still in curlers, her quilted robe gathered tightly about her. "Where did you learn that?"

"Learn what?"

"You were singing about the union."

"I was not. I was singing about the grapes of wrath."

Her mother's brown eyes, so like Rosemary's, narrowed. "I heard you."

Rosemary held her mother's gaze. She strummed, a hard chord. Deliberately, she sang, "We are trampling out the vintage where the grapes of wrath are stored."

"You smell like cigarette smoke and beer."

"It's your cigarettes you're smelling," Rosemary countered.

"Give me that." Her mother held out her hand. "Give me the guitar."

Rosemary clenched the instrument tighter. "Why?"

"Don't sass me, Rosemary. Give it to me. If you're going to play communist songs—"

"I told you, I was playing 'Battle Hymn of the Republic.'"

"Solidarity forever. Solidarity forever. Solidarity forever. For the union makes us strong." Mom sang low and soft. The words coming from her mouth were weirdly shocking.

"The world is changing, Mom. You can't just pretend it's not happening."

Her mother crossed her arms. The look on her face—what was that look? Assessing, thoughtful. "Oh, Rosemary, quite contrary."

"Don't say that. I hate that."

"Who taught you that song? Some boy?"

Rosemary tried to push the thought of David away. "I don't know any boys. I never go anywhere. I never do anything."

Another slow, thoughtful look. Very quietly, Mom said, "You be careful. You'll do things for boys that you never thought you'd do. That you don't mean. That aren't you."

Rosemary only glared back.

Mom sighed. "You know what, Rosie? Play me a song."

It was a trick, Rosemary knew it. She regarded her mother sullenly. "What song?"

"That one you learned in church. The one you used to play all the time."

Rosemary frowned. "'Jesus Loves the Little Children'?"

"That's the one."

"Why?"

"I want to see if you remember it."

"Of course I remember it."

"Show me. I don't want you to forget who you are or what you want."

"What I want?"

"College. A life that you choose for yourself. Not one a boy chooses for you. A boy who teaches you a song like 'Solidarity Forever' will take all that away. Communists will take that all away. That's what they're trying to do, you know. Make everyone the same. Everything you've worked so hard for—"

"Everything *you've* worked so hard for, you mean."

"You're meant for so much more, Rosie, but they'll make you just like them. They don't even believe in Jesus. They don't believe in anything—"

Rosemary cut her off with a strong, loud strum, the first chord in "Jesus Loves the Little Children." Oh, yes, here was the lesson; she should have known.

Mom went rigid.

Rosemary sang, "Jesus loves the little children, all the children of the world. Let them stand and let them fight. Change the world and make it right. Jesus is a great big lie—"

The slap was so quick and hard she didn't see it coming. Rosemary's head jerked with her mother's force; she saw stars. Mom seized the guitar from Rosemary's surprised hands and threw it with all her might across the room. There was a twang of strings, a crack as the instrument crashed against Rosemary's sturdy walnut desk.

Rosemary's hand went to her blistering cheek, her eyes blurring with tears. She stared in horror at the guitar, the neck broken at a sickening angle, wood splintered, strings looped loosely from the tuning pegs.

Mom slammed the bedroom door shut. Rosemary heard the turn of the key in the lock. Then her mother's furious stomping down the stairs.

Rosemary didn't wait. She packed a few things, then slipped out the window and jumped to the first-story roof over the porch and to the ground, spraining her ankle, but not badly enough that she couldn't walk the few blocks to the nearby park, where she waited for the trolley to start its morning run.

Chapter 4

Seattle, WA—September 1954

Rosemary settled the twinset into the suitcase and closed it and then glanced around her bedroom. Over the last weeks, she'd already moved everything else to Mercer Rocks, toured the school, and met most of the administrative staff. Tomorrow would begin this new adventure, and it was about time. In the three months she'd been here with her parents, Rosemary had felt her mother's eyes on her constantly. That Mom wanted her away at Mercer Rocks was so obvious Rosemary thought more than once about saying, "I've changed my mind. I'm not going to work there," simply to see what her mother would do.

But there was no point to it but contrariness, and she felt Mom half expected that too, and frankly Rosemary was more than ready to be gone. Her mother seemed fine. Tired, but fine. Still smoking, still cooking dinner every night, still picking at Rosemary every moment she could. Mom no longer needed her help—if she ever had.

Rosemary went into the living room, where her parents sat waiting. Dad was driving her to the school. Mom sat smoking on the davenport, idly glancing through the newspaper. The smell of simmering stew filled the house, though the early evening was warm, hot even. "It's fall," Mom had announced earlier when Rosemary wondered if beef stew was too heavy for the weather. Her mother liked her routines.

Well, Rosemary wasn't going to be here to eat it. Dinner was being served for the teaching staff tonight. It was her first opportunity to meet them.

Dad rose. "Ready to go?"

Rosemary nodded as Mom set aside the newspaper and balanced her cigarette on the ashtray. Her expression was tight and anxious. "I can't believe the day is here already."

"As you said, it's fall," Rosemary said brightly.

"Yes, but . . ." Mom threw a troubled glance at Dad. "Rosemary, there's something I've been meaning to say."

"I really don't need any advice, Mom," Rosemary assured her. "I've been a teacher for ten years now."

Again, Mom seemed oddly nervous. "It's not that . . ."

"You've given me a hundred warnings. I'll be on my best behavior, I promise."

"She's going to be late if we don't get going," Dad said.

Mom took a deep breath. A short, definitive nod. "Yes. Well, later, then. Go on. Have a good first day."

"I will," Rosemary said, relieved to be done, to be gone. She followed her father to the door. "Sundays are my day off. I'll come by then and tell you all about it."

"That would be nice." Mom picked up her cigarette again. The ash had grown long; it tumbled to the floor. She didn't seem to see it. "You do that."

~

The drive to the school was uneventful. It wasn't until they pulled into the circular drive fronting the school and her father said, "You *do* mean to come by next Sunday?" that Rosemary understood Dad also thought Mom's nervousness had been strange.

She nodded. "I'll want to see how Mom's been doing without me."

"Good. There's something on her mind. I don't know what it is, but I think she's worried about this place." He glanced up at the brick building with dormers, its arched and pillared entrance and mullioned windows. Matching buildings were on either side—a connected dormitory and the building that contained the gymnasium, stage, and four classrooms. "Kind of creepy, isn't it?"

Again, Rosemary felt the school's separateness, the border of maples that screened it from the neighborhood, the lack of signs, but now, in the evening, it was more than just detachment. Her father was right: There was a gray and heavy air to it. The windows reflected the silhouettes of the trees sightlessly back; the stillness of the place felt like abandonment. Ferns grew against the brick, ivy twined up one side. It looked as if it had been here for a hundred years or more.

"You going to be all right here, Rosie?" he asked.

"It's just an old building, Dad." She opened the car door and stepped out, then reached for her suitcase in the back seat. "I'll be fine. Tell Mom that too. I'll see you both on Sunday." She shut the door with her hip. Her father waited until she went up the steps to the doors. The only sound she heard as she went inside was the engine of the Buick as her father drove away.

It was an old building, yes, and it smelled old, of mildew and damp, chalk dust and sweat, and the thousands of school lunches that had crept into its corners and crannies to produce that definitive funk that Rosemary associated with every school in which she'd ever taught. The freshly mopped, scuffed wooden floors and mullioned windows belonged to the previous century, and the ceilings were high. But it was so strangely quiet that Rosemary thought she must have the date of the staff dinner wrong. It should not be so quiet. What was worse was that the quiet was not *still*. It pressed, it tugged, it was not the least bit restful. The air here gripped the remnants of adolescent rage in a way she didn't remember of any other school.

Or maybe it was only that her mother's anxiety had affected her. Rosemary tried to shrug it off as she went down the hall to the stairs, but her heels clacked and echoed eerily, and that restiveness did not abate as she climbed to the second-floor dormitories for the older girls. The younger girls would be in the attached annex building.

There were twenty-three double dormitory rooms and four bigger ones, and due to the lack of students this year (Because there were rumors the school was closing in four months? Because there were fewer "wayward" girls? Rosemary didn't know, and Stella Bullard had not said), each of the twenty older girls enrolled would have their own room, furnished with one plain metal bed, a dresser, desk, and chair. There were no curtains, only dingy roller blinds, and every door had an outside lock so the girls could be confined.

The second floor hadn't escaped the unrest of the first. The hall light did not quite reach the corners and painted the high ceiling in smoky gloom. The windows were old and wavy with reflections.

The rooms for the housemothers—Rosemary and the housekeeper, Mrs. Sackett, whose job it was to keep the dorms running smoothly— were in the attic, as well as the bathroom they shared, with a claw-footed bathtub and a feeble shower. Rosemary's own room was small, a bed, dresser, and narrow closet. There was also a desk with a chair, a bookcase, and a lamp. She'd arranged everything on previous visits: her guitar leaned in its case against the wall, the portable record player on top of the bookcase, her records and her books neatly shelved. A vase of yellow "Welcome!" roses were on the desk. The flowers were already fading but were somehow more fragrant in dying.

Her view was of the back: the main school grounds, the meadow, tennis courts, and some brick fireplaces near a huge willow. Beyond was the lake with its volcanic-rock formations that the school had been named for. To the right, a dilapidated boathouse posted with "Keep Out" signs was half hidden by the towering branches of a grove of white oaks. A small orchard and a greenhouse were to the left, along with the gardener's cottage. She saw the man now, treading the edge of the field with a teenage boy, both carrying buckets. As they disappeared into the oaks, Rosemary was suddenly and inexplicably swept with panic.

She was far too hot. She pulled loose her blouse and sank onto the bed, unbuttoning the waistband of her pencil skirt. Not that it helped. Her panty girdle kept her tightly gripped. She let her purse fall, one she'd borrowed from her mother's vast collection, a barely used calfskin box bag. The gold turn latch clanked gently against the floor, the sound shuddering into her nerves, triggering that familiar but intensely unsettling restlessness. She had no idea why the sight of the groundskeeper provoked it.

She grabbed cigarettes from the purse, along with a crumpled book of matches—from the Cloud Room at the Camlin Hotel downtown, which she didn't want to think about—and when the cigarette was lit she closed her eyes, inhaling gratefully.

It was only this building, she told herself, and it was probably just her imagination abetted by her mother's anxiety and Dad's worry. It was the encroaching twilight that made all this creepy, and she'd never taught at a boarding school, and this was all new. That was all. She hadn't got the date wrong. She would go down to dinner and the other teachers would be there, everyone would be friendly and she would forget all this, and tomorrow the students would arrive and everything would be fine.

~

When she went downstairs, people were indeed in the staff room, and warming trays on the counter held chicken noodle casserole and green beans. Crowded around the coffee urn were several white coffee cups. Five teachers, three women and two men, gathered at round tables hazed in cigarette smoke.

Only five? This couldn't be all of them, yet Stella Bullard had made it clear that the whole teaching staff would be here tonight. Rosemary must be a bit early. She filled a plate with casserole and green beans and grabbed coffee and then went to the first table she came upon, where a younger, striking, dark-haired woman sat with a tall balding man and another woman in her late forties. They stopped talking when Rosemary approached.

"I'm Rosemary Chivers, the new home-ec teacher and one of the housemothers in the main dorm," she announced with a smile.

The striking young woman adjusted the brightly colored paisley scarf tossed carelessly about her throat and drew on her cigarette. "Ah, you're the new girl. Fresh meat."

"Oh, be nice, Alicia," said the older woman. She fussed with her tight riot of graying pin curls as she scrutinized Rosemary. "She looks hardier than the last home-ec teacher, thank goodness. Hello, Rosemary—I may call you that, mayn't I? I'm Pearl Hoskins, English. This is Alicia Avilla, who teaches physical education and art, if you can't tell by that ridiculous scarf she's wearing, and that's Quincy Reese, who's languages."

The man rose and pulled out a chair for Rosemary. He had quite nice eyes, large and brown and heavily lashed. His curly brown hair tufted about his mostly bald head like a monk's tonsure. Obviously premature balding; Rosemary guessed him to be only a few years older than she. His three-button Brooks Brothers suit was stylishly boxy, his knitted tie the latest in men's office fashion. "I'm new here too," he told her.

Rosemary sat down, surprised to discover the plates of the other three were mostly empty; they'd already eaten. She was later than she'd realized.

Pearl Hoskins fingered the fake pearls at her throat and indicated the next table, where sat a woman with short, blindingly bright red hair and an older bearded man in tweed. "Andrew Covington is geography, and Gloria Weedman is math. She and Alicia are housemothers in the annex."

"I see. Are the others running late?"

"Others?" Alicia Avilla blew smoke in a long thin stream.

"The other teachers."

Pearl Hoskins laughed lightly. That she'd been pretty as a girl was obvious, though now that prettiness had coarsened, and brown spots mottled the skin about her temples and her hands. "We're it, I'm afraid. There are no other teachers. Matters are delicate this year."

"Because of the financial difficulties, you mean?" Rosemary asked.

Pearl exchanged a quick glance with Alicia Avilla. "Among other things."

Alicia stubbed out her cigarette onto a dirty pressed-aluminum ashtray that already held several lipstick-stained butts. "The school's reputation is fading. There are newer, more 'modern' schools now. Fewer students, fewer teachers."

"I wondered. When will I see the student records? I expected them by now." Rosemary picked at the casserole.

"I did too," Quincy said. "I've been asking. It's been hard to prepare without them."

Another glance between Pearl and Alicia.

"What?" Rosemary asked.

"You'll never see those records," Alicia said. "None of us do."

"Why not?"

"Because it isn't supposed to matter." Alicia shrugged. "The school is supposed to be very private. Nothing leaks from Mercer Rocks. That's why the girls are brought here. Whatever they've done is locked away, never to be seen again."

Rosemary could not tell what she heard in Alicia's voice. Resentment? Frustration? Relief?

"Their futures are assured. You understand, it would not do for a teacher to have information to . . . well, to hold over them," Pearl added.

Rosemary remembered what Stella Bullard had said about the pasts of the girls being erased, about starting in the world anew. Her mother's words: *They can't afford for those futures to be derailed. You should not forget that.*

Again, Rosemary felt that nagging, troubling sense that there was something else here, something her mother was not saying. She would have plenty of questions for next Sunday.

Alicia took a pack of cigarettes from her satchel-like purse. "Anyway, it's not as if we're trying to psychoanalyze them. We don't need that information to turn them into good little girls, and that's all anyone cares about."

Pearl sighed. "This year especially, given the school's troubles."

"Do they even use their real names?" Quincy asked.

Alicia snorted again as she lit another cigarette. "One can never be sure."

A memory raced back, quick and unexpectedly stunning. *You'll be Mary here. No one uses their real names.*

"She's joking," Pearl admonished. "Of course they use their real names."

"I understood they were problems for their parents, but have they broken laws?" Rosemary asked.

"I assume they haven't murdered anyone, or they'd be in jail," Quincy said.

Alicia laughed wryly. "With parents like theirs? I wouldn't assume that. They have *connections*. Jean Karlstad's father is on the House Un-American Activities Committee. He's too busy looking for communists and deviants to discipline his daughter, but you can bet he'll be making sure we do. The 'molding of young minds,' and all that. They're always watching."

Alicia was not exaggerating, Rosemary knew. Six years ago, Washington State's answer to un-American activities, the Canwell Committee, had rousted "communist" professors at the University

A Dangerous Education

of Washington, and—much to Rosemary's horror—had ruined the
Seattle Repertory Playhouse leaders who'd run the Negro unit of the
FTP so long ago. That committee was gone now, but the federal House
Un-American Activities Committee had long arms and paid infor-
mants, and had visited Seattle several times already to hold hearings.
Their last visit had been only two months ago. She'd stayed well out of
their way and meant to continue. Just knowing a student's father was
on HUAC made her nervous.

Alicia took yet another cigarette from the pack and lit it. "These
aren't innocent little girls. If you want my advice, you won't forget that.
They pick a favorite teacher as their victim every year—"

Car brakes screeched. Through the windows they all saw the
Cadillac—so shiny it nearly blinded—fishtail into the drive. Even
before it jerked to a stop, the back door swung open, and a girl leaped
out. Her straight dark hair swung around her face at the force of her
motion as she slammed the car door shut; her full, dark red corduroy
skirt flared.

Alicia swore beneath her breath.

The girl turned sharply on her heel and was halfway to the school
entrance before the man driving the car jumped out, shouting. He
grabbed her arm. The girl yanked away and reached for her hat—a
calot that matched her skirt—keeping her hand on it while she turned
to yell at the man.

The two of them stood in the drive shouting at one another.

"Oh, for goodness' sake, where is Lois?" Just as Pearl asked, Lois
Vance, the vice principal, stepped out, tall, thin, and imperious, and
the man and the girl, who wore one of the most mutinous expressions
Rosemary had ever seen, stopped shouting and turned to look at Lois.

Alicia said, "Well, Rosemary, I do hope you're ready. That's one of
your girls. Maisie Neal. Looks like you won't be alone in the dormitory
tonight after all."

Chapter 5

The foreboding Rosemary had felt earlier in the evening rushed back. She heard the flurried murmurs echoing in the hallway, the clatter of heels. The gunning of the engine and the spinning squeal of tires as the Cadillac sped away made her jump.

Two cream-colored suitcases with tan straps sat abandoned in the drive. The school custodian, Tom Gear—a vibrant dark-haired Duwamish native in his fifties—rushed out to retrieve them.

"Maisie looks to be in a good mood already," Alicia observed through another plume of smoke.

Rosemary turned to the art teacher. "You sound as if you don't like her."

"Maisie is a bitch," Alicia said. At Pearl's *Ssshhh*, Alicia shrugged. "What? It's true."

"She's a senior, and she knows every trick," Pearl warned. "She can be very charming. That's what you have to watch out for."

Alicia stubbed out her cigarette almost viciously. "Don't believe anything she tells you."

~

Though there was only one girl there, her presence loomed disproportionately in the empty building, and the bergamot and lavender of Jean Naté perfume added a new layer to the scents of floor wax and perpetually shaded musty corners and the drifting aromas of dinner.

All the room doors on the second floor were open in anticipation of their tenants tomorrow. The building was L-shaped, with the room for the hall guard and its locked closet for contraband near the main stairs and another set of stairs at the very end of the L, also with a locked door to prevent girls from sneaking out, though Lois Vance said that they always managed it anyway.

The hall guard's light was on, as was that of the floor's only bathroom—four toilet stalls, four sinks, three showers, and single bathtub. But Cheryl Fields, the security guard hired by the school, was nowhere to be seen, and neither was Maisie Neal.

"Not those! Please! My uncle gave them to me!" The voice, it had to be Maisie's voice, came from around the turn. There, at the end of the L, a light blazed from the last room on the floor, the one directly across from the set of locked stairs.

"You know the rules, miss. You shouldn't have brought it." Cheryl Fields's deeper voice rumbled.

Rosemary followed the voices. Her gaze swept past Cheryl, tall and husky, her blond hair braided tightly about her head, to the girl who watched the security guard rifle though one of those open cream-and-tan suitcases on the bed.

Maisie Neal was pretty, tall and slim, with brown eyes and clear, faintly tanned skin, high cheekbones, and a challenging expression that she turned quickly to Rosemary.

"Who are you?" Maisie demanded as if no one had ever refused her anything.

"I'm your new teacher and housemother. Miss Chivers."

"You're the housemother for this dorm?"

Rosemary nodded.

"*Miss?* Are you engaged?"

The only surprise in Maisie's question was that she asked it instead of waiting for Rosemary to explain why she wasn't married. It was not a safe question to ask aloud these days. "No."

"Are you a lesbian?"

"Watch your tongue." Cheryl Fields pulled from the suitcase a cigarette holder–makeup case of gold and mother-of-pearl, dangling it from its chain to admire before she dumped it into a pile containing a cream-colored cashmere sweater, a bottle of Jean Naté, black eyeliner, gold hoop earrings, and a pair of high-heeled sandals with a bracelet strap that were against school regulations.

"Why would you ask such a thing?" Rosemary asked.

Maisie folded her arms over her chest. "You're too pretty to be single, as old as you are. You must have a reason. Are you?"

"I don't think it's any of your business."

"So you *are* a lesbian."

This was dangerous. It was too familiar an accusation, if always before a tacit one, and in these times it was an out-and-out threat. Any aberrant behavior could bring the attention of McCarthy acolytes or witnesses for the House Un-American Activities Committee. Homosexuality especially imperiled national security. It left one open to blackmail and was a first step toward communism. Being unmarried was suspicious enough, and it wasn't as if the rest of Rosemary's life— not to mention her past—could stand up to scrutiny either.

Maisie went on, "You know I'll have to tell Mrs. Bullard what I think. I wouldn't get too comfortable here if I were you."

"Have I done something to offend you, Miss Neal?"

"Everything about this school offends me, Miss Chivers. That I'm here offends me. She"—a nod toward Mrs. Fields—"offends me. There's nothing in the cigarette case, Fields, and my mother sent it from somewhere in Europe, so if you please—"

"It'll be in the safe with all the other things." Cheryl put all she'd collected into a canvas bag. "You know the rules, Miss Neal. You'll get it back at the break to take home, where it belongs. You're allowed uniforms and underwear and shoes. That's all. The rest is provided." As Cheryl spoke, she dropped a bar of lavender-scented soap into the bag.

"No! That's from *France*! And I *hate* the soap here! It ruins my skin!"

"You know how to fix that," Cheryl said. "Learn to behave like a lady, and you can go home and use all the flower soap you want."

The guard quirked her mouth at Rosemary and left with the bag of contraband.

Maisie gave Rosemary the same mutinous look she'd worn in the driveway. "Yes? Is there something else you wanted?"

"I just wanted to introduce myself. If you need anything, Miss Neal, I'm here to help." Rosemary turned away.

"Really?"

Rosemary turned back. "Yes, of course."

"You really want to help? Or are you like everyone else here, just saying the words and then doing nothing?"

"I hope not," Rosemary told her.

Maisie Neal considered. Then: "You know I wasn't supposed to be here until tomorrow. The man who brought me here, my uncle—"

"Is that who it was? I saw you arrive. You didn't look very happy with him."

"I hate him." Maisie spoke matter-of-factly, the way she might say someone was tall or had acne. "He doesn't like me any better these days, but he's in charge of me now, so he *thinks* I have to do what he says."

"Why is he in charge of you?"

Maisie rolled her eyes. "Because my parents say so."

"Where are they?"

"God knows. Timbuktu today, the wilds of the Amazon tomorrow."

"But—"

"I don't *know*. Anyway, my uncle kidnapped me and brought me here—did they tell you that?"

"Kidnapped you?"

"I was having a perfectly lovely time on the beach in Oregon. My friend has a house there, and I sat in the sun and listened to the waves and it was perfect, and then Uncle Ed ruined it."

"I see." Rosemary regarded her uncertainly.

"I don't think you do." Maisie's brown eyes narrowed. "He came and he forced me to come back to school. He took me against my will."

Rosemary felt an instant sympathy. How well she remembered being this age. All that powerlessness, not yet an adult but no longer a child, so much frustration—

"She's exaggerating, of course," Mrs. Sackett, this dorm's other housemother, said from behind Rosemary. Mrs. Sackett was short and plump and looked like the portrait of a kindly grandmother on a box of pancake mix. She had been sweet and friendly to Rosemary, but her expression was unyielding as she handed the towels she carried to Maisie; the woman was more formidable than she appeared. "Here you are, Miss Neal."

Maisie stepped past Rosemary to take them. "Thank you, Mrs. Sackett."

"You shouldn't be telling tales to the new teachers. Miss Chivers'll be thinking she needs to call the police."

Maisie dropped the towels on the bed. "Maybe she should."

Mrs. Sackett shook her gray head. "They've all got their tales of woe, Miss Chivers. They'll be vying to see who has the best summer sob story before the week is out, isn't that right, Miss Neal?"

"I'm sure Jean will try to beat me again," Maisie admitted. "But she didn't get dragged from the Oregon coast and embarrassed in front of all her friends."

"We all have our crosses to bear. You should have everything you need now. We'll be back to the usual after tomorrow." To Rosemary, Mrs. Sackett said in a voice low enough to keep Maisie from hearing, "Don't let them work you, Miss Chivers." Then she walked away, and Rosemary remembered Alicia's words: *These aren't innocent little girls.*

"What did she say?" Maisie asked.

Rosemary smiled. "I think I'll let you get organized. We'll have plenty of time to get to know one another."

"Just so you know, I'm not a lesbian," Maisie said.

"I'll make a note of it," Rosemary told her. "Sleep well, Miss Neal."

∼

On her way to her room, Rosemary passed Cheryl, who was putting Maisie's things in the contraband closet. "There'll be plenty more tomorrow," she informed Rosemary brightly. "You'd be surprised what they think they can sneak in."

Rosemary tried to smile. "At least it wasn't weapons."

Cheryl laughed. "Oh, these girls don't need guns or knives or such as that. They've got weapons of a much better kind."

"What are those?"

"Their smiles, Miss Chivers," Cheryl said, turning the key in the lock. "Their smiles."

Chapter 6

Rosemary woke several times throughout the night, the lambent light of the tennis courts sneaking past the crack in the blind unfamiliar, everything strange and therefore startling. Yesterday's foreboding hadn't left her, and she couldn't pinpoint it except to say that maybe it had something to do with the challenging Maisie Neal and Alicia's words *fresh meat* . . . and Cheryl Fields's comment that the girls used smiles as their weapons.

When the day finally began, Rosemary was already tired, but the rest of the students were due to arrive, and so she roused herself and washed and dressed. A few sprays of perfume—her favorite Shalimar— for confidence as she prepared to meet them. Tables had been set up at the top of the stairs to search the students' luggage before they were assigned their rooms. Cheryl, Mrs. Sackett, and Rosemary stood ready—or at least, Rosemary thought she was ready.

They came in a rush, a whirl, a flood of sullenness, insolence, and the heavy chicken-soup stink of adolescent sweat mingled with Soir de Paris, Lily of the Valley, and Noxzema. There were no new students; all the girls had been at Mercer Rocks before, and they knew the drill. They lined up before the three tables obediently, though there was nothing obedient in their attitudes. They slouched, they popped gum, they argued as their suitcases were opened and searched. Mrs. Sackett and Cheryl had warned Rosemary of their tricks.

"Oh, that's just for my cough, Miss Chivers," one girl said as Rosemary pulled out a tin of hard candy.

Rosemary eyed her and opened the tin, which was full of lemon drops. She put it in the contraband box behind her and watched the girl's face fall. Those were the rules, though she couldn't imagine what harm it would do to let the girl keep lemon drops, and she felt like a jailer as she took away one thing after another, some trinkets obviously precious and beloved. Some, like the candy, comforting.

Others not so harmless.

Rosemary pulled a pill box loose from a tangle of socks. "What are these?"

"My medication," the girl before her said, raising her chin.

"For what?"

"A skin condition."

"I see." Those, too, went into the box. "All medicines are registered with Nurse Rita. They'll be in the infirmary if you need them."

By ten that morning, Rosemary had collected over twenty tubes of lipstick from rolled socks, toothbrush containers, carefully folded underwear, and false hairpieces coiled like little weasels in suitcase corners; six cigarette lighters; a dozen shoes that raised arguments about heel allowances; and assorted makeup. Candy and gum in volumes too great to count. Cigarettes by the hundreds. Liquor bottles. And all this from only fifteen girls. She wished just one would tell a lie she could believe—she had been such an excellent liar at their age. Someone should have taught them better.

"It's mouthwash, Miss Chivers, really!"

Rosemary pulled off the cap of a sculpted and frosted glass bottle. "Lavender mouthwash?"

Such innocent eyes. "I promise."

Rosemary dropped it into the contraband box labeled with the girl's name.

She had Lizzie Etheridge's suitcase open on the table and was emptying a curler full of Camels into the contraband box while sixteen-year-old Lizzie muttered, "Dammit," when suddenly Rosemary heard a heavy thud on the stairs, then a crack, glass breaking, what sounded like marbles clattering down the stairs, and finally a flurry of curses. Then, another thud, and *"Aaahhh!"*

Rosemary's senses sharpened almost painfully. Cheryl was at the contraband closet. Mrs. Sackett had her hands full of foil-wrapped balls of chocolate she'd discovered in another girl's suitcase.

Mrs. Sackett said, "You'd better go see."

Rosemary closed Lizzie Etheridge's suitcase and hurried to the top of the stairs.

On the landing below sprawled a girl, an open suitcase, scattered clothing—and a smashed bottle of rum. More astonishing than all that was the opened case of curlers, and the dozens of curlers still bouncing down the stairs, along with the dozens of mini liquor bottles falling from their insides.

The girl looked up through a mass of frizzy brown hair. She had a face like Audrey Hepburn, at the same time delicate and big featured. She was very pale, and her eyes were blue and unfocused. She squinted as if trying to right an upended world. "I don' know you," she slurred.

Rosemary laughed in disbelief as she went down the stairs. "You're drunk."

"No." The girl pulled herself up with clumsy dignity.

The rum pooled on the floor and soaked into the clothes around it. Shards of glass glittered everywhere. The girl swayed on her feet as Rosemary pulled her up. Rosemary wondered how much of that bottle she'd drunk before she'd fallen.

"Come on now. Let's get you to the infirmary." If there was one thing Rosemary knew how to do, it was manage drunkenness.

"The infirma—what? No!" The girl yanked away. "I'll getta demerit the firs' day!"

"Maybe you shouldn't have shown up drunk. What's your name?"

"I need to lie down," the girl said.

"I'm sure you do."

"I mean now." The girl gripped Rosemary's arm hard, leaned over, and vomited all over the landing, the scattered clothes, and Rosemary's favorite slingback pumps.

But she managed to miss herself.

"Oh, for heaven's sake." Mrs. Sackett spoke from the top of the stairs. "Sandra Wilson, what have you done this time?"

Rosemary had been in this same drunken, confused state. She knew exactly how the girl was feeling—sick to her stomach, world spinning, trying to forget some fundamental hurt, and desperate to appear in control when all she really wanted was to be somewhere else.

Sandra Wilson said, "I needa drink."

"The only drink you need is water." Rosemary hoisted Sandra up the stairs and said quietly to Mrs. Sackett, "We need to get rid of all this on the stairs."

The housekeeper nodded.

Rosemary led a heavy, limp Sandra down the hall. As they approached the bathroom, Maisie stepped out.

"Sandy!" Maisie swooped upon them.

Sandra detached herself from Rosemary, letting Maisie take her. "Thank God you're here."

"I came last night. Uncle Ed dragged me from Sarah's. You won't believe the story. My God, you stink."

"I brought some rum."

Maisie wrinkled her nose. "I'll see to her from here, Miss Chivers. Can I put her in the room across from mine?"

"If no one else has been assigned it yet, I don't see why not."

Maisie turned her attention to Sandra, and Rosemary let them go, watching them walk slowly down the hall, Maisie's arm tightly about Sandra's waist, Sandra wavering. It did not surprise her that the two girls were friends. They seemed to belong to one another. Sandra fit next to Maisie so familiarly, as if they'd walked that way a hundred times, as if Maisie had supported her, just so, many times before.

Suddenly Rosemary realized that Sandra Wilson had been the only one of the girls today who had arrived already wearing the school uniform of white blouse, pleated dark green skirt, and sweater of gold, white, and green argyle, though she was terribly disheveled. The front of the skirt had twisted to the back; the blouse was untucked. Rosemary wondered what that meant, if anything, that Sandra had chosen to follow one rule while so spectacularly shunning another.

Wayward girls, she thought. *Troubled girls.*

Or maybe like she had been, just girls who felt powerless, who wanted something they couldn't define, something other people either couldn't understand or didn't want to.

"Make sure she drinks some water!" Rosemary called and went back to the line.

The Past

It was called Common House. Most of those who lived there were University of Washington students or friends of students, those who worked for the Seattle Repertory Playhouse or on other FTP programs, or hangers-on who could contribute to rent or food. The house had a leaky roof in the winter and a sagging porch and drafty windows and doors, but it was near the university, the landlord left them alone, and it cost almost nothing when the rent was split by everyone.

The main guy was Frank. Rosemary never knew his last name, only that he and David were both members of the Young People's Socialist League. When she and David showed up at the door, he welcomed them with a hearty "Come in, come in. Join the rest of us proletariats!" He gave them a small room in the basement that could only be reached by going through a labyrinth of boxes of flyers and old furniture, and all the light bulbs down there were burned out, so they had to feel their way through the dark until they memorized the path.

They found an old mattress, and it was their own private cave, a place to escape after late nights of talking and communal meals made up of whatever anybody could scrounge, and someone always had a guitar, so they sang and talked about revolution and Spain and the horrors of capitalism and the oppression of women and Negroes until Rosemary thought she would cry at the unfairness of it all, and only huddling in David's arms at night and losing herself in him kept her despair at bay.

It had been six months since she'd run away. Six months of living here with David, and she'd learned so much in that time about what the world was really like, what it really needed, and she knew that she'd been naive and sheltered before. But now she was helping to change things at last.

There had been picketers at the *Seattle Post-Intelligencer* plant every day since the newspaper workers' strike began in August, and since they wanted to be sure there were always enough picketers to surround the building, they welcomed the students.

Today there were meetings and hearings about the strike, and so the mood among the picketers was sharper and more urgent. The day was fair, the morning's fog burned off, leaving in its wake a keen tension. Tempers flared at little things. Rosemary concentrated on the sign she carried and tried to ignore her hunger and the nicely dressed men and women going in and out of the Frederick & Nelson department store across the street.

Then someone shouted, "Red bastards!" and the words heightened the uneasiness, bruising the air. She reached for David's hand, meaning to steady him, but then someone else yelled, "Commies! Go back to Russia!" and one of the students called back, "Workers unite!" and after everyone swarmed, the protest lines broke apart in a melee, and everyone everywhere was throwing punches. Bottles became projectiles. In the confusion, Rosemary lost David.

A bottle cracked on her arm; she cried out in pain and saw the flash of police blue and broke from it all, cradling her throbbing arm as she raced across the street to the department store and huddled next to the glass display windows. She watched the fight in a haze, unable to do anything but stare as the police broke it up.

Then, finally, she saw David limping into the street. Blood ran down his face from a gash in his head. She ran to him in dismay; he pulled her tightly into him. "I'm all right. Are you?"

She nodded, though her arm hurt like crazy and she was afraid it might be broken. She was so relieved to see him she said nothing of it, just wrapped her other arm around his waist, and together they made their slow way back to the old truck that had brought them there. She dabbed at his head with the edge of her sleeve, and he only smiled lazily at her and said, "It looks worse than it is. What's wrong with your arm?"

"Someone hit me with a bottle," she told him as the truck started up, rocking everyone in the back against the wooden slats, knocking them against each other.

David bent over her arm and pulled the sleeve up to reveal a huge bruise, red around the edges, that looked like it might turn black. "Ouch."

"It hurts," she told him.

He leaned down to kiss it and then smiled up at her. "That will make it all better."

She laughed, and it was true, her arm hurt less then, and suddenly the worry and the fear of the last hour gave way to excitement, the aftermath of terror, and everyone in the back of the truck began jabbering about the riot and the thrill of it, and by the time they got back everyone was roused, the stories bubbled from them, words crashed against every corner of the room as they talked over each other. David was the center of attention, with his bleeding head and his limp and Rosemary's swelling bruise— *"They did that to a girl!"*

She saw in David's eyes the need to escape, to be alone, just the two of them, and finally she managed to slip down those stairs, negotiate the puzzle of shadows into their room, where she waited breathlessly for him, and then he was there—she heard his breath, she felt him in the darkness, his electricity fusing with hers as it always did, and then they were on the thin mattress, hot and wanting, and he was inside her and she was rising with him, pulling him deeper the way she'd learned to do, and when it was over and his soft pulsing filled her, he whispered against her ear, his warm breath against her throat, "I love you so much, Rosie. You belong to me."

"We belong to each other," she said back. "I'm not ever letting you go."

It was the spell they chanted, their talisman against the future, against fate, against whatever might come between them. They said it a hundred times, a thousand, in those months, the best months of Rosemary's life.

What never occurred to her was that something they might make together would be the thing that tore them apart, because this is what she knew, and all she knew: When she was twelve, she woke up with a terrible stomachache, and when she went to the bathroom, her underwear was red with blood. When she told her mother, Mom lifted her foot from the treadle of the sewing machine distractedly, and said, "Every woman gets that, Rosemary. It's your period. Now that you have it, you have to stay away from boys or you'll get pregnant."

Rosemary put her mother's words together in the most logical way she could: bleeding and boys meant getting pregnant. So she was very careful never to have sex with David when she was bleeding. Which was gross to think about, and she felt awful and hurt too much anyway. One must really want a baby badly to do it.

She and David had decided their future and a baby was not part of it. They were saving money, and then they were going to Spain, to fight with the Republicans. Then, when that was over, they would go wherever the world needed them. They had plans. So many, many plans.

Chapter 7

Rosemary's classroom was fully equipped for home economics, with two stoves, a refrigerator, two sinks, plenty of pots and pans and mixers and measuring cups and spoons. Windows overlooking the tennis courts opened to let out steam or smoke from the inevitable disasters. There were also sewing machines, tables for cutting fabric, irons and ironing boards, and those textbooks from the dark ages, along with sewing patterns and home hygiene and nursing manuals. Some were dusty enough that it looked as if they hadn't been touched for years, and the sewing machines all needed oiling. What kind of home-ec teacher had been here before her? One who never used a sewing machine?

Rosemary's first two classes were the younger girls, and so she was surprised to see an obviously older girl come in with them.

The girl had bright blond hair, fashionably cut in a pageboy with a side part and curled at the ends. The first three buttons of her blouse were unbuttoned, the dark green pleated skirt was rolled at the waist to shorten it, exposing a large expanse of smooth, pale thigh, and her socks had been rolled to resemble bobby socks. She wore mascara and bright red lipstick. How had those been missed in the search?

She sat at the table with a tired nonchalance.

The other girls in the class threw half-awed, half-anxious glances at her. She ignored them, leaned back in her chair, tapping her perfectly manicured nails on the tabletop, and regarded Rosemary with huge, wide-set eyes of deep brown.

Rosemary asked, "Could you be in the wrong class, miss?"

The girl glanced about, and then straightened when she realized Rosemary was speaking to her. "What?"

"Is this where you're supposed to be? Home economics, first period?"

"Oh." The girl shrugged. "Isn't it?"

"What's your name?" Rosemary asked, taking up the class list for the period.

"Jean Karlstad."

Jean Karlstad. This was the girl whose father was on the school's board, and more importantly, the House Un-American Activities Committee, with its very long, very intrusive reach and witch-hunt tactics. Not someone Rosemary wanted to rile. In fact, she'd rather have nothing to do with the girl, who was a senior and supposed to be in her fourth period.

"Miss"—Jean's gaze went to the blackboard, where Rosemary had written her name—"Chivers?"

A voice crackled over the intercom. "Good morning, girls. Please rise for the Pledge of Allegiance."

The girls shuffled to their feet and dutifully faced the flag hanging in the corner near the door, hands upon hearts, chiming monotonously, "I pledge allegiance to the flag . . . ," all of them, Rosemary included, stumbling over the new addition of *under God*, the rote pledge requiring sudden concentration, ". . . with liberty and justice for all."

They sat in a rustling of skirts and tittering, someone coughed. Rosemary caught a whiff of cigarette smoke. Lois Vance droned on over the loudspeaker with announcements. A welcome-back message, a reminder that smoking was not allowed, and anyone feeling ill should go to the infirmary instead of throwing up in the bathroom—there had been an incident that very morning. Rosemary immediately thought of Sandra. Bullying was not tolerated, and obviously some girls should refamiliarize themselves with the school handbook. And starting tomorrow, charts on the dorm bulletin board would list chore assignments. "Have a wonderful first day! We are all looking forward to our welcome-back barbecue on Friday!"

It was enough time for Rosemary to gather herself. Whoever Jean Karlstad's father was, Rosemary couldn't allow the girl to take control. It was a teacher's first and most important rule. Never let a student get away with something, or they would always try.

She turned to Jean and said, "I'm sorry, Miss Karlstad, but you're not in this class. You're in fourth period. After lunch."

The girl exhaled heavily. "Well. I don't want to go to math first thing in the morning. It's deadly boring, and I haven't the energy for it. Can't I just take home ec twice? You can teach me how to—I don't know, whip up Jell-O or something?"

"I think Mrs. Weedman is expecting you in math."

The younger girls watched excitedly, waiting for a confrontation, and Rosemary fought an overwhelming weariness.

Jean said, "I'd rather stay here if you don't mind."

"This class is for the younger girls, Miss Karlstad. I'm certain you'll be more engaged in the home-ec class for girls your own age."

"I don't know. Try me."

Jean's gaze was unblinking. The challenge was softly spoken, more lazy dismissal than a test.

Rosemary turned her attention to the other students. "Good morning, girls. I'm Miss Chivers. Welcome to home economics. On the table before you is a class syllabus. As you'll note, the most important thing we'll discuss in every segment of this class is cleanliness and hygiene, and so today, we'll begin with the most efficient way to wash dishes. Miss Karlstad, I believe you've been through this part of the course before. Would you help me demonstrate the proper steps to prepare a sink for the rinsing and stacking of plates?"

Jean's three-alarm-red lips parted in surprise. "But . . . my manicure!"

"You said you wanted to be in this class."

Jean gathered herself up with an exaggerated sigh. "I'm sorry, Miss Chivers, but I believe Mrs. Weedman expects me to conjugate numbers or something this morning."

"Then I'll see you fourth period."

Jean gave her a short nod and a quirk of a smile. "Wonderful."

~

The girls arrived for fourth period in a flurry of pleated green skirts and talk, bringing with them the smell of sun and the meadow and the pea soup they'd had for lunch. It was a class of ten, three seniors—Maisie, Sandra, and Jean—and the rest juniors, and when Maisie and Jean walked in, there was an immediate difference between them and the others, a separateness. Rosemary didn't want to call it *maturity*, but it was an attitude. Maisie wore her uniform with a confidence that screamed *If I must wear this thing, I'll at least pretend I want to.* And someone had got to Jean since this morning. The lipstick had been wiped away, and the skirt had descended an inch or two, though the shirt was still unbuttoned—or unbuttoned again—and the socks were still rolled.

The girls took their seats, Maisie and Jean together, and Jean gave Rosemary a little wave.

"I'm ready for the Jell-O, Miss Chivers," she said—a bit of impudence there, but charming. Rosemary only smiled and motioned for Jean to button her shirt.

Jean smirked but followed instructions.

Maisie plopped her notebook on the chair beside her, shooing away anyone who tried to claim the seat. Nine girls. Where was the tenth?

The bell rang. Rosemary rose to shut the door as Sandra finally slid inside. "I'm here, I'm here. I'm not late."

She wasn't drunk. At least not that Rosemary could tell. But she was just as disheveled as she'd been yesterday. The blouse half untucked, the knee socks slumped, the sweater unbuttoned.

Rosemary smiled. "Good afternoon, Miss Wilson. I trust you're feeling better today?"

Sandra turned a chilling stare. "Excuse me?"

"I asked if you were feeling better."

"Than what?"

"Than when you arrived."

Maisie choked a laugh.

Sandra didn't flinch. "I don't know what you mean. Who are you? You're new."

Either Sandra had been too drunk to remember or she was pretending not to. Rosemary indicated her name on the blackboard. "Please take a seat, Miss Wilson."

"How does she know my name?" Sandra muttered as she went to the chair Maisie had saved for her.

"I think you made an impression," Maisie told her, obviously trying not to laugh.

"What happened?" Jean asked.

That the three of them were good friends was apparent. Jean so obviously belonged to the other two that Rosemary was surprised she had not realized they must be a threesome the moment she'd seen her. Separate, they called attention to themselves; together, they commanded it, Maisie the darkest and the tallest, Jean the blondest, and Sandra the middle in coloring and height. All of them seventeen. This was the last year the school or their parents could hold them, and Rosemary wondered why they were really at Mercer Rocks. Was it the obvious— Maisie's high drama and Sandra's drunken disdain and Jean's obvious wish to capture the attention of every breathing male within a hundred yards? Or was there something more?

"Miss Chivers, are you just going to stare at us all day, or are we going to learn about Jell-O?" Jean asked.

Rosemary tore her gaze away from the trio—and from Maisie, especially, whose brown gaze bored assessingly into her—and cleared her throat. "Good afternoon. I'm Miss Chivers, and this is home economics. I'm going to read the attendance. Could you please raise your hand when I call your name?"

When that was done, the girls wriggled in their chairs and whispered to one another but for Maisie and Jean and Sandra, who folded their arms on the table and smiled at her with big innocent eyes. There was an unnerving brazenness in it. Rosemary knew that expression; she'd faced her own mother with it a hundred times, but she'd never had it turned on her so effectively. She didn't know whether to admire or dislike the turnabout, but she didn't miss the irony that her mother had already pointed out to her.

"This term we're starting with a new unit on nuclear preparedness by the Federal Civil Defense Administration and the Department of Education," Rosemary announced. "Women's involvement in home protection and saving lives is critical to the civil defense effort, and over the next few weeks we'll learn how to protect ourselves and our families in case of a nuclear attack. We'll learn about medical care, cooking in a disaster zone, building and maintaining an emergency shelter, shelter living, and surviving the new landscape—"

"'The new landscape'?" Sandra asked incredulously. "Is that a joke?"

"No," Rosemary said firmly, trying not to think of the civil defense committee's pamphlet on outdoor shelters that her mother was probably even at this minute reading.

"Do you think it's really going to happen, Miss Chivers?" asked Lizzie Etheridge, blond and ethereally pretty.

"Daddy says so. Especially if we don't get rid of all the commie spies here plotting with Soviets," said Jean without interest. "He says there are hundreds of them."

"Hundreds of spies?" Lizzie asked.

Jean nodded. "And even more communists. And if you take into account all the homosexuals and lesbians—"

"Miss Karlstad, can we return to the lesson?" Rosemary asked.

"You see how she doesn't like talking about lesbians?" Maisie said quietly but not quietly enough.

Sandra's expression lit with interest. "Why? Is she one?"

"Or maybe she's a Red," Maisie mused.

"Girls," Rosemary said. "Please."

"Have you ever been to a hootenanny?" Maisie asked the question the same way she'd asked if Rosemary was a lesbian the other night, without shyness or hesitation, and Rosemary noted the way the other girls in the room hung on her words. Maisie was obviously a leader, and this was also a question they'd already discussed between themselves. A bet, maybe.

"You can live through a nuclear attack—"

"Daddy doesn't like communists, but I think they're interesting," Jean said. "Don't you, Miss Chivers?"

"You mean you think they're sexy," Sandra teased.

Jean grinned. "Don't tell Daddy."

Rosemary tapped the blackboard loudly. "You can live through a nuclear attack without a Geiger counter or protective clothing or special training. Here's what you must know." She scrawled the words on the board:

1) KNOW THE BOMB'S TRUE DANGERS.

2) KNOW THE STEPS YOU CAN TAKE TO ESCAPE THEM.

"First, we'll talk about the bomb's true dangers."

"Decimation." Sandra dragged her finger idly across the top of the table. "Ravagement and horror. Look what happened to the Japanese."

Rosemary sighed before she could stop it. "Please, Miss Wilson."

"We decided we were God, we made the whole world crap, and we're all going to die. If the bomb doesn't get us, polio will."

"Ick, Sandy," Jean said.

Maisie grimaced. "Sandy's right. What is the point of this lesson? Can we really survive an atomic bomb?"

"Well?" Sandra met Rosemary's gaze, challenging, goading.

The other girls waited.

"I certainly hope so. Just as we should hope that the polio vaccine they're developing comes out soon, Miss Wilson. We should all hope for miracles if we can. In any case, surely these lessons can't hurt."

"Wait—what did you say?" Maisie asked.

Rosemary dropped all pretense. The day had been long and the class was spiraling out of control. These girls were older; they required a more subtle touch than the younger girls. She dropped the chalk onto the wooden tray of the blackboard and brushed its dust from her fingers. "It's the first day. Maybe we won't start with annihilation just yet."

"No, wait—you said . . . did you just say you weren't sure we would survive an attack?"

"I said I hoped we would. But actually, I don't know."

"You aren't lying to us." Sandra's expression sharpened, as if she suddenly saw one of the miracles Rosemary had suggested they hope for.

The look made Rosemary vaguely uncomfortable, but now she had their attention, and she saw the opportunity. Despite what Alicia and the others had said, Rosemary suspected these girls were less "troubled" than social misfits. Not all transgressions were equal. Now was her chance to find out if she was correct. "Why don't you tell me a little about yourselves? This is a small class, and some of you will be graduating this year—"

"If the school stays open," Jean interrupted.

"Are the rumors true, Miss Chivers?" Maisie asked. "Is the school going to close?"

"Wouldn't that be nice," Sandra said.

"Then we'd just have to go home. I'd rather be here." Lizzie Etheridge was glum.

"You would?" Jean was clearly surprised.

"Even I'd rather be home, and it's a pure misery," Maisie said.

Sandra rolled her eyes. "A misery? You get to do whatever you want, and the housekeeper throws money at you."

"Because she hopes I'll leave. You should see her face whenever Uncle Ed brings me home. I swear, every time I run away she's praying I stay gone."

Rosemary sat on the edge of her desk. A runaway. Something she'd once had in common with Maisie Neal. "Do you run away a lot?"

"Whenever I can," Maisie answered.

"Why?"

Maisie eyed her dispassionately—no, not dispassionate, though the girl tried desperately to seem so. There was anger burning in those eyes. "Because I want to be free of all this." She waved her hand at the room. But she looked away too quickly, and her anger wasn't for the school, and Rosemary understood that Maisie was not saying the true reason and also why that might be.

Sandra said, "Yes, you're so mistreated."

"At least I'm not a drunk."

Sandra's blue eyes blazed. "Shut up, Maisie."

"What are you going to do without all those little bottles of booze Mrs. Sackett threw away?" Maisie needled. "Sneak into the kitchen for the cooking sherry?"

Sandra snorted. "There's no cooking sherry in this kitchen. Everything tastes like crap, or haven't you noticed?"

"Stop it! Stop it!" Jean put her hands to her ears. "I hate it when you do this!"

"Oh, stop having kittens, you sex fiend," Sandra snapped.

Jean said, "You can be such a bitch, Sandy."

"I think that's enough." Too late, Rosemary realized, but she'd forgotten herself, drawn in, for the moment one of them.

"Mrs. Bullard'll put you in isolation for saying that word," said a dark-haired girl in the back, Barbara Trask.

"I said that's enough." Rosemary spoke sharply, more irritated with herself than with them.

"I suppose you'll send us to the office now." Maisie crossed her arms, pure sass touched with bravado.

"It's the first day of school," Rosemary said. "I should make an example of you."

Jean and Sandra watched warily.

"Fine." Maisie started to rise.

"Sit down," Rosemary ordered.

Maisie looked at her in surprise. "But—"

"I think there's no need to start with demerits so soon, and Miss Wilson already has several. Let's put today behind us, all right? But no more language like that, or I'll send you straightaway to Mrs. Bullard. That goes for everyone in this room. Understood?"

The students nodded. Even though Rosemary had started the conversation, she could not be rewarding them for behavior like this.

Not only that, but Maisie, Sandra, and Jean—the trio, as she was beginning to think of them—especially fascinated her, and that was troubling in a way Rosemary had not expected. The runaway, the drunkard, and the sex fiend. They reminded her of herself in many ways. There were always students like this, in every city, in every school, those who called to Rosemary in some inexplicable way, those who called to that deep ache that she tried to ignore because it could only cause trouble, and now she found herself wondering once again why her mother had thought sending her here would be a good idea.

Maisie

Maisie stares out her window toward the trees stretching along the lake and waits for the darkness to grow dense and fixed. She tenses when she hears Mrs. Fields's measured footsteps. Every fifteen minutes precisely. Fields doesn't check the doors unless someone is in isolation and locked in her room; she checks only for lights, for movement, for sound. Maisie has had three years at this school to learn every routine, to learn just what she can get away with. She has made this place her own. This is the first year there's been anything different.

Miss Chivers.

Miss Chivers with her wavy golden-red brown hair and large cat-like brown eyes and her wide mouth, and what Maisie likes best: a way of moving that calls attention to itself, an ease with her body and a swaying walk that reminds Maisie of Jean and gives Maisie the same hot feeling she doesn't really want to understand. Maisie can't stop looking at the new teacher.

More importantly, Maisie is good at sensing people's weaknesses, and she senses one in Miss Chivers, though she doesn't know yet what it is. There's a *wanting* in Miss Chivers. Maisie recognizes it because she feels it herself. She doesn't yet know what the teacher wants, but Maisie knows what she herself wants. The world at her feet. Someone to give it to her. So far, no one has managed it. God knows her parents can't or won't, and they're too busy traveling to even know Maisie. But in Miss Chivers, Maisie sees opportunity.

She glances at the clock on the windowsill. With the second hand's sweep comes the scratching at the door she's been waiting for. Jean and Sandy wait in the dim hall. They've done this many times now, and wordlessly they hurry the few feet to the stairway door. Sandy slips the lock. She's the best thief in the school. If you want something, you go to Sandy.

Silently, they go down the stairs. Sandy hands Maisie the flashlight she's stolen; Maisie is always the leader. Jean tucks a bit of folded cardboard into the lock to block it so they can get back in. Then they race out into the night, past the tennis courts and the brick fireplaces and picnic tables and the big willow tree in the middle of the grounds. None of them speak. The only sounds are the rush of their breathing, the shush of their shoes through the grass. The school lights lend enough illumination that they don't need the flashlight. But at the boathouse, where the path disappears into the grove of white oaks, Maisie switches it on. The beam bounces against the gray weathered planks of the boathouse, glints upon the chain blocking the steps, the sign reading "*Danger.* Keep Out."

Jean slaps at her hand, forcing the beam away. "Stop it," she says in a harsh whisper.

Maisie laughs quietly. "What's wrong, Jeanie?"

"Turn it off," Sandy says. "Someone will see."

"Look—no one's repaired it yet."

"They've left it like that on purpose," Jean says crossly.

"Turn it off," Sandy says again.

Maisie keeps it on another moment to show that it's her decision, not Sandy's and not Jean's, and then she does turn it off until they round the corner, until they're out of sight of the school, and it's really too dark to see the path—the break line of trees that shield it from the school and the bushes edging the lake both blocking the clear night sky.

When Maisie turns on the light again, its narrow beam shows a wide and beaten dirt path bordered by blackberry and salal, ferns and maple and alder, and then the trees thin and the lake begins to peek through, as do the rocks and short jetties of its shore, and beyond the brush a pebbled beach and rock stairs leading to a small cove, and looming from the dark water, denser shadows in the darkness, the jagged formations known as the Mercer Rocks.

Jean shivers dramatically. Maisie and Sandy go down the stairs to sit on the fallen tree on the shore, but Jean stays on the top stair the way she always does, and Maisie laughs at her the way she always does.

"Still afraid of the Rocks? How old are you?"

Jean's bright blond hair has its own illumination in the darkness. She is just so beautiful, with her big dark eyes in her pale face. "There's something out there. There's a reason the Indians called this place Taboo Container."

"A kraken. It's coming to get you!" Sandy raises her hands like claws and lurches toward Jean, who leans away even though Sandy is nowhere near her.

Maisie says, "Listen—Jean, come closer. I don't want anyone to hear."

"There's no one out here," Jean says.

"Sam's always lurking about."

"Sam can keep a secret."

"Not this." Maisie motions with the flashlight, and Jean sighs and wiggles down to the bottom step.

Sandy reaches into the brush behind the fallen log, and brings out a bottle with a little smile of triumph. Rum.

Jean gasps with delight and surprise. "When did you put that here?"

"Before I checked in yesterday. I came here first. Just in case." Sandy is already twisting the cap. She takes a gulp and passes it to Maisie, and suddenly the sweet smell of the alcohol is everywhere.

Maisie takes a small sip. She doesn't want to lose her focus yet. She hands it to Jean.

Sandy says, "So . . . what do we think about her? Is she for real?"

Maisie is surprised. First that she has no doubt whom Sandy is talking about. Second that the new teacher is on her friend's mind too. She is even more surprised when Jean says, "We've been fooled before," as she hands the bottle around again, and Maisie realizes everyone is thinking about Miss Chivers.

"She's not like Miss Avilla," Sandy says.

Maisie plays the flashlight along the rocky beach, picking up glints of quartz and glass. She glances at Sandra, whose hair has come forward to hide her face. "What do you mean?"

"There's something strange about her." Sandy's voice is nearly a whisper.

"Like what?"

"I don't know."

"She's got a secret," Maisie says confidently. "And once we find out what it is, we can use it. She'll belong to us."

Jean giggles. "You really think she's a lesbian?"

"I don't know, but if it's not that, it's something else. I'm never wrong, am I?"

The others are quiet. With squirming unease, Maisie thinks of Miss Avilla. But neither Sandy nor Jean brings up the art teacher, and Maisie is grateful for that.

She says, "So . . . anyone have any objection?"

"No," Jean says quickly.

Sandy gulps again from the bottle. Maisie swipes it from her. "Sandy?"

Sandy's eyes reflect the lambent light, but they reveal nothing. She shakes her head. "No objection."

"Good." Maisie raises the flashlight beam beneath her chin so it sends ghoulish shadows over her face. "Then you know what to do."

Sandy smiles. "I've already begun."

Chapter 8

The bathroom was a mess by the time the girls were in bed, piles of used towels in the bin, liquid soap pooling on the sinks and dripping down the porcelain. Moisture fogged the walls and the windows and turned the tiled floors slippery. Someone had written *Bev is a slut* in the steam clouding one of the mirrors. Rosemary wiped it clear and cracked the windows, which only opened an inch or two to keep girls from jumping, escaping, or throwing things.

Tomorrow chores would be assigned, but tonight was for settling in, and so it was late by the time she went upstairs. Mrs. Sackett was already in the bathroom they shared. The housekeeper stood at the sink in a battered chenille robe, looking mournfully at her reflection in her mirror as she pulled at the sagging skin of her jaw.

"No problems tonight," Rosemary told her.

Mrs. Sackett harrumphed. "Don't you believe it. But maybe they'll be good since it's the start of the year."

"Is there anything special I should know?" Rosemary asked.

Mrs. Sackett turned from the mirror. "They'll lie about everything. All of them."

"I've taught high school before."

"Not like this," Mrs. Sackett said. "Their parents couldn't manage these girls."

Rosemary made no comment to that. She knew too well what parental management could and could not do. "What about the seniors? Maisie, Jean, and Sandra? They seem quite close."

"Now there's a trio." Mrs. Sackett's voice was dry. "They love and they hate each other, those girls."

It was not news after what Rosemary had seen today.

"You ask me, after last year those girls should be kept apart, but I'm just the housekeeper. No one listens to me."

"What happened last year?"

Mrs. Sackett hesitated, then she sighed. "Honestly? I couldn't say exactly. They said it was an accident. I suppose it was. And I shouldn't be telling tales."

"What kind of an accident?" Rosemary pressed.

Mrs. Sackett offered an uneasy smile. "I'm just being silly. But it does seem those three get in more trouble when they're together. I'll be glad to see them go." She tucked her toiletries into a pink vinyl bag and set it on the shelf above the toilet. "Sleep well, Rosemary. You'll need your strength."

Rosemary wanted to ask more questions, but Mrs. Sackett was obviously done talking. No one else had mentioned an accident last year. Surely if it had been important, someone would have said something. Still . . .

The moment Rosemary opened the door to her room, something felt wrong. She could not say exactly what. Her guitar leaned against the wall just as she'd left it. The portable record player, her records, her books . . . nothing seemed disturbed. Her barrettes and hairbrush still on the dresser, the pen and notebook on the desk were all as she'd left them. But it was off. Someone had been in her room. She didn't know how she knew it, but she did. It felt uncomfortable, crackly, like just before the electric zap of a touch in cold, dry weather.

Maybe it was just too quiet. Rosemary opened the record player and pulled her *A Pete Seeger Concert* album from its sleeve. She put it on at a low volume, not wanting to disturb Mrs. Sackett. Pete Seeger surrounded her with comforting familiarity as Rosemary changed into thin cotton pajamas. She went to the window and stared out at the tennis courts softly glowing in the night, and her room began to feel like her own again. She began to think she'd imagined everything. Tomorrow she would start locking the door.

Pete Seeger broke into "Kisses Sweeter than Wine," and a light flashed in the darkness of the meadow outside. Rosemary blinked, thinking she was seeing things, but no, there it was again. The gardener, probably with a flashlight. The light bounced haphazardly, disembodied, over the boathouse wall before it shut off abruptly. But no one used the boathouse. "Keep Out" signs were posted all over it, and the door was chained shut.

Rosemary waited for the light to return until she realized the needle had reached the end of the record, and she'd been listening to its staticky *thwump, thwump, thwump* for some time. She rescued the record. She should go downstairs and check that the girls were in their beds. But if they weren't, what then? What would she do? Rouse the rest of the staff? Cause a scene? Such a way to start the year, and she didn't want to be an enemy. Besides, wasn't it Cheryl Fields's job to catch them?

Yes, leave it to Cheryl.

It was probably the gardener anyway. And if it wasn't, well, just this once, Rosemary would let them be.

Chapter 9

Burgers sizzled on grills set over the fireplaces, smoke tangled in the branches of the willow, and the scents of dripping fat and bubbling cheese and toasted bread wafted over picnic tables set with paper plates, along with bowls of Mrs. Dennis the cook's famous potato salad, and plates piled high with buttered corn on the cob. Pitchers of iced lemonade wept from their places at the end of each table.

"The girls love the yearly barbecue," Gloria Weedman confided, but it seemed to Rosemary that mostly the girls were taking it as an opportunity to break rules, because Tom Gear and the gardener, Martin McCree—in his forties, with shaggy blond hair and a taciturn attitude—kept retrieving sullen girls who'd tried to sneak away for a cigarette, and Andrew Covington constantly tested the lemonade to make sure it hadn't been spiked. The smell of cigarette smoke was unmistakable, and Lizzie Etheridge and Sarah Waller were quite obviously drunk.

When the burgers were eaten and cookies brought out, and everyone gathered around the fires, Rosemary ended up sitting with Maisie, Sandra, and Jean at one of the firepits. It was obvious they'd engineered it, and Rosemary vacillated between feeling flattered, trepidation over Alicia's warning that they picked a new "favorite" teacher every year, and her own misgivings about becoming too attached to students. Then again, what could it matter really? It was only for four months.

Maisie nibbled at a snickerdoodle. "I wish we had some music."

"Don't say it so loud," Jean cautioned. "If Mrs. Vance hears, she'll make us sing the school song."

"What's the school song?" Rosemary asked.

"You don't want to know," Jean said. "It's all about Mercer Rocks girls brave and true, lalalala. It gives me the creeps."

"It doesn't go anything like that," Sandy said.

"Well, it's awful anyway."

"What we need is a guitar," Maisie said. "And not Miss Avilla."

"She only plays Spanish songs," Jean informed Rosemary in a low voice. "And dumb things like 'Sur le pont d'Avignon.'"

Spanish songs. Spain. Rosemary resisted a pang of heartache. "Why Spanish songs?"

"It's where she's from. Some little Spanish town."

Sandra turned to her. "You have a guitar, don't you, Miss Chivers?"

Rosemary was taken aback. "How do you know that?"

Sandra shrugged. "There are no secrets at the Rocks."

Rosemary remembered last night, the feeling that someone had been in her room.

"I'll bet you don't play just Spanish songs," Maisie said.

"You're so cool," Jean said. "I'll bet you'd play something we could dance to."

Despite herself, Rosemary felt a warmth that wasn't from the fire.

"Yeah, like 'Crazy Man Crazy,'" Maisie added.

"I can play that," Rosemary admitted.

Jean clapped her hands. "Oh, you have to play it for us!"

"You could bring your guitar to class," Sandra suggested. "Couldn't you?"

Rosemary glanced toward Stella Bullard with Andrew Covington and Pearl Hoskins near the far picnic table. "I don't know what 'Crazy Man Crazy' has to do with nuclear preparedness."

"Then you could play something else. I'll bet you know a lot of songs. Like . . . 'The Roving Kind'?"

"I love that song," Jean enthused.

"Me too!" Maisie said.

"Of course I know it," Rosemary said.

"What about 'The Hammer Song'?" Sandra's gaze riveted to Rosemary's, and though she was smiling, there was something provocative there Rosemary could not quite catch, a dare, maybe?

Rosemary frowned.

"You know, 'If I had a hammer . . .'"

"Yes, I know." Rosemary wondered why the girl would bring up that protest song, and thought of the records in her room, that particular one among them, as had been Guy Mitchell's version of "The Roving Kind."

"It's a communist song," Jean said. "I remember Daddy going on about it."

Time to change the subject. Rosemary said, "I know many songs. I got a guitar for my tenth birthday, so I've been playing since then."

"Such a long time!" Jean blurted.

Rosemary laughed. "I'm not that old."

"How old are you?" Maisie asked.

"Thirty-four. How old are you?" Of course she knew, but she wondered how Maisie would answer.

"Eighteen in July. You know what's funny? We're all Cancers—Sandra, Jean, and me. For a while I had this theory that it meant something, you know?" Maisie sighed. "But it doesn't. It's just a coincidence. I guess it's what makes us friends."

"Miss Chivers? Rosemary?" Lois Vance marched over before Rosemary had a chance to respond to Maisie. The vice principal looked more turtle-like than usual, her weak chin softened into nonexistence by firelight. "There's a call for you from your father in the main office."

Rosemary frowned. "My father?"

Lois nodded. "I think you'd better take it."

It was so odd for her father to call that Rosemary knew it could only mean one thing. She hurried to the office, where Irene sat waiting by the phone. The secretary handed the receiver to Rosemary wordlessly and left to give her privacy, and Rosemary's heart pounded in her ears as she whispered, "Dad?"

"It's your mom." Grief was in his voice. "I rushed her to the hospital."

"Which hospital? I'll be right there."

"It's too late, Rosie," he said. "She's gone."

~

Rosemary did not understand it. Four months ago, her instincts that there was something wrong in her parents not answering the phone had brought her racing home. She'd been right then. Her mother had been in the hospital, and yet tonight, her mother had died, and there had been nothing to warn her, no premonition, no apprehension, no dread. Nothing. She had been talking to troubled girls about music, which might have been the greatest irony of all. On the phone, Dad told her to stay at school until Sunday; there was nothing she could do. *It's only the day after tomorrow. No need to turn everything upside down. She'd planned for this.*

But I haven't planned for this, Rosemary wanted to say. Despite all evidence to the contrary, she had somehow expected her mother to live forever, if for no other reason than to spite her, and she could not believe Mom was not sitting at home watching *Schlitz Playhouse of Stars*, smoking her Kools, and drinking Gallo.

Stella had been teary-eyed herself, and had said to Rosemary, "Lois can take over your classes for a few days. But frankly, Rosemary, we can't really spare you. I hope you won't leave us, but if you wish to take longer, we'd have to replace you."

Rosemary had been too distraught to reply one way or another. Just now the school was a burden Rosemary didn't want. She had never really wanted it, but her mother had been so insistent . . . and now . . . Truthfully Rosemary had not expected Mom's death to be such a shocking blow. That a force like Dorothy Chivers could be gone so suddenly, just gone—the quiet of the world was suddenly too quiet.

Rosemary could not be still, so she went into the night and walked toward the boathouse, the path through the white oaks. The trees gathered darkly, blocking out the sky, and the boathouse loomed ominous and silent, but from the radiant light it was not hard to find her way, and easy to see once she was through the tunnel of oaks, and the sky opened up again, the overcast chased by the wind, the night sky bright, stars breaking through. The rocky shoreline became broad dark shapes, angled and solid; the water a flat plane of shining opacity lapping against the pebbled beach. Across its expanse was the shadow of the far shore, lights twinkling—Rosemary, who had lived in Seattle all her life, but for college and jobs sprinkled throughout the state, could not figure out what she was looking at; she was turned around by the night, by sorrow and distraction.

She kept walking until she reached what looked like stairs, stairs of stone, and gingerly she went down them to a broader beach, a cove, and was caught by the shadows before her, great, jagged shadows jabbing from the lake into the sky. Contrasts of darkness—dark shining lake, the shadow of the far shore, and these dense, hard shadows with a distinct presence. She had only seen the Mercer Rocks in the daytime before, and from the path, but at night they were menacing. They had a distinct sound as well—the swish of water, the suck, the rush of current, the soft slap—a language of both temptation and threat.

They were beautiful too. Beautiful and terrible, and she stood watching and listening, shaken and undone, for a long time, her grief the only solid thing.

The Past

It took seven weeks before she admitted to herself that she was pregnant. David was busy with the FTP, and she had been so distracted with trying to find a job that she didn't realize at first that her period was late; then, when she did realize it, she told herself she'd simply miscalculated. She'd lost track of time. It could not be true. When she told David, he put his hand on her stomach and became deeply thoughtful.

Rosemary began to cry.

He looked up at her through his lashes. "I love you. What do you want to do? We could get married."

She allowed herself to imagine that. Married with a baby. They had no money. They lived with at least a dozen other people. They had nothing. But she knew that if she wanted it, David would make it possible. For a moment, she hugged that idea tight. For a moment, she dwelled in that fantasy.

But then she thought of her father going to work every day and her mother sitting at the table with a faraway look in her eyes and a dream for her daughter that Rosemary had run from. She didn't want that life. David's dreams had become her own. She loved him and she wanted to be with him, and his fight had become hers. Between yesterday and today, nothing had changed to make her want to bring a child into this world. Nothing had changed except that she now knew she was pregnant, and this child was hers and David's.

But was that enough to shift everything she'd come to believe?

No. There would be other children when they were ready.

She met David's gaze. "I don't want this. Not yet."

"Are you sure, Rosie?" he asked.

"I'm sure. If . . . if it's what you want too."

Softly, he said, "Someday. Not yet."

The decision settled heavy and certain between them, and suddenly she was frightened that this meant the end of something, that it held a danger she could not see. "This will ruin everything."

David drew his hand away, and when she grabbed it and held it tight, he squeezed back as if he understood her fear. "You belong to me. This doesn't change anything. I'll fix it."

"How?"

"Trust me." He kissed her.

Two weeks later, he'd found the way. "A guy at the YPSL meeting told me about a woman who takes care of things like this if we can get the money."

But Rosemary had heard of people like that too. "I don't want to die."

"Do you think I'd send you if I thought that would happen? This woman's safe. He's had other girls go there. It's all fine. I promise."

"Where is she?"

"It's a secret. The police are watching all the time. But I trust what he says. I trust him with you. Unless you've changed your mind? We could see this through."

"No. Anyway, my parents would never allow it."

"They might, if they knew."

Rosemary shook her head and laughed shortly. "Not my parents. Besides, I don't want a baby now, and neither do you." She had only ever been so certain of one other thing in her life, and that was her love for him. "We'll get the money, and I'll go."

It took them another ten days. David picked up whatever odd jobs he could, and Rosemary begged on the streets, and in the end they had to borrow money from a friend, but they managed it.

She was to wait at the Associated gas station in Queen Anne at eight o'clock on Saturday night with a nightgown and some sanitary pads in a bag. She would be picked up there and then delivered to the Richland gas station in Fremont the next morning, where David would meet her.

He walked her to the Associated. There were three other women there already, waiting with bags, looking nervous, all of them older than Rosemary.

David kissed her, and she held his hand and kissed him back hard, unable to ease her apprehension. "I don't want you to go."

"You'll be okay," he reassured her. "I can't go with you. I'll see you tomorrow morning. I promise. I love you, Rosie."

"You belong to me," she whispered, but she wasn't sure he heard it; he was already turning into the darkness beyond the streetlamp.

Rosemary and the other women didn't look at one another, as if by not looking they couldn't be held accountable for what they were doing. At eight o'clock sharp, another woman approached them through the darkness. She had dark hair and wore a black coat with a turned-up collar and a hat. She swept them all with a cursory gaze and said to Rosemary, "How old are you?"

"Eighteen." Her instincts told her to lie, though she didn't think there was an age limit. But how would she know? It seemed best not to test it.

The woman laughed, and Rosemary was afraid she was going to tell her she was too young and turn her away, but she only said, "This way, ladies."

They followed her across the street to a parking lot, where she ushered them into a two-toned Chevy sedan. In the darkness Rosemary could not make out the colors, except that they were dark. One woman got the front seat and the rest of them got in to the back.

"You all have your money?" asked the woman who'd picked them up.

Rosemary's hand trembled as she handed it over. The woman counted it, then reached into a bag and took out four cardboard Halloween masks: a black cat, a devil, a witch, and a Raggedy Ann. Rosemary got the devil.

"Put them on. It's just so you can't report where you went," the woman said.

"Why would we want to do that?" squeaked one of Rosemary's companions.

"I didn't say you would want to," said the woman. "This just makes it easier."

Rosemary put on the mask. The eyeholes were taped over. The tight elastic band forced the cardboard to curve to blind her peripheral vision. She felt she was smothering. The engine started.

"Down on the floor, please."

Obediently, Rosemary followed instructions, knocking knees and elbows with the other two in the back seat. It was clumsy, uncomfortable, and cold. The car didn't have heat, the only warmth came from the bodies beside her. Rosemary caught the scent of beer, and she wished she'd thought to drink away her nerves too.

The car rocked and jolted; she closed her eyes against the taped eyeholes and listened to the breathing of the others and thought about tomorrow, being clean and cleared of this burden, running into David's arms at the gas station. If she imagined it as being already over, it was easier.

The woman driving said, "It won't hurt. We'll give you gas, and it'll knock you right out, and then what she'll do is she'll scrape your womb."

One of the women *eek*ed.

"It won't hurt," the woman said again. "You won't be awake. You'll be kept blindfolded so you can't identify anyone, okay?"

No one said anything.

She went on, "You'll wake up in a bed, and once we're sure you're only bleeding normally, we'll take you back. You'll want to wear a pad for a few days. It'll be like a period, maybe a bit heavy. A warm bath will help with the cramping."

That was all she said. They drove on for a while. Rosemary didn't try to track where they were going or how long it took. She didn't care. She just wanted it to be over, to be back at Common House, to have it be done. She wished there were an easier way, something not so scary. Maybe a pill to take or a potion to drink, and poof! All gone.

Finally, the car stopped. She had no idea where they were, only that she heard muffled music.

The car door opened. "Easy now," said the woman, taking Rosemary's arm. She led her out carefully. "There's a walk here, that's right. Now a step."

Rosemary stumbled a little. When she put out her hand, she felt rough, wet siding.

"Wait here," said the woman, and Rosemary heard her helping the others from the car.

A door opened. The music blasted. "Goody Goody." Benny Goodman and His Orchestra. Another woman came up beside her.

"Come on," said a voice—a man's, low and deep. "Who's first?"

"The little girl," called the woman who'd brought them from the car.

"Okay."

Another hand grabbed Rosemary's arm. She shrank away.

"You want this or not?" he asked.

She nodded. She took one step.

A scraping sear of sound, sirens, wheels skidding and braking, something flashing through the darkness of the mask, lights and confusion.

"Shit!" The hand on her arm dropped. Footsteps running, a car door opening, another one.

"This is the police!" a man shouted. "Stop immediately and come out with your hands up!"

Rosemary tore off the mask. She took in the white house, the narrow porch, the police cars blocking the road, lights flashing, cops everywhere, the woman who'd brought them being handcuffed and another woman crying.

She ran.

She got as far as the trees at the edge of the yard, and then a cop was yanking her back, grasping her around her waist and pulling her off her feet. She was in the back of a police car before she knew it, handcuffed herself, sullen and silent, her pulse pounding in her head so she could hardly hear anything else.

"What's your name, sweetheart?" asked one of the officers.

She pressed her lips together tightly.

"Haven't I seen you before?" asked another, turning to look at her over the seat. "You know, I think I have. Look at her, Mark—isn't she that runaway we got posted all over the station?"

Rosemary threw up in the back seat.

~

Back at the station, they kept her locked in a cell until her parents came. She'd been gone for over six months, but they looked just the same. Well, perhaps her mother was thinner. Dad only sighed heavily when he saw her.

Mom put her hand to her mouth and her eyes overflowed with tears. "Oh, Rosemary, what have you done?"

She didn't meet David the next morning at the Richland gas station in Fremont. In fact, she never saw him again.

Chapter 10

Seattle, WA—1954

The next morning Rosemary took the trolley to her parents' house. The sky was a deep September blue and people went about their business as if nothing were different, and when she walked through the front door, the radio was on, tuned to KIRO, as always: *See the USA in your Chevrolet. America is asking you to call* . . . She didn't see her father anywhere.

"Dad?"

There was no answer. Rosemary took off her coat and hung it in the closet.

She tried again. "Dad!"

Still nothing. The house felt empty; the force of Mom's presence dissipated even here, despite the fact that her things were everywhere, her coat, her rain boots, her ashtray, a half-crumpled pack of Kools and the latest *Life* magazine folded over to hold her place. She felt so strangely absent. But then, why should Rosemary be surprised? Mom was—*had been*—like rain in Seattle. So constant and unceasing and *there* that it was easy sometimes to forget about the sun.

The kitchen sink held only her father's cereal bowl and a spoon, and the percolator was full of cold coffee. So Dad was here somewhere;

a manila envelope from the hospital was on the Formica table of the kitchen nook, and his car was parked out front. Then she saw him out the back-door window. He was sitting in the backyard, staring into space.

Rosemary hesitated, and then she opened the door and stepped out on the aggregate patio. "Dad?" she called softly.

He started, then twisted in the chair. "Rosemary? What are you doing here?"

"What do you mean, what am I doing here? Of course I'm here."

"I said Sunday."

"I couldn't stay at school, Dad."

He rose; for the first time he seemed creaky and slow, an older man in his late fifties. He gestured toward the yard, the browning grass of September, the long-stemmed, fluff-headed dandelions he'd been ignoring. "She talked about putting a bomb shelter back here."

"I saw her reading that pamphlet."

"Right there." He took off his glasses, rubbed them, and put them back on. "She wanted one big enough for all of us."

Rosemary winced at how quickly and instinctually a retort about hell being weeks enclosed in a small space with her mother sprang to her lips. "Come on. I'll make some coffee. You can tell me what happened."

Dad frowned so that for a moment she thought she'd actually made the comment about her mother, but no, she hadn't, and Dad glanced away. "She had a heart attack."

"I know that. I mean . . . where was she when it happened? How long did she . . . did she say anything?"

Dad had never been good at talking about emotional things. Again, he took off his glasses.

"You just cleaned them, Dad," she said.

"Oh, I—I did?" He put them back on.

"Come in the house." She went into the kitchen and poured out the coffee in the percolator. It wasn't until she'd emptied the basket and refilled it that Dad came back inside.

"Rosie," he said slowly. "There's something . . . your mom said something . . ."

Rosemary put water in the pot and set it on the stove.

"She said your girl was at that school."

It took a moment for the words to register, and even then, at first they meant nothing. They were so out of context, so foreign, the subject so taboo that Rosemary did not make any connection. Then, before she herself understood, her heart did. It began to beat this staccato double dance and halt; she was suddenly light-headed. She turned to her father, the coffeepot lid still in her hand. "What?"

"That's what she said. It's why she wanted you to work there, I guess."

It was all a confusion, a shock. *Your girl.* "I don't . . . I don't understand."

How uncomfortable he looked. "She's there, at Mercer Rocks. Your daughter. That's what your mother said."

"But . . . she never said anything to me."

"Me neither. Not until yesterday. I didn't know anything about it."

"What . . . what *exactly* did she say?"

"She said to tell you your girl was there."

"But . . ." Rosemary shook her head, surprised to find she was near tears. "That can't be."

"Why can't it?"

Rosemary struggled to put her thoughts into words, but they were bludgeoned by shock, by disbelief, by confusion. "I just . . . How did Mom know?"

"I don't know."

"Why didn't she tell me?"

Reluctantly, Dad said, "I think she meant to. I think she was waiting until you were ready."

"Until I was *ready*? Ready for what?" Rosemary's confusion turned suddenly to frustration. "I don't understand. God, I'm so tired of how she tries to control my life! Is she ever going to be done?"

"She's done now, Rosemary."

Her father's voice was so soft that it caught Rosemary hard, and she sagged and pushed the lid onto the coffeepot with trembling hands. She did not know what to feel. She was shocked and angry with her mother, but there also were hope and joy and fear, and those were too big to hold on to, and she'd spent too many years twisting and squeezing them to nothing. Mom had been the first one to say *"Put it behind you. Forget it ever happened."* They'd never spoken of it. It had been the forbidden topic, the family secret, the family scandal. Rosemary's daughter had stopped existing. Had never existed. In the face of such staunch opposition, Rosemary had been unable to keep insisting otherwise. It had become unbearable, finally, to long for her return, to keep searching. And yet . . . Mom had searched for her? Mom had found her? After all that? *Mom?*

Rosemary could not have spoken if she'd wanted. *Rosemary, quite contrary, how does your garden grow? With silver bells and cockle shells and little maids all in a row.*

One little maid had gone missing. Rosemary had thought she was the only one who cared, and she could not now reconcile herself to knowing that her mother had not only cared but had tracked that little maid and said nothing. Mom had insisted Rosemary take the job at Mercer Rocks and said *nothing.*

Rosemary could not see through sudden tears. She felt her father's hand heavy on her shoulder. "I thought maybe you knew already."

"How would I know?" she asked bitterly. "Mom and all her stupid secrets . . ."

"I thought you might have guessed, you know, since you've met her by now."

Rosemary straightened and blinked away her blindness. "Met her?" And suddenly it dawned on her what her confusion was about. Her daughter was at Mercer Rocks, and she'd met every student there, and yet—

"Maybe you recognized her? Or suspected? Was there a girl who looked like you? I mean, she'd be what by now . . . seventeen?"

Yes, she would be seventeen, and there were only three seventeen-year-old girls at Mercer Rocks.

Maisie Neal. Sandra Wilson. Jean Karlstad.

Rosemary had always believed that she would know her daughter in a glance. She would have his hair or eyes, or Rosemary would see herself in the shape of her daughter's face. Her heart would know, instinctively she knew she would recognize her child. She'd felt her daughter's every movement for nine months, every hiccup, every stretch. How could she not know?

But she hadn't. She hadn't recognized her daughter in any of them. The only things she'd found familiar in those three girls were the inclinations that might have brought them to Mercer Rocks. Maisie the runaway. Sandra the drunk. Jean the sex fiend. Going by their physical looks, none could be her daughter. But if she judged by their personalities, any of them could be.

"There are three the right age. But none of them look like me, or like . . . him. I don't know which one it could be. I suppose . . . if I could get into the records, I could find out their birthdays . . ." Her mind spun. Maisie had said July, hadn't she? She'd said they were all Cancers. *All of them*—her thoughts stopped at the look on her father's face. "What?"

"A birthdate wouldn't tell you," he said sheepishly.

"What do you mean?"

He sat heavily at the kitchen table. "You have to understand, Rosemary, we thought it best. You were just a child. You had your whole life before you. College, and your mom especially wanted you to have choices she never had. She was so disappointed when you decided on home ec—"

"What are you saying?"

"We gave the agency a false birthday."

"Why?"

"You were sixteen when you ran away, Rosemary. Sixteen. Think about how young you were. We didn't want you to find her."

Rosemary didn't know whether to laugh or cry. "You're joking."

Dad shook his head. "We were trying to protect you."

It took her a minute to process that. "Okay. Well, what day did you choose?"

"I don't know."

She stared at him. "Dad, please. I'm not sixteen anymore."

"I'm telling you the truth. Mom took care of it. I don't know what day she chose. I never asked her and she never told me."

"I don't believe you."

"I'd tell you if I knew, Rosie. I promise I would."

He was not lying; Rosemary knew by the look on his face. The sudden obstacle rocked her, the bewilderment of being given a gift so unexpectedly and having it taken away in the very next moment. Her one sure way of determining which of them was hers gone, and she had nothing else. She hadn't recognized her own daughter. Of course, she hadn't known to really *look*, but the fact was that nothing of her had been strong enough to pass down in any obvious way. It was as if nothing about her had been worth keeping, or—the thought occurred to her and would not budge—as if the universe or fate or whatever had judged her a bad mother at seventeen and had stepped in to make sure that nothing stayed.

With the notion came that restless flutter in her blood, that edge that would not let her be still. She forced it away. "Then how will I ever know which one is mine?"

Dad said nothing for a moment, and then, heavily, "Maybe it's best. Maybe, after all this time, it's best to let things be."

Walk away, he meant. Leave her daughter alone. "What? You can't possibly mean that now! Mom *found* her. Obviously she didn't want me to let things be. She insisted I work at Mercer Rocks!"

"I thought you didn't want your mother controlling your life any longer."

"Nice, Dad."

He shrugged. "What would you do if you found out which one was yours, Rosie? What difference would it make? How would it change your life? Or hers?"

"Maybe she needs help. She's in a home for wayward girls!"

"*Wayward* doesn't mean unhappy. Remember how you were."

She couldn't deny that. She hadn't been unhappy. Simply restless. Frustrated. And she knew better than most that *wayward* meant only that someone didn't walk the path laid out for them.

"She has a family, Rosie. She doesn't know you exist. Even if she does, are you going to go in there and upend her? She has a better life than you can give her. It was true then and it's still true, isn't it?" Dad's words were blunt, and that he looked sorry to be saying them didn't ease the pain they caused.

He was right; Rosemary knew that. She would be interfering in lives she had no business interfering in, and she knew better than to do that. It would only end up hurting her, and she'd already made a mistake like that before and had no desire to relive it. But Mercer Rocks was a reform school, and now that she knew her daughter was there, how could she just walk away without knowing who she really was? "I just . . . I just want to know her, Dad. I just want to know that her family cares about her, that she's really okay."

"You really think you can figure out which girl is yours and not get involved in her life? You think you can keep your distance?"

"Yes, I can. I promise I can."

That look on his face, that deep-set worry that took her back what seemed a thousand years, that spoke of his care and his love and the pure pointlessness of her resistance . . .

"I think this is a bad idea, Rosie. You don't have to work there. You can stay here with me as long as it takes to get your next steps sorted out."

"I think I have to do this," she said.

He sighed. Then, reluctantly: "I mean it, Rosemary. This isn't just play. This is someone else's life. You made a promise back then to let her go, remember."

"I know," she said.

"You did something good when you gave her up. Don't forget that."

She did not tell him that was not how she remembered it.

The Past

Seventeen years earlier
White Shield Home
Tacoma, WA—July 3, 1937

Long Silence Follows Amelia's Radio SOS, read the headline in the *Seattle Daily Times*, and Rosemary gathered around the scratched console of the RCA Victor radio with the others, jockeying for space among the large and growing larger bellies and hoping for some reassurance from the announcer. It was a fine day in early July, though they were expecting the clouds to roll in for the Fourth as always.

A cramp, at first slight, uncomfortable more than painful. Rosemary's hand went protectively to her protruding stomach, pressing. The baby pushed back.

"You all right, Mary?" the nurse asked. None of the girls used their real names here.

Rosemary nodded, but truthfully she did not feel all right. She moved to the window and stared down at the parklike landscaping, wishing, hoping, as she had every day, that he might materialize before her, that lazy stride, that dark blond hair clipped short on the sides, those longer curls on top flopping onto his forehead, untamable by any hair cream.

Come to me.

The father of Elizabeth's baby had arrived just last week, so it wasn't as if it didn't happen. He'd showed up just before the child was born and whisked her away on a milk wagon. "I'm to be the wife of a milkman!" she'd announced happily, though there were shadows in her eyes, too, and Rosemary knew that until then Elizabeth had feared he would be like most of the other fathers. Absent. Disappeared.

Another cramp, intense enough to make Rosemary gasp. Not yet. She hadn't told them her decision. She needed another day to find the courage, though she'd been saying that for days now. She needed him to somehow read her thoughts, brave all perils, find his way to her through some magical power of location. She didn't know if she could do this alone. Mom would be angry. Dad would argue. But they had put her here and forced her to live with her memories, and she had felt this child moving inside her and known that if it was all she had left, she could not let it go. She could not bear the thought of being alone, or of her child—their child—being without her.

Another cramp, more fierce, and then something gave way, and a whoosh of warm wetness sluiced down her legs, soaking her underwear, and she stood in a pool of thick, slippery liquid.

"Oh!" She bit the sound back and clenched her fist hard.

"What's this?" The nurse hurried over. "Oh, looks like you're going to have a Fourth of July baby after all! Won't that be lovely! The baby can celebrate with the whole country!"

"I can't." Rosemary stared out the window, wishing so hard it seemed her soul reached through the glass. *Come to me.* "He's not here yet."

The nurse tsked. "Oh, honey, he's not coming. You know that. They never do."

"But Elizabeth's did—"

"Let's get you over to delivery. Nurse Williams, can you call Mary's parents and tell them she's in delivery?"

It was a first labor, and she was barely seventeen. They thought it would take many hours. The contractions began in earnest and they hurt and Rosemary was scared and he wasn't here and she hadn't told them what she wanted, but her body was making the decisions now. She couldn't stop it. Her body was not her own. Still, she tried. *You're going to have to wait,* she told the baby. *I love you now, and I have to tell them.*

"Nurse Lancer," she tried as the woman hustled her into the delivery. "I need to tell you something—"

"You just relax," the nurse cooed. "It's going to be all right."

Before Rosemary knew it, she was in a bed and they were shaving her pubic hair and giving her an enema. No one had said anything about any of this. They did it all with a detached efficiency that was even more embarrassing, as if she wasn't a person but just a body to move to and fro: "Roll on your side now," "Open your legs," and she wanted to cover her head with the pillow and die, and instead she cried, which embarrassed her even more. She did not want them to see, but she couldn't seem to control her tears, and then she realized they weren't looking at her face. She could have been anybody or nobody at all. They deliberately avoided her eyes.

"Wait." She grabbed another nurse's arm. "I need to talk to someone. My mom. Where's my mom?"

"She's not here yet."

"Please, listen. I don't want—"

"It will be over soon," the woman said, patting Rosemary's arm. "No need to worry."

"That's not what I mean. I mean I've changed my mind. I mean—"

"Have you the pills, Doris?" the nurse called.

"Right here." Another nurse came hurrying over. "Here, Mary. Take these like a good girl."

Rosemary looked down at the pills. "What are these for?"

"They'll help with the pain."

"All right, but . . . you heard what I said, didn't you, about changing my mind? I want to keep the bab—"

"Just take the pills. It'll make it easier." The nurse bent to her with a needle. "Go on now."

She did. And after that . . . after that she remembered nothing at all.

~

When she woke, she was in a different room, and another nurse was fussing between her legs. Blearily Rosemary realized that the woman was changing a sanitary napkin—another humiliation—and also, confusedly, that her stomach was flatter. "My baby." Her throat was sore; the words were hard to say. "My baby?"

The nurse glanced over. "A healthy baby girl."

A girl. Rosemary touched her stomach gingerly, disbelieving. "Where is she?"

"She's doing fine, dear."

"I want to see her."

The nurse busily lowered Rosemary's gown and hiked up the thin blanket of the hospital bed. "You should go to sleep. I'm sure you're tired. Giving birth is hard work."

She remembered not a bit of it. She'd slept through the entire thing. "But I just woke up. Where is she? I want to see her."

"It's late. Past midnight."

It was only then that Rosemary noticed the blinds were down, and the other girl in the room was sleeping. "Was she . . . is she a Fourth of July baby, then?"

The nurse shook her head. "No. Missed it by a few hours. But nothing wrong with the third. Go on to sleep."

"Where is she? Where's my mom? Did they tell you what I said? Did they tell you I changed my mind?"

"Go to sleep, dear," the nurse said soothingly. "Go to sleep. Things'll be clearer in the morning."

Rosemary closed her eyes again. She drifted into dreams where she was unburdened and flying, and a little girl holding fast to her ankle, her fingers slipping while Rosemary tried to slow down and give the girl time to tighten her hold, but she couldn't go slow enough, and the child fell away.

Rosemary woke with a start to see her mother sitting at the side of the bed, dressed impeccably, as always, in a hat with a navy ribbon that exactly matched the big buttons and polka dots of her cream linen weave dress—as if fashion mattered when there were constant labor strikes and homeless people crowded in Hooverville and fascism gaining ground all over the world. Rosemary had no doubt that Mom's shoes and purse were equally matched; Dorothy Chivers's closet was the envy of all her friends, and she'd made certain to keep it so, even in the midst of a depression.

The hat had a veil that fogged her mother's hard eyes and the lines of her face, and Rosemary could not help saying, "I see you didn't want anyone to recognize you."

"Rosemary, please. You needn't make this unpleasant."

"Did they tell you that I decided to keep her?"

"We've already discussed this. You're seventeen."

"I'm not giving her up."

"And what do you think will happen, then?" Mom lowered her voice. "How do you expect to support her and yourself? You've no money. You'll be going to college. What will you do with her?"

"His family—"

"His family doesn't want you or her, and he's gone off to Spain. He's abandoned you, Rosemary. He was in such a hurry to get away he went to war where he's certain to get himself killed."

The words hurt. "That's not true. Who told you that?"

"We've spoken with his parents, of course," Mom said in exasperation. "Really, Rosemary, your father sees Mr. Tapper sweeping up at the university most days."

Sweeping up. Rosemary knew Mom had said it on purpose to remind her of the differences between their families. Stubbornly, she said, "He loves me. I'm keeping our baby, and when he comes home—"

"We all agreed this was best. You agreed." Mom sighed. "You're only tired and emotional. It's natural, given what you've been through, but tomorrow you'll think differently."

"I won't. I won't. I know it," Rosemary insisted.

"What do you know about anything? You're still a child. I'll hear no more about it. You're to stay here for the next few days, recovering. Then we'll take you home."

"Home? I'm not going back there."

"You certainly are."

"I want to see her. Bring me my baby."

Another sigh. Mom's gloves were in her lap; she picked them up and smoothed them as if they were riddled with intolerable wrinkles. "You don't have a baby."

Rosemary snapped, "I had her last night. She's here. I want to see her now."

"It never happened, Rosemary. This is why you're here. This is what we discussed. The whole point is to forget it happened and move on."

"That's what *you* wanted," Rosemary insisted sullenly.

"Is it? I'm not the one who was arrested at an . . . an . . ." Her mother's face contorted. "I can't even say it, it's so obscene. You did not want this child either. You should be happy we provided this for you. You've made a mistake, and now you can go on. Your life needn't be affected in the slightest. You can go to college. You can want something more. You can be something."

Rosemary turned away. "That's your dream, not mine."

"Your dream too," Mom said tightly. "You're not meant to destroy your life like this."

"Then you should have let me do what I wanted. Now I've changed my mind. Now I do want her."

"Well, you can't have her. You signed the papers."

"We can tear them up."

"We can't. It's too late."

"Where's Dad? I want to talk to him."

"He's taking care of the last details. This is for the best, Rosemary. You know this. We have discussed this ad nauseam. You're seventeen years old, for God's sake. You're still a child yourself. Now stop with all this."

"I just want to look at her—"

"No, you don't." Mom leaned close, her hand on Rosemary's, squeezing. "You think you do, but it will only torment you, and this will be easier, I promise you. It's time to put this behind you. Best to forget it happened. *Ssshhh*"—stroking now, those long thin fingers on Rosemary's arm, gentle, soothing, and when Rosemary looked, she saw only the blur of her mother's face, not only because of the veil but because of the tears she hadn't realized she was crying—"*Ssshhh*, that's right, it's all right. Ah, my sweet Rosemary, quite contrary. It's better this way. You know I'm right, and you'll thank me for this. You will. I know it doesn't seem so now, but you can go on, and you can have the life you're meant to have and you'll never have to talk about any of this again . . ."

So many words, words murmured and stumbled over and whispered, and though Rosemary did not mean for them to linger or to stay, somehow they got tangled up with everything else she had promised, and pulled her into a well of grief until she surrendered and drowned there. She stopped asking to see her baby and in fact said almost nothing else the rest of her time there. When the week was up, and her stay at White Shield was over, she packed up her things and got into the Chevy sedan with her father, and when he said, "A nice restful stay for you, eh, Rosie?"

She said, "Oh, yes."

But she did not forget the grief, nor the shame of how easily she'd surrendered.

Chapter 11

Dorothy Chivers had not liked being a housewife and mother, that was clear. She had wanted to be a scientist, but the only education she'd been able to afford was typing school, and before her waitressing job had earned her enough savings even for that, the Spanish flu pandemic in '18 stalled everything. She'd met Dad at the hospital, where they'd both been taken with the flu; they'd survived thanks to their will to be together, Dad joked. Then she had Rosemary. The flu had weakened Mom badly—it was only now that Rosemary wondered if it had something to do with her heart condition—and Mom said often that Rosemary was a difficult baby and worse child. There had been no further education at all.

Mom had no family here, or so Rosemary assumed; the only time her mother talked about her family was to say she didn't want to talk about them. They lived in Michigan, or Minnesota . . . some state that began with an *M* . . . Rosemary couldn't remember and wouldn't have been able to say it was the truth anyway. Mom had been the queen of obfuscation. Dad said that Mom told him she'd come to Seattle because it was as far as the train could take her from where she'd been. Neither he nor Rosemary had known whom to contact at her mother's death, and no one claiming to belong to Mom had shown up for the funeral. The only family there was Dad's sister, Aunt Pat.

At the service, her mother's friends talked about Dorothy Chivers as an organizational genius, an intellect and autodidact. All those things were a revelation to Rosemary. It wasn't that she hadn't known her mother was smart. From the time Rosemary could remember, her parents flung about names like Einstein and Bohr and Schrödinger and Heisenberg and had deep conversations about the chemistry classes her scientist father taught at the university. But most of Rosemary's memories were of her mother sitting at the table smoking cigarettes and staring at nothing, and herself bearing the weight of Mom's hopes and stunted dreams. Perhaps Rosemary had not known her mother, but the opposite was true as well; she had often wondered if her mother knew her at all. Her mother had not been much of a mother, and so who could blame Rosemary if she, too, hadn't enough mothering instincts to recognize her own daughter?

Stella Bullard had come to the funeral, and at the reception following had asked Rosemary if she'd decided about returning to Mercer Rocks. "I understand if this is a difficult time for you, and I'm sorry to ask you to make a decision now—"

"Do we still only have through December?" Rosemary asked.

Stella seemed taken aback by her bluntness. "We're trying to find funding, and the board is working very hard, but for now, yes."

Before, four months had seemed perfect. Now, even this week spent away from the school felt too long, given that Rosemary had to start from nothing to discover which of those girls was her own. She needed more time. "I'll be back on Monday."

Stella's relief was obvious.

But Rosemary's dilemma was not so easily solved as the principal's. She spent the days at home tearing through the house, looking for any information her mother had left behind: papers, notes, photographs, anything. There was nothing to indicate how her mother had discovered

Rosemary's daughter was at Mercer Rocks. Rosemary remembered no photographs of Mom's family, but she searched the boxes in the attic, looking for anything Mom might have forgotten she had, any old photo of a grandmother, or a cousin or aunt who might give her a clue, some physical family trait that might point her to Maisie or Sandra or Jean. She found none. "My guess is that she wanted to leave it all behind her," Aunt Pat told Rosemary. "I know she left when she was eighteen. Her mom had remarried—that's all she ever said about it. Some people don't like to remember, Rosie."

Rosemary found old science textbooks of her father's and ancient sewing patterns, Mom's used makeup and a bagful of old shoes, and a collection of magazines and the copy of her parents' marriage license, but nothing that helped her identify which of those girls was hers.

She would study them more closely, of course, now that she knew she was looking for herself or David in their faces, but she desperately needed more concrete information. Short of asking which was adopted—and they might not know; it wasn't as if parents volunteered such information. No one admitted to adopting; it was a well-kept secret in most families. She could ask their parents directly, but that would only get her fired, and why should the parents tell her the truth anyway? She was a threat. Why should they tell her anything? Her only recourse was the adoption papers themselves, and she already knew how useless that avenue of pursuit was.

"They're sealed, miss. You signed your rights away, miss. I couldn't get them for you even if I wanted to. No one can."

"But I'm her mother."

"You're no one's mother, miss. You signed the papers saying so."

Rosemary pushed the memory away, that office at White Shield, the way the words ricocheted against the walls, the hollowness of the sound. But they didn't leave her, and once the reception was over, the house silent, the serving plates washed and dried, and the casserole dishes brought by the neighbors neatly stacked in the freezer, Rosemary's restlessness and grief returned, a combination she could not manage. She could not be still. She thought of the headstone she and her father had picked out for the plot at Washelli Cemetery: *Beloved Wife and Mother*, and the secrets they'd kept from one another mocked her. The word *Mother* mocked her too—something she both was and wasn't— until Dad finally said, "What's got into you, Rosie?" and suddenly she could not bear standing there another moment, she could not stand herself. She could no longer ignore her restlessness; she was unraveling. She both longed for someone to hold her tight and knew she would break apart at a touch.

"I have to go out for a bit," she said.

Her father said, "Rosemary."

"Not for long. I just need a smoke and . . . and a drink." She headed to the front door, grabbing her coat before he could stop her. "I'll be back soon."

"Rosemary, why don't we—"

"I'm a grown woman, Dad," Rosemary snapped. "I'll be fine."

She left the house and started walking.

It wasn't as if she went there deliberately. Her thoughts were too full for real intention, but when she saw the familiar brick facade and neon sign sporting the half-clad woman on the blue crescent moon, Rosemary stopped. There was knowing, and there was *knowing*, and now that she was here, there was the choice. *Turn around. Go home.*

You let her go. You don't even know which one she is.

She stepped inside and was assailed immediately by loud music from the jukebox, the smoke-and-beer-saturated scent of wooden booths scratched with graffiti, the hodgepodge of framed photos and books and ephemera crowding the walls, the grubby, stinking dark of the Blue Moon Tavern.

Mostly men—students from the University of Washington, professors—and a few women sprawled in the booths, smoking and downing schooners of beer, poets and writers and playwrights and probably anarchists and socialists, though these days no one asked and no one would tell you even if you did. The Blue Moon was, and had been forever, a Bohemian oasis, and Rosemary looked out of place in her severe suit, though once, long ago, when she was sixteen, she had fit in easily, and there had been times this last summer when she'd shown up in dungarees. How easy it was to hide if one wanted.

For a moment, the present dissolved; the grubby booths and benches melted into the past, into a crowd of set and prop builders and actors, some of them Negroes, because the Blue Moon was one of the few places that would serve mixed clientele. And there she was, sliding into the bench, her beer cold in her hand, and there was David, reaching to pull her close . . . Rosemary blinked away the vision, but it left a heaviness, a smear across her vision. There was a small table in the corner booth; she took it. The waitress eyed her dubiously until Rosemary said, "I'll have a beer."

The waitress returned a few minutes later with a schooner she plopped on the scarred table. Rosemary shrugged off her coat and studied the graffiti to see what was new since the last time she'd been here. She drank the beer quickly, ordered another. By the third, her restlessness began to turn as she'd known it would. The conversations around her grew louder. A group of men over there were obviously professors. Another group—students. One man at the bar, lanky, dark-haired, and wearing glasses, reading and nursing a beer. Another over by the door, leaning against the wall, watching her through the fog of his cigarette smoke.

The bench was hard. The jukebox blared Tony Bennett's "Stranger in Paradise." Rosemary lit a cigarette and waited. The one at the bar closed his book and left. But the other one . . . She exhaled a long stream of smoke, focusing her gaze on him. Tall. Solidly built. In the gloom she could make out little else.

The men at the table next to her argued about *From Here to Eternity*. She couldn't tell if they argued over the movie or the book. Rosemary kept her eye on the man by the door. She drank more. Smoked more. The restlessness that was no longer restlessness but something else—she didn't know what to call it. Longing seemed too vague. Lust too concrete. Desire—no, it hadn't that kind of intention and nothing to do with pleasure—tingled through her fingers and prickled her skin. As if the man at the door felt it, he stirred, pushing himself off the wall. Rosemary straightened, tilted her head in coy welcome, waited.

He was dark too. She liked dark, for contrast, and with that sleepless look that said student, though he was too old to be an undergraduate. A grad student, then. She liked that too. Too much to do to try to find her again.

He stubbed out his cigarette in her ashtray. "You were looking at me."

"What's your name?"

"Vincent. Vincent Th—"

"Vincent is enough," Rosemary said quickly. "Vincent, are you busy?"

"Not at the moment."

"Do you live near here?"

He jerked his head. "Just up the street."

She dragged on her cigarette. She said the next words quickly too, before she had time to think, before she could swallow them. "How would you like to take me home?"

Chapter 12

Monday morning she was back at the school, breathing in its familiar scents of fried bologna, sweat, and soap, and uneasy again in the disquietude of its hallways, worse now that she knew her daughter walked those halls too. Rosemary wondered if her daughter felt that unrest, if it unsettled her the same way. She wondered too many things, could not stop listing everything she knew about the three girls: clever Maisie, a runaway; cynical Sandra, with a liking for alcohol; pretty Jean and her inappropriate sexuality. Rosemary did not want to linger on what she understood about those particular flaws, but instead on why. Why were these girls in Mercer Rocks? Were those the reasons, or were there others? Was there a clue in their records?

There was nothing in those files, Alicia had said. But how could Rosemary know that unless she checked for herself? Who knew what she would discover, or what might be important? She had no other choice but to look. Before classes began, she went to the office. Irene was fiddling with the catch of the open window. Rosemary glanced toward Stella's door. The principal wasn't there. It was a relief; Rosemary had more confidence that she could convince the secretary to show her the records if there was going to be an issue.

"Good morning, Irene," she began cheerfully. "Is something wrong with the window?"

Irene let out a breath. "No, the latch is funny, that's all. It keeps getting stuck. Did you need something?"

It had been made plain the records were off-limits, so Rosemary knew she couldn't just ask to see them. "I'm planning a special home-ec project," she lied confidently. "For the senior girls. I wanted to check their records for any allergies."

Irene hesitated. "Oh. Well, I'm afraid you'd need Stella's permission. Or Lois's."

"It's such a small matter. I hadn't thought to trouble them with it."

"I'm sorry." For what it was worth, the secretary truly did look sorry. Also immovable. "You'll have to talk to Stella. Oh, and Miss Chivers? I'm sorry about your mother. Stella spoke so highly of her."

Rosemary tried to smile through her disappointment. "Thank you."

She left the office. Perhaps she would talk to Stella, but given the principal's lecture about Mercer Rocks and its mission, Rosemary would have to come up with a better reason than a home-ec project. When she got to her classroom, she riffled through her papers until she found the class list for fourth period and searched it again, wondering if she'd somehow read it incorrectly. There was no mistake. Only three girls were seniors. Only three girls were seventeen. It had to be one of them, unless her mother had lied, and why would she do that? In her last moments, and after so long, when she could have just left it . . . No, Rosemary did not believe it was a lie.

Whatever the reason her mother had waited until now to reveal this secret, Rosemary was glad for it. It was true what she'd said to her father; she wanted to know that her daughter was okay. Rosemary wanted to know that she had not given her up for nothing. For now, she had no recourse but to discover which one was her daughter from the girls themselves, and so she waited anxiously to see them again.

~

Rosemary sweated in her short-sleeved sheath dress, the thick white belt around her waist too tight, wisps of hair slipping from her updo to cling to her sweaty neck and cheeks. The damn radiator hissed as the afternoon sun blasted relentlessly into the room. The windows were open as far as they would go. Some of the girls pressed the handouts Rosemary had placed on the tables to their faces, sniffing the compellingly sweet scent of fresh dittoes. Maisie, Jean, and Sandra sat in front, smiling.

"Oh, Miss Chivers, you're back!" Maisie said—so pretty, with those dark brown eyes and that clear skin. "It was so awful with Mrs. Vance here instead. We missed you so!"

"Though we're very sorry your mother died," Jean said quickly.

"Thank you, Miss Karlstad."

"Mourning is always such a trial. That's what Daddy says."

Daddy. If the girl was her daughter, it would bring Rosemary into closer proximity with a member of the House Un-American Activities Committee than she had any wish to be. Teachers were especially vulnerable to investigation—as Alicia had said, they were "molding minds," and there was the little matter of perjuring herself on the loyalty oath.

Not only that. Rosemary thought uncomfortably of the Blue Moon Tavern and the reason her contract had not been renewed in Yakima. She would have to watch herself. She could not risk the kind of rumors here that had dogged her everywhere else.

Rosemary pushed the thought away. First things first. "I understand that last week you talked about the forms of radiation with Mrs. Vance. Today we'll talk about the treatment of radiation burns. The first page of the ditto on your desk—don't inhale it, Margaret—lists the three types of nuclear radiation: alpha, beta, and gamma."

As she went through the information, she studied the three girls covertly. Blond hair, brown hair. Two with brown eyes like Rosemary's own. One with blue eyes, which were not in Rosemary's family, nor in David's. So maybe not Sandra. Sandra and Maisie both had oval faces; Jean's was heart-shaped. But again, Rosemary did not see herself in any of them, and she wondered . . . had it been too long? She tried to bring his image into her head and couldn't, but then again, she was distracted. She had no photographs of David, but she saw him in her dreams often enough to know she could not forget his face.

The girls dragged their fingernails down the dittoes, making purple scratches in the paper; some of them doodled idly on the edges.

"When are we going to get to cooking?" Lizzie Etheridge whined.

"Never, I hope," Jean said listlessly.

"It might be never, if the school closes," Sandra put in.

"Girls, please focus. Let's talk about the difference between contamination and exposure." Rosemary tried to concentrate. "A person wearing perfume, for example—"

"What kind of perfume?" Jean perked up.

"Any kind."

"Jean Naté is my favorite," Maisie said.

"Jean Naté, then."

"What perfume do you wear, Miss Chivers?" Jean asked. "I love it."

Rosemary sighed. "For the purposes of comparing it to nuclear radiation, a person wearing perfume is contaminated, because the perfume is actually on their skin. Someone close enough to smell the perfume is close enough to receive rays of radiation."

Maisie's eyes lit mischievously. "So if a boy is close enough to smell your perfume, he's exposed."

"Well, yes. But we're not talking about that."

"He'll die of radiation poisoning just from being too close." Maisie flipped her dark hair. "That will teach him."

Giggles all around.

"At least he'll know," Jean said. "He'll know when he smells it that he's too close. He'll have some warning. My cousin said a friend of his got gonorrhea just from sharing a Popsicle with some girl. He didn't even know she had it."

"Radiation doesn't really smell like perfume, Miss Karlstad. It was just an example. And your cousin's friend did not get gonorrhea from sharing a Popsicle. You can't get it that way."

Jean looked flummoxed. "Then . . . then how do you get it?"

Rosemary had spoken without thinking, and now she realized she should not have. This was not the curriculum the board had approved. The only reference those texts made to gonorrhea was listing it under "sex troubles and worries," and saying it should be avoided at all costs. She couldn't talk about this. She could be fired for it.

"Oh. Well . . ." Rosemary struggled to think of something to say that would be acceptable to Stella and the board. Some easy deflection, some half-truth.

"How?" Maisie demanded. She leaned forward, her dark eyes intense, her expression all curiosity, anxiety, pleading, reminding Rosemary suddenly of the girl she'd been when she'd first run away, the thrill of excitement but yes, the fear too, the filthy streets and the soup kitchens and the homeless and the smell of paint and rain-soaked canvas baking in the sun and nervous sweat. The knowledge that the world was not as she'd thought, which was both exhilarating and terrifying. Then she'd believed it was hers to own and to change. Even the stars in the black expanse of the sky she'd believed she could spin about as she wanted, and yet how powerless she'd been.

How abjectly, completely, tragically powerless. Like these girls, giddy with rebelliousness but with nothing to rebel against but their own youth and ignorance. Drugstore lipstick was their call to arms. A cashmere sweater and a scarf tied just the right way. Fighting over skirt length and teasing the girl whose breasts grew first because *of course, she must sleep around, look at how the boys watch her!* Their only power was in hurting their friends. Hurting their parents. Hurting anyone who might care for them, when what they really wanted was to show the world they were not to be trifled with, and yet their whole world was so small and trifling still. Emotions that turned on a dime and movie-star gossip in *Photoplay* and the lurid covers of the paperbacks they hid beneath their beds, and it all felt so big.

How big it had felt to her then too. How much she'd wanted. How afraid she'd been in the end to take it. How easily she'd let it go.

No, they'd taken it from her. Everything she'd loved. Every decision that had been hers to make. They'd thought her too young. They'd thought she couldn't possibly know what she wanted.

But no one had told her anything. She'd never been given the information she needed, not by her parents, not by teachers or doctors. She'd been kept innocent and stupid and she hadn't known any better. She'd been too ignorant and afraid to fight them, and for that, she didn't know whom she hated more: the society that encouraged it—that required it—or herself, for being such a willing victim.

She could not lie to these girls. She could not deflect. One of them was her daughter. She could not do to her daughter what her mother—what the world—had done to her. She would not.

Before she could talk herself out of it, she said, "From sexual intercourse."

Her students looked at her blankly.

Finally, Maisie—of course, Maisie—said, "Oh . . . yes."

"So when a boy is getting fresh . . ." Jean's uncertainty was obvious.

"Or like French kissing?" one of the other girls asked.

Rosemary sighed. "No. Sexual intercourse is when a man puts his penis into a woman's vagina."

The shocked silence in the room was deafening.

"Yes, but . . . how"—Lizzie flushed a brilliant red—"how does he get it in?"

"Ah." Rosemary took a deep, steadying breath. "The penis, when it's aroused, gets hard, and the vagina, when it's aroused, gets wet, and the man can slide his penis inside easily."

"Aroused?" one of them asked faintly. "How does it do that?"

"Sex feels good." Rosemary hesitated. How much was enough? Their faces were so earnest, their curiosity not just curiosity but an eager craving for information. Maybe just a bit more. "There are nerves on parts of the genitalia that are designed for pleasure, and when you touch them, or rub them, it feels very nice. That's arousal. For both men and women."

"Oh my God," Sandra said.

Rosemary pretended to be oblivious to their embarrassed horror. "If either you or your partner has gonorrhea, and you have sexual intercourse, you can be infected. The bacterium lives in the genitals. Fortunately, there are medicines now, so it's not as dire as it used to be."

"You mean we won't die from it?" Jean clearly grappled with the revelation.

"You won't die from it, no. There's a cure."

"But I thought you could die!"

"Why are you so surprised? Adults lie. They lie to us about everything." Sandra's voice was brittle with anger.

They lie. Rosemary didn't bother to contradict her. "Your teacher from last year didn't tell you any of this? The seniors at least?"

"She left before we got to this part. We weren't even to cooking yet. She didn't care about us at all," Maisie explained.

"She wasn't as honest as you, Miss Chivers," Sandy said.

"She wasn't even pretty," Jean put in.

"I think she was more interested in dancing than teaching." Maisie snickered.

"We got a substitute teacher who taught us how to make paper snowflakes and sand candles. So boring," Jean said.

Lizzie Etheridge raised her hand. "So . . . so you can't get gonorrhea from a girdle? A friend of mine has this rash, and she thought . . ."

Rosemary shook her head. "Not from a girdle—"

The buzzing from the intercom speaker cut her off.

Stella Bullard's imperious voice crackled tinnily from the speaker. "Atomic bomb–attack drill, students! Duck and cover! Duck and cover!"

Chapter 13

Rosemary marched them out to join the other classes in the gymnasium.

"Duck and cover! Remember Bert the Turtle! Duck and cover!" Andrew Covington shouted, referring to the government film about nuclear-bomb safety every school showed at least once a year.

"Bert the Turtle can go straight to hell!" someone called out.

"He's a homo!" another one shouted.

The girls laughed.

"Down!" Covington ordered.

"But the floor's so dirty!" one of the girls complained.

"I said down! *Duck and cover!*"

With a collective groan, the girls curled into balls against the walls of the gym, putting their hands behind their necks.

Gloria Weedman's fine porcelain skin shone with sweat. She glanced toward the closed gym doors with longing. "As if this would save us."

Rosemary thought of her mother's bomb-shelter pamphlet and the unit she was supposed to be teaching. One Christmas, she remembered, Dad had bought Mom a pin "inspired" by the bomb, a pearlized stone bursting into faux gems of all colors. *As daring to wear as it was to drop the first atomic bomb,* the box said, but that was when everyone had been dazzled by the sheer audacity of such a weapon, before they'd known to fear it. She didn't suppose anyone would wear a pin like that now.

She looked over the giggling, jiggling girls, whispering to each other, not taking any of this seriously. There were Maisie and Jean. Rosemary looked automatically for Sandra but didn't see her.

Quincy Reese sauntered over to Gloria and Rosemary, calling, "Be still, girls! Remain in position!" He glanced at the caged clock high on the wall. "Maybe they'll wait to give the all clear until the period is over."

"Wouldn't that be nice," Gloria said.

"Aren't you supposed to be ducking and covering too, Miss Chivers?" Maisie called.

Rosemary ignored her.

Gloria shook her head. "That girl."

"It's the other one I have trouble with," Quincy said in a low voice. "Miss Karlstad. If she bats her eyes at me one more time . . ."

"All clear!" Lois Vance's voice blasted across the gymnasium speakers. "Please return to your classrooms in an orderly fashion."

Quincy groaned.

"All right, girls, everybody up." Gloria clapped her hands; the girls scrambled to their feet. "Line up, please!"

Already the gym was rank with the musk of teenage sweat not quite mastered by deodorant. Covington threw open the doors. The buzz of a lawn mower on the far edge of the property drifted inside, mixing with the talk and laughter of the girls as they brushed dust from their skirts.

But it was impossible now to restore order. When they reached the classroom, the bell for the end of fourth period rang, and there was only enough time for the girls to grab their things and hurry to their last class.

"Bye, Miss Chivers!" Maisie waved as she went out, and Rosemary struggled to remember if she'd seen Sandra return and couldn't. But she must have. Where else would she have gone?

Fifth was Rosemary's planning period. But the room was too hot; her own bedroom, even stuck as it was in the attic, would be better. She gathered her papers, still unnerved that she'd somehow lost sight of Sandra.

She left the windows open in the hopes that the cool evening air might combat the radiator and departed. As she passed the tennis courts, she caught sight of Sandra wearing the dark green cotton school gym suit, leaning against the fence with Maisie and a row of other girls, watching Alicia demonstrate a serve.

Rosemary relaxed. Nothing to worry about. Sandra was right there.

The golden Indian-summer afternoon was edged with the slight touch of fall—not quite a chill, but a tinge that marked the change in season. In the dorm, a few girls talked idly or studied. Mrs. Sackett was always there during the day to monitor them, so Rosemary continued to her room. She unlocked the door, dropped her books and papers onto the bed—

And stopped.

Someone had been there. She'd been back a day, and it had happened again. Even though she'd locked the door, the feeling was unmistakable. Rosemary looked around. Guitar. Records. Record player. Everything as she'd left it. But there . . . on her dresser . . . she didn't know why, but something led her to her leather alligator-print vanity case, though it was still in its place, the gold latch closed.

Rosemary unlatched it, opening the lid slowly. Her cosmetics were all there, the Revlon powder compact, the eyebrow brush, foundation . . . but on the edge of the cream-colored acetate lining was a smear of pink that had not been there before. The case had been her mother's and unused, the lining still pristine; Rosemary had not had it long enough to mar it.

She searched through it. One lipstick, two, but the third was missing. It was the deep pink color that matched the smear on the lining. Revlon's Cherries in the Snow.

She went through the case again, pulling everything out, searching for the lipstick. It was definitely gone. She went to her purse, thinking it might be there. It wasn't, and the only way for it not to be was if someone had taken it.

Sandra. The thought came before she could stop it, but no, even if Sandra had managed to disappear during the drill, there wouldn't have been time for her to sneak to Rosemary's room and then be back for tennis.

Rosemary must have mislaid the lipstick. It was her favorite too. Maybe it had fallen out of her purse. Maybe at the Blue Moon, or . . . or later . . . She shook that thought away. The lipstick hadn't been that expensive. She could easily buy another. She eased off her heels and undid the belt cinching her waist, then unhooked her stockings from her garters and wriggled free of the panty girdle. She opened the top drawer of her dresser for another bra, and—

Her perfume was gone.

This she could not have mislaid. She kept the bottle in her underwear drawer on purpose—she liked the way its scent somehow managed to imbue everything. But the distinctive shell-like bottle of Shalimar was gone, leaving behind only the sillage of its warm and spicy fragrance.

This was not so easy or cheap to replace. Not only that, but Rosemary felt the loss as the invasion it was. Someone rifling through her underwear. Someone searching for something—for what? It made her acutely uncomfortable to think of other hands, hands she didn't know, touching her things, doing . . . what? . . . to her things . . . taking her perfume, and why? For what reason?

She closed the drawer slowly and went to the window to look out at the tennis courts. Yes, there. Jean and Sandra against the fence, talking. Maisie on the court, her ponytail swinging as she backhanded the ball.

There hadn't been enough time. Yet even as Rosemary told herself that, unease scuttled over her skin, and Sandra looked up. Too far away, there was no way she could see Rosemary in the window, but still the directness of the girl's gaze pinned Rosemary in place. Sandra turned to Jean, and then Jean, too, looked up, and Rosemary felt like a beacon, too bright, too loud, impossible to miss.

She backed away from the window and went to change.

Chapter 14

The next morning, only Alicia and Gloria were in the staff room when Rosemary entered, but the room was thick with smoke from Alicia's cigarettes, and the tin ashtray was already full. Several notebooks were spread over the table, and Alicia scrawled madly in one of them.

Gloria waved Rosemary over. "Help me convince Alicia that all is not lost."

"I don't see any room to put my coffee," Rosemary joked, sitting down.

Alicia glanced up grumpily from her rabid note-taking.

"You're teaching a nuclear unit now, aren't you, Rosemary?" Gloria asked.

"*Personal and Family Survival,*" Rosemary quoted the title. "Such cheery curriculum."

"Stella asked me to include a unit on keeping art alive after an atomic attack." Alicia puffed anxiously on her cigarette.

"At least math doesn't change after an apocalypse," Gloria said, sipping her coffee.

Alicia exhaled a cloud of smoke. "It's hard enough to teach these delinquents to care about art, without having to teach them how to paint with sticks and ashes—assuming even those are left."

Rosemary said, "I wish I knew what to tell you. I don't know anything about art."

"Apparently that's not the only thing you're stupid about."

Rosemary gasped at the insult that came from nowhere. Her face heated.

"Alicia!" Gloria scolded.

Alicia sighed and stubbed out her cigarette. "I'm sorry. I didn't mean it to sound so harsh. But so far you haven't been very good at listening, Rosemary." She turned to Gloria. "Are you going to tell her?"

"Tell me what?" Rosemary asked.

Alicia lowered her voice, though they were the only ones in the staff room. "You should not be bringing any attention to yourself here. There are too many people watching. I'm doing you a favor by saying it." A stabbing glance at Gloria. "Since no one else will."

Rosemary frowned. "What do you mean?"

Alicia leaned even closer. "Did you really teach them about gonorrhea?"

"Oh, that—"

"*That.* God. There are still HUAC hearings going on in Seattle. Have you forgotten these girls belong to important families? Do you think they'll just ignore this? Some girl will tell her parents, and before you know it, you'll be in front of a congressional committee trying to explain how teaching girls about debauchery isn't a threat to national security."

"I was answering a question," Rosemary explained. "Isn't that what a teacher is supposed to do? Who else will if we don't?"

"It's unsanctioned curriculum," Alicia said.

Gloria said nothing, but looked sympathetic, and just then Lois Vance peeked into the staff room and said, "Rosemary! There you are. I was just coming to find you."

Alicia gave Rosemary a pointed look. Gloria sighed.

The vice principal's mouth was tight above her receding chin. "Stella would like to talk to you."

Rosemary's heart sank. She should have gone straight to Stella's office the moment class ended.

She followed Lois to the office. The vice principal ushered Rosemary inside and shut the door firmly behind her.

Stella Bullard's face was expressionless. "Ah, Rosemary. I'll get right to the point, as I know you have class in a few minutes. Maryanne Brown was in the infirmary last night—were you aware of this?"

Rosemary shook her head, but any hope she had that this meeting was not regarding teaching about gonorrhea fled. Maryanne was in her fourth period.

"She was there because she worried she might have gonorrhea."

Which meant, of course, that Maryanne had not needed the discussion about how sexual intercourse worked. Rosemary worked to keep her expression even. "I see."

"She said that yesterday in your class there was a discussion about it. Might I ask why you're discussing gonorrhea in your class? I don't believe that is in the curriculum decided upon by the board."

"The question came up," Rosemary told her. "I felt it would be best to give them an honest answer."

"We are not here for honesty, Rosemary. We are here to teach them the curriculum."

"But the curriculum says almost nothing about gonorrhea, and what it does say is at least ten years old."

"That's what the board decided upon."

"Stella, surely you must see that it's wrong to leave them in ignorance and fear—"

"It's what you were hired to teach," Stella persisted.

"But—"

"Do I have to say it again? Our patrons trust us to make their daughters good citizens. Wives and mothers. Valuable members of society."

"I wasn't aware that included ignorance of disease," Rosemary said quietly.

"You also"—the principal glanced down at her notes—"spoke to them about sex, I believe."

"It was part of the discussion."

"Is it in the curriculum?"

"Family planning is, in fact—"

"The discussion of sex 'feeling good' is in the curriculum?"

Maryanne Brown had apparently said a great deal. "I believe there are references to boys getting 'carried away' and girls needing to stop them."

Stella nodded. "Yes, that's what I thought. That's what you're to teach them."

Rosemary worked to control her temper and her habitual contrariness. "I don't believe it helps to keep the facts from them. Better that they know the truth, don't you think? So they know how to . . . handle things."

"It's up to their husbands to teach them about sex, not us," Stella said firmly, then she softened. "I know you must be having a difficult time this soon after your mother's death, and so I'm willing to put this off to distraction."

Rosemary took the lead Stella offered. "Thank you. It has been . . . difficult."

"But I do not want to have this conversation again. You have been a fine addition to our staff thus far, Rosemary. But there are limits to what is acceptable. If the board were to get wind of this kind of deviance in a teacher, they would be very concerned. We're trying to raise funding to get past December, and having to fire a teacher or take disciplinary action so early in the year, *especially* for deviance, would put that at risk. Do you understand?"

"Yes, of course. I understand. It was a mistake. It won't happen again."

"It cannot happen again," Stella said, and Rosemary heard the warning. "Very well. You'd best go or you'll be late."

A nod of dismissal. Rosemary left as quickly as she could without looking like she was running, but her pulse raced and the weight of her secrets pressed. This was not just another job, and she could not lose this chance to know her daughter. If she were fired, she would never discover the truth.

Chapter 15

By lunchtime, the gonorrhea scandal had been replaced by the flurry over girls who'd been caught with contraband during a room search. Rosemary was monitoring lunch when she was startled to find that she was in the thick of it.

"Miss Chivers, thank God!" Maisie rushed into the dining room, Sandra on her heels. Both looked upset.

"They've got Jean," Sandra burst out.

"Who's got Jean?"

"Mrs. Bullard," Maisie explained. "They did a room search this morning, and they found some things."

"Like what?" Rosemary knew the answer before Maisie answered.

"A bottle of perfume. And lipstick."

Shalimar, Rosemary would bet. And Cherries in the Snow. But . . . it had been Sandra who'd disappeared, not Jean.

"And malted milk balls she got from Lizzie Etheridge," Sandra added.

"God, Sandy, don't be such a tattletale," Maisie snapped at her.

"All right," Rosemary said. "So?"

"So do something," Maisie said urgently.

"What would you like me to do? Mrs. Bullard and Mrs. Vance are in charge of discipline."

"But they're going to put Jean on field duty," Sandra protested. "She'll have to work with Old Martin on the grounds. For a week. Everyone hates that job. It's dirty and sweaty."

"We thought you could help. She'd rather work with Mrs. Dennis in the kitchen. Or maybe . . ." Maisie lowered her voice thoughtfully. "Or maybe she could be assigned to you."

"To me?" Rosemary asked.

"To—I don't know—make decorations or something? Isn't that something the home-ec teacher does?"

"She'd really like that," Sandra agreed.

Rosemary hesitated. "I'm not sure how I could help." She was pleased these girls had come to her, and she couldn't help attributing some deeper meaning to it, but Stella's warning was in her head, and it was dangerous for her to interfere.

Maisie and Sandra exchanged glances. Maisie said, "Please, Miss Chivers, you're our favorite teacher. You listen to us. After the other day when you told us the truth . . . we like you. You're the only one we trust."

Rosemary felt herself weakening.

"Jean admires you so much, Miss Chivers. I know she would be so grateful."

Again, Maisie flashed a glance at Sandra.

"We all would be," Sandra added.

Such pretty faces. Such words . . . they caught at Rosemary's heart and twisted. Jean could be her daughter. Sandra could be. Maisie. How could she not do them this favor?

But there was Stella's warning. The timing was all wrong.

"I'm sorry," she said quietly. "I can't—"

"You can't? You mean you won't," Maisie accused.

"If you would just let me explain—"

"Don't bother. You're just like the others. You don't give a damn."

"We thought you were different," Sandra said with contempt.

The two of them spun away without another word, not a single glance back.

Rosemary was surprised at how much it wounded.

~

Rosemary could not make a plea to Stella Bullard without endangering herself, but maybe there was another way. As soon as she could, Rosemary went in search of the gardener, Martin McCree.

The clouds had grown fuller, a mottled gray that promised showers at some point but not full-on rain. In her long-sleeved, blue-striped blouse and gray flannel slacks, Rosemary wasn't cold, but the breeze coming up from the lake held the bite of fall.

The sounds of tennis balls thudding on the court and against rackets grew fainter as she ventured closer to the trees bordering the slope down to the shore. She saw no sign of the gardener, but then she heard the faint thwacking of cutting and she followed the sound to where the path from the lake came out at the orchard. Beyond was a stand of alders and maples and cottonwoods. There was the gardener, alone, hacking at a clump of blackberry bushes.

"Hello!" Rosemary called, carefully making her way down the stone stairs laid into the path. The gardener straightened and put the wicked-looking machete next to a bucket. He wore gray coveralls with the school crest embroidered in green over the pocket. Martin McCree was not tall, but he had broad shoulders and back and narrow hips. His craggy face and the lines about his blue eyes spoke of a life spent outdoors.

"Hello there. Miss Chivers, is it?" McCree's Scottish burr had been mellowed by a long residence in America, but it was still unmistakable.

"Rosemary." She offered her hand, which he shook. "And you must be Martin."

He nodded shortly.

A man of few words, it seemed, and one not prone to small talk. Rosemary said, "I understand you've got Jean Karlstad working field duty this week."

"Aye, she's on the list."

"I wanted to ask if you could go easy on her."

He reached into a pocket for a pack of cigarettes, shook one free, and offered it to her. Rosemary took it, waited as he pulled out a silver lighter and flipped the lid to light them both. "Go easy on her? There's not much easier than clearing shrub and pulling weeds."

"Maybe she could . . . I don't know, water things."

He eyed her through a cloud of cigarette smoke. "What'd she do this time?"

"She was caught with perfume and lipstick. They were mine." She hadn't meant to say the last. She wasn't sure why she did.

"Yours?"

"It's a long story."

He blew out a long stream of smoke. "You see, Rosemary, it's like this: if I give these girls something easy to do, it's not much of a punishment, is it? They keep getting into trouble, which means they keep getting field work and coming out here to bother me. Which I don't want. They're a pain in the ass. I don't want to listen to them bitch, and I don't like keeping an eye on them. And I don't want them around my son."

That surprised her. Then she remembered the young man she'd seen working alongside him. "Your son?"

"Samson. He works with me when he's home from school. He's fifteen and a good lad. Works hard."

"How does he feel about working at a girls' school?"

McCree snorted a laugh. "These girls scare him, if you want to know the truth. He keeps his distance. Wouldn't know what to do with one of 'em, I think. I'd like to keep it that way."

"I understand." She did. She also knew by his expression that he was unlikely to change his mind about going easy on Jean. She couldn't blame him for that. "Still, if you see ways to make things lighter for her . . . I can promise you she won't be out here again."

"How can you promise that?"

"She likes me. I think she'll listen to me." Rosemary was anything but certain about this, but if Jean knew she had tried to help . . .

"Ah." He grew thoughtful and flicked away ash. "Now why would you want to do that?"

"What do you mean?"

"Why d'you care about this girl? This Jean Karlstad?"

"I care about all of them," she lied.

"You're not here asking me about the other one on field duty this week, are you?"

Rosemary hadn't even known there was another girl on field duty, or who it was. She took a drag from her cigarette to keep from answering. It had lost its flavor. She tossed it and ground it out.

"No littering the grounds." He bent to pick it up and tucked it into his pocket.

"I'm sorry." Though she was more annoyed with him for asking her a question she did not want to answer. "Why not just throw it in the bucket?"

"It's full of oak apples." He gave the bucket a little kick.

She leaned to see. It was full of brownish apple-looking things. Some were round, some more misshapen. "What are oak apples?"

"Galls. Wasps grow 'em in the oak trees. Plant their eggs in 'em, and when the larva gets big enough, it drills itself out. See?" He got one and held it out for her. It was light and hard, and there was a small hole in it. "These are dead and used up. They're much prettier when they're alive. I once saw a pink-and-red one looked like a beating heart growing on the tree branch. Beautiful really."

Rosemary looked at him in surprise. She had not suspected the man had a poetic streak. "Why are you collecting them?"

"They're Sam's project for school. He makes ink with 'em. Like they used in the old days."

She thought of Alicia complaining about art and the apocalypse. "You should tell Alicia about that. She needs an art project for her atomic-bomb unit. Maybe your son could show her how."

Martin made an amused and dismissive shrug. "Probably could. Stuff's endlessly fascinating to him. He has bottles of it sitting around. He's the best student in his class. Means to go to college. He'll be the first one in the family to do it too."

"You must be very proud."

He crushed out his cigarette on the path, picked up the butt to shove into his pocket with hers, and retrieved his machete. He turned back to the half-lopped blackberry bushes.

The conversation was obviously over.

"I hope you'll consider what I said. About Miss Karlstad," Rosemary said.

"You want my advice, you'll leave things alone." He didn't look at her as he spoke. "You don't want to be one of those teachers."

"One of what teachers?"

"Ask Alicia. She'll tell you."

"Alicia?"

He didn't answer but hacked at a blackberry vine viciously enough that Rosemary stepped away. The breeze picked up, carrying with it the algae-and-reed scent of the lake, and she thought she heard the whistling too, from the Rocks, that high and lonely sound, but no, that was just her imagination. She hurried back up the path, annoyed with Martin McCree and disappointed that her efforts had won her nothing.

Chapter 16

As Rosemary neared the school, she saw Alicia on the tennis courts, cleaning up errant balls after class.

Rosemary approached her. "I was just talking to Martin McCree. Did you know his son makes ink from oak apples? I thought it might be a good idea for your art project."

Alicia bounced a ball into a basket that contained a dozen others. "Why were you talking to Martin?"

"I was just—"

"I heard Stella gave you a warning. You'd think after that, you'd know better than to do those girls favors."

Rosemary tried to hide her surprise. "I don't know what you're talking about."

Alicia sighed. "Come on, Rosemary. Why else would you be talking to Martin? Do you think they haven't tried this same thing before with other teachers? There's not a trick they don't know. These girls are trouble. How often must I say it? You need to remember that."

You don't want to be one of those teachers. Ask Alicia. "You said they pick a favorite victim every year. Who was it last year?"

Alicia's expression went carefully neutral. "The old home-ec teacher."

Funny, the girls had not spoken as if they'd cared about her that much. "What did they do?"

"I don't know. But she left quickly and without notice."

She's lying, Rosemary thought. She had no idea why.

But she realized that Alicia was right about one thing: Rosemary should not have talked to Martin about going easy on Jean. Rosemary had been too easily persuaded. There was too much at stake for her; she wanted her daughter to like her, and she saw now that maybe she couldn't trust herself completely to stay detached. Her need to know these girls could only cause her problems. The sooner she discovered which was hers the better; she could waste no more time. She had to get to those records.

~

Rosemary had always been good at getting in and out of places. When she was young, she'd mastered the art of escaping her room, no matter how many ways her mother found to lock her in. Rosemary smiled ruefully at the thought. It was astonishing that she hadn't been thrown into a reform school herself. Of course, had she not run away, she might have been.

The office would not be that difficult to break into. Unlike the windows on the dormitory floor, those in the office were not designed to keep girls from climbing out. They were just regular windows, and Rosemary remembered Irene fiddling with one. *"The latch is funny."* Perfect.

She knew that Tom Gear cleaned the first floor around eight o'clock because she'd seen him mopping, lingering outside the lounge when the girls who'd earned merit points were allowed to watch television—he always seemed to be there for *I Love Lucy.*

All Rosemary had to do was sneak in the window after Tom was done. As for getting into the records themselves . . . she would decide how to do that when she got there. It wasn't much of a plan, but she had nothing better.

After lights out, when Cheryl started her rounds, Rosemary went quietly down the stairs to the first floor. She wore her pajamas and a robe—if she were caught, it would be easier to make excuses clad this way. She could claim she was going to the kitchen for a snack.

The first floor was dark and empty and silent. The cloudy night sent almost no light through the windows, and the school's aura of unease was worse at night, disconcerting and creepy, and shadows seemed to move within shadows. The slightly antiseptic scent of the cleaner Tom used on the floors pricked at her nose. As she suspected, the office door was locked.

Rosemary went back down the hall to the front door and unlatched it. The brick stoop outside was rough and chill against her bare feet. She stumbled on little pebbles on the walk as she hurried to the office window, and hoped that the bordering maples kept her mostly hidden from any passersby, though the property lights were on and the circular drive and parking area were well lit.

She found the right window easily. She retrieved the shoehorn she'd put in her pocket and flattened it, then jiggled it between the windowsill and the edge of the sash, jimmying it tighter into the crack, and suddenly she was sixteen again, climbing the trellis to the garage roof and shoving the rusted shoehorn into the crevice of her windowsill. She levered up the office window, relieved when it lifted; she was glad Irene had not reported the faulty latch but wondered why—this was a reform school, for God's sake.

Rosemary put the shoehorn back into her pocket and then lifted the window sash high enough to crawl through. She half pulled, half hoisted herself up, cursing her weakness, and managed to squeeze and wiggle inside while the frame scraped her stomach and thighs through her robe.

She fell to the floor with a thud, and sat there catching her breath, heart pounding, hoping no one had heard.

The office was dark; the shadows of Irene's desk, the covered type-writer, loomed. There was no sound, and finally Rosemary's breathing calmed. She moved warily to the narrow door of the records closet. Even in the darkness, it seemed forbidding. She reached for the brass knob, dented and nicked, held her breath, and twisted.

The door didn't budge. Locked, just as she'd feared. Rosemary crouched to peer closer. She felt all over the knob, then felt the keyhole above it, old-fashioned decorative metal. A skeleton key maybe? It was hard to tell. She could try to pick it. All she needed was a bobby pin—

A click at the office door sent Rosemary spinning.

The door opened. A flashlight beam shone directly in her eyes, blinding her, freezing her in place.

"Miss Chivers?" The voice was familiar, but Rosemary was too shocked to recognize it until she saw the three shadows that came in with it. The glimmer of institutional white-cotton nightgowns and pale bare feet. Bright blond hair with its own light.

Maisie, Sandra, and Jean.

Chapter 17

"What are you doing here?" Maisie asked.

"I could ask you the same question," Rosemary said, tense and shaken. "How did you get in?"

The three girls looked at each other. Sandy shrugged. "The door was open."

A lie so obvious that Rosemary tsked.

Maisie glanced to the open window. "Did you climb in the window?"

"Of course not. I was looking at a file."

"In the dark?" Sandra asked. "In your pajamas?"

Maisie laughed with obvious delight. "Oh my God! You're a delinquent too!"

Jean's sly smile looked dangerous in the harsh light. "Does Mrs. Bullard know you're here?"

"Of course she doesn't," Maisie said.

"She'd probably like to know that her new teacher was breaking and entering," Sandra added.

"Into the office, no less!" Maisie chided.

Their talk had been rat-a-tat, no time to get in a word edgewise, but now Rosemary summoned her authority. "I'm not the only one breaking into the office, it seems. It's after lights out. You girls should be in bed. Why are you here?"

Jean went to Irene's desk, pulled open the deep second drawer and reached inside. Her pale fingers glimmered as she gestured for the flashlight, which Maisie handed her. They were so calm, so completely unfazed; Rosemary was the teacher, but that she was at a disadvantage was undeniable.

The drawer was full of contraband confiscated from room searches: gum, candy, cigarettes, makeup. Jean searched through it, pulling out a pack of cigarettes, a tube of lipstick, and a bottle of perfume. Shalimar.

"I believe that belongs to me," Rosemary said quietly. "The lipstick too."

"We're rescuing them for you," Maisie said.

Rosemary did not believe that for a moment. "Why did you have them to begin with?" she asked Jean.

"Sandy got them for me. I like the way you look. I like the way you smell," Jean answered.

Rosemary looked at Sandra. "You can't just go into someone's room and take things—"

"She's the best thief in the school." Maisie's voice rang with pride.

Sandra only smiled.

Rosemary ordered, "Put them back. You can't break into the office, and you can't take these things. You're not idiots, but you're behaving like it. What happens when they find out?"

"But we're doing it for you," Maisie protested.

"Is that so?" Rosemary made a sound of disbelief. "Well, I don't want you to do it. Now I have to report it—"

"No you don't," Maisie said.

"I certainly do—"

"Then we'll just report you." Maisie's dark eyes glittered as she moved toward Rosemary. "What are you doing in the office near—what time is it, Sandy?"

"After eleven," Sandy reported.

"After eleven, with the window open and no lights on? What do you think Mrs. Bullard would say if we told her about this?"

Rosemary knew exactly what Mrs. Bullard would say. *You're fired.* But she said, "I would tell her that you're lying. That I came upon you breaking in to the office."

"Hmmm." Maisie twisted her mouth in mock puzzlement. "Maybe she'd believe that. But . . . didn't you get a warning from Mrs. Bullard today, Miss Chivers? That's the rumor."

"That's what I heard too," Sandra added.

"We all did," Jean agreed.

Maisie preened at Rosemary's obvious surprise. "How worried you look! I guess you really don't want Mrs. Bullard to know about this. Why, whatever shall we do? What do you think, Sandy?"

"I think Mrs. Bullard would want to know that Miss Chivers was sneaking around here in the dark."

"Funny. I think she'd care more about you girls sneaking around here in the dark," Rosemary said evenly.

"It's like the Cold War, isn't it?" Jean offered. "Like—what do you call it, Sandy? The reason we don't bomb the Soviets and they don't bomb us?"

"Mutually assured destruction," Sandy said cheerfully.

"That's it."

"Why, Miss Chivers." Sandy laughed. "It seems you belong in Mercer Rocks too."

There it was, a connection Rosemary felt, the one thing she knew for certain about these three girls. She *was* like them. She had always been. They were like her. The risks they took, the things they cared about, that singular driving resistance, where the only thing you knew to do was whatever anyone told you not to . . . oh, she understood it too well, and even as it brought her closer to them, even as it fascinated her, Rosemary knew it should frighten her. It wasn't just that one of them belonged to her, it was that her understanding made her care, and that was the most dangerous thing of all, because it made her vulnerable.

"Mutually assured destruction." Yes, it was almost that. For them, this was all a game. But it could get her fired, especially because she didn't know how far they would go. She didn't know their rules. They risked nothing, but she could lose everything.

Chapter 18

It ended much as it began. Rosemary closed the window and went through the door with the girls, hearing the lock click shut behind her. Everyone sneaked back to their rooms, no files for Rosemary and no perfume or makeup for the girls—detente for now, so to speak, though Rosemary did tuck the Shalimar surreptitiously into her robe pocket before they left. There were so many things from room searches in that drawer it would never be missed, and it would be expensive to replace.

That night she tossed and turned, feeling her disadvantage and wondering what to do about it. That the girls now had a way to manipulate her was indisputable and untenable; she did not know how to stop them.

The next day, Maisie and Sandra and Jean whispered among themselves during fourth period, distracting the whole class. Because Rosemary didn't trust that they wouldn't bring up last night, she didn't attempt to scold them. It was only the first of what she knew would be many ways to control her if she didn't settle it. They needed to talk, to reach an accommodation. Before lights out, she went to Maisie's room. The three were gathered on Maisie's bed, and when Rosemary arrived, they looked up expectantly.

"There she is!" Maisie announced. "Our own Le Chat!"

In confusion, Jean said, "The cat?"

Maisie sighed heavily. "From that book *To Catch a Thief.* You read it. I gave it to you."

Jean brightened. "Oh, yes. I remember. That guy who could break in anywhere."

Rosemary smiled wryly. "We need to talk."

"Yes, we do." Maisie sat up straighter. "In fact, we've just been having a discussion, haven't we?"

Sandra had been brushing out her frizzy curls, and now she put aside the brush. "Miss Chivers, we have a proposition for you."

She tore the sheet of paper from a notebook Rosemary noticed on the bed between them and handed it to Maisie, who slid from the mattress and thrust it at Rosemary.

"What's this?" Rosemary took the paper warily.

"We thought you could explain to us what these words mean *exactly.* We know, sort of, but . . . we want the details, so no one can take advantage of us."

It was a list of slang. The first words leaped out at Rosemary: *screw, come, faggot, cherry, blow-job, dyke.*

It would take almost an entire sex-ed course to explain these—if she were ever allowed to teach anything but abstinence before the "marriage act."

She glanced at the girls, wondering how much *"we know, sort of"* actually meant. Maybe they were only playing with her. Maybe this was a test, a trap. But the gazes regarding her held that frustrated curiosity. Whatever they knew—or didn't—they were being honest about their desire to learn more.

"We'll get to this later in the semester," she hedged. "When we come to family planning."

Sandra said, "We've seen those books, Miss Chivers. 'The Case for Chastity'? You know Jean's already practically made every argument against it."

"Ha ha," Jean said.

"Don't be cruel, Miss Wilson. We'll get to your questions. You just have to be patient." Another hedge.

"Will we, though?"

Ah, Sandra's skepticism. How did one become so distrustful so young?

But then, wasn't she right? The textbooks wouldn't teach them what they wanted to know, and Rosemary would not be telling them either. Stella Bullard and the board had given Rosemary curriculum guaranteed to keep them ignorant.

Maisie said, "The school might close in December. Do you plan to get to it before then?"

Rosemary did not. Not then. Not ever.

Sandra must have seen it in her face, because she said, "You see?"

"We're going to be eighteen soon. All of us. We'll be women. We'll be out of this school and on our own." Maisie's gaze was frank as she stood there wearing the white nightgown with "Mercer Rocks School" across the left breast in green thread. She looked both a child and a woman, and Rosemary had a sudden memory of herself, a pink nightgown of dotted swiss and *"I'm not a child! You can't make me!"* Mom's laughter still rang in her ears, and Rosemary hated that memory and hated that it came back now—as contrast or comparison, it didn't matter.

No one would tell them these things. No one spoke of these things. They would learn the way she had, by making mistakes. Some of them terrible. Some impossible to live with.

"I don't think you understand," Maisie said patiently. "This is our price. If you want us to keep quiet about last night, this is what we want. Information."

"You teach us what we want to know, and our lips are sealed." Sandra mimed the turning of a key.

"You've been so honest with us. We'd still be thinking we could get gonorrhea from a Popsicle if not for you," Jean said.

"Yes, well, that's what Mrs. Bullard's warning was about. If I teach you these things, I'll be fired."

"It will be our secret. Just like last night," Maisie promised.

Rosemary regarded them. Maybe it had been a test after all. Regardless, Rosemary was neatly trapped.

Agreeing to this would make her more vulnerable than she was already. The power it gave them, the secrets they would share . . . But if she said no, they would go to Stella, and when Rosemary weighed her chances with the principal, they weren't good.

Then Sandra said quietly, "We weren't the ones who told on you before. That was Maryanne. We wanted to know more. We didn't want you to get in trouble. We kept the secret. You know we're not like the others."

It was as if Sandra somehow knew what would affect Rosemary best.

"We aren't, are we?" Sandra insisted. "We're not like the others."

It was true, for more reasons than Sandra could possibly know.

Sandra edged closer as if she sensed an opening, and Rosemary felt it in herself, uncertainty, vulnerability, longing. Maisie and Jean closed in.

"Miss Chivers?" Mrs. Sackett's voice echoed down the hall. "It's lights out!"

"In a minute!" Rosemary called back.

"We'll be graduating soon, and there's so much we don't know and no one will tell us," Maisie said. "Everyone lies to us but you, Miss Chivers. Won't you help us? Please?"

"We could have our own class," Sandra said quietly, urgently. "Just the three of us. You could tell us everything we need to know as women in the world."

Rosemary hesitated. *Don't do this.* But as she looked at those faces, Jean, hiding interest behind languid nonchalance, Sandra's intensity, Maisie with those fathomless dark eyes, and all of them with a wanting that Rosemary understood so deeply she knew she could not walk away. It wasn't only the threat of exposure. There was her own life stretching behind her. Here were these girls, one of them hers, asking for the help and guidance she had wanted and never received. She was to help make them American Dream wives. Maybe that's what they were meant to be, but what if they were not? What if that cleverness was meant for something else?

"You're meant for so much more." Her mother's words to her, and with a little shock Rosemary appreciated for the first time her mother's hopes.

Don't get involved.

"Miss Chivers!" Mrs. Sackett called again.

Rosemary turned from the door. There was no choice, was there? "Go to your rooms now," she said in a low voice, and then, "Tomorrow, we'll talk about where to meet."

~

She handed back the girls' assignments with a jotted *See me after class,* written above the grade, and when they'd gathered, she suggested meeting at the Rocks during the free hour after dinner.

The season had turned nearly overnight. The lone patch of blackberries Martin McCree kept for Mrs. Dennis were dying off now for the season, any remaining berries dried or swollen and rotting, left for the spiders. The edges of the oak leaves were turning brown; the yellowing leaves of the cottonwoods at the lakeshore flapped softly in the light, chilly breeze. Rosemary stepped gingerly down the stairs and sat on a driftwood stump with octopus-like roots. The cinch of her girdle clutched tight; not a comfortable position, and her skirt bound so that she couldn't cross her legs, but she didn't move.

The Rocks were less malevolent in the daytime, black, craggy, and broken against the deep blue of the sky brushed by clouds. The sound of them, the gurgle of the currents at the base, the slap of the water, the slight hiss and suck was harder to hear in the daytime, with the noise from the school in the background, but she had heard it in the night and knew what to listen for, and she found the music as arresting as ever.

She listened so closely that she didn't hear the scuffling footsteps at first, or the shushed laughter. From the corner of her eye, she caught movement and turned to see her girls, Maisie leading.

"We're here," Maisie announced unnecessarily. They made their way carefully in their smooth-soled shoes.

"It will get too cold to be meeting here before long," Rosemary said. "We'll have to find someplace else soon, but for now it will do."

"No one will think to look for us here." Jean shivered and drew her school sweater closer. "But it is getting cold. I miss the summer already."

Sandra arranged herself on the end of a fallen log, and Maisie seated herself beside her, which left Jean to perch on the edge of the stone stairs. The lake lapped against the shore, and the wind whistled softly through the hole in one of the rocks. Rosemary heard her father's warning in it, and she ignored it and looked over the three girls, who looked back at her, ready for anything, the whole world waiting for them, and she saw her own bravery at sixteen in their faces, that confidence that came from nothing truly bad having ever happened to them, that faith that nothing ever would, and the need to protect them swept her so strongly that for a moment Rosemary could not breathe.

"What is it, Miss Chivers?" Sandra asked. "Are you all right?"

"I just want to make sure we all understand: these meetings must be secret. No one must know. I mean *no one*."

Maisie nodded. "We've already agreed to that."

"I want a promise," Rosemary insisted.

"We won't say a word," Jean agreed.

"I promise," Maisie said.

"Here's to mutually assured destruction." Sandra grinned, and it was pure joy; there was nothing calculated or mean in it. She was such a regular adolescent girl in that moment that Rosemary could not help grinning back.

"Well, where would you like to begin?"

"I think with *come*," Maisie said—so much self-assurance. She glanced at the other two. "Don't you think?"

Jean giggled. Sandra nodded in agreement.

"Yes, that one," Maisie said. "Please."

Their gazes were a mix of anticipation and expectation and innocence that called to the yearning Rosemary had thought she'd buried long ago.

The Rocks stood steady and silent. The breeze lulled and with it the whistle through the hole in the rock. But the water still swirled and slurped, and it said to her *Be careful. Remember.* She shook the yearning away. She reminded herself of how she'd come to this point.

And she began to tell them what they wanted to know.

The Past

Central Washington College of Education
Ellensburg, WA—1942

The baby's name was Mary McConnell. Her last name came from that of the arts and science building because College Elementary School, where the practice house was with its kitchen and nursery, was too unwieldy. Mary was the practice baby, six months old when she was brought from the orphanage for the Child in the Home class, where home-ec majors learned the newest methods in motherhood. Mary was on a strict schedule. Each of the girls in the class was the baby manager for ten days, rotating through the semester. At the end of Mary's time at the college, she would be returned to the orphanage to be adopted by one of the many families vying for a child who'd been cared for by the newest scientific methods.

She was the prettiest baby Rosemary had ever seen. She smiled all the time. She had light brown hair and brown eyes, and a little cleft in her chin that reminded Rosemary of David.

Rosemary had refused to go back to her old high school in Seattle, where the rumors and memories were too much to bear, and had moved to Ellensburg to live with her aunt Pat and graduate. After that, she stayed to go to Central Washington College. It pleased her parents, and the classes distracted her from the hollowness that had taken up residence inside her. There were other things that distracted too—drinking, for one, and Ellensburg was full of young men, some college students, but mostly those jobless and anxious about the war and the draft and drowning their fears in beer and vodka and looking for ways to forget, just as she was. Rosemary had special permission to live with her aunt instead of in the dorm, and it was easy to sneak out.

Rosemary hated weekends especially, too much time to think and to ache, and Sundays were the worst, so many little girls in pinafores and ruffles at church, and all Rosemary could think was *She would be three now. She would be four.* She imagined her daughter in every little girl she saw. Her hunger was a misery and unappeasable, and the only thing for it was to drink and bury herself in a warm body until she forgot, but it never went away. There was always waking up.

She avoided home in those years, and the topic no one mentioned. Instead, she caught the bus when she could afford it and went to White Shield Home to beg for information and hear the same words over and over. *You signed the papers. You aren't a mother.* When she did go home, she searched the house whenever Mom and Dad were gone, but her parents had done as they promised and made her daughter disappear. It was as if she had never existed.

And so . . . when Rosemary saw baby Mary, everything Rosemary had tried to forget rushed back. When Rosemary first looked into Mary's face, the baby smiled—dimples, she had dimples like David! The teacher said it was just gas, Rosemary knew it wasn't. Mary recognized her. Mary knew her. Rosemary knew Mary couldn't be her daughter, of course not, but surely it wasn't a coincidence that the baby had the same name Rosemary had assumed at White Shield. They were connected. Rosemary was meant to love her.

Whenever it was Rosemary's turn to live in the practice house, taking sole care of Mary, her hollowness eased.

Rosemary sang to the baby as she bathed her. She cooed as she fed and changed her. She played with Mary, laughed with Mary, kissed the baby's face, delighted when Mary curled her hand around Rosemary's finger. Rosemary had a preternatural ability to soothe the baby—all the girls said it. When Mary was fussy, Rosemary was the first to sense it.

Mrs. Redmond, the instructor, looking concerned, told Rosemary, "You know Mary is going back to the orphanage at the end of the year, Miss Chivers. I worry that you're getting so attached."

"I know, Mrs. Redmond," Rosemary said. "I won't get attached." But oh, there was that precious girl, smiling every time she heard Rosemary's voice, holding out her arms to be lifted, to be kissed—not what they were supposed to do; these were not the scientific methods they were supposed to be using. Children were not to be spoiled by affection, but nurtured by bottles and strict schedules. Rosemary broke the rules every day, but the thought of not holding Mary, of not squeezing her and tickling her . . . How could she not, when that little girl lit up at the sight of her? No one had ever loved Rosemary so much. Rosemary had never been the center of anyone's world the way she was the center of Mary's.

Then the semester ended, and new students were set to begin A Child in the Home.

"I'd like to retake the class," Rosemary told Mrs. Redmond.

"You don't need to take it again. You got an A," the teacher said.

"But I want to. I think there are things I haven't quite grasped."

Mrs. Redmond considered her. "An A is an A, Miss Chivers. It doesn't become more than that. You've been an excellent student in this class, but now it's time to move on to other things. Your organic chemistry, for example. You show such promise in that course. Dr. Rogers believes you've a real talent for it."

The hollowness returned, and it was more terrible than before, because now Rosemary knew what it was; she knew what was missing. The smile that was gone, the soft skin and chubby arms, the sound of burbling giggles, even the quickly cooling spit-up on her blouse. She wanted that baby so much, and nothing made that longing go away, not drink, not sex. But now Rosemary knew how to appease it. Mary was right here on campus. Mary was within reach.

Rosemary began sneaking into the College Elementary School building. She waited until after the assigned baby manager put Mary to bed and went to bed herself, and then Rosemary climbed through the window, which was never latched—she had always locked the windows. There were kidnappings all the time, people grasping for money any way they could get it; weren't they aware? When the pseudomothers were sleeping, Rosemary sneaked into the baby's room, and woke Mary up and played with her until neither could keep their eyes open, and then Rosemary rocked the baby to sleep with quiet lullabies. Even with weariness weighting her limbs, it was all Rosemary could do to leave her. Each time was worse than the last.

Mary grew fussier and fussier, her smiles harder to find. Rosemary grew more frustrated. One night, it took her what seemed hours to make Mary laugh, and by then Rosemary was so tired, and Mary wouldn't go to sleep, no matter how Rosemary rocked her. She sang every lullaby she knew. The baby fussed. Rosemary struggled to keep her quiet, not wanting to wake the baby manager. Finally, Mary fell asleep, and Rosemary, exhausted herself, closed her eyes for just a moment—just a moment.

She woke to "Rosemary Chivers!" and an angry and flustered Beverly Simon, that week's baby manager. The next thing Rosemary knew, she was called in front of Mrs. Redmond and then the department chair. Everyone was grim-faced and disturbed, and it dawned on Rosemary that she'd done something terrible, and that the price would be terrible too.

Baby Mary was sent back to the orphanage. Rosemary was not even allowed to say goodbye, and she was banned from the practice nursery. The other girls looked at her with pitying glances, and Rosemary was thrown back to her days at White Shield Home, those terrible days when there was only loss, and here it was again. Once again loss.

She felt scoured by grief. As the weeks passed, she could not climb out of it. The nurse at the student health service asked her a hundred questions, and at the end of it gave her pills to help her sleep. The dean of women told her she had to forget Mary. "You must move on, my dear."

Forget. Move on. Familiar words, and painful ones. "But I—"

"You'll have your own family someday."

Except she'd already had her own family, and it had been taken from her.

"You aren't her mother, after all. You do know that, don't you?"

You aren't a mother. You signed the papers. You gave her away.

Aunt Pat said, "You're too intense, Rosie. You've always been that way, even when you were little. Never satisfied with anything. Couldn't be still. Drove your mom crazy, not that she was exactly a patient person herself . . . You've got to learn to stop."

"Stop feeling?" Rosemary asked dully.

"Stop feeling so *much*. Grow up, Rosie, before the world crushes you into nothing. Nobody gets everything they want. What makes you think you're different?"

The words landed. Probably because Rosemary was tired. She was tired of hurting. Tired of grief. She wondered if everyone was right after all. If the thing to do was forget. To stop searching, stop aching. Stop tormenting herself with the past and with the way things should have been. They were not that way, and she couldn't change it.

Rosemary had been a child, but she was no longer a child. Her life was her own, and it was time she took control. The truth was that she had frightened herself with Mary, with the intensity of her wanting, with the fact that she had not realized it was wrong.

From now on, she would do as her aunt suggested. Put all this behind her. Stop wanting so much. Stop feeling so much.

Starting now.

Chapter 19

The girls sat shivering in the chill breeze blowing from the lake. Fall had taken hold at last.

"We need to find someplace else to meet." Rosemary huddled into her sweater.

"It'll be December in no time." Sandra stared moodily out at the darkening water.

Maisie said, "We'd have to find someplace hidden."

"Our own secret lair." Sandra looked at Jean. "Like the kraken in the lake."

"Stop it, Sandy," Jean scolded.

"Jean thinks a kraken lives in the Rocks," Sandra told Rosemary.

"I do not," Jean protested. "But there has to be a reason the Indians call this place Taboo Container."

"Really?" Rosemary glanced at the jutting Rocks. "How interesting. I wonder why."

Maisie propped her elbow on her knee and rested her chin in her hand. "Maybe it was because this was where they sent people to punish them. You know, like a jail or something."

"Or like a school for wayward girls," Sandra said derisively.

"So we're the taboo thing," Jean said.

Maisie shrugged. "Maybe. Or maybe it was something like those tribes Miss Avilla told us about. Remember, where they banished the women to a separate hut when they were having their period?"

"I think that was a lie." Jean dragged a stick idly through the pebbles at her feet. "She was such a liar."

"Jean," Maisie said quietly.

The warning in Maisie's voice caught Rosemary's attention.

"Well, she was," Jean argued.

Rosemary said carefully, "What she told you about the tribes isn't a lie. That's true. Why do you think Miss Avilla is a liar?"

"I think Jean just meant in general," Sandra said quickly. "We don't like liars."

"We know you're not a liar, Miss Chivers," Jean said just as quickly.

Rosemary smiled, but the words troubled her. "Well, you probably misunderstood."

Sandra snorted.

Rosemary opened her mouth to ask more, but then Maisie pulled a battered book from her pocket.

The lurid cover of the twenty-five-cent paperback depicted two women hovering next to one another, a man with a gun lurking in the background. The title was *The Price of Salt*. Across the top were the words: *The Novel of a Love Society Forbids*.

Rosemary had heard of the book. Who hadn't? *The Price of Salt* had raised a fuss, a lesbian love story that had ended without one of them hanging herself, or dying miserably, or living unhappily ever after.

"Is it good?" she asked.

Maisie said, "You're the first person to ask me that. Everyone else just asks why I'm reading a book about nymphomaniacs. I don't even know what a nymphomaniac is."

"Neither do I," Sandra said.

Rosemary said, "A nymphomaniac is a woman who really likes sex. Who has to have it all the time, I guess."

"So . . ." Maisie paused. "So . . . women who want women . . . that way, like the women in this book—"

"Lesbians," Rosemary provided.

"Lesbians. They're nymphomaniacs?"

"Maybe some of them. But I would think that mostly they're just like women who want men. Sometimes they want sex and sometimes they don't."

Maisie was quiet for a moment. "That makes sense. Because these women in the book were just regular women who fell in love. There didn't seem to be anything terrible in it. Or even wrong. It was . . . it was really kind of beautiful."

"Kinsey's report said that it's not uncommon. Or abnormal. It's just that no one talks about it." The book studying female sexual behavior had come out last year and caused as much of an uproar as the one on men had five years before.

"No one will let us near that book, Miss Chivers." Sandra laughed ruefully.

"The man at the bookstore refused to sell it to me without Daddy's permission," Jean said. "He told me I was too young."

Maisie said, "But you'll tell us all about what it says, won't you?"

Such hopeful eyes, relieved ones too. Rosemary had not dared to bring that book here where it would only cause trouble, but she realized that Maisie had been afraid of the things *The Price of Salt* had made her feel, and Rosemary remembered her own early adolescent world, those first touches, the play with her girlfriends, where they had clamped their hands over each other's mouths and pretended to kiss so they would know how to do it with a boy. All that hideous confusion and not knowing what was right and wrong and the fear that you were on the road to hell when there was no clear map laid before you. No map at all, but only shadowy paths and emotion and touch that you wanted so much to trust.

How desperately they wanted to know the truth. Rosemary saw that, and saw, too, that they wanted to trust her, that they were half afraid but hopeful, and she didn't want to disappoint them.

"Yes," she said. "I'll tell you. But first we need to find a warmer place to meet. I wondered about the boathouse. I know it's boarded up, but do you know why? Is it just abandoned, or . . ."

She trailed off. The girls did not look at each other or at her, but the tension was palpable and infected all three. Jean dug the stick she'd been playing with almost viciously into the gravelly beach.

"What is it?" Rosemary asked.

"It's off-limits," Maisie said with a hard shrug. "We're not allowed to go there."

"You're following rules?"

"Are you asking us to *break* them?" There was an insolence in Sandra that struck Rosemary oddly—it was creepy somehow, uncomfortable.

"No. No, of course not."

"Plus, it smells like kerosene." Jean did not look up from her stick. "It's awful in there. Dark and spooky."

"We'll think of somewhere else." Maisie's voice rang with finality. "Just forget the boathouse, Miss Chivers."

~

The agitation of the discussion stayed with Rosemary; that evening, she asked Mrs. Sackett about the boathouse.

"I don't know why they don't tear that place down," Mrs. Sackett said. "One day girls are going to sneak off there to get drunk and we'll all be in trouble. There's hardly any floor left."

"What happened to it?"

"There was a fire last year. Burned all the boats and mostly gutted the inside. A pity too. It was a pleasure to watch the girls learning to sail those little boats, though there was always the chance they'd try to escape on them. I suppose it's all for the best." Mrs. Sackett sighed. "Not that it matters if the school closes."

"Have you heard any news?" Rosemary asked.

Mrs. Sackett shook her head. "We've heard the same rumors."

Yes, Rosemary had. The school had been sold. The school had received a new grant. The school was being bulldozed for a new housing project . . . She had shrugged them off, as nothing ever came from them. The rumors ran rampant for a few days and then dissipated.

Rosemary smiled and murmured a good night and went into her room. Mrs. Sackett's story hadn't enlightened her as to why the girls had become so tense at the mention of the boathouse, but Rosemary suspected there was more to it than the housemother either knew or said. She imagined she could wiggle the tale out of the girls eventually—not that it mattered. There wasn't enough time to care about it. The weeks were moving too quickly as it was.

She glanced toward the orchard, and the greenhouse beyond—the greenhouse. Maybe. Mrs. Dennis kept a kitchen garden there. As far as Rosemary knew, the only teacher who ever held a class inside was Mrs. Weedman, and only occasionally. It would be warm. Rosemary could think of many reasons for home-ec students to meet in the greenhouse.

The next afternoon, she paid it a visit. The greenhouse was gable-roofed, with a hip-high brick foundation, and then all glass above. The door was unlocked; she stepped into warmth and humidity, the smell of dirt and fecundity, tomato and dill and wet. Metal piping formed a jungle gym throughout; dripping hoses hung in coils and snaked over the floor. Buckets full of fragrant compost crowded one corner; gardening forks, small shovels, a green watering can, and an abandoned pair of stained leather gloves cluttered one of the raised platforms just inside the door. Plants were everywhere, hanging, in pots on tables, in wooden beds running down the middle of the slate floor. There wasn't much room. A narrow pathway ran between the platforms lining the walls and the beds in the center, but at the far end there was a cast-iron bench and a matching chair, behind them piled bags of compost and lime and fertilizer.

The door opened behind her; Martin McCree and his son stepped inside. It was the first time Rosemary had seen Samson up close. The boy was nearly Martin's double, with a more delicate face, and awkward in his fifteen-year-oldness. He avoided her gaze as if he'd learned to avoid looking at women in general—probably not a bad idea given where he lived.

Martin smiled at her. "Hello there, Rosemary. What brings you to the greenhouse on this lovely gray day?"

Rosemary smiled back at him. "I hope you don't mind. I was wondering if the greenhouse might be suitable for a class."

"Ah. Rather small, but if you can find the room . . ."

"It would be all right, you think? We'd stay out of your way."

He rubbed his nose and shrugged. "It belongs to the school."

Samson frowned. "You want to bring girls here?"

"Sam, manners," Martin admonished. "Miss Chivers, this is my boy, Samson."

Samson bowed his head in greeting. "Miss Chivers."

"It's nice to meet you, Samson. I'm only bringing a few girls. A couple of them are interested in plants and flowers."

"Are they?" Martin looked frankly doubtful. "Didn't think they were interested in much but movie stars."

"I think you just have to find the right subjects," Rosemary said.

"I'll go tend to that Gravenstein." Samson seemed as if he could hardly wait to escape as he hurried out again.

"He's a fine-looking boy," Rosemary said. "Seems he got your green thumb."

Martin raised a shaggy brow.

"Tending to the Gravenstein."

He chuckled. "He's got a green thumb, but it's more that you scared him."

"Do I look like I bite?"

"I told you, he keeps his distance from the schoolgirls." He picked up a pair of clippers and went to tend a pot of bolting dill.

"I see." Everything in the greenhouse looked so settled, as if it had been here for years and years and would be here for years more. But there might not be years more. There might not even be months more. "What will you do if the school closes?"

"They'll still need someone to take care of the grounds. For a while anyway."

Rosemary nodded. "It must be nice, not to be worried."

"I'd be happy for the quiet." He clipped the dill, then looked at her again. "What will you do?"

"I'll land on my feet. I always do."

His crinkly eyes swept her. "Been through some hard times, have you?"

Rosemary was taken aback. "Why do you say that?"

"A bit of sadness about you." He took her in with a gesture the way an artist might, the clippers his chisel.

She didn't know what to say to that. She didn't know why he said it. She'd worked hard to banish that sadness; she refused to feel it or to give it purchase. But perhaps being around her daughter—whichever one she was—had touched something, some nerve, some muscle. Perhaps her attempt to determine which girl was hers had triggered some reflex, and that was what he sensed.

It made her uncomfortable that he'd said it. She hoped no one else saw it. There was nothing she wanted him, or anyone else, to know.

He didn't seem to expect her to reveal a secret, or even to answer. He only bent again to the dill. "The greenhouse is yours whenever you want it. Just don't let your girls hurt anything."

"No, of course not. Why would they hurt anything?"

"It's who they are," he said.

Chapter 20

The cold air whisked into the greenhouse with Maisie's entrance. "I've never been in here before."

Rosemary motioned for the girl to join her on the cast-iron bench. "It's not that comfortable, I'm afraid, but it will do."

"Old Martin won't kick us out?"

"No. He told me we were welcome to it. Why do you call him that? He's hardly old."

"He always looks so disapproving." Maisie scrunched her face and lowered her voice to imitate the gardener. "'You girls now, stay away from that tree before you break a branch!' I swear he thinks we mean to destroy the grounds."

The door opened again; Sandra and Jean came inside. Jean wrinkled her nose. "It smells in here. What is that?"

"Manure," Sandra said.

"Manure? Whatever for?"

"They keep it to bury the bodies in. They decompose faster that way."

"What?" Jean stopped short.

"It's for fertilizer," Rosemary corrected. "Stop teasing her."

"I can't help it. She's so gullible." Sandra plopped onto the chair, Jean sat more delicately on Rosemary's other side, though the bench was not long, and she and Maisie and Jean were pressed together close enough that Rosemary caught the competing scents of the cream rinse in their hair. It was the same stuff used by the entire school. It came in great, industrial-sized bottles. Funny how it smelled different on each girl.

"What's this?" Sandra reached behind Maisie, to a radio resting on a narrow shelf. Rosemary had not noticed it before. Sandra stretched to turn it on; it was already tuned to KJR.

"Old Martin listens to KJR?" Maisie asked disbelievingly.

"It's probably Sam," Jean said.

"Do you mind, Miss Chivers?" Sandra asked. "We'll turn it down low."

The radio played Kitty Kallen's "Little Things Mean a Lot," a song that had been ubiquitous on the radio for months, and of which Rosemary was heartily tired, but it made the greenhouse feel cozier, so she said, "It adds a nice touch."

Jean grinned. "We knew you were one of us."

"I love music." Sandra closed her eyes and swayed to the rhythm. "It makes everything better, doesn't it?"

The comment caught Rosemary. Did preferences come through the blood too? Not just hair color and eyes but a love for music or a talent for playing the guitar?

"Do you play an instrument?" Rosemary asked her.

Sandra opened her eyes and grimaced. "Too much practicing. Why would I turn something I love into something awful?"

"It's a good skill to have, and you might find that you enjoy it."

"Um—no. You sound like my mom now. Everything's always got to be good for you in some way. Why can't some things just be?"

"Do either of your parents play an instrument?"

Sandra scoffed. "That would make them interesting, and they're not. They're boring. Dad's an architect and Mom does a lot of charity stuff and that's all they do."

"At least they're home," Maisie said. "My parents travel all the time. It's been so long since I've seen them, I can hardly remember what they look like."

"Maybe like you?" Rosemary suggested.

Maisie shrugged.

It was not at all helpful.

"I have a picture of my mom, but I don't look anything like her," Jean said. "I hardly knew her. She died when I was three. Daddy thinks she's like a guardian angel watching over me, but honestly I don't feel her or anything."

Somewhere a hose dripped. Drip, drip, drip. A beat to Rosemary's nervous excitement. "Do you look like your dad?"

"He's blond like me. But you know, he's a man and I'm a woman. I can't see it if he does."

This line of questioning was getting Rosemary nowhere, so she plunged in. "Why did your parents send you girls to Mercer Rocks?"

Sandra said, "Because I like to go to parties and I drink too much."

"Why? Are you unhappy?"

Sandra stared at Rosemary as if the question had never occurred to her before. "No. I don't know. I just do it."

"What do you get from it?"

"I don't know."

"You must like something about it. What is it?"

Sandra's whole face wrinkled in concentration. "I think I want . . . I want . . . quiet. When I drink, it's quiet."

Such a soft answer, one that turned Rosemary soft too. She nodded and looked at Jean. "What about you?"

Jean's fair skin colored. "I like boys too well. And they like me. I mean boys have always looked at me, but mostly I like it. I think maybe I really am a sex fiend. That's . . . that's okay, isn't it?"

Jean's uncertainty and fear touched Rosemary's heart. Another soft spot. Another sore one. Gently she said, "I think you're pretty normal. And yes, it's okay."

Jean sighed with what sounded like relief. "But I'm not . . . I mean . . . I've never . . . I'm still a virgin." She said it quickly, on a rush of breath. "Daddy would *kill* me otherwise."

"You know you don't have to tell him everything," Maisie pointed out.

Jean rolled her eyes.

"Why are you here?" Rosemary asked Maisie.

"I keep running away."

"Why?"

"I don't know. I've done it practically since I was old enough to realize I could."

"What are you looking for?"

Maisie was thoughtful for a long moment. Then, "I don't know really. Maybe someone who wants me to stay."

The sore spot in Rosemary ached now. She glanced away, catching how Sandra raised and lowered her heel, pressing on the ball of her foot like a dancer, flexing her calf. Something Rosemary had noticed before; Sandra was almost never completely still.

"Anyway, Miss Chivers, now we have a question for you," Maisie announced, breaking the somber silence, directing, as usual. Something that reminded Rosemary of David. All that confidence. So much charisma . . .

"There's always a question," Sandra said, still nervously flexing. "What if we never get all the answers?"

Maisie groaned. "That's why we're here, to get as many as we can. God, Sandy, why are you always so gloomy about everything?"

Jean said, "You should tell Miss Chivers about your nightmares, Sandy."

"What nightmares?" Rosemary asked.

Sandra waved them away. "They're nothing."

"They are too something," Jean insisted. "You have them all the time."

"She woke up screaming last night." Maisie stretched her arm across the back of the bench. "It scared the whole floor."

Rosemary frowned. "No one said anything to me."

"Because it didn't scare the whole floor." Sandra let out a breath of exasperation. "Do you have to exaggerate everything, Maisie? It didn't scare anyone."

Rosemary glanced at Jean for confirmation. Jean nodded. "It didn't. Sandy just told us about it this morning."

"Why did you have to lie like that?" Sandra snapped at Maisie. "I wasn't even screaming. God. Sometimes you're such a—"

"What was the nightmare?" Rosemary asked gently.

Sandra's foot waggled faster. "It's nothing new. I'm walking home and everyone starts yelling and pointing at the sky and I get down in a gutter the way they say. But this part was different: I look up and everyone is on fire. Then I'm running and trying to find the school so I can go into the basement and make that shelter the way we talked about in class, you know, with the piece of cardboard and the crates and stuff, but before I get there, all my skin starts falling off."

"You weren't following directions. Bert the Turtle says to find shelter right away." Maisie's voice was sarcastic.

Sandra glared at her. "Bert the Turtle can go straight to hell. There isn't time to do anything."

They went quiet. Then Jean said, "What if Sandra's dream is right? What if there's no time for anything? I mean, what if there is no future?"

"Then I guess we just have fun while we can," Maisie said.

Jean leaned forward, her blond hair swinging against her jaw, her wide eyes lighting. "That's what I think too. Why be good? Why not do whatever we want? Travel and have a passionate love affair and just *be*. I'll bet you've had a love affair, haven't you, Miss Chivers? I know you have. And it ended unhappily—he died in the war, maybe? Or you were tragically torn apart? That's why you're single—because you've never loved anyone else and you never will? Oh, please tell me you're not just an old spinster who's never kissed anyone! If you tell us you're still a virgin, I will just die!"

How quickly that had turned too. Rosemary had gone from listening intently to having three pairs of eyes riveted to her, searching, curious, demanding. The answer they wanted was not one she was prepared to give; she had closed that door and she did not want the pain of remembering, and yet . . . one of them deserved to know. One of them was owed the answer.

Which one?

The radio buzzed into white noise. As evenly as she could, she said, "No, I'm not a virgin."

"I knew it!" Jean crowed. "I told you, Maisie."

"I didn't say she was," Maisie protested.

"You thought she was a lesbian," Sandra said. "Like the ones in that book."

"Then you know," Jean pressed. "You truly know about the things you're telling us. About pleasure and about . . . how it is and . . ."

"Yes," Rosemary said quietly.

Jean pressed. "And you don't have any children, so it's not true what they say. There are ways to . . . to do it without getting pregnant."

The words were an unexpected blow. Rosemary froze, but her mind was leaping in a hundred directions, a hundred things that could be said that she would not say, not yet, not now. She struggled for the right thing. The radio played on, relentlessly mocking now, "Make Love to Me."

"They say you can't get pregnant the first time," Maisie suggested.

"Is that true?" Sandra asked.

Rosemary managed to find her voice. "It's not true." How raw she sounded, how uncertain. She tried again. "No, it's not true. You can get pregnant. But yes, there are ways to prevent it, as long as you use them. Unfortunately, it will be your job to make sure of it. Boys won't want to stop. Neither will you, but you'll have to try, because in the end, it will be you who pays the price. He can just walk away if he wants." She went on, telling them about condoms, the diaphragm that doctors would only prescribe for women who were married or engaged, and the best lies to tell to get an appointment and a prescription, and how you could easily buy a fake engagement or wedding ring at a pawnshop. She told them about pulling out, which was very undependable, and the rhythm method, which meant knowing your body perfectly and being able to say no, even when someone had his hands on you and you were feeling good and wanting to just do it. When she was finished, the girls stared at her as if she were some sort of magician showing them the secrets to her illusions, a kind of dawning awe, along with an awareness of difficulty and required cunning they had never imagined might be necessary. The kind of lies and manipulations needed to get what they might want. She told them everything she wished someone had told her, everything she'd learned after David and the baby, everything she'd done herself as a single woman who wanted a life of her own, unfettered by the conventions that so changed the path she might have taken.

They were flabbergasted. They were stunned. There, too, she saw incipient anger, the realization of the unfair responsibility they bore.

There was a burst of static from the radio, the announcer's voice breaking on a soap advertisement, and then some nattering about the weather: *Cloudy tonight, with a low of forty-seven degrees. Tomorrow we're looking at much the same. And now, for your listening pleasure, your favorite* . . .

The music started, a blaring horn, voices in a rhythmic *hey da dee ding dong* . . .

"'Sh-Boom'!" Sandra broke the spell for all of them. She leaped to her feet, swaying to the music of the Crew Cuts, then singing along and dancing, and Jean made a little cry of joy and joined her, grabbing her hands until the two of them were shuffling along the stack of empty peat seedling pots, swinging into an exuberant dance and singing at the top of their lungs about how life could be a dream if only she loved him.

Suddenly, inexplicably, Rosemary wanted to cry.

Then, Sandra winced as something hit her shoulder. "Ouch!" She drew back as something else hit her, and then it hit Jean too, small and dark, one after another, a fusillade of what looked like rocks coming fast and furious, pummeling them until both girls raised their arms to fend them off.

"Maisie! Stop!" Sandra shouted.

One hit Jean in the face. She clapped her hand to her cheek. "Ouch! Maisie!"

Rosemary turned to see Maisie tossing handfuls of galls from a tin bucket. She was grinning, but it was a mean grin, her eyes dark with a spite that took Rosemary aback.

"That hurts!" One bounced off Sandra's hair and pinged off the window.

Jean yelled, "Stop it!"

Rosemary said, "Miss Neal, that's enough—" just as Sandra lunged for Maisie, tripping over Rosemary's outstretched feet, falling across the arm of the bench and into Maisie, who stumbled backward into the bags of manure and soil. A bag of vermiculite split beneath her weight, spilling onto the slate floor.

"Ow, dammit!" Sandra pulled herself up, holding her hip. "Ow, ow. My hip!"

Rosemary helped her sit down.

Sandra glared at Maisie. "You're such a bitch, Maisie."

"Oh, I'm fine. Don't worry about me." Maisie stood and brushed away the vermiculite clinging to her wool skirt.

"No one cares," Jean said, smoothing her hair. "It's all your fault."

"It was just so funny."

"It was not. It hurt." Jean fingered her cheek. "Is it red?"

"A little pink," Rosemary assured her. "You can hardly tell." She had promised Martin the girls wouldn't hurt anything. "You girls had better go. It's getting late. They'll be expecting you in the dorm. I'll clean up."

Sandra groaned as she rose, but when Maisie put her arm around her, she didn't flinch away. Jean adjusted her skirt, which had fallen to its regulation length while she'd been dancing, rolling the waistband to reveal more of her thighs, stealing a glance at Rosemary.

"Miss Karlstad," Rosemary scolded on cue.

Jean smirked; that smile said as clearly as words how absurd it was that Rosemary should chastise for a raised hem after what she'd just told them.

"A secret, girls. Remember," Rosemary cautioned—also on cue.

"We won't forget, Miss Chivers," Maisie said.

The three left the greenhouse. By the time they'd rounded the corner, they were chattering away, friends again.

It took another half an hour to clean up the mess. Rosemary left a note for Martin telling him the bag had split, and then turned off the radio and went out into the gathering darkness.

She'd reached the tennis courts when a prickling on the back of her neck made her glance around. There was no one about; the courts were quiet, but the lights shadowed more than they lit. No one in the windows.

Just the creepiness of the empty grounds and the general unease of the school and Maisie's meanness in the greenhouse. Jealousy, spite, anger . . . all of it had been in Maisie's face as she threw those galls. Rosemary sighed and opened the back door into the school. For a moment so fleeting she thought she imagined it, the shadows coalesced into a presence. She smelled cigarette smoke.

But when she jerked to look, there was nothing there.

Jean

Jean sneaks up to the roof after lights out. She is not the only one up there; it's a well-known spot for illicit smoking—well known to the staff too. Often, Mr. Gear comes to chase them all back down, and if they're caught, it's isolation for sure, which they all hate. There's nothing so boring as being locked in your room for days at a time with nothing to do but daily lessons. But tonight it's cold and damp and there are only a few die-hard smokers shivering in their nightgowns and sweaters, and no one's talking or laughing or paying attention to anyone else. A quick smoke and then they climb down the fire escape and through the bathroom window with the broken hinge. If you jiggle it just right, it opens wider than six inches, and when you push it back into place, no one's the wiser. It's dangerous, of course. You don't want to fall. But no one ever has in the time Jean's been at Mercer Rocks.

There are stairs to the roof too, which are easier, but few girls take those, because you have to get past Mrs. Fields and get into the custodian stairwell, which is always locked, though Jean thinks Sandy could manage it. Briefly Jean feels a spark of envy. She has no real talents. Not like Sandy, though Sandy is so tightly wound sometimes it feels like she might explode. Unlike Maisie, who's so controlled—well, usually. There was that time last year, but Jean tries not to think about that. It was scary and they don't talk about it. Jean sometimes wonders why Sandy and Maisie want her around. What does she add? She could lure in the boys, if there were any, but there aren't except for Sam, and she isn't sure Sandy or Maisie would care even if there were. But it's Jean's best talent, and always has been.

Lately she's been bored. It started last summer. She'd been at home in Olympia, and Daddy had thrown a party and it was all old men and their wives, and they'd been drinking and smoking and Daddy would have kittens if he caught her doing either, and she was already in enough trouble, so she'd gone into the den and turned on the radio and was just dancing by herself when she felt someone watching her. When she turned, there was Mr. Langdon, a gin and tonic in his hand and a look on his face that Jean understood.

The most she'd ever done was let Donny Remington get fresh, and of course Daddy had walked in on them, and that—along with a few other things, like Daddy's friend Mr. Porter sliding his fingers down the back of her swimsuit bottoms and her too-ready smiles for the delivery boy and the pool boy, oh, and the boys at school who crowded round—had put her in Mercer Rocks.

And so . . . Mr. Langdon. He was tall and paunchy. Not the best looking of Daddy's friends but not the worst, and he offered her a sip of that G&T and she took it, and then he offered her more, and soon he was kissing her and it was interesting because grown men kissed so differently from boys. It wasn't so messy, and the way he used his tongue sent shivers all through her, and by the time he pulled up her shirt and got fresh she was ready to spread her legs for him. Then Mr. Langdon's wife came looking for him and Daddy put Jean in lockdown for the remaining two weeks in summer.

But she hasn't forgotten Mr. Langdon's skill, the way he excited her. A man, not a boy, and she has decided that's what she wants the first time, and she's ready. She's wanted it forever now. She's wondered if that means there's something wrong with her. She's sick or immoral or even evil. Women aren't supposed to want it the way she does. They aren't supposed to think about it all the time. But now Miss Chivers has reassured her that there's nothing wrong with desire, that there's nothing wrong with her, that she's normal for wanting it.

The question is, who should be her first? The only men here are teachers, and Mr. Covington is a straight-up no. He's too old and she hates beards, and Mr. Gear is also old, though his being an Indian is interesting and she likes his stories about the Duwamish when he tells them. Mr. McCree is also too old and anyway he hates her because of Sam. But maybe Mr. Reese, who is new and seems nice, though Maisie gets upset whenever Jean mentions it, and Jean is starting to think that maybe Maisie's obsession with that *Salt* book says something Jean doesn't really want to know. Sandy only rolls her eyes and tells her she's asking for trouble, which she is, Jean knows that, but there's something inside her that burns. She thinks Miss Chivers must understand, because the home-ec teacher always says exactly the right thing, she always gives the answer Jean is looking for just when Jean most wants it. It's like they have this secret connection. Jean is glad Maisie decided to make Miss Chivers this year's favorite. She's been the best one so far, even if they only have until December.

Though maybe not. Daddy tells her he's working hard—*desperately* was the word he'd used—with the board to find a way to keep the school going, and Jean knows by how he says it that what he is desperate about is the idea of having her home again because he doesn't know what to do with a daughter who is a sex fiend and he's worried she'll cause a scandal someday and ruin his career, and the way he looks at her sometimes, like she's Jezebel or Bathsheba . . . she knows all the whores in the Bible; he's made sure of it.

Jean hates Mercer Rocks. But she hates that look on Daddy's face more, and when she's eighteen, she's leaving. She's looking for the passionate love affair that takes her away from her father's stiff-necked views and this school. For now, Miss Chivers and Maisie and Sandy are the only things good about it.

Jean finds a shadowed corner on the roof and settles herself into it, out of sight of any of the other girls up there, not that they would care about this—or not most of them anyway—and waits. It's only a few minutes before she sees another shadow sidle over the edge of the roof and lean into the slant of the asphalt shingles to climb. It starts to drizzle as Samson slides in beside her. He smells of wool and peat and fifteen-year-old boy, and she thinks it's a pity that he's not older because she does like his smile.

"Hey," he says. "I left you something in the greenhouse. Did you get it?"

Jean shakes her head, and his face falls. "What was it?"

"A marigold in a pot. Didn't you see my note?"

"Where did you put it?"

"Over by the pail of galls. I thought you'd look there for sure."

Jean remembers Maisie pelting them with the oak apples. "Oh, I'm sure Maisie saw it and didn't tell me."

"That bitch."

"She's my best friend. Her and Sandy."

"I'm sorry, but she's still a bitch. What does she have against me? She knows I love you."

"Sammy, you're only fifteen," Jean says gently.

"So what?"

"So I'm seventeen."

"That's only two years."

"It might as well be a million. I'm a woman now. I'm too old for you. You really have to forget me. I won't be back next year."

Sam sighs. "I don't want to forget you."

"We've talked about this before." She touches his hand. "I'm sorry. I like you, Sam, but you're not what I'm looking for."

He twists his wrist and grabs her fingers, holding them tight. "Tell me what you want and I'll be it."

She laughs shortly. "I want you to be thirty-five."

He ducks his head. "Oh. Well."

"I'm sorry, but that's just how it is."

"I thought maybe tonight we could make out again." His eyes are so hopeful. "You think it was easy to sneak out? Da watches me every minute."

"Oh, baby, you don't know what being watched is." Jean has promised herself not to lead him on, but he is a handsome boy, and she does like being touched, and . . . and why not? It was fun last time. "Okay. One kiss. But no French tonight. You promise?"

The way he straightens, his excitement . . . he nods and leans in, and his lips are soft and he clutches her waist and presses hard, opening his mouth, which is very wet, no finesse at all, and very enthusiastic, and it only firms Jean's resolve to have a real man, but she does like to kiss, and it feels good, and he's here when no other boy is—

"Is that you, Jean Karlstad? And is that . . . *Samson?*"

The voice is too loud. Sam springs away. Jean looks up lazily to see Lizzie Etheridge staring at them in the darkness, a lit cigarette in her hand.

Of course it has to be Lizzie who spots them.

"Oh my God," Lizzie says. "No boys are allowed. If Mrs. Bullard finds out—"

Just then there's a rustling on the roof, scrabbling. One of the other smokers shouts, "It's a raid!"

The door from the custodian stairs is opening. Mr. Gear. Or Mrs. Fields. Or both.

"Shit!" Sam lurches to his feet. Jean grabs his arm to pull herself up. They ignore Lizzie and race to the fire-escape ladder, where everyone else is racing. Jean scrambles down; Sam is right above her. At the bathroom window, she slings herself in behind another girl. She has no idea where Lizzie is and she doesn't care. Lizzie is an easy problem to fix.

"Bye!" she tells Sam, whose face is stricken as he hurls himself down the ladder toward the ground. Everyone scatters, bolting out the bathroom door and past Mrs. Fields in the hall, but thankfully Mrs. Fields only has two hands and can't catch them all.

Jean puts her sweater over her head to hide her distinctive hair and slides by, dashing down the hall. As she skids around the corner, Maisie is waiting outside Jean's door. Jean sighs with relief, even when she sees the scold on Maisie's face, the *I told you so*.

"Tell Sandy to get Lizzie some rum," Jean gasps.

Maisie swears quietly. "Again? Lizzie's becoming a problem, Jeanie."

Jean only smiles.

Chapter 21

The next morning, Rosemary walked into the staff room to find Alicia and Gloria Weedman standing in front of a sign announcing a staff meeting after classes.

"Maybe they've found funding for the rest of the year," Gloria suggested.

"Or maybe they're closing earlier."

"Maybe it's not about anything like that at all," Rosemary speculated.

Alicia turned to Rosemary with a frown. "It can't possibly be good news."

About that, Rosemary had to agree. For the rest of the day, she and the other teachers were on edge. That afternoon, most of the others were already in the staff room when Rosemary arrived. Gloria Weedman tapped her fingers impatiently and looked repeatedly at her watch. Andrew Covington packed tobacco into his pipe with annoying deliberation. Quincy Reese waved her over. He sat next to Alicia, who was smoking, of course. Rosemary grabbed a cup of coffee and went to join them.

"Any more news?" she asked as she sat down.

"It's all a great mystery." Quincy reached for his own coffee.

Pearl Hoskins walked in, followed by Lois Vance, Stella Bullard, and a man Rosemary had never seen before. He looked about her age, midthirties or so, with dark brown hair and eyes. Like every professional man these days, he wore his charcoal suit boxy, with the ubiquitous knitted tie—he was nearly Quincy's twin when it came to dress—and a crisp white shirt. Unlike Quincy, he stood out in a way that negated the conformity of the suit. There was something provocative there; he caught one's attention and held it.

Alicia stubbed out her cigarette and straightened.

Stella closed the door, and Pearl hurried to sit at Rosemary's table while the vice principal and the stranger sat at the head of the room.

"Who is that?" Alicia whispered to Pearl.

Pearl whispered back, "A numbers guy," just as Stella Bullard cleared her throat.

"I know you've all been anxious about your futures here at Mercer Rocks, and about the school's future in general. As you know, we've undergone some financial hardships. Enrollment is down for the fourth straight year. Costs are always rising, of course, and we have had to let some custodial staff go this year. Fortunately, Mr. Gear, our laundress Mrs. James, Mr. McCree, and Mrs. Dennis do a remarkable job keeping us going, and they are working doubly hard. We would be lost without them, and I do hope you all show them appreciation."

The stranger glanced about the room, taking them all in. The touch of his gaze was momentarily studious when it landed upon Rosemary. It was not quite comfortable; she looked away.

"First, I am pleased to announce that we have received more funding, a quite generous grant from the Elliott Foundation, as well as one from Wakefield Industries. We will not be shutting down, but will be continuing for the full academic year, through June. I'm sure you will all be relieved at this very good news."

There were murmurs of relief and surprise.

Stella went on, "The board is concerned that our cost-cutting measures aren't enough, and they have hired an additional administrator to watch our finances. I would like to introduce you all to Robert Frances.

He will be with us the rest of the school year as a second vice principal, primarily responsible for helping us achieve greater financial efficiency. I expect you to welcome him with your usual warmth and to offer him whatever assistance he needs. Mr. Frances."

Robert Frances rose with a smile. "Thank you, Mrs. Bullard. Let me just say that I'm happy to be here, and I want you all to know that I'm not looking to be disruptive. I want to work with you, not against you. We're just going to try to streamline things a bit. I look forward to getting to know you. And please, 'Mr. Frances' makes me sound like my father. Call me Bobby."

Very charming, without arrogance. A smooth, easy voice and manner. They were all smiling in response.

"Well, well." Alicia spoke quietly; she was grinning. "At least they hired someone easy to look at."

Pearl slapped her hand playfully, whispering, "Now you've got two to choose from."

"Two?" Rosemary asked, equally quiet.

Pearl gave her a wicked smile, mouthing, "Martin."

"Oh, be quiet," Alicia scolded, but she hadn't lost that grin. "Just look at this one!"

Stella said, "So you see, there's no fear that we'll be closing the school anytime soon, and certainly not this year. I expect that with Mr. Fran—Bobby's—help, we will find a level of efficiency that will ensure your jobs are secure. Are there any questions?"

"Is he married?" Alicia asked under her breath.

"No? Then I'll leave Bobby to introduce himself to you each separately."

The meeting was over; Stella and Lois and Bobby Frances departed, leaving the rest of them to talk among themselves. Pearl knew the most about him, though it wasn't much. "He's a veteran, that's what Stella told me."

"Which war? Korea?" Alicia asked.

"Korea wasn't a war, it was a *conflict*," Pearl corrected primly. "And no, he wasn't there. He was in the Philippines or someplace like that in the big war. I don't know if he's married or not. Probably. Why wouldn't he be?"

"If he's watching costs, I guess that means my request for new oil paints is going to be denied," Alicia said with a sigh.

"Maybe you can charm him," Rosemary suggested.

"I imagine you're nervous, Rosemary," Quincy said.

She looked at him curiously. "Why should I be?"

"Home ec has the highest expenses of all the classes. All that food and fabric and stuff. He'll no doubt be double-checking your accounts."

"Wonderful."

Truthfully, Rosemary didn't care about the finances of her class. But the last thing she wanted was a curious new vice principal, particularly one whose job it was to look into her business.

Chapter 22

For the first time, Rosemary's classroom was cold. It might have been a relief but for the fact that it was frosty outside, and now that she actually wanted heat, the radiators were dead. She pulled her cardigan more closely about her and glanced out the window to see Martin McCree and Bobby Frances talking earnestly near the tennis courts.

The greenhouse meetings crept uncomfortably into her mind. But why would Martin say anything to Bobby Frances about those? Martin never interrupted them, not him or his son. He'd never said a word about the broken sack of vermiculite. She didn't know if he remembered they met there. Why should it be a topic of discussion with the new vice principal?

It wouldn't, she decided. She was being foolish and paranoid. Bobby Frances was simply learning school operations; of course the gardener would be part of those discussions.

Because of the gym below and the mezzanine, this building was never really quiet. You could hear movement in any part of it. She'd left her classroom door open, so she heard the whooshing thunk of the gymnasium doors, the echoed steps on stairs that normally sang with the rush of girls' feet. Rosemary tensed. She'd never seen Martin inside this building, and so she knew it must be Bobby Frances, and there was no way to leave the classroom now without being seen.

Even knowing he was there, the sound of him at the door made her jump. She berated herself silently. The best way to reveal a secret was to be aware that you had one.

"Someone *is* here," he said, coming inside. "I thought I heard noises. Oh—sorry. I didn't mean to startle you."

She crossed the room toward him. Again, she had the concerning sense of him as more than the *"numbers guy"* Pearl had dubbed him. That self-confidence. Disarming. She should be wary. "No, no, I . . . wasn't expecting anyone. Just getting ready for class."

"You're Miss Chivers, right?" he asked.

"Rosemary," she corrected, flustered.

His smile was wry. "Rosemary. I've made you nervous. Maybe I should go out and come in again."

"No." Rosemary composed herself and smiled. "No. It's fine. I'm afraid my thoughts were far away. How can I help you, Mr. Frances?"

"Bobby," he said. "I was just looking around. Counting desks and radiators, things like that."

"There are three in this room."

He gave her a blank look.

"Radiators," she provided.

"Oh." He laughed. "No, I don't actually care how many radiators there are. This is your first year at Mercer Rocks?"

The change of subject caught her off guard. "Oh, yes."

"And before that?"

"I was taking care of my sick mother." She wasn't sure why she said it; it had nothing to do with anything. Maybe to blunt the force of him.

It seemed to work. "I hope she's feeling better."

"She died at the start of the school year."

"God, I'm sorry. I didn't mean—"

"I taught in Yakima until my mother's illness. I do have an extensive résumé. I'm sure Stella has it on file if you wish to look at it."

"I'm sorry again." He sighed and swept a hand over his thick hair, smoothing it, though there was not a hair out of place. "People get anxious when I come in. They think it means they're losing something."

"Isn't that because they usually are? Isn't it your job to take things away?"

"Sometimes. People don't like change, but I wouldn't have thought you've been here long enough to be attached."

"Attached to what? Cake mix? I think I can live through any cutbacks you suggest."

"Everyone has their own little fiefdom—"

Rosemary waved her hands about the room. "I'm surrounded by textbooks from the thirties and sewing machines that haven't been replaced since Coolidge was president. I am the queen of teaching modern girls with ancient equipment. Please, release me from my fiefdom. I beg you."

He laughed softly. "Okay. Okay."

She relaxed. "How long have you been doing this?"

"A few years. Not long. I was . . . well, I discovered I had an aptitude for it. Detail-oriented, I guess you could say."

"I see. Pearl Hoskins says you're a veteran."

His full lips tightened. He nodded.

"You must have been young."

"Weren't we all? I enlisted after Pearl Harbor. I was angry, ready to take on the world, well"—a shrug—"when I got out, I went to college on the GI Bill, and here I am."

There was still anger there, she thought, and something else too, something interesting, though she didn't know what it was. She knew that quick averting of his eyes. There was something he wasn't saying. Bobby Frances had secrets too.

"It's lucky for us that you are." At his sudden bewilderment, she clarified, "If we want to stay open and keep our jobs, I mean. Streamlining and all that. You'll let me know what I can do, I'm sure."

He was all business again. "I appreciate that. I'll want to see your budget reports for this quarter."

"Of course."

"And those you've projected for the coming quarter."

"Until yesterday I didn't even know there would be another quarter. But I'll get them to you as soon as I can."

"Good. Thank you." He turned to go, and then turned back again. "And . . . McCree—the gardener?"

Rosemary struggled to keep a pleasant smile. "Yes?"

"He says you've been teaching some girls extra gardening classes?"

Rosemary raised a questioning brow.

"I'm assuming that's not in your regular budget. I'd like to see the numbers for that class as well."

"There are none," Rosemary told him, trying for casual unconcern. "I've spent nothing. It's mostly discussing the plants that are already there. But if I end up with costs, I'll let you know."

"Okay. Just thought I'd ask. They've given me the office next to Lois's. You can drop off your reports there, or if you have any questions for me . . ."

"I doubt I will, but thank you. It was nice to meet you, Mr.—"

"Bobby," he said again.

"Bobby." Rosemary mustered her most brilliant smile. "Welcome to Mercer Rocks."

He looked a little stunned—Rosemary had rarely used her smile to such good purpose, and it delighted her that she'd managed it. So that force in him could be arrested. It was good to know he was vulnerable to flirtation if she ever needed to use it.

He seemed at a loss for words. "I—I guess I'll see you later, then."

"Don't eat the creamed corn at lunch," she warned. "Mrs. Dennis is usually a good cook, but she puts far too much pepper in it."

"Thanks for the warning." He started to the door. "Oh, and Rosemary . . . You're using the board's approved curriculum, aren't you?"

Rosemary's satisfaction fled. "Of course. Why?"

"Just checking. Lois said something about a deviation, and I'm just making sure there aren't new costs associated with it—"

"No." The radiator had ramped up into enthusiastic action. The room had grown suddenly hot. Rosemary resisted the urge to pull off her cardigan. "We're pondering all the ways to use canned peas to survive the bomb, just as the board directed."

"Ah. Good." Another quick smile, and then he left.

Rosemary listened to his retreating footsteps, but she still felt his force in the room, not so vulnerable after all.

Chapter 23

The glass was foggy and humid against the outside cold and growing more so with the heat of their breath as they talked eagerly about virginity and the first time and the hypocrisy of men enjoying sex and wanting someone with experience and yet expecting their wives to be pure.

"Kinsey's study showed that women who'd had orgasms before they married were more likely to have them when they were married—and they were happier," Rosemary said.

"That's why I want someone older the first time," Jean said thoughtfully. "Not some clumsy boy."

Sandra cringed. "It's just . . . embarrassing to think about. I mean, it's one thing to be all romantic like in the movies, but really it would be like *Excuse me, mister, but before you stick your thing into me, do you have any rubbers?*"

"*Penis*, Sandy," Maisie corrected with a teasing grin. "Use the right words so there's no misunderstanding."

"That's why you pick someone experienced, so you don't have to ask," Jean said. "He would just know to do it."

"I wouldn't count on that," Rosemary said wryly.

"I'll bet Mr. Frances would," Jean went on pensively, ignoring Rosemary. "Don't you think so? He's such a dreamboat."

"Well, he's got a cool car," Sandra admitted. "A '49 Deluxe Coupe."

"You know his car?" Rosemary asked, surprised.

"He's too old," Maisie said. "And anyway, Jean, didn't you say he was a friend of your dad's?"

Another surprise. Rosemary frowned. "He is?"

"Daddy was the one who recommended him for this job," Jean told her.

"You know him?"

Jean sighed. "I wish. I'd never seen him before. Daddy called to tell me that he was the reason Mr. Frances was here and the school was saved, so I should be good."

Rosemary did not like that Bobby Frances was connected to John Karlstad and therefore the HUAC. That was a danger she hadn't expected. It was one thing when he was just asking questions about finances; this was something else completely. If he found out about these secret meetings, it could mean more than just losing her job. HUAC would not hesitate to destroy her if it felt she was an immoral influence. Jean's involvement only made their meetings more perilous.

"Mr. McCree told Mr. Frances about our meetings here," Rosemary said, considering the complications.

"I really hate Old Martin," Maisie said. "He's such a busybody. Why would he do that?"

"We're not spending any money, so why should he care?" Jean asked.

"Our meetings are supposed to be secret, you big boob," Maisie noted.

"Exactly," Rosemary agreed. "If Mr. Frances gets suspicious, we could all be in trouble."

"We'll think of a lie, then," Sandra said. "Maybe we *are* talking about gardening."

"Do you really think anyone would believe that, after Miss Chivers was warned not to talk about gonorrhea?" Maisie asked.

The girl was so quick, so clever. No wonder she was the leader.

"I think we should stop meeting for a while," Rosemary suggested. "At least until Mr. Frances is settled in and I know how curious he is."

"No!" Jean burst out.

"Can't we just meet somewhere else?" Sandra asked. "Somewhere he doesn't know? We can't stop. I learn so much, and . . . and honestly I'd miss you."

"*We'd* miss you," Jean said, not to be outdone.

Rosemary loved their devotion, but this was dangerous, and she couldn't allow herself to be swayed or seduced. It would be hard; she had to admit that the meetings were about more now than trying to discover which of them was hers; she found an immense satisfaction in teaching them. It was as if she were somehow making it up to the girl she'd been. Saving them in a way she had not been able to save herself.

But she had time now. Months until the end of the school year. "I think it's better just to take a break—"

"No, Miss Chivers," Maisie said firmly. "You can't do this to us. Not now. You're the only thing we care about here. We have to keep meeting. We'll die if we don't. We'll just die. No one will find out. We promise, don't we?"

Sandra and Jean nodded in unison.

"We'll make sure of it," Sandra said.

"We swear," Jean said.

"You see?" Maisie offered. "Once we make a promise, Miss Chivers, we never break it. *Never.* And you can't either."

Chapter 24

Rosemary avoided Bobby Frances over the next days as much as she could, on the theory that if he didn't see her or couldn't find her, he couldn't ask questions. It was easier than she'd expected. Rosemary dropped off her reports when he wasn't in the office. He was in meetings most of the time, sometimes with the board, according to Irene. Rosemary wondered if John Karlstad was home from DC and at those meetings. She stayed away from the staff room and the office and tensed every time she heard footsteps on the mezzanine stairs before or after classes. But Bobby didn't seek her out. She imagined hopefully that he was too busy with everything else to ask questions about the home-ec teacher.

She was grateful when Thanksgiving came, and the students and non-live-in staff—which meant the new vice principal—took a four-day break.

The girls who could go home for Thanksgiving, which included Sandra and Jean, left. Maisie, along with a few others whose parents weren't around, remained.

The school was serving a turkey dinner for those students and allowing them to watch television. It would be a night of *The Life of Riley*, *Amos 'n' Andy*, and *Dragnet*, along with popcorn and soda. Maisie was not appeased by the special treat.

"It will be the most boring night ever," she said, rolling her eyes. "At least you'll stay, won't you, Miss Chivers? You can play guitar and we can sing songs. Maybe we could build a fire."

"My father is expecting me," Rosemary told her sympathetically.

Maisie sighed. "I used to go to a movie with my friends on Thanksgiving. It was so fun. I wish I could do that again. I don't suppose . . ." She looked hopefully at Rosemary.

The thought of a movie with Maisie tempted. For a moment Rosemary allowed herself to imagine it. The two of them sitting together. Laughing at the same scenes, crying, whispering, shoulder to shoulder like any mother and daughter . . .

"Oh, it would be so fun! We could get popcorn and Raisinets—if you like them, I mean. I love them, but maybe you like something else?"

"Raisinets?" Rosemary started from her imaginings. David had loved Raisinets.

"I could check the newspaper and see what's playing." Maisie's excitement was palpable.

"No." Rosemary spoke more bluntly than she meant and was sorry when Maisie's face fell. "I'm sorry, but no. I'll be fired. You must know that. You'll have fun here, and I'll see you in the evening."

Maisie's disappointment was hard to turn away from, but Rosemary did so with a forgive-me smile. She was halfway down the hall when she heard, "Have a good time, Miss Chivers. Think of me here, miserable without you."

When she turned again, Maisie had already gone back into her room.

~

Last year they'd known nothing about Mom's heart. Mom had been tired and drawn, but she had insisted she was fine and still she'd done everything, the entire dinner, the turkey and every traditional side dish and two pies for just the three of them. She hadn't let Rosemary lift a finger. Last year the gravy was lumpy and the potatoes undercooked, which was unusual, as Mom had never made a less than perfect dinner, and she and Rosemary had got into a fight, which was not.

What the day would be like this year, Rosemary didn't know.

It was quieter. She and her father drank coffee and picked at a cinnamon coffee cake he'd bought, as they watched the Macy's Thanksgiving Day Parade on television.

Dad had told her over the phone that he did not want a big meal. "What am I going to do with it all after?"

"Eat it maybe? You're too thin."

"I've got plenty of canned stuff here. I'll buy a couple of TV dinners."

"Dad—"

"No, Rosie. It'd be good for both of us to relax. I don't want it. Please."

Rosemary didn't argue. He was right. He wouldn't appreciate the dinner and she didn't really want to cook.

Instead, compulsively, she went through Mom's belongings again. She could not lose the feeling that she was missing something, and when she found a box of her mother's costume jewelry socked away in a sewing kit, it only told her she was right. Mom had hidden things— who knew why? Here was the atomic-bomb brooch Rosemary had been thinking about during the school drill, and three flower pins with enameled green leaves and rhinestone petals. One blue, one yellow, and one pink. Rosemary didn't remember seeing them before, but when she did . . .

Three matching pins and three girls. It seemed weirdly destined.

She stared down at the brooches glittering in her hand. It was a bad idea to give the girls these pins. A very, very bad idea. It could only lead to trouble.

She jiggled the pins, tossing about the sparkling light from the rhinestones. It was certainly against the school rules, although truthfully she didn't remember a rule about gifts. There didn't have to be a specific rule. No jewelry was allowed; this was exactly the kind of thing Rosemary herself would have taken away the first day and thrown in a box to be locked up. These would be confiscated if they were discovered.

Then again . . . no one had to know, and it was just costume jewelry, and there *was* that sense of fate about it. If Rosemary held the girls to secrecy. If she made them promise not to wear them at school, to hide them until they could take them home and squirrel them away . . .

They'd kept the secret of the meetings, hadn't they? They'd kept every promise they'd made, and Rosemary liked the idea of handing something of her mother's down to her daughter. One of them was certainly owed it, wasn't she?

They were nothing expensive and maybe the girls wouldn't even want them, and Rosemary didn't have to decide now, did she? She could take them with her, think on it a while.

She put them in her purse.

Dad put two TV Thanksgiving dinners into the oven: slices of turkey and gravy, mashed potatoes, and corn-bread dressing and peas. He'd bought a can of cranberry sauce and chocolate pudding mix, which she'd made earlier and put in the refrigerator to set. They ate in silence, listening to the radio. It had been only a day, but Rosemary missed her girls. She could not stop thinking of Maisie's suggestion of a movie. The dark theater, images on a screen, watching in rapt wonder and companionship, mother and maybe-daughter. She glanced at her father and felt the emptiness of the house, the lack of Mom's presence, and wondered how he spent his days without his wife of thirty-five years.

"Why don't we go to a movie, Dad?"

He peered at her in surprise—as well he should. She couldn't think of the last time she had suggested they do anything together. Perhaps when she was ten and they'd listened to a baseball game on the radio.

"A movie?"

"Yes, why not? Where's the paper? Let's see what's playing." She didn't wait for him to answer but fetched the *Seattle Daily Times* and shook open the newspaper to the Amusements page. "Look—*The Last Time I Saw Paris* opens tonight at the Music Hall. It's got Elizabeth Taylor. What do you think?"

"Well, I—" Dad paused, and then he put his napkin down. "Have we ever gone to a movie together, Rosie?"

She couldn't answer. She'd suddenly realized that the dream she'd had of a mother and daughter at a movie had only ever happened in her imagination. Nor had she ever gone to a movie with her father. These family memories had never been hers; they had only been stories in her head and wishes that had never come true and a future that was nothing but an illusion.

~

Half an hour later, they were in Dad's gray-and-blue Buick in front of the movie house. The lights flaring in the darkness made the Music Hall look even more like a fortress, highlighting the intricacies of its Spanish baroque detailing, fairy-tale-like amid the office buildings on the street. A crowd formed at the entrance. She bought their tickets while he parked the car, and when he objected, she told him he could buy the popcorn and her Hot Tamales. "Oh, and some Raisinets. Get a box of those too, please."

The red-carpeted foyer was dimly lit; murals of Spanish conquistadores decorated the walls of the stairways, and mossy green and rose velvet drapes decorated the rest. Rosemary and her father settled into the plush seats. He sucked on a Coke and said, "This is fun, isn't it?" and smiled, and Rosemary wondered why she hadn't suggested this before.

After the movie ended, Dad was quiet and thoughtful as they left the theater. Rosemary's eyes still blurred with tears over the melodrama.

Cold, damp air crept into the crevices between Rosemary's scarf and her collar, and the street filled with cars, headlights illuminating the faint mist, people rushing across the street and down the sidewalk, huddled against the glowing streetlights and shadows of the late November night. Her father tucked her into the Buick, and they were nearly back at the school before he said, "I didn't really care for the movie much. Everyone in it was only thinking of what they wanted. No one was thinking of that child."

Rosemary heard what he was not very subtly saying. "I know you and Mom thought I would be a bad mother. I know you thought I wasn't ready. Maybe I wasn't. I know that's what I thought at first, but I wanted her at the end. Maybe it wouldn't have been a mistake."

He was quiet. Then, after what seemed like a long time, he said, "Not a bad mother, Rosie. But you were young, and alone. Without that boy—"

"He would have stayed." She spoke with confidence, but that memory, too, was a hard one.

"Maybe."

She heard his doubt. If Dad had met David even once, everything would have been different—or maybe not. She remembered when she'd been in White Shield, he'd told her that David's family wasn't their kind and this was not a fairy tale. Rosemary shoved those thoughts away. "I still don't know which one she is, Dad. They all could be. It's . . . difficult."

They fell into silence, but it was a tender one.

As he pulled up the circular drive to the school and stopped, he said, "It was good tonight, wasn't it, Rosie?"

"Yes, it was." She reached for the handle to open the door. "Good night, Dad."

She got out of the car and went into the flood of the school lights, and he waited until she was through the front door before he drove away. The building was quiet; it was late and everyone had already gone to bed. She wondered how the day had gone for her girls and whether they had thought about her at all. The Raisinets were in her coat pocket; she reached inside, taking the box into her hand to keep the candy from rattling. Quietly, she went upstairs. With every step she was gripped by a pressing foreboding, hard and persistent. This damn building seemed to breathe with the gathered resentment and anger of years. *Keep going up,* she told herself when she reached the second-floor landing. *Go to bed.* But instead she went down the hall. There were the Raisinets. They could wait until tomorrow, but she wanted to surprise Maisie with them now.

As she passed Cheryl Fields's open door, the woman looked up from the desk. "Rosemary?"

"I found something of Miss Neal's on the stairs," Rosemary lied. "I'm going to drop it outside her door."

The guard nodded and went back to her book.

Rosemary hurried to Maisie's room. The door was closed. She tapped on it gently. When there was no answer, she tried the knob. The door wasn't locked. She opened the door enough to peek inside. The room was dark, but the roller blind had not been pulled, so the ambient light from outside seeped in, illuminating the bed, empty and still made.

Rosemary blinked disbelievingly. She looked again. Maisie was nowhere in the room.

She backed away from the door. The girl must be in the bathroom. Or perhaps she was ill and she'd gone to the nurse. But Cheryl would have said something.

Then Rosemary thought of that light she'd seen the first night. She'd not seen it since, but then again, she hadn't looked for it. She glanced toward the window. There was no movement outside. No flashlight.

Rosemary's foreboding intensified. Maisie had run off. It was surprising only in that Rosemary had thought there was a connection between them that would keep Maisie here, and now . . . Rosemary could pretend she hadn't seen this, but she'd just told Cheryl she was coming to Maisie's room, and if Maisie were caught out of bed, there would be questions about what Rosemary knew and when. If Rosemary didn't report this to the guard . . .

She had to make a choice now. Tell Cheryl Fields that Maisie was gone or hope that Maisie was safe and wouldn't get caught being out of her room.

Rosemary closed the door softly, torn and angry with Maisie for forcing her to make the choice. It was only then that she noticed Jean's door was ajar, which was odd, because Jean was at home. Rosemary went to close it—and caught a glimpse of the bed, where Maisie lay, sound asleep, Jean's pillow held tightly to her chest.

Rosemary knew then, with dismay, what choice she would have made. She would have pretended she hadn't noted Maisie's disappearance. She would have protected Maisie from punishment, at whatever cost to herself.

She was in far too deep.

Rosemary closed Jean's door. She went back to Maisie's room and hid the Raisinets under the blanket near the pillow, where Maisie would be sure to find them.

The Past

When David came back, they would find their daughter together. That was the dream and the hope that Rosemary clutched. Everything would be fine when David returned from Spain. It was the only thing that saved her. She scoured the newspaper for what the Republicans were doing, where the fighting was. She could not get there herself, but in her head she was beside him.

And then . . . a very bad day.

She had been forced to come home for Easter, and she and Mom had gone shopping. Rosemary had no interest in Best's, and so she agreed to meet Mom at the Tea Room in Frederick & Nelson's next door. Rosemary ordered an olive sandwich and angel food cake, then took off her gloves and laid them primly in her lap and drank her iced cocoa with whipped cream, only half listening to the women talking at the next table until one of them made some comment about the International Brigades fighting in Spain, and the foolish Americans who had gone there with the red passports issued by the Soviets and how they were all going to die the wretched death a communist deserved. Rosemary had to restrain herself from screaming that while they were cramming club sandwiches into their mouths, those brave men were dying for a cause—and then she realized that she was doing the same thing. Sitting in the Tea Room drinking iced cocoa, living a safe and stupid life here, while the man she loved was fighting, maybe dying.

When Mom bustled in, complaining about the prices in Best's and ordering her own club sandwich and iced tea with such assurance and privilege, Rosemary could not bear it.

"When David gets back, we're going to find our daughter, and then we're going to travel the world and fight men like Franco and . . ." Rosemary trailed off at the look on her mother's face, which was not what she expected. It was not exasperation or anger. It was pity. "What?"

Mom seemed suddenly fascinated by a waitress filling saltshakers.

"What?" Rosemary asked again with an increasing sense of dread.

Her mother sighed heavily. "David Tapper is dead, Rosemary."

Rosemary stared at her mother in shock.

Mom turned to her. "He's dead."

Slowly, the words began to make sense, only they didn't, how could they? Rosemary managed, "I don't . . . understand."

"A few months ago," Mom said matter-of-factly, pulling off her gloves with tense precision.

"That's not possible."

"Taken prisoner and executed."

"No." Rosemary shook her head. "No, that's not possible. That's not possible. I would know. I would feel it."

"Well, you didn't," Mom said brutally. "His parents got word last week."

Rosemary went very still. "When did you get word?"

Her mother said nothing.

"When did you hear?" Rosemary asked again.

Silence.

"Last week." Rosemary could barely say the words. "You knew last week, and you didn't tell me?"

Mom spoke but all Rosemary heard was buzzing. It went on and on, buzzing and buzzing until she couldn't stand it any longer. Her gloves fell from her lap onto the floor as she rose and raced mindlessly from the restaurant, out of the store and into the city streets, not understanding where she was going until she came to herself and understood where she needed to be and caught a trolley.

She'd only been to the Tappers' house once, but she remembered it clearly. He'd taken her there to meet his parents, and his mother had not seemed to like Rosemary. His father had been polite but obviously concerned about some aspect of his son's romance that Rosemary had assumed had been the difference in their social position. No doubt he felt ill at ease over the fact that her father was a professor at the school where he worked as a janitor.

The house was not in a good part of Seattle, but after Common House, bad parts of town didn't frighten her. She got off the bus and tried to find the street. It was a nice late afternoon, and a couple of children in threadbare clothes stopped short when they saw her, and one of them called, "You lost, miss?"

Then she recognized an ugly mustard-colored house on the corner. Not David's, but his was two away, tiny and needing paint and with a roof patched with plywood. An abandoned tricycle lay on its side in the front yard.

"Just a minute!" a woman called from inside when Rosemary knocked.

Rosemary bit the inside of her cheek and waited nervously. It seemed to take a long time. She took in the wooden rocker bench on the porch, a clay pot of something dead. Something narrow and about three inches long was nailed to the inside right of the doorframe, a rectangular tube unlike anything she'd ever seen before, intricately carved and pretty. Just as Rosemary touched it, the door creaked open. Rosemary yanked back her hand.

But the woman caught the motion and frowned. "It's not witchcraft."

The way she said it, with such bitterness and deep-in sadness . . . it stripped Rosemary of her anger. "What is it?"

David's mother had his long face, but her hair was darker, her eyes too. She looked older than the last time Rosemary had seen her, more worn. Or maybe it was only that sadness. "There are verses from the Torah inside. It's tradition."

The Torah. That was . . . wasn't that Jewish? Rosemary frowned.

"What do you want, Rosemary?" Mrs. Tapper asked. "Why are you here?" There was no gentleness in Mrs. Tapper's voice, nor curiosity really. That she felt Rosemary was an intrusion was obvious.

But Rosemary could not take her eyes from the Torah thing, from her sudden realization that David's family was Jewish, and he'd never said. Not once had he even implied it. Now, Dad's words made a terrible sense. *"They aren't our kind."*

She should have known. She should have realized. But she hadn't, and shame and desolation swept her because David had said nothing and she'd never guessed, never even suspected. It hadn't mattered to her, but she knew it would matter to her parents, and she could have done something if she'd known, she could have tried to make them see . . . and now it was too late.

She'd been in a battle she hadn't known she was fighting. No wonder she had lost.

Mrs. Tapper stared at her expectantly, and through her misery Rosemary managed, "I—I came to ask about David. My mom told me—"

"Yes, he's dead." Mrs. Tapper said the words as brutally as Rosemary's mother had. But, unlike Mom's, Mrs. Tapper's eyes filled with tears. "Now maybe you can leave him alone, the way you should have from the start."

"I loved him."

Mrs. Tapper sighed wearily. She started to close the door.

Rosemary put out her hand to stop it. "No. No, don't. Please. I need you to know. I loved him. We—"

"You only encouraged him. All those stupid ideas. And he's gone now, thanks to you. Ran off to Spain when you went away. Broke his heart."

"I didn't have any part of that. I didn't know that. My parents—"

Mrs. Tapper snorted. "We were told you didn't want him."

Rosemary stared at her in shock. The world upended, and then just as quickly fell into a different order, one she understood for the first time. She had been so stupid, but now she saw it. Why David had not come to White Shield. Why he'd never even written to her. Her parents had lied to him. They'd lied to her. They'd lied to keep them apart. "But—but that's not true! They lied! That was never true! I waited for him. I wanted to keep our baby."

"Oh? Is that so? Where's that baby now?" Mrs. Tapper looked around, searching.

Rosemary swallowed her tears. How to explain how easily she'd surrendered? And now David was dead.

"That's what I thought. Just as well. Don't come back here again."

The door closed hard in Rosemary's face.

Chapter 25

Mercer Rocks School for Wayward Girls
Seattle, WA—1954

Rosemary woke with a start, her dream of David and the grief of losing him lingering like a ghost, and with it that restlessness and too-familiar feeling that something was wrong—or going to be wrong.

School did not begin again until Monday. The few girls who were here were already at breakfast; Rosemary entered the dining room to see that Maisie wasn't among them. Alicia was there. Rosemary got coffee and joined her.

"You look pale," Alicia commented. "A rough Thanksgiving?"

"Actually, no. We went to a movie. *The Last Time I Saw Paris.*"

"Elizabeth Taylor, right? Was it good?"

Rosemary nodded and sipped her coffee. "Big drama. Not really my dad's favorite. How were things here?"

"Lizzie Etheridge got caught with a bottle of rum. She's in isolation."

"For how long?"

"Lois thought the rest of the break would be long enough."

Two girls appeared in the doorway—Maisie and, surprisingly, Sandra Wilson. Maisie was laughing, but Sandra looked terrible: very pale, shadows beneath her eyes, her hair tied back in a lumpy, frizzy mass as if she couldn't be bothered to brush it.

Alicia followed Rosemary's gaze. "She came back this morning. Decided to end her break early."

"Did she say why?"

Alicia shrugged. "Probably a fight with her parents. Had to be bad to make her choose here over home."

Rosemary watched Sandra and Maisie sit at a table apart from the other girls.

Sandra glanced over, catching Rosemary's eye. Rosemary looked away quickly, pretending she hadn't been watching, and it was then that Sandra leaped up from the table and raced from the dining hall. Maisie watched her go with only cursory interest and went back to buttering her toast.

Don't follow. Leave her alone.

But Rosemary found herself rising. "I'd better—"

"Rosemary," Alicia said urgently enough that Rosemary turned to look at her. "Don't. I mean it. You should leave her be."

"But—"

"You're getting too involved with those three. I'm telling you—"

"She looks ill to me. Doesn't she to you?"

"I'm sure whatever it is, she did it to herself."

"Alicia!"

"Rosemary, listen to me. You don't understand. You really don't."

"I'm sorry. I've got to see to her." Rosemary's concern over Sandra had her hurrying out. There was no sign of Sandra in the hall, but the bathroom was only two doors away; Rosemary heard retching from inside. It had to be Sandra. One of the stall doors was closed; Rosemary waited near the sinks. Finally the stall opened, and Sandra, bleary-eyed, red-nosed, stepped out.

She started when she saw Rosemary and wiped self-consciously at her mouth. "Oh, Miss Chivers, I—"

"Are you ill?" Rosemary asked.

Sandra hesitated.

Rosemary knew that hesitation; she'd seen it in herself a hundred times. "You're drunk."

"Not anymore." Sandra went to the sink and turned on the water to splash her face. She gratefully took the towel Rosemary handed her. "I'm just hungover now."

"I see."

"Don't look at me like that. I'm sure you've never been hungover."

Rosemary laughed. "Do you want some aspirin?"

Sandra looked wary. "I can't get aspirin without going to the nurse, and she—"

"I have some in my room."

"You won't report this?"

"Did you get drunk at school?"

Sandra shook her head. "I got drunk at Thanksgiving dinner. Or . . . I guess after, really. It's why I'm back early."

"Then there's nothing to report, is there? You didn't break any rules."

"Oh, thank you, Miss Chivers." Sandra's face sagged in gratitude.

"Let's go, before they miss you." Rosemary led the way to her bedroom. Once they were there, she handed Sandra two aspirin and the cup of water Rosemary kept by her bed.

Sandra swallowed aspirin and water, handed the cup back to Rosemary, and asked carefully, "I don't suppose you have any cigarettes?"

"Let's not overdo it," Rosemary advised.

"I suppose not." Sandra sighed and glanced around the room. "Can I look at your records?"

"Haven't you already seen them?"

Sandra widened her eyes, ready to protest. But then she smiled slowly in acknowledgment. "I wanted to know about you."

"Why?"

"Because you were a new teacher. Because the first time I saw you, I knew I was going to like you."

The confession warmed Rosemary and made her wonder if there was some meaning in it, if Sandra felt a connection between them. "How did you know that?"

Sandra shrugged. "I just knew. But . . . I've been wrong about teachers before, and I didn't want to be surprised. So . . ." She waved at the room limply.

"How would searching my room and stealing my perfume keep you from being surprised?" Rosemary asked.

"I'm tired of liars. I wanted to make sure you weren't one."

Again, the talk of liars. Again, Rosemary wondered what Alicia had done last year to upset them so.

"But I didn't have time to really look through your records, and, you know, I like music. May I?"

"Go ahead."

Sandra pulled out an old album from the Almanac Singers and turned it over to look at the list of songs. "'Union Maid,' 'Talking Union,' 'Which Side Are You On?' . . . These are all communist songs, aren't they? Does Mrs. Bullard know you have these?"

"If you've been sent by the House Un-American Activities Committee to question me, you should be more subtle."

Sandra snorted. "Ha! I leave that kind of thing to Jean's dad."

"They're *union* songs. Protest songs. That's an old record. And no one asked me my music taste when they hired me."

"Hmmm. And the Weavers too. Why, Miss Chivers, you are a commie!"

The girl was teasing, but even a tease had bite in these days, and the past, peril. Rosemary tried to smile. "My father would have me deported."

Sandra sat back on her heels. "My mother would like to do the same to me, I think."

"Because you're a Red?" Rosemary tried to keep her voice light, but the way Sandra looked at her told her she hadn't quite succeeded.

"Because I don't want to be like her. Do you ever feel like the world is too small for you? Like everyone wants to put you in such a little box and you just can't breathe there?"

How familiar that sounded. How exact. *Stop staring,* but oh, to see into Sandra's brain, deep and deep, into the circuits there, into the genes that made her who she was. What was familiar, what was true, what belonged to her? Excitement tingled, hope—was there an answer here at last? "What's your mom like? Why don't you want to be like her?"

"Honestly? I don't know. She doesn't understand me and I don't understand her. I guess that's it. Did you understand your mom when you were my age?"

Rosemary laughed shortly. "No."

"Do you understand her now? I mean . . . I'm sorry, that didn't come out right. I know she's passed, and umm . . . but—does being an adult help you understand her?"

Rosemary hesitated. How to answer that question?

Sandra went on, "My mom always says she remembers what it was like to be seventeen. I don't think she does. Do you?"

The plaintive expression on Sandra's face squeezed Rosemary's heart. "Oh, yes," she said quietly. "Too well, I imagine."

Sandra considered that for a moment. "Yeah. Well, my mom's not like you. No one's like you."

Those words climbed inside Rosemary and nested, and in that moment she wanted her daughter to be Sandra with such intensity she could hardly breathe.

Dangerous, she warned herself. The intensity of feeling was too dangerous, and suddenly she was remembering being awakened in the College Elementary School building with baby Mary in her arms. Her aunt's admonition *"Stop feeling so much. Grow up, Rosie, before the world crushes you."* Fear made her step back, force a smile, and say, "Well. We should be getting back before we're missed."

"Oh. Yes, I guess so." Such disappointment in the girl's voice. "Thank you for the aspirin, Miss Chivers. And for . . . not telling anyone."

"Your secret is safe with me," Rosemary said, but as Sandra left, Rosemary's fear faded and she was sorry she had retreated. She was sorry she had not said, *I know that feeling of being in a small box. I felt it all the time when I was your age. I feel it now.*

But then again, it was not her place to say such things. If Sandra was not her daughter, it would never be Rosemary's place to say them. If Sandra *was* her daughter, Rosemary had given her up. She had lost the right. She wondered now: If she had the answer of which girl was hers, what would she do with it?

It frightened her to realize that she didn't know.

Chapter 26

A cold rain sluiced down the greenhouse glass, blown in spurts by a wind that lifted the branches of the orchard trees outside. Maisie and Sandra watched while Jean bent over the guitar, stretching her fingers into a simple G chord.

"It's harder than I thought," Jean complained. "Plus it hurts to press so hard. Show us again."

"All right. One more time. Watch carefully." Rosemary took the guitar and led them again into 'This Land Is Your Land.'

They were all competent singers, Jean perhaps the best of them, with a high and clear soprano that had a sweet pureness to it, and a poise, too, that reminded Rosemary—maybe—of sandy-haired boys who moved through the world too easily, though the girl truly had no talent at all for the guitar. Maisie was better at stretching those long fingers to make the chords. Sandra didn't have any interest in trying.

Their voices had a nice acoustic in the greenhouse, bouncing off the hard glass with the rain adding a beat, and when they were done, Rosemary put the guitar aside. Her mother's pins were in her purse, but she still hadn't decided if she would give them. On one hand, the rules. On the other, it was such silly costume jewelry, how could it matter? Yet, that was the part that caught her each time. It *did* matter to her.

"Oh, I don't want to leave for Christmas break—and I never thought I would say that," Sandra said mournfully.

Maisie sighed. "My uncle's supposed to be home from London. I wonder if we can manage not to spend the whole time screaming at each other. Probably not."

"Lock yourself in your room and refuse to come out until he brings you presents. That usually works." Jean tossed her blond hair with a flourish.

"I'll be lucky if he remembers it's Christmas," Maisie said.

"The Christmas tree will remind him."

"What Christmas tree?"

"You mean you don't have one?" asked Jean, aghast.

"Oh, I don't know. Maybe. The housekeeper might remember it if she's still there. He threatened to fire her last summer, and of course, I wasn't home for Thanksgiving, so I don't know if he did. Last year, he left me there alone while he was in Paris, and I celebrated with the cook until she went home to her family."

"Sounds delightful." Jean wrinkled her nose.

"Let's see, what did I do last year? Mom and Dad were having a party, as usual, and I drank eggnog with rum until I was sick all over the stairs, and my cousin Richard carried me up to bed and tried to get fresh. One of the best times of my life." Sandra stared morosely at the rain. "I'm sure he'll show up again this year."

"I opened so many presents that it took the maid an hour to clean up all the wrapping paper." Jean was thoughtful. "And you know, I don't remember a single thing Daddy gave me. I only remember that I didn't get what I wanted."

Rosemary ached for her. "What was it that you wanted?"

"The pearls that belonged to my mom. He says he doesn't know where they are, but I think he sold them."

Pearls. Mom. The words struck powerfully.

"Anyway, we're going to my uncle's this year. My mom's side of the family. I'm to get my mom's trust fund next year, so he says I have to go and be nice because it's a family thing, you know? She got it from her grandmother, and now it's going to come to me."

A trust fund. What a thing for a mother to leave a child. Grandmother to mother to daughter. Rosemary had nothing like that to give to any of these girls beyond costume jewelry. Not a trust fund, but it was jewelry that had belonged to her child's grandmother, passed from mother to daughter. It, too, was an inheritance, if a small one.

The only one she had.

Impulsively, Rosemary reached for the purse at her feet. "I got a small gift for each of you."

"A present!" Jean squealed and clapped her hands like a child.

"It's nothing much," Rosemary warned, fishing about for the small boxes she'd wrapped in tissue paper that morning. Yellow for Jean, pink for Maisie, blue for Sandra, all tied with a bit of ribbon she'd curled into corkscrews with a scissor blade. She handed them around.

"Oh, Miss Chivers!" Maisie looked ready to cry.

Rosemary watched while they opened their gifts, spilling onto the floor the tissue paper and the ribbon she'd curled so carefully. Jean gasped with delight as she opened the box.

"Why, it's a pin! A flower!" She held it up for the others to see—rose-tinted gold with enameled green leaves and petals of yellow rhinestones.

"It's not real," Rosemary explained. "It's not what you're used to, I'm sure—"

"I love it!" Jean clasped it tight in her hands, then pinned it onto her sweater. "Oh, look how it sparkles! Isn't it just perfect?"

Rosemary could not help smiling.

"I'll think of you every time I look at it, and all the things you've taught me," Jean declared, pressing her hand to her heart. "I'll keep it forever. Thank you, Miss Chivers."

Maisie's eyes threatened to overflow. Sandra stared down at the pin in the palm of her hand, serious, contained, until Rosemary thought something was wrong.

"Do you not like the color?"

"It's perfect," Sandra said quietly, meeting her gaze. "Thank you."

It was true, they both seemed as enchanted as Jean had been, both overwhelmed. Both pinned them immediately above their breasts. Rosemary had never given gifts that brought such satisfaction, and suddenly she was thinking of all the Christmases past, the ones she'd spent alone, the efforts she'd put into forgetting, all the Santa Clauses with their lines of waiting children that she'd walked by, ignoring, telling herself she had no reason to notice them or to care, that she had gone on, that she was living her life the way they'd told her to.

Now she knew she had only been pretending.

Sandra

Sandy's window overlooks the entry court of the main building. She likes to see who comes and goes from the school. Maisie chose the room for Sandy on purpose, because along with Sandra's skill at breaking in—the lock on her parents' liquor cabinet has been changed so many times, in so many ways, that she has honed her skills on nearly every lock imaginable—she likes to watch people, and she remembers what she sees, and Maisie finds such information useful. Maisie is the real genius among them, and mostly Sandra is content to give Maisie what she wants and let her make the plans, but sometimes Sandra thinks that Maisie misses what's important. All Maisie sees is what she can use.

For Maisie, everything is about power, and Sandy knows Maisie regards those pins Miss Chivers gave them as power. It worries Sandy, because she loves that pin, and she knows that ultimately she'll do whatever Maisie wants her to do, and she feels guilty already for a surrender that hasn't happened yet, and guilty because they owe Miss Chivers so much, and how can they possibly repay her?—and they need to repay her; Sandy feels that to her center.

It's one of those things she just knows, like she knows she lies and she hates it and can't seem to stop it. Like she knows she brings sadness into her mother's face, but she doesn't know what to do about it or how to change it. Most importantly, like she knows Miss Chivers holds the answer to a question Sandy hasn't yet quite defined. When she told Miss

Chivers how drinking made the noise in her head quiet, Miss Chivers gave her such a look . . . the teacher understood, and Sandy wants to know why; she wants to know how. Miss Chivers is so self-possessed and forthright. She seems to live her life without caring what anyone else thinks. She's so honest. Sandy doesn't believe Miss Chivers would ever lie, and when she's in Miss Chivers's room, the noise in her head dulls a little, so she's been sneaking in there to think sometimes. Just to sit and think.

Now Sandy stands at her window, tapping her fingers against her skin until she feels she might go mad, and watches Miss Chivers on the front step, the smoke from her cigarette spiraling away in what must be a damp, chill wind, because Miss Chivers shivers in her cardigan. Her hair is down, that pretty-colored hair that Maisie is always talking about, *"How does she get it so smooth?"*

An uncomfortable shiver strikes Sandra, as if she, too, stands in that damp, chill wind. The gift Miss Chivers gave them is a promise, Sandy sees that. A promise of loyalty and dedication, and Sandy knows that they need to give the teacher a promise in return, something to show her that they belong to her as completely as she belongs to them.

Sandy has been thinking all night, and she thinks she knows a way.

Chapter 27

The Christmas decorations that had been brought out of storage had apparently been used to decorate the school since its founding, and the limp garlands, snowflakes losing their glitter, and *Ho Ho Ho*s in faded red and green lent a forced gaiety that only made the already morose halls more grim.

The staff room, too, looked sadly moribund with holiday cheer. More drooping garlands. A small fake silver tree hung with sparkling ornaments on the cabinet. Dusty Santa Claus candles and Christmas tree centerpieces on the tables. It was only a few days before Christmas break and everyone was restless and ready for the vacation except Rosemary, who dreaded the time without her girls.

She'd been so caught up with them that she'd nearly forgotten about Bobby Frances. She hadn't needed to avoid him; he was the busiest man in the school, always in meetings, and Rosemary had, for the most part, decided that she was of no interest to him and was delighted to know it.

She should have realized that she'd relaxed too soon.

"Do you mind if I join you?" he asked as he stepped into the staff room. "Or am I interrupting something important?"

She gestured for him to sit and pretended that just the sight of him did not make her nervous. "Just grading."

"Maybe I could help?"

Rosemary showed him a paper. "Question: 'What other types of information about family members might prove helpful in a bomb shelter?' Barbara Trask's answer: 'Whether there is enough whiskey to last your dad ninety days.'"

Bobby started to laugh and then stopped when he realized she wasn't joking. "Really?"

Rosemary caught a whiff of his spicy aftershave as he sat. "She's not wrong. But I can hardly give her a proper grade for that."

"No, I suppose not. Teaching these girls must be quite a trick." He stared into his coffee cup, which he spun slowly on the table.

"Sometimes. Most of the time, actually. How were my budget projections?"

"I've been so busy I haven't had time to go through everything," he admitted. "Too many meetings."

"So I've heard. With your friend John Karlstad and the board?"

He gave her an odd look. "Karlstad isn't my friend, and he's rarely at board meetings."

That was a relief. She wondered whether to believe him. There was that look, which was strange, a little too sharp. "I would have thought he'd be more of a presence, given that his daughter is here."

Bobby shrugged. "I guess his legislative committees keep him pretty busy in DC."

Rosemary said nothing.

Bobby stared again into his coffee. Rosemary felt there was something he wanted to say, and she waited for him to say it. His square fingers tapped on the white porcelain of the coffee mug. "Are you staying at your father's over the break?"

The change of subject surprised her. "Yes."

"No plans to travel?"

She laughed a little. "My dad isn't much on going places."

"You'll be just . . . hanging around?"

"I suppose. What about you? Going anywhere?"

He looked thoughtful and then shook his head. "No, but I wondered . . . can I see you? During the break, I mean? Maybe we could have dinner or a drink or something?"

Rosemary stared at him, surprised. "You mean . . . a date?"

His smile was wry. "I suppose you could call it that."

She tried to think if she'd had any hint of his interest. She had the impression he was charming with everyone. She'd had no indication that he'd been especially attracted to her in particular. It was dangerous to date him, of course, and she didn't want to. Not only because she didn't date anyone, but because he was the vice principal, and she still didn't know whether to believe his words about Karlstad.

"You're my boss," she said carefully. "Isn't it against the rules?"

"Not any that I know. I don't think I have the power to fire you or anything."

"So I don't have to worry about disappointing you at dinner," she joked.

He grinned. "You don't drool when you eat, do you?"

"Hardly ever."

"Then I think we're good."

She considered. What could it hurt really? Dinner. A drink. It was just once. It would be a good opportunity to test him, to find out his loyalties. She could at least determine how great a threat he was, or if he was one at all. It would be during the break. No one had to know.

"Okay," she said. "But if I order the crab, I don't want to hear any complaining about the price."

Chapter 28

That morning after breakfast, parents or their proxies would arrive to pick up their daughters for Christmas break, and the mood in the dining room was high. Rosemary monitored the door, too busy making sure girls didn't take the opportunity to sneak out and disappear to think much about the impending holiday. When Maisie, Jean, and Sandra approached her, she was so distracted that for a moment she didn't notice that they wore the pins she'd given them—not until Jean's caught the sparkle of the winter sun through the windows, spinning a reflection into Rosemary's eyes.

"What are you doing?" she asked in a low voice. "You aren't supposed to be wearing those."

"It's the last day. No one will even notice." Maisie pushed back her dark hair. Her sleeve slipped to reveal one of the school's dark green ribbon headbands wrapped around her wrist like a bracelet, the "chic" little pressed bow perched at the side. "Barb Trask has on a St. Christopher's medal and no one's said a word."

Rosemary glanced at Barbara Trask, who did indeed have on a necklace.

"Anyway, we have something to tell you." Sandra glanced over her shoulder furtively.

Jean played with the headband on her wrist. "But we should probably do it in private."

It was then that Rosemary noticed Sandra also had a school head-band wrapped around her wrist. Rosemary frowned. "What are those about?"

"That's what we have to tell you." Jean grinned; all of them seemed jittery with excitement. Sandra bounced on the balls of her feet; Maisie fiddled with her hair.

"What is it? I can't leave now. I'm monitor."

"But my driver's going to be here any minute, and he's picking up Sandy too, so we don't have much time," Maisie said. "We have to show you."

Rosemary glanced about. Most of the students were eating. "Just outside the door." The girls followed her into the hall, which was filled with suitcases, and Tom Gear and Martin McCree were coming down-stairs loaded with more. "What is it?"

Maisie touched the pin glittering on her breast. "We wanted to give you something."

"To show you how much you mean to us," Jean added.

"How important you are," Sandra put in. "You've been loyal to us and we wanted to show that we're loyal to you."

Carefully, as if it hurt, Jean unwrapped the headband from her left wrist, and then turned her arm so that Rosemary could see the under-side, the blue veins spidering beneath Jean's pale skin, and there a raised cut, bright pink, scabbing over. She moved closer so Rosemary could see it better. "It's an *F*. We wanted to do an *R* too, but it was too hard to get it right with just the pin, and the *F* was much easier and Sandy said it would make you just as happy—does it? Do you like it?"

An *F*. With a pin. It had obviously been a painful effort, but there it was, cut into Jean's flesh, small and deep, but yes, a blistering *F*. In confusion, Rosemary raised her gaze to Jean's. "An *F*?"

"For *Flowers*," Jean told her, smiling proudly. "Rosemary's Flowers. It was Sandy's idea. We all did it."

Maisie pulled off the headband covering her wrist, as did Sandra. Both had scratched *F*s deep into the inside of their wrists, in the same place as had Jean.

"But . . . I don't understand," Rosemary whispered.

"Because you belong to us," Sandra said quietly.

"And now we belong to you," said Maisie.

Jean nodded. "Forever."

~

Rosemary had no idea what to say or what to do. That they'd disfigured themselves was bad enough. That they'd done it for her was . . . she didn't have the words. It frightened her in ways she could not describe. She kept picturing the three of them bent over their wrists, piercing with the pins, scraping deep enough to scar. There was something so wrong in it. Something sick or dangerous—

She should report this. She should go to Stella . . . or Lois . . . or even Bobby . . . but what would she say? *Three girls I've been having secret meetings with cut Fs into their wrists for me after I gave them gifts for Christmas. Gifts I should not have given them, but I did, because one of them is my daughter . . .*

It was the start of break. Two weeks. Maybe that was enough time to cool things down. Time for this to become one of those stupid spur-of-the-moment things they would regret later.

And maybe the scars would fade until there was nothing left to see.

She told herself those lies, but she could not make herself believe them. Before she'd had a chance to react, Maisie's driver had arrived, and the girls ran out to the car with Sandra following, hugging and laughing like regular girls, and for a moment Rosemary imagined they were the kind of girls who would have responded to a gift from a teacher with candy or an apple. But all she had was the image of a bloody *F* against pale white skin.

~

Rosemary tried not to think of any of it when she got home. Dad had already pulled out the boxes of Christmas decorations and put them up: Mom's North Pole ceramic houses arranged on their shelves lined with white floss snow, the outside lights strung and blinking, the fake tree erected and decorated with all the ornaments they'd amassed over the years and hung with copious amounts of tinsel that was constantly falling to the rug and getting caught in the vacuum cleaner.

She didn't sleep, and she longed for something to distract her from the memory of their excited faces, their joy when they revealed those *F*s to her; they'd seen nothing wrong or creepy in it and that was what troubled her most. They'd thought it a *gift*.

It seemed more imperative than ever that she determine which of them belonged to her. She spent the days going through Mom's things, even those she'd already searched.

Dad had touched nothing since Mom died, and this was the first real break Rosemary had long enough to really explore. She found old recipe files and what looked like an entire junk drawer tossed into a box, with rubber bands and ticket stubs to plays her parents had seen and old menus stolen from restaurants and a program from Longacres racetrack, and her mother's life came into focus as separate from motherhood in a way Rosemary had never noted before, in a way that felt strangely and uncomfortably like her own.

It was not a feeling she appreciated. Her fraught relationship with her mother kept Rosemary firmly in the right when it came to their disagreements. She did not really like this idea of seeing Mom as a whole person, as someone who'd kept the menu for the Club Maynard nightclub and circled *Amblin In* on the Longacres program, penning five exclamation points alongside. Who was her mother, and what would she say to Rosemary now about Maisie, Sandra, and Jean?

Rosemary told herself she didn't care. Mom had lost the right to give advice the moment she'd had Rosemary sign those adoption papers. The moment she'd told Rosemary to put it behind her and forget.

But then . . . then she'd given Rosemary's daughter back to her. Rosemary hadn't had the chance to ask what Mom meant by it, nor to ask what she should do. Rosemary didn't think she would have even if she had. She'd never wanted her mother's help.

Until now.

Rosemary could not keep those raw-looking *F*s from her thoughts. If she could only find some clue as to which was her daughter . . . maybe then, she would know what to do. At least she would know how to direct her fears.

Then, one morning, the phone rang in the living room, and with the sudden blast of sound came apprehension.

She did not think the phone had rung since she'd been here. She heard Dad pick it up, his gruff "Chivers residence." Then a long pause. "Yes, she's here. One moment."

He came back into the kitchen. "It's for you. Someone from the school."

Someone had discovered the *F*s. A parent had reported it to the school. It was all over. Rosemary forced herself to the phone. "Hello? Hello, what is it?"

"Rosemary?" The voice was male, which she didn't expect, and it sounded far away. "It's Bobby."

She had forgotten all about him and now she wished he had forgotten about her. "Oh. Bobby."

"You sound disappointed."

"No. No, not at all."

A pause. "Well, I . . . it's New Year's Eve."

So it was. It didn't matter. Most of her New Year's Eves were best left unremembered. "I guess it is."

"Have lunch with me."

"I didn't know lunch was a New Year's Eve thing."

"We don't really know each other well enough for a midnight party, do we? Honestly, I don't even know where there is a midnight party and I . . . I don't really like crowds—or fireworks, for that matter. There's a diner downtown. The Dog House—have you heard of it?"

"Yes."

"Good." He sounded relieved. "So . . . lunch?"

"Okay."

"Good," Bobby Frances said. "I'll pick you up at noon."

"You don't have my address."

"I have it. Office files."

"The perks of administration." The last thing in the world she wanted right now was someone digging through her files. She had too many things in the air, too many secrets. The *F*s, the girls, her past . . . she was in over her head and she didn't know what to do about any of it and Bobby Frances was just one more thing to manage—going out with him seemed a waste of time now. Better to keep him at a distance; he was too big a risk. But she'd already told him she would see him.

Keep him out of her business, discover how close he was to Karlstad and what he wanted from her, and neutralize him as best she could . . . a formidable list of things to accomplish on a date. Rosemary was not at all confident.

Chapter 29

She was tense and he was disarming. It was almost as if he knew she meant to keep him at a distance and was deliberately trying to thwart her every attempt, and he was very good at it.

In well-fitting gray slacks and burgundy corduroy sport coat, with his shirt unbuttoned at the throat to reveal the chest hair peeking from the collar of his undershirt, he was both more good-looking than she'd first thought him and more self-possessed, with an easy smile that made it seem rude not to smile back, despite her resolution not to be swayed by his charm.

He sat across from her in the booth at the restaurant and ordered the truly atrocious-sounding spaghetti with chili so that Rosemary made a face and said, "You're really going to eat that?"

"It's delicious," he told her. "Want some?"

"It looks like something served up by a mess hall."

"You've eaten in a lot of mess halls, have you?"

Rosemary shook her head. "I've only seen newsreels."

"This is *much* better than mess halls. But that"—he pointed to her minced ham and pickle sandwich—"*that* looks disgusting. It reminds me of the bologna salad my mom used to make."

The ham was so thickly spread it was falling out the sides. Rosemary poked it back in with a finger. "My dad loves bologna salad. I made it for him all the time last summer. I make a really good one."

Bobby grimaced and lifted a bite of spaghetti dripping with chili. "You would have to be a miracle worker."

"You know, cooking is part of what I do for a living. Bologna salad is one of the first lessons in the home-ec curriculum. I've perfected it."

"Hell would be preferable—and I've come close enough to know."

He'd given her the perfect opening. "Oh, yes? From where you were stationed during the war? Where was that?"

His full lips tightened. "Manila. Are you sure you don't want a milkshake?"

He was deflecting, but for now she let him. It was clear he didn't want to discuss the war, and she didn't want to upset him. "Why do you keep asking me that?"

"Because you keep looking at that guy's at the next table like you want it. I think you had a Coke just because I ordered one. You know, to be polite."

"I see. You think I'm following the rules."

"There are rules? What rules?"

"According to one of the ancient textbooks I'm supposed to be using, there are." Rosemary put down her sandwich. "*Facts of Life and Love for Teenagers* has pages and pages of rules about how to go on a date."

"Is there a rule about milkshakes?"

"Well, no, but it does say that I'm supposed to follow your lead, so that whatever you suggest, I'll know just what you're prepared to spend, and I can order the same."

Bobby sat back. "So that's what women have been doing all this time!"

"Oh, yes, we're all following the same guide. Right now, instead of being concerned that I don't have a milkshake, you're supposed to be very smug and satisfied that I've picked up your cues and haven't made you spend too much. I'm sure you can appreciate that, given that your job is watching finances."

"I'd rather you have a milkshake if you want one."

"The Coke is fine," she said.

"What do we do now, according to the book?"

"Now we're to talk about a movie we've just seen, or mutual friends, or interests we might share." She tried to lead him. "You said you met John Karlstad when you spoke at a fundraiser for veterans?"

"I'd rather talk about movies," he said, another easy deflection.

Rosemary parried, "Well, I haven't yet seen *It Came from Outer Space*, so . . ."

He laughed. "That's what you think I'm interested in?"

"Did you see it?"

"With the son of a friend, who loved it, by the way. I thought the aliens were a little underwhelming. What did you think of *Tarzan and the She-Devil*?"

Now it was Rosemary's turn to laugh. "Should I be insulted?"

"You're the one who accused me of watching aliens."

"Well, you had."

"So, I think you've seen *Tarzan*," he teased. "Am I right?"

"As it happens, yes," Rosemary admitted, only partly embarrassed. "I've always had a crush on Tarzan."

"Of course."

"It's really the leopard-skin toga . . . I don't know . . . I just find it appealing."

"I think the she-devil is a little more my style."

"She's pure evil, you know."

"She has a heart of gold, I'm sure. Besides, who doesn't like romance in the jungle?"

Rosemary took a sip of her drink. "Nothing better, as long as there are Hot Tamales and popcorn to go along with it."

He grinned. "I'll remember that."

It was too easy to talk with him, and flirting with him came naturally, and both things worried Rosemary. But as the afternoon wound on, she forgot to be worried and got caught up in their talk, and found herself telling him about playing protest songs, and her mother demanding she play "Jesus Loves the Little Children."

She made it a funny story.

"What did you do?" Bobby leaned over the table with interest.

Rosemary gave him a sly smile. "I played it. But I changed the words. I was halfway through before she realized I was singing about unions forever."

He laughed.

"She wasn't happy, but I'd won." Rosemary didn't tell the rest. She liked that he laughed, which was what she intended, but then she wished she hadn't told this story, or that she'd told the truth instead, because it wasn't funny at all.

She played with her straw and went on contemplatively, "You know, I found out later that the minister who wrote it stole the tune from a Civil War marching song, so it seemed only right that I'd stolen it in turn."

"It's true, isn't it, that everything circles back?" Bobby noted. "So what do you think of protest songs now?"

He asked it casually, but she realized suddenly that the story had been better not told, not to this man, with his connections. She'd lost all sense of why she was here. Her tension returned.

"I still like the music," she confessed because her room was full of such records. Then, carefully, because it seemed as if he was waiting for something more, and she remembered him saying that he'd been angry after Pearl Harbor and ready to take on the world—fascism? Communism? What did he care about? "I like the idea of everyone having what they need, but"—she shook her head—"anyone who ever thought about communism then had to think again after Stalin, didn't they?"

"Yeah," Bobby agreed, and she saw that he was not suspicious of her, and Rosemary relaxed, but he'd given her nothing really, and she realized she wanted to stay there longer with him, to bury her ghosts in reframed stories and talk about movies, but the waitress was giving them a side-eye and the check had been paid, and though she sensed that he didn't want to go either, there seemed no good excuse to stay. They walked out of the restaurant into the cold early-evening air. The sky had taken on a lavender cast, the wind had picked up. It was bracing; in tacit agreement they walked past Bobby's pale green Plymouth toward the water, the breeze rushing up Wall Street, and festively dressed people were starting to gather for a celebratory dinner meant to stretch well into the night. It was New Year's Eve, she remembered again. The city was still lit for the holidays. Tonight, everyone would be drinking and celebrating. But she would be sitting on the couch, maybe watching television. If she was lucky, drinking, but not enough for it to help, because Dad would be there.

Her memories pressed, those ghosts brushing her shoulder, too close, whispers in her ear. Rosemary shivered involuntarily, and Bobby asked, "Are you cold?"

"No," she said, attempting a smile, and the way he looked at her . . . she knew that look. It fluttered right through her, leaving heat in its wake.

"Look, I've got a jug of Almaden burgundy—half a jug anyway—at home. I'm not much of a cook, but I'm sure I have something to make for dinner, if you wanted to . . . if . . ." He drew his hand across his mouth as if he meant to stop himself from—what? Kissing her? And Rosemary felt it too, that pull of attraction, and thought *Dear God, this is trouble.* This was not something she could do.

"Bologna, maybe?" she teased, because she was not good at saying no to things she wanted, and this time she had to say no.

He rolled his eyes, laughed lightly. "Uh—no, but . . . we can get some if you really want it. I'll even try it. Maybe."

"Now you're just pandering, Mr. Frances," she teased, but her heart wasn't really in it. Better not to prolong this. "But I'm not falling for it.

I'm not that kind of girl." It was the biggest lie she'd ever told, because she was that kind of girl. She completely was. But she couldn't be that girl with him. He was her boss. She saw him every day. He was too big a risk and she could not afford it and this was supposed to be one date.

"Just dinner," he said quietly, but Rosemary knew better. She knew herself too well.

"I really must get back." She offered a smile.

A moment's pause, and then he nodded. "Let's go, then."

The car ride back was quiet. He turned the radio down as if they might want to talk, and she wished he'd left it loud so she could pretend to be absorbed in the music. She was reaching for the door before he pulled to the curb in front of her father's house. "Thank you. It was a wonderful day—"

"Rosemary—"

"—but we can't do it again."

She got out quickly.

"Happy new year," he said, and she had the sudden and intense perception that she was abandoning him, that he had not wanted to be alone, that maybe he was afraid to be.

Rosemary closed the door with force and walked away without a word. She wanted him to drive off, but he sat there, watching, until she opened the front door and went inside.

Chapter 30

She did not think of Bobby the last few days of the break. In fact, she made every attempt not to think of him. Going out with him had been a mistake. She waited for the phone to ring, and when it did not, she was relieved—he'd at least taken her seriously when she'd said it was only the one time. She didn't need the complications of a relationship with her boss, especially now.

Everything in her life felt so precarious suddenly; she had to step so carefully.

Rosemary had not yet seen Bobby when she met with the girls the second day back from the break. She'd been avoiding the staff room and the offices, though she'd been jumpy and nervous waiting to run into him.

But when she saw Maisie, Sandra, and Jean again, she forgot Bobby at the sight of the headbands with their girlish flat bows still around their wrists, hiding the *F*s, though those scars flamed like beacons in Rosemary's mind. They were all wearing the pins too.

"Don't you love them?" Jean asked, showing off new strappy heels. "I asked for them specially, but I didn't think Daddy would get them for me. He says I'm trying to be too old too soon."

"They're gorgeous," Maisie agreed.

"They're beautiful," Rosemary chimed in. "But they're not regulation. How did you get them through inspection?"

Jean cocked her head, eyeing Rosemary coyly. "I'm not sure I should say."

Maisie laughed. "Oh, Miss Chivers won't tell! She belongs to us. Besides, it's so clever."

She belongs to us.

Jean smiled broadly. "Well . . . I wore them. Inside my rain boots."

"That is clever," Rosemary agreed. "But now you should hide them so they aren't found on the next room search."

"I have the perfect place. In the—"

"Don't tell me!" Rosemary threw up her hands. "It may be me doing the search, you know."

"But then you'll know where not to look."

Once it would have pleased her that they trusted her not to turn them in. "I don't want to know."

"I got a new radio," Sandra told them. "But since I'm not allowed to bring it to school, it's just sitting in my bedroom at home, where I never am. Can you believe it?"

Jean twisted her ankle to and fro, still admiring her shoes. "It's ridiculous."

"Well, you won't be here forever," Rosemary soothed. "Besides, someone might try to steal it if it were here."

"No one would dare." Sandra slumped back against the cast iron, swinging her foot.

Maisie barked a short laugh. "No, they wouldn't."

The three of them exchanged smug glances—what was that all about? Rosemary wondered.

"Ugh." Maisie rose and wandered among the Christmas cactuses, which were blooming on a nearby shelf. She put out her finger to touch one and jerked it back again. "At least your parents care enough to get you a gift. Mine sent a check from London. My uncle didn't even show up. He sent a tin of Almond Roca. I ate it in two days. Oh, and a bottle of Jean Naté. But that's all right. We only fight when he's there, and that meant I could do whatever I wanted."

Sandra said, "I hope you took advantage of it. I was practically a prisoner."

With a stab of empathy, Rosemary remembered Sandra's confession that her mother didn't understand her.

"Well"—Maisie took on a confidential tone—"honestly there was a bit of a scandal. A friend of a friend—no one I really know, just this girl . . . I guess her boyfriend had been pushing her to . . . you know . . . have sex. He promised her he wouldn't get her pregnant. He put a sock over his p-penis, so she believed him."

Rosemary winced. "That can't be true."

"That's what I heard!"

"It might as well be nothing at all," Rosemary said. "Not only that but . . . it would be uncomfortable."

"I wondered! Anyway, she's pregnant. So now they're going to"—Maisie's voice fell to a whisper—"get rid of it."

"You mean . . . an abortion?" Sandra was equally hushed.

"What else would I mean?" Maisie snapped.

"But . . . that's illegal," Jean said. "Where will she go?"

"There are places," Maisie said with smug superiority. "You just have to know the right people."

Sandra snorted. "As if you know."

"Those places can be dangerous," Rosemary said quietly. "There are people who take advantage of desperate women. You could die if you choose the wrong one. You have to be careful."

"I don't understand how they do it," Jean said. "How do they get it out of you? Do they cut you open?"

Maisie shook her head. "They give you poison to drink. Or they make you run up and down stairs until you fall, and that jolts the baby out."

It was appalling, how little they knew, how dangerous what they did know was. "Who told you such foolishness? Poison? For God's sake. Stairs? Those might cause miscarriages—maybe, but you could die doing those things too. That's not what they do for an abortion."

"You mean you know?" Sandra asked.

They were looking at Rosemary now, looking to her, waiting for an answer, and what was she to say? What Maisie had just said was the kind of misinformation that led to tragedy. These girls trusted her to be honest, and she could not be otherwise, not about this.

She told them about abortion the way she'd told them about sexual intercourse and gonorrhea and condoms and diaphragms—with clinical precision.

"It's best, of course, if you never have to make that decision," she finished. "It is illegal and it's dangerous because no one regulates it and too many women die. The better idea is to use contraception—if you can get it, even if you have to lie—until you decide you want a child."

Her words fell into silence. Sandra looked at her quizzically with those big blue eyes, so serious. "Would you do it, Miss Chivers? Would you have an abortion?"

"Yes." She watched them relax and settle as the subject changed from a fearful mystery into solid knowledge, something explained and understood.

"I think most people just get married," Jean said.

"But they don't have to," Rosemary insisted. "There's no reason a woman has to be trapped her whole life when there are other choices."

"I suppose there are a lot more abortions than we hear about," Maisie said thoughtfully.

"Yes," Rosemary said. "And there are plenty of adoptions too. That's another choice women make."

"I don't know anyone who's adopted," Sandra said doubtfully.

"No one talks about that either, but I'm sure you all know at least one person who's adopted." It was all she could do not to say, *One of you.* Rosemary watched them thinking, hoping against hope that this would be the moment she'd waited for, that she would be able to turn this into the information she needed, but then she saw the frowns on their faces, and she knew with a sinking despair that they did not know. Of course they did not know.

"I wish I was," Maisie answered with a snort. "But I think if I was, they wouldn't keep bringing me back when I run away."

Jean said, "Maybe my cousin. He doesn't look like a Karlstad. He's got a great big head. But I'd be afraid to ask. Isn't it . . . I mean . . . no one wants to be, do they?"

"Besides, why would you go to the trouble of having a baby if you weren't going to keep it?" Maisie asked. "How could you just give it away? How could you not want it?"

"I would die if I knew my mother didn't want me," Sandra said. "If she just gave me up like that."

"Which is worse? That she didn't want you or that she kept you but doesn't care about you?" Maisie asked.

"Or that she died?" Jean put in.

Rosemary rose abruptly and went to the radio, fiddling with the dial, snippets of songs and news, the start of an ad for Pine-Sol, and then the weather—

"What are you doing, Miss Chivers?" Sandra protested. "Put it back on KJR."

Rosemary stared blankly at her. "I—"

"Here, I'll do it." Sandra twisted on the bench and leaned over to turn the dial again until the music came in clearly, and once again Rosemary caught the whiff of Sandra's hair, the lingering scent of whatever shampoo she'd used at home, the faint trace of lavender not yet washed away by the school's fruity rinse. Rosemary fought the urge to wind her fingers through Sandra's frizzy waves. *I would die if I knew my mother didn't want me.*

Rosemary couldn't bear to hear any more. It hurt too much to remain silent, but she couldn't speak about it either. "This is one conversation that *must* stay between us. And . . . we need to talk about your wrists."

"We haven't told anyone," Maisie said.

The other two nodded in agreement.

"That's not the point. Well, I mean, I'm grateful for that, truly, and it really must stay a secret. But as . . . overwhelmed . . . as I am by your gesture, you can't scar yourselves for me. Please, no more of that. *Please.*"

They exchanged glances. Rosemary couldn't tell—was that understanding or puzzlement in their expressions? She decided on understanding.

"And the brooches," she continued. "I'm so glad you like them, and it's all right to wear them here, but you need to hide them. They'll be confiscated—"

"We know," Maisie said, rolling her eyes. "Believe me, Miss Chivers, we're very careful. Aren't we?"

Sandra and Jean nodded in agreement.

Rosemary went on, though the last thing she wanted to do was bring up Bobby Frances, "We need to be especially careful now because the new vice principal—"

"Oh my God, did you see him today?" Jean asked, nearly swooning. "I almost died. He has the best hair."

"Dreaming of running your fingers through it?" Sandra teased.

"I don't know why you're not," Jean teased back. "He's as good-looking as Marlon Brando."

Maisie noted, "Darker, though. More like the guy in that movie with Lana Turner. You remember—oh, what was it? The Spanish one. *Latin Lovers!*"

"What he is, is the vice principal and completely inappropriate for any of you," Rosemary said wryly.

"Maybe." Jean examined her fingernails. "I wish I had my lipstick back. You should see the way some of Daddy's friends look at me when I wear it."

"That's why you're at Mercer Rocks," Sandra reminded her.

Jean made a face.

Rosemary said, "Remember, he knows about these meetings. If he were to find out what they were really about—"

"We're studying radishes and tomatoes," Maisie intoned.

"And how to grow your own garden after the bomb," Jean added.

"Which will be hard to do when your skin is peeling off," Sandra said.

From the main building, the bell for dinner rang.

"Eww, Sandy! Do you have to be so gross?" Jean protested.

Sandra curtsied. "I do it just for you. I hope dinner isn't that awful buttered fish again."

"It's not Friday," Maisie told her.

The three girls chattered as they started for the door.

"Jean, hide the shoes!" Rosemary shouted after. "And don't forget the pins!"

They waved her off, assuring her they would remember as they went out into the cold and cloudy January day.

How quickly they left everything behind them, the talk of abortion and adoption and Bobby Frances, how close it lingered here, how it wrapped Rosemary about, their hopes and their questions and quick and brutal judgments, and she wondered how she had ever believed that she had locked her past safely and well behind her.

Chapter 31

Sunday dawned clear and cold. The girls were in chapel; the droning of the minister echoed into the hall. Rosemary had long since given up on church; even for the sake of appearances, she couldn't bring herself to attend the morning services. Sunday was her day off, but it was best to disappear; no one could judge her lack of piety if she couldn't be found. She had just spent all break with her father and she had no errands to run and the morning was crisp and beautiful, the bare branches of the oaks skeletal against a deep blue sky. The only staff around were live-in, so she didn't have to worry about Bobby Frances either.

She put on her red wool swing coat and fur-trimmed boots and stepped out into the meadow behind the school. Almost immediately she caught the scent of cigarette smoke. She glanced in its direction; there, near the willow, Bobby Frances and Martin McCree stood deep in conversation, smoking.

She ducked onto the path toward the lakeshore, walking quickly in the hopes that they wouldn't notice her—though there was little chance of that, given that her coat was bright red. Or maybe they would assume that she didn't want company, which was true.

The breeze coming off the lake rattled the bushes and pushed small waves ashore, and it smelled of water and algae and wet stone. It was cold enough that her lungs burned when she breathed deeply, which she liked; it cut through all the muck of the week, clearing her head. She went to the stairs, the Rocks with their whistling hello—just for her, weirdly both malevolent and reassuring, casting darker slate reflections on the slate water, their rough edges tossing ruffled foam, the hole you could see through to the other side.

Rosemary sat on the octopus stump, pressing her wool-trousered legs more tightly together against the cold, digging her chin into her scarf. She wished she'd worn a hat, but she'd left her hair down and she liked the way the wind blew it about, like those days when riding a bicycle through the neighborhood, hair streaming, had been like racing into an unknown world, wild and unbound and with nothing to hold you back until suddenly every kid in the neighborhood was calling out, *"Rosemary, your mom's ringing the bell!"* and then it was like dropping, landing hard and pushing uphill, every pedal a grinding pump in the effort to get home before Mom stepped out on that porch a third time to ring that bell, when being late meant punishment.

Now why had she thought of that?

Rosemary shook her head to free the memory, and then heard the scrunch of footsteps behind her, the roll of pebbles.

"There you are," Bobby Frances said. "I saw you come down this way. I don't mean to intrude . . ."

Rosemary tensed. No more avoiding. "Why are you here on Sunday?"

"I had some work to do."

"And here you are, down at the beach."

"I was having a smoke with Martin, and I saw you and thought I'd take a break."

"Ah, I see."

He indicated the fallen log. "Do you mind?"

"Go ahead."

He wore denim and a belted brown gabardine jacket with a shearling collar. Rather grubby-looking boots. No hat, so the wind attacked his thick hair despite the cream he used to tame it. "So these are the famous Mercer Rocks."

"Taboo Container is what the Indians used to call this place. Or at least, that's what the girls tell me."

He raised a brow. "'Taboo Container'?"

"Apparently they believed that some supernatural being lived in the Rocks." Rosemary looked out at them. "The girls wondered if it was called that because people were sent here to be punished. Taboo people. Outcasts. Like reform-school girls. It seems appropriate, doesn't it?"

She felt his gaze, but he said nothing for so long that she turned to him. Her hair whipped across her face, blinding her so she didn't see his expression. She pushed it away, but by then he'd glanced quickly back at the water as if to hide whatever he'd been thinking.

"You've been avoiding me."

Here it was, then. Rosemary shook her head. "No. Yes, I mean. It's awkward. I'm sorry. It shouldn't be. We're both adults, and I told you we couldn't go out again, so that should be it."

"Why not?"

"Why not?" Rosemary repeated blankly.

"Yes." He regarded her frankly. "Why can't we go out again? I had fun. I thought you did too. Didn't you? You said you did. You said it was a wonderful day. Were you lying?"

"No. No, I—"

"Then why not?"

"Bobby, surely you must see the complications. You're my boss."

"I was right, there's no rule against it. I've looked."

"You've looked?"

He nodded.

Rosemary laughed without amusement. "Oh, for God's sake. You can't possibly—"

"Listen, Rosemary—" He paused as if he were thinking better of what he was going to say, then blurted, "I can't stop thinking about you."

Disarming her again. He was so good at it. "Well. I—"

"I don't want to stop seeing you."

When was the last time a man had said that to her? When was the last time she'd allowed it? Never. She always picked strangers. She rarely saw them twice.

"I tried to do what you said. I tried to think of it as one time. But I just kept thinking . . . We had a connection, don't you think? There's something . . ." He glanced away; she felt his thoughts travel somewhere else briefly, circle back. "It's rare, you know? I don't think we should walk away from it."

"I don't think I'm what you want," Rosemary said carefully.

"How do you know? Maybe I'm not what you want either. What can it hurt to at least see?"

Rosemary did not know what to say. "Listen, Bobby, I'm not looking for a relationship—"

"Not a relationship, then. We're just playing. Nothing serious."

He'd taken her objections and turned them about, and no one had ever done that and she had no defense against it. How did he make it so that *No* seemed not just an unreasonable answer, but one that she did not want to make? *Karlstad,* she reminded herself. Bobby was her boss. Her secrets. Her girls. She didn't want a relationship. There were a hundred reasons to refuse.

But there was that easy smile that reminded her of the way he'd leaned on the table at the Dog House as if he wanted to catch her every word, and she remembered her sense that he hadn't wanted to be alone, and Rosemary heard herself say—inexplicably—"Okay."

"Good." His smile widened. "You said you have Sundays off?"

She nodded.

"Next Sunday? Around noon? I'll pick you up here at the school."

She nodded again.

The wind caught hold of his hair then, so he had to smooth it back, and he started up the stone stairs. Then he paused as if arrested by a sudden thought. "What's the perfume you wear?"

"Shalimar."

"Shalimar." He spoke the word as if savoring it. "I like it." A final grin, a wave, and then he was gone, down the path and around the corner, into the cottonwoods.

Chapter 32

Rosemary was halfway across the meadow back to the school when Alicia marched out to greet her. The art teacher's face was pinched with worry. "Have you seen Lizzie Etheridge?"

"No. Why?"

"She was signed up for art today, but she didn't show." Sunday was a day for relatives to visit or for structured activities the girls signed up for. "No one's seen her. She wasn't in chapel."

"Where else have you looked?"

Alicia mused, "It's strange. Lizzie never misses art. I just have this feeling . . . It's not like her."

Rosemary helped Alicia search, but there was no sign of Lizzie in the dorms, nor in the recreation room in the basement, where there was a small library, a Ping-Pong table, and a shelf of board games. The lounge with the television was empty, and the dining hall held only a few students with their parents, none of them Lizzie.

"Maybe she's gone off the school grounds," Rosemary suggested.

Alicia frowned and shook her head. "Lizzie? She was threatened with expulsion when she was caught with that rum at Thanksgiving. I don't think she would."

Rosemary caught sight of a familiar blond head leaning against the wall by the offices. Jean with her skirt hiked up too far, as usual. "Miss Karlstad," she called.

The girl turned, wide-eyed. "Oh, hello, Miss Chivers. What are you doing here on Sunday? Is something wrong?"

"Lizzie Etheridge is missing," Alicia said shortly—almost meanly. "Have you seen her?"

"Lizzie? No, not at all."

"Where are Miss Neal and Miss Wilson?" Rosemary asked, puzzled by Jean's lone appearance. She almost never saw the three apart.

"In their rooms." Jean played with the headband on her wrist. "At least they were a few minutes ago."

"What are you doing down here?" Alicia asked.

"I was hoping to talk to Mr. Frances."

"He's not here on Sunday." Alicia's voice was tight. "Go upstairs. You've no business here right now."

Jean did not argue. She only made a moue of mild protest and left.

Rosemary did not say that Bobby had been there that morning. She glanced at Alicia, wondering why she'd been so abrupt with Jean, wondering once again what was between Alicia and the girls.

"Trouble," was all Alicia said.

Lizzie did not show at dinner. By then the whole staff was looking for her.

The clear, cold day became a clear, cold night. A little after seven, Martin and Alicia came into the gymnasium, where Rosemary and Tom Gear were looking behind piles of worn blue floor mats. Martin was as grim as Rosemary had ever seen him, and Alicia as well.

"It's past time to call the police," Martin told Tom. "They've got searchlights for the lake."

"The lake?" Rosemary asked faintly.

"Hopefully not," Alicia said.

"Has anyone checked the roof?" Tom suggested.

Cheryl Fields came into the gym just in time to hear this. "Already looked. She's not there."

"What about the boathouse?" Rosemary asked.

Alicia stiffened. "Why would she be in the boathouse?"

Martin said, "It's locked up tight."

"The door to the roof is locked too," Rosemary reminded him, curious over Alicia's obvious upset at the mention of the boathouse. "It's locked every night, and still they manage to get up there to smoke."

"There's hardly a floor in the boathouse," Alicia argued.

"I'll go if you'll give me the key," Rosemary said to Martin.

"I'll go too," he said. "It's dangerous."

Alicia followed. "I can't just sit there and wait." Alicia's voice trembled, but she hurried with them down the path through the oak grove to where the boathouse stood on stilts over the lake, its gray weathered sides shimmering in the bright starlight.

The chains usually looped across the bottom of the stairs had been moved aside.

"No," Alicia whispered. "She wouldn't have been so stupid."

Martin cursed beneath his breath and rushed up the stairs. He had the key in his hand but there was no need. When he pushed the door, it swung slowly open.

Martin's flashlight illuminated the scene, and in a quick glance Rosemary caught it all—the floorboards in the middle of the boathouse gone, the edges of the hole blackened and burned, the rafters above as well.

And there, on the far side of the hole, near where a ladder had once led down to the dock and the water, where boats had once been kept ready for sailing, sat Lizzie Etheridge, her feet dangling over the edge, her pale hair haloed in the shine of the light. She wore only the regulation school slip, white against her white skin. The flashlight beam glanced off the bottle beside her. The air stank of mildew and algae, burned wood and rum.

She twisted to see them, tried to rise just as Alicia shouted, "Don't move!"

The board beneath her cracked; Lizzie lost her balance and fell.

Rosemary shouted, "Lizzie!"

A crack, a splash, and Lizzie screamed.

Martin pushed past them, back out the door, slipping and sliding down the steps. Rosemary and Alicia were close behind. Lizzie flailed in the lake below, just past the building's stilts. Without hesitation, Martin pushed the flashlight into Rosemary's hands and flung himself into the water after the girl.

He hauled her unceremoniously back onto shore. Lizzie shook so violently Rosemary heard her teeth chatter. The girl's skin was blue-white in the darkness.

"What have you done, Lizzie?" Alicia asked. "What have you done?"

"They m-ma-made m-m-me." Lizzie could barely get out the words.

"The girl's freezing," Martin said gruffly.

And obviously drunk. Rosemary wrapped her coat around Lizzie. "She's probably got hypothermia. We have to get her to the infirmary."

Martin lifted the girl. Lizzie didn't struggle, but huddled into him, and they ran back, meeting the others on the way.

When Lizzie was finally in an infirmary bed, cared for by Rita Everett, the nurse, Rosemary went exhaustedly upstairs to the now quiet dorm.

Mrs. Sackett, in curlers, waited outside their bathroom. "What happened?"

"She was in the boathouse with a bottle of rum. She fell into the water. She'll be all right. She's in the infirmary now."

"What was she doing there?" Mrs. Sackett asked.

"She didn't say. Too drunk. And cold. She'll be questioned in the morning."

Mrs. Sackett said, "Well, I guess we'll know soon enough. No doubt a dare."

Rosemary thought of the girl's only words and could not ignore her dread. "What makes you think that?"

"It's happened before. No girl goes to the boathouse without being dared. It's dangerous. The punishment won't be easy either."

Rosemary remembered Alicia's fear. "What happened in the boathouse last year? You said there was a fire . . . ?"

Mrs. Sackett pushed the bobby pin that held a loose curler more firmly into place. "I didn't hear the whole story."

"But you sound like you don't believe what you did hear."

"I don't know what to believe. They said it was an accident and the girls were there to paint for a class. But who goes to paint a picture of the *inside* of a boathouse at night?"

Painting a picture for a class. What other class could that be but art? *Alicia.*

"I don't know." Rosemary did not want to ask the next question. "What girls?"

"Your three. Maisie Neal, Sandra Wilson, Jean Karlstad. Your Flowers."

Those words turned Rosemary cold.

"*My* Flowers?" She barely managed the words.

Mrs. Sackett turned a weary gaze. "That's what they're calling themselves. 'Rosemary's Flowers.' They wear those pins you gave them."

How did Mrs. Sackett know this? What else did she know? "Who told you that?"

"They did. They tell everyone."

Rosemary was confused. "But they weren't supposed to. They were supposed to—"

"Hide them?" Mrs. Sackett provided.

"Take them home," Rosemary said, feeling the telltale heat in her face. "So they weren't confiscated."

"Instead, they've formed a special club." Mrs. Sackett didn't look disapproving, only concerned. "It sounds as if you don't know any of this."

"I don't," Rosemary said. "I had no idea. They told me . . . they promised . . ."

"Then they lied. As these girls do. People have been talking about the three of them. And you."

They lied. They'd promised her and they'd lied and she'd been stupid to believe them. But she had. Uneasily, not knowing what else to say, Rosemary said, "I see. Thank you for telling me."

Mrs. Sackett nodded shortly. "I'm glad Miss Etheridge is found. Now maybe she'll think twice before taking a dare. Good night—and Rosemary, you'd best be careful."

Rosemary nodded, still stunned. "Yes, I will. Good night."

Rosemary went to her room. That strange feeling was back, the sense that someone had been here—Sandra?

Woodenly, Rosemary stood at the window, staring out. Her dread had developed into suspicions she did not want to examine; she could not unsee Lizzie Etheridge plunging off the edge of the boat platform, or unhear the terrifying splash, and those images held a special kind of horror when combined with what she'd just learned and with the memory of Jean standing nonchalantly in the hallway twisting the headband bracelet. *"Lizzie? No, not at all."* Had those wide eyes been just a little too innocent?

Rosemary lit a cigarette to dispel the scent of rum and lake water and Lizzie's ice-cold skin still in her nose, and tried to deny the questions in her head, the questions to which she did not want answers.

Chapter 33

Maisie, Sandra, and Jean were not in fourth period the next day, and Rosemary was called to Stella Bullard's office that afternoon, after classes.

It wasn't much of a surprise. Everyone had been summoned during the day at some point to discuss Lizzie. Rosemary had still not heard the entire story. Her suspicions only grew worse when her girls didn't appear in home ec.

When she stepped inside Stella's office and saw the three pins on the principal's desk, her heart sank. Her mother's pins. Blue, pink, and yellow, the rhinestones sparkling in the lamplight, the enameled green leaves glinting.

There was no plausible way to deny or justify this. Her girls had been involved—and she had given them those pins and encouraged them to form a club even if she hadn't realized it. She had made them special, so special they scarred themselves to declare it. Rosemary was sickly certain that whatever had happened with Lizzie was because of it.

Stella waved her to the uncomfortable chair on the opposite side of the desk. "Would you like coffee?"

"No." The pins blinked charmingly. The principal had to know Rosemary saw them. Dully, Rosemary asked, "Are you going to fire me, Stella?"

Stella raised a reddish penciled eyebrow. "Do you think I should?"

The answer was an easy one. *Yes.* "I hope you don't."

"I understand you were part of the search that found Miss Etheridge last night."

"Yes."

"And that it was your idea to search the boathouse. Can you tell me why you thought she might be there?"

Rosemary frowned. "I . . . I just thought it was a place to look."

"You had no reason to believe she would be there."

"No, should I have?"

Stella sat back in her chair. "It's only that I find it a bit coincidental. Given your relationship with the girls who destroyed it last year."

"I knew nothing about that until Mrs. Sackett told me last night."

Another raised brow. "Really?"

"I knew it was ruined in a fire. I had no idea those girls were involved."

"It's a bit hard to believe that Alicia said nothing of it."

"No, she didn't." All she'd got from Alicia was vague warnings. The girls were trouble. Don't get involved with them. But never that Alicia had had a personal experience. The girls themselves had said it, hadn't they? *Miss Avilla is a liar.*

Rosemary waited for Stella to explain it all, but annoyingly, all the principal said was "Now you must know why I ask the questions, given that you've become unseemly close to those same girls. They even have a club name. Rosemary's Flowers, I'm told. What would you like to tell me about that?"

"I didn't know about that either. Not until yesterday."

Stella's eyes glittered behind those cat-eye frames. She motioned to the pins before her. "I understand that you gave them gifts for Christmas, which, as I'm sure you know, is completely against school policy. We do not play favorites at Mercer Rocks. The staff here prides itself on its equal treatment of all students. I thought I made that clear when you joined us."

"Yes," Rosemary managed. "You did."

"Then perhaps you can explain to me what you're doing."

There was nothing she could say. Not a single excuse that Stella Bullard would accept, and the truth—*One of them is my daughter*—was even worse. If they found out, she would be fired. She would never be allowed to see them again, and she could not explain, even to herself, what a bad idea that would be just now. She had made a mistake, but she could undo it. She *would* undo it. She would talk to them and explain what a dangerous game they played. They knew she cared about them. They had scarred themselves for her. They would listen.

"Rosemary?"

"I don't know what I was doing, Stella," she said simply. "You're right, of course. The girls were older and I thought they would like the gifts, but I was wrong to do it."

"And this club they've formed . . ."

"I'll break it up immediately," Rosemary promised. "There will be no more trouble about it."

"I hope not. These pins . . ." Stella gestured to them. "The girls are using them to lord over the others. It's quite unacceptable. You have become a favorite."

It was not a compliment, that was obvious. "I think it's only because I'm new."

"Hmmm. Well." Stella opened a desk drawer and made to sweep the pins into it.

"Oh—" Rosemary raised a hand to stop her. "If you don't mind, might I have those back? They were my mother's."

"You gave your mother's brooches to schoolgirls?" Stella was incredulous.

Rosemary tried to look penitent. "I regretted it the moment I did it, but there was no way to ask for them back without . . . well, you see. But I would like to have them. Please, Stella. I'll take them home. The girls will never know."

Stella hesitated. Had the principal not known Dorothy Chivers, Rosemary was certain Stella would have refused her. But the principal sighed and gave the pins to Rosemary instead. "I don't want to see them on those girls again. In fact, I don't want to see them again at all."

"Of course not," Rosemary promised.

"We will have no cliques at Mercer Rocks. Am I clear?"

"Very," Rosemary said.

Stella gazed at her again with those piercing eyes, measuring once more. "The next time, you'll be fired," she said, the words no less deadly for how soft they were.

Rosemary could only nod.

"In the meantime, Miss Etheridge has informed us that last night's shenanigans were the result of a dare. She had a fever this morning and is quite nauseated. She will be in the infirmary the rest of the week as her punishment. The other girls involved are in isolation through next Sunday."

Though Rosemary knew already, she hazarded, "The other girls?"

"Maisie Neal, Sandra Wilson, and Jean Karlstad." Stella said the names precisely, crisply, each so pointed it was as if she meant to stab Rosemary with them. Then, as if she did not trust Rosemary to understand, "Your 'Flowers.'"

An echo of Mrs. Sackett last night. Rosemary worked to keep her expression even.

"They're in isolation, Rosemary," Stella emphasized. "Do you understand?"

"Yes," Rosemary told her.

"I sincerely hope you do. Mrs. Sackett and Mrs. Fields exclusively will be tending to them during this time."

"But surely it's unfair to make them do all the work when I'm also a housemother in the dorm," Rosemary objected. "It's my responsibility—"

"Your favoritism toward these girls has proved to be a problem, wouldn't you say? The punishment is for you as well, Rosemary. Shall we leave it at that?"

Rosemary curled the pins in her palm as she left Stella's office, squeezing them so tightly that one of them pricked her.

Chapter 34

Rosemary did as Stella Bullard instructed. She left the care of her girls to Mrs. Sackett and Cheryl Fields. Rosemary did not run to answer the bells when Maisie or Jean or Sandra rang to use the bathroom. She did not bring them meals. She did not check on them throughout the day.

Tuesday night, she watched Mrs. Sackett ushering Maisie to the bathroom. Maisie looked miserable, her dark hair loose, her expression sullen until she saw Rosemary. Then her eyes brightened as if she'd spotted a savior. She mouthed, "Miss Chivers, please!" and Rosemary had to look away.

Wednesday, Mrs. Sackett took Jean's lunch—uneaten, and not just uneaten, but mashed into a mess on the plate—away from her room. "She's not eating, but she will, don't worry. This never lasts."

Rosemary tried not to think about it.

Three full days without her girls in her class was bad enough. What was worse was Rosemary's growing disquiet, that foreboding she hated because it never seemed to mean anything or lead anywhere. She was afraid for them. Afraid of those cursed *F*s and what they signified. The halls crushed and suffocated. Only a few more days until it was over, she told herself. She wrapped her mother's pins in a scarf and put them in a far corner of her dresser drawer and hoped Sandra wouldn't find them before Rosemary had a chance to talk to her and the others.

On Friday, she saw Sandra, looking more disheveled than usual as she trailed sullenly behind Mrs. Fields to the bathroom.

The girl's white shirttails hung out, the edges marked with what looked like spatters of spilled ketchup; her skirt had twisted so the button clasp was at the side; she wore slippers on bare feet; and her hair looked as if it hadn't been brushed since she'd been put in isolation.

Sandra's gaze caught Rosemary's as she passed. Those blue eyes were luminous with angry tears, and her expression was hurt and furious, the face of a girl who meant to have her way with the world when she was set loose upon it again, who believed no one was on her side. A girl who feared she was alone.

Rosemary took one step, then caught Cheryl Fields's disbelieving glance, the raised hand *stop*, and Rosemary stepped back again, though it hurt to do it.

Her last warning, Stella had said. There were only two more days in isolation, and the girls would be free.

The day after tomorrow was Sunday, and her date with Bobby. She felt guilty for abandoning her girls to go on a date and had thought of canceling a hundred times. The only reason she didn't was because she frankly needed the distraction. Better to be gone from here than to witness this punishment, even though Rosemary knew it was meant for her too.

~

She wished she'd said earlier than noon. It would have been better to go when everyone was in chapel. At noon, everyone would be gathered in the dining hall, girls wandering about; someone would see. She left the school during church and walked a few blocks down the street.

She leaned against the fence of someone's yard and waited. For two hours. In the damp cold. It wasn't raining, but she was freezing by the time he drove up in his light green Plymouth, almost driving by her before she waved him down, and he stopped abruptly in the middle of the street, the car jerking.

She hurried, breathless and shivering, into the passenger seat. "Oh, thank goodness. I can't feel my hands."

"Why are you out here?"

"I didn't want anyone to see."

"How long have you been waiting?"

"Since chapel."

He gave her an incredulous look. "You could have called me. I would have met you anywhere."

"I didn't have your number."

"The office—"

"Was locked. And no, I wasn't going to rouse the whole school to get your number when all it will do is cause gossip, and no, I don't want anyone to know about this."

"I see." He nodded shortly and began to drive. "You look like you could use some coffee."

"Please." She leaned back against the seat, relaxing. "Do you have heat? Can you turn it on?"

He chuckled and reached over to flip the switch and soon the defroster was blasting in her face, and Rosemary closed her eyes and luxuriated in it. "Where are we going?"

"Well." He paused. "I'd thought we'd go downtown, walk around in broad daylight, go to one of those restaurants with windows fronting the street, make a big show of being together—"

"You're joking." Rosemary opened her eyes to see he was grinning.

"I didn't realize you were so keen on keeping this secret."

"Don't tell me you aren't. You know how everyone is. The gossip . . ."

"What does it matter?"

"Because we aren't dating, remember?" she said firmly.

"Ah. Then I guess . . . let's go to my house. I make a good cup of coffee. It's one of the only things I can do, but I went out this morning and got Dick's hamburgers and fries and two milkshakes—you seem like a strawberry girl to me—and I thought we'd talk, listen to some jazz, maybe later have some wine . . . I don't know—how does that sound? It will be private, anyway."

"You never meant for us to go anywhere," she accused.

Another grin. "Guilty as charged. I'll take you back to the school if you'd rather, but . . ."

"No," she said. "I love strawberry."

~

Maybe it was because he'd guessed she liked strawberry. Maybe it was that grin. Maybe it was simply that he was so agreeable about everything. All Rosemary knew was that she was composed and in control when they walked through his door, and then she took in the small duplex, spotlessly clean, the living room with its matching davenport and chair nearly the same color as his car, the three-way television console with records carefully piled on top, ready to be played, straight through to a kitchen at the back and the blue chairs and mottled gray-and-white Formica table with chrome accents no different from anyone else's, with a vase of flowers and the paper bag from Dick's Drive-In upon it, and her loneliness welled and dipped; she wanted to cry at the care with which he'd planned it all—my God, when had anyone done this for her?

He was a good man. When had she last been with someone like that?

David.

The thought terrified her. Bobby Frances was exactly wrong for her. She didn't deserve a man like this, and he certainly deserved a better woman.

Still. She was here. He was here. He'd see the truth of her soon enough, and it would be over, but in the meantime why not let herself be seduced?

Because she didn't trust him. He was dangerous, a terrible risk just when she could least afford one.

That, she told herself, was the best reason to take what she suddenly and indisputably wanted right now. Why not give in to it? Once he realized what she was, he would run; why prolong it? Why not show him before he had the chance to do any damage?

He had taken her coat and hung it with his on the hooks by the door. He said, "Milkshake or coffee first?" and started to step past her, and she grabbed his hand to stop him, and when he turned in question, she gripped his hand harder; she could not quite see him; he was blurry.

"What?" he asked. "What is it?"

His plaid shirt was open at the throat; she pressed her mouth there, heard his small intake of breath, felt his fingers flex in hers.

"Rosemary. I didn't intend—"

"Of course you did." She kissed him hard. She felt him hesitate, a sudden tensing in his body, and in that split second she knew he was going to refuse it and back away, but then he didn't. He relaxed, and his hand went to her waist and his other hand came to her jaw and he leaned into the kiss. His mouth parted under the pressure of hers; she tasted his tongue, and the result was just what it always was, what she expected it to be, that suffusing, encompassing heat, a desire to be lost in, to drown in—she had long since lost the words for it—filling her so she could think of nothing else, possessing her so she could manage nothing else. She undid the buttons on his shirt and pushed her hands inside and fumbled with the buckle of his narrow belt.

He pulled away and held her hands still, and said in this husky voice, "Are you sure?"

Such nice eyes, the color of burnt caramel—questioning, pausing, giving her time to say no, which was exactly what she did not want. She kissed him again, and he gave in, and then she was shoving off one fur-trimmed boot with her foot and then the other, a flurry of undoing, his shirt, his belt, his pants, her skirt and slip, her nylons and panty girdle, too many things, and they fell on the narrow davenport.

He breathed, "Wait, I've got—" but she was too impatient; she pulled him inside her at the same time he was taking off his undershirt, and the fullness of him felt so good she cried out and arched against him and he groaned and forgot his shirt, still looped around his neck. She yanked it off; she wanted the dark hair of his chest, her fingers in the trail of it narrowing from his stomach. His mouth on her breasts, his hands beneath her hips, bringing her to meet him, the slap of flesh and the gasp of breath, and she was coming before she knew it, coming before she was ready, before she wanted to, *not yet, not yet*, every part of her so sensitive she felt she might blow apart, but there was no stopping it and she let herself go, those soft mews of pleasure she couldn't keep from making, then fading, and he was moving faster, his own gasps louder in her ear, into her consciousness when she hadn't quite heard them before, and then of course, just then, just then, *so stupid*, she remembered and managed, "Pull out—"

He jerked from her the same time she spoke, shuddering; she felt the hot wet of him on her stomach that went almost immediately cold; his trembling. The muscles in his arms taut, his pomaded hair falling now in his face; she couldn't see his eyes and she no longer wanted to. A moment, his shuddering breath, and then he collapsed upon her, his heart beating hard against hers.

~

Remorse came immediately. Here she was, sticky and wet and embarrassed at her urgency. The couch was too narrow; he was on top of her, legs tangled with hers, heavy, and she could not breathe. She lifted her hips slightly, and obligingly he moved, rolling off, falling to the floor with a thud and grunt and a "Dammit!" and really it was comical and absurd. He reached for his trousers and rummaged in the pocket, pulling out his wallet and from that a small packet, which he flipped onto the coffee table with a wry laugh, a condom. "I did tell you to wait."

"You planned for this!" she accused half teasingly.

He gave her a smile over his shoulder. "For some time. I wasn't thinking today, exactly. But . . . you can't blame me for hoping."

A good man. Rosemary's nerves twitched uncomfortably. She rose to her elbows to grab her blouse from the floor, the words in her mouth: *I'm sorry, but I can't do this. I want you to take me home.*

Before she could, he gave her the handkerchief from his other trouser pocket, motioned to her stomach, and rose, walking completely naked and without the least bit of embarrassment into the kitchen. She cleaned herself quickly as she heard the opening of the refrigerator, and then he was back. She had run her fingers through his hair, ruining the smooth look. Because of the pomade he used, the mess she'd made of it stayed in places, ruffled and sticking up, like a child just waking from sleep, but this was no child standing in front of her, the dark hair on his chest trailing to his pelvis and all . . . the rest of him—she caught her breath—holding two milkshakes in paper cups that sweated in his hands.

"I bought the strawberry for you, but I have chocolate too, if you'd rather." He held them out to her.

Helplessly, she took the strawberry. "Bobby—"

"You sure? You don't prefer the chocolate? You don't have to be polite."

"No, thank you."

He sat again on the floor, stretching his arm out against her body. The intimate warmth of him held her there.

The paper cup was squishy and melting and cold in her hand. She sucked on the straw. The creamy sweetness burst into flavor in her mouth, and she closed her eyes, savoring it, shivering a little at the cold. She moved her leg closer into his arm, into his warmth.

He smiled at her. "Good?"

"The best milkshake I've ever had."

He told her about the time his mother had made him a chocolate milkshake just after he'd returned from the war, and she didn't have the lid on the blender tightly enough, and it had exploded all over the kitchen—"It was everywhere. Not just dripping down the walls, but into the cracks in the molding and the baseboards. Two days later we realized some of it had dried on the ceiling. You could not get the dog out of the kitchen for a week, though. She kept waiting for it to happen again."

She laughed. "What kind of a dog?"

"A cocker spaniel. Sheila. A nasty little thing, but I was her favorite."

"I'm not surprised."

"All girls love me," he teased.

This was how she ended up forgetting that she was going to go home. This was how she ended up spending the afternoon in her slip and his shirt, while he wore only trousers, and they ate hamburgers and limp hand-cut fries of perfect, greasy saltiness. Then he put on a record that took her back to those hootenanny days, and the bands playing in the sweaty, smoky halls, the music that chased its tail in her dreams for days after, irresistible, and she could not keep from jumping to her feet and dancing, and he joined her, twirling her about and then pulling her back into his chest, swinging her and dipping her, and they danced until they were both breathless and laughing—how much she loved dancing; she'd forgotten that—and then lazed about in the weak winter sunlight coming through the windows in the living room and drank wine. She forgot about flower pins and punishment and her guilt and her fears and all the things that had led her here to this moment.

"Do you want to go somewhere?" he asked her as she sank against him on the sofa. "A movie? A restaurant?"

She shook her head. "This is actually a perfect day."

"Yeah, it is." He took a sip of wine and leaned his head back. His other arm tightened around her shoulders. "Watch."

"Watch what?"

He nodded toward the window. "Just watch."

She rolled a mouthful of Almaden burgundy on her tongue, lazy and satisfied, looking where he indicated, to the small window, where the setting sun suddenly burst through the clouds, illuminating a shaft of light on the floor, along with the silhouette of the tree branch angling across. It was beautiful, but she knew it wasn't what he was telling her to watch, because just then, a squirrel raced across that branch. He was fat and chattering; his shadow, too, scampered over the floor; then he jumped from the branch, and she heard him bustling against the house, chittering.

"What's he doing?"

"There's a pumpkin down there. I left it from Halloween," Bobby told her. "I left it for him. It's pretty rotten now, but he comes every day at this time to pick at it. His family too. Of course, *he* might be a *she*. I've no idea."

Rosemary smiled. "You've got a soft heart."

The half smile on his face disappeared. He took a convulsive gulp of wine. "It hasn't always been a good thing." Those shadows on his face, that faraway look she'd seen once before. "I guess I'd better get you back before they think you've been kidnapped."

"Not quite yet," she told him, and pulled him closer.

~

He dropped her a block away from the school. She laughed a little when she kissed him goodbye and said, "Remember, we're not dating."

"Absolutely not." He pulled her back again, deepening this kiss, and when he finally let her go, it was with a whisper. "Next Sunday?"

"Maybe," she said. "Yes."

She got out of the car and walked back to the school in the tunnel of his headlights, still lost in the dream of the day, not yet awake.

Chapter 35

Her day with Bobby had distracted her from her girls, but once she entered the uneasy, restless halls of the school, it all came rushing back: Maisie's pleading glance, Sandra's horrible dishabille, Jean's not eating, and Rosemary's guilt and fear over all of it. Tomorrow their isolation was over, but she was anxious about seeing them. She hadn't been able to help them with this at all. Though Rosemary wasn't sure what she could have done that wouldn't have ended with her being fired, it didn't make her feel any better.

She did not want to imagine what they might think or say if they knew that while they'd been miserable and unhappy, she'd spent the day making love and dancing—and with the vice principal she'd been warning them about, whom Jean had a crush on. That they would see it as a betrayal, she had no doubt.

One more secret to keep.

But then, they had betrayed her too. They had not kept their promise about the pins.

∼

The girls looked mostly themselves Monday morning, but Rosemary did not miss the shadows in their eyes from the days of isolation, or maybe it was anger.

Maisie said flatly, "I expect you had a fine week."

Rosemary caught the edge in her voice. "Of course I didn't. I was worried for all of you."

"Were you?" Jean asked.

"Worried and angry, given that the pins were supposed to be a secret."

Sandra looked at the floor. Jean twirled her hair. Even Maisie looked ashamed.

But by Friday, it chilled Rosemary to see that every girl in the school was wearing a school-regulation headband bracelet. When she finally, warily asked Jean if they had all scratched *F*s into their wrists as well, Jean laughed in delight and said, "They would if we asked them to, but why would we? *We're* Rosemary's Flowers."

Rosemary was horrified. "You spent a week in isolation for that," she said as evenly as she could manage. "Do the other students know about the *F*?"

"Of course they know. They're all jealous."

Now Rosemary was more than horrified, she was angry. "I see your promises mean little if anything. Do you have *any* idea what will happen if one of the staff discover it—"

"Everyone's sworn to secrecy, Miss Chivers," Jean assured her. "They know what will happen if they tell."

Rosemary could not help asking, "What will happen?"

"They all saw Lizzie."

"Yes, about that." Rosemary spoke softly. "What exactly happened with Lizzie?"

Jean glanced toward Maisie, who was gathering her books and talking to Sandra. Just then Maisie glanced up, catching Rosemary's gaze. Something in Maisie's dark eyes—a knowing, a slyness . . . what was it?—made Rosemary shiver, and she thought, *What if she's mine?* and found herself alarmed and overwhelmed by the thought.

Those *F*s were like little barbs snagged into her own skin, stinging. Maisie's cunning leadership. Sandra's idea to disfigure themselves with the *F*s. Jean's joy in the power of the group. It was not just the thought of Maisie as her daughter that alarmed Rosemary.

This had gone on too long. "We need to meet today."

~

"Honestly!" Jean was saying as she and Sandra stepped into the greenhouse, bringing the freshness of rain and the must of wet wool coats and berets into the humid closeness of the greenhouse. "I thought I was going to die."

Sandra let the door shut hard behind them. "You really are a sex fiend."

"You should have seen the way he looked at me. He's got the most beautiful eyes."

Rosemary straightened from running her hand through a bed of fragrant mint and turned to greet them. "Where's Maisie?"

"She'll be here soon. Miss Avilla made her run twenty laps around the gym," Sandra said.

"For what?"

"Sassing her, I guess. I don't know. All Maisie said was that she didn't think it was fair that she was always the one who had to put the birdies away."

"Maybe it was that she said 'shuttle*cocks.*'" Sandra grinned.

Jean laughed. "We've put your lessons to good use, Miss Chivers."

Rosemary winced. "That's not exactly—"

The blur of Maisie rushed to the glass door. She hurried in, breathing hard, pulling off her hat in one motion. "I'm sorry I'm late. I'm sorry. That bitch Miss Avilla made me stay after class. Jesus Christ, she can be so—"

"Maze." Sandra's voice was very soft, but it brought Maisie up short.

"You shouldn't call Miss Avilla a bitch," Rosemary said. "What's the real story about Lizzie and the boathouse? And what does the boathouse have to do with Miss Avilla last year?"

Sandra stilled. Maisie and Jean exchanged a glance.

The greenhouse fell into silence but for the light drip of hoses and the rain pattering on the glass roof.

"We were defending you, Miss Chivers," Maisie explained.

"Defending me?"

Maisie nodded. "Lizzie said that we were stupid to trust you and, in the end, you would be just like all the other teachers. She said you gave us the pins because you were trying to buy us and make us into snitches. Of course, we couldn't tell her the truth because it's our secret."

Sandra leaned against one of the plant-laden tables and crossed her arms, twisting her foot reflexively, silent.

Maisie went on, "Anyway, we told her that we were special and she wasn't, but maybe, if she was lucky and good, that might change. But she had to prove her loyalty first. So we dared her to go to the boathouse."

Jean plopped onto the end of the bench and twisted the headband on her wrist about her finger. "It's all over now."

"That's all it was," Maisie said. "She was just jealous, Miss Chivers."

This was even worse than Rosemary had imagined. "You can't do things like that. What happened with Lizzie was dangerous."

"It was just a game," Maisie said. "But Lizzie was stupid."

"Lizzie could have died."

"She was perfectly safe if she stayed close to the walls. We told her that. It's not our fault she went right up to the edge," Jean said.

"Stupid," Maisie said again.

Rosemary frowned. She had expected at least some remorse. "I don't think you understand. She was terrified. It was freezing cold and she was very drunk. That water was—"

"We didn't want to hurt her," Maisie said.

"She's learned her lesson." Jean spoke with disconcerting satisfaction.

Rosemary said slowly, afraid to ask, "And Miss Avilla last year?"

"Oh, that. That was an accident," Maisie said. "The can of kerosene got kicked over somehow."

"We didn't mean for it to happen," Jean said, glancing at Maisie as if for reassurance—or permission? "It was scary. I thought we were going to burn down with it. We were only there because Miss Avilla wanted us to paint the boathouse."

"I assume she meant the outside of the boathouse."

"We wanted to impress her and do something different." Maisie lifted her chin, a challenge. "She's always going on about art being thinking beyond what other people see, and we were trying to do that. But really she wanted us to think like everyone else."

Was it true or not? Maisie did not look away, but Jean did. Perhaps a lie. Perhaps only part of the truth. "She probably didn't expect you to burn down the boathouse and maybe yourselves with it. Maybe she was worried."

"She wasn't." Sandra spoke flatly. "Are you really going to lecture us too?"

Sandra's censure was in the stiff lines of her body, her attitude that changed the air in the greenhouse. Rosemary felt the warning in it; she'd overstepped some line she hadn't seen.

"We don't usually get punished." Maisie studied her nails. "We didn't expect to be this time either, to be honest."

"We thought *you'd* help us," Jean said.

"I might have been able to, had you not worn the pins and called yourself Rosemary's Flowers." Rosemary waited for that to land.

Then Jean smiled, that slow, lazy smile.

"Well," she said, pulling up the headband to reveal the *F*. "At least they can't take this away."

"No one can," Maisie agreed.

Chapter 36

They had not been remorseful or sorry in the least. They had been *satisfied*. The realization left Rosemary adrift and even terrified. They had sent Lizzie Etheridge to that boathouse and had not cared if she were hurt. They were using the *F*s on their wrists to control the other girls, and Rosemary had played into it all so beautifully and well, and she didn't know how to stop it or even if she could.

Sunday morning, she went to her father's. "What are you doing here?" he asked. "It's early for you."

"I have a date later."

He whistled. "A date? Anyone I know?"

"Who do you know, Dad, except professors at the U?"

"You're not going out with one of those Reds, are you?"

"He's the vice principal at Mercer Rocks—what? Why are you giving me that look?"

"Is this that guy who picked you up on New Year's Eve? It must be serious."

"Yes. And no."

"He had a nice car, I remember. A Plymouth Deluxe Coupe. A '49, I think." Dad gave her a wry grin and held out his coffee. "You want a cup? It's instant. You'll have to boil some more water."

Instant coffee. Something else new. "I'm fine," she said.

"You aren't, or you wouldn't be here," he pointed out. "What's happened?"

Rosemary went quiet. He was right, of course, and she wasn't even sure what had possessed her to get on the trolley almost with the dawn except that she hadn't been able to sleep, and she didn't know where else to turn. Only her father knew the truth of why she was at Mercer Rocks. "I don't know what to do."

He took a slow sip of coffee and regarded her owlishly behind his dark-framed glasses.

"I've sort of . . . formed a group. Or a . . . a club . . . with these girls, and . . ."

"By 'these girls' you mean the three who might be yours?"

"It was a way to get to know them, to figure out which was mine. But it got out of hand." Rosemary sank onto the bench seat across from her father and stared at the spotted beige, orange, and white of the Formica tabletop. She thought of the *F* engraved in Jean's pale skin, in Sandra's and Maisie's.

Despondency took her words. How had this happened exactly? She had never been like this, had she? She had never done anything so distressing, so frightening, so creepy.

Dad frowned. "Your mother was always worried—"

"I do not want to hear what Mom worried about." She was too on edge. That wretched school, her dread . . . At Dad's concern, she tempered her voice. "She cared more about her plans for me than what I wanted."

Rosemary thought he wouldn't respond, and she felt guilty for saying it, no matter how honest she'd been.

When he finally spoke, she almost didn't hear him. "She knew the decision was wrong for you in the end. That's why she told you about Mercer Rocks. She never told me. I didn't know she was watching out for her. I don't know how long she was doing it. Maybe she had been from the start. She was not a sentimental woman, Rosie, but she loved you. She wanted so much for you. Maybe too much. Don't you forget that. Maybe one day you'll understand her."

Rosemary snorted. "There's a better chance the Soviets will bomb us all into oblivion than that I'll ever understand Mom."

"Well, those commie bastards are going to do it, so I guess there's hope."

Rosemary couldn't help a laugh.

Her father sighed. "You know, the whole foundation of the atomic bomb—"

"Not the bomb, Dad, not now. Please."

"Just listen—this has something to do with you, I promise. It all comes from some of the earliest work in physics and the nature of reality."

"Dad, for God's sake, a physics lesson?"

He held up his hand to quiet her. "Niels Bohr—a rat bastard communist, but his quantum theory is worth reading—"

"If you're a scientist, I'm sure."

"—he posited that there was such a thing as entanglement. Einstein didn't trust it. He called it 'spooky action at a distance,' but even he can't deny it exists."

"I have no idea what you're talking about."

"Be patient. You were always so impatient, even as a little girl. Once two particles have been entwined, they are forever entwined, so that when one is impacted by something, the other reacts, no matter how far apart they are, and instantaneously, so that they are, in essence, the same particle, though they might be thousands of miles apart."

Rosemary stared at him blankly. "That's enlightening, Dad. Thank you."

"You don't see what I'm saying."

"Not really."

He leaned forward. "When you were little, your mom always knew when you were hurt. You'd skin your knee when you were playing outside, and suddenly she'd frown and say, 'Where's Rosemary?' in this voice that I knew meant something was wrong, and you'd come in seconds later crying. When you ran away, she was the one who kept saying you were alive when no one really believed it, when even the police said you were either kidnapped or dead—"

Rosemary stared at him, startled. Obviously she'd been wrong in thinking she'd never done anything worrying or frightening. She'd been safe with David, but she'd never thought of it from her parents' point of view. "But I—"

"Let me finish. She knew. She said: 'She's alive. I would know if she wasn't. I would feel it.' I wonder if maybe because the two of you were once one particle, so to speak—you know, you were part of her—if maybe there's something to this entanglement thing."

What he was saying dawned on Rosemary slowly. "You mean, we were physically connected somehow."

"Yes." He nodded, pleased. "Maybe you've got that with one of those girls. Because one of them was a part of you, Rosie. Maybe you'd just know if you let yourself feel it."

"But I don't. I thought I would. I thought I would feel that exactly, but I don't."

"You stopped letting yourself feel anything important a long time ago, honey. But now you've been given a gift. I didn't agree with it at first, but I've come to see that your mom was right. You're afraid to know which is yours, that's all. But if you don't find a way to not be afraid, it will be too late."

Chapter 37

Her father's words stayed with her but were not much help. He was right; she was afraid to know which of those girls was hers, because it was easier to imagine a daughter than to take responsibility for one or to feel for what had happened to her.

She was distracted and frustrated when she met Bobby that afternoon at the Fifth Avenue Theatre for a movie. Rosemary could barely concentrate upon *Carmen Jones*. She chewed Hot Tamales reflexively, conscious every moment of Bobby's warmth beside her, and the rustle of his package of licorice Crows, hearing her father's words "*. . . if you don't find a way not to be afraid, it will be too late*" over and over again, and when the film ended, and Harry Belafonte's Joe was standing over the body of Dorothy Dandridge's Carmen, whom he'd just strangled, Bobby turned to her and said, "What's going on? You've been a hundred miles away."

She was surprised. "How do you know? You were watching the movie."

"Not really. You were twitching and sighing so much I couldn't concentrate." He rose and offered a hand to help her from her seat.

"I just feel restless today."

"Hmmm." He led her from the Chinese-inspired baroque theater into the cold and overcast day, rain spitting intermittently from the sky. "Tell me what's wrong."

Too many things she couldn't say. They hadn't talked about Lizzie Etheridge or the confiscated pins or isolation, though he had to know about all of it, and she didn't want to bring it up because she was afraid of his response.

"I don't suppose it has something to do with Rosemary's Flowers," he said.

"You've broken our rule," she protested.

"What rule is that?"

"We don't talk about Mercer Rocks." It was not really a rule; it was more as if they'd tacitly agreed it was a separate world, and that was how she liked it.

He took her arm and drew her against a building, out of the way of the theatergoers. "I had a friend in my unit—a good guy. Where we were stationed there were all these dogs . . . I guess you could call them strays, but some were feral, and you had to be careful with them. He made friends with one of them. He fed it and played with it, and that little dog followed us around everywhere. Then one day the truck ahead of us veered off the road and overturned. It was a loud crash, and it scared the dog. He turned on Ron and ripped open his arm. The guy sitting beside him managed to get the dog off, but Ron's arm got infected and he ended up losing it."

"Are you comparing those girls to feral dogs?"

His smile was small. "Didn't Stella tell you to stay away from them?"

"Yes, but—"

"Then maybe you should. In fact, I think you definitely should."

"You don't understand. I've got a special bond with them, and—"

"What special bond is that?"

She wasn't sure how to explain. The truth could not be said; not to him, not to anyone. She settled for "I'm . . . sympathetic. They trust me to tell them the truth about things. You know, they want so much from the world, and they don't know how to get it, and . . ."

"There are maybe better ways than stealing and lying. They're in reform school, Rosemary."

"I know, but—"

"Let them be."

"Don't you want to help the girls here? What happened to that soft heart of yours?" she asked.

"It's soft enough to care what happens to you," he said quietly. "These girls are problems, and you're too involved with them."

His gaze asked questions, too many and too intently. Rosemary looked away. "What do you think about going for a bite?"

Bobby said, "There's something you're not telling me."

"No." She attempted a smile. "You're right. I shouldn't get so involved."

He did not quite believe her, she knew. His voice was wary when he said, "Okay. Good."

"Maybe we could get a beer too. You can tell me more war stories."

He let out a quiet half laugh, and the shadows came into his eyes again. He looked down at the sidewalk, and she wished she hadn't said it.

She put her hand on his wrist. "Bobby . . ."

He said, "No more war stories, if you don't mind. The sooner I forget, the better."

His words made Rosemary suddenly sad. She squeezed his wrist and smiled at him and said, "Whatever you want," and didn't tell him what she now believed: that it didn't matter how you tried, forgetting wasn't possible, and even if you locked the doors to your past, they never stayed closed.

~

Her dread and confusion returned as Rosemary climbed the stairs to her room that night. The stairwell felt narrow and close, the school stench of years of meals and old plaster and wood and sweat and disinfectant swirled with the currents of anger and resentment, and the blissful few hours of forgetting that she'd spent with Bobby faded with the memory of *F*s on wrists and too-intense loyalty and her mistakes.

Rosemary stopped on the second floor. It was past lights out. The dorm was quiet. The light from Cheryl Fields's room slanted across the hall floor, the shadow of her moving within it, and Rosemary thought about asking the guard if anything unusual had happened today, then realized she didn't want to know.

Upstairs it was dark but for the light peeking from beneath Mrs. Sackett's door, but the darkness had a shifting mistiness to it that seemed to pulse with her breath, as if it were animate.

Rosemary tried to shrug away her uneasiness and readied for bed. When she came out of the bathroom, she heard the radio—music, which was strange for Mrs. Sackett. She usually had on news, or one of the late church services. Not popular music, which this was. By the time Rosemary opened her bedroom door she realized two things: the song was "The Roving Kind," and it wasn't coming from Mrs. Sackett's radio, but from Rosemary's own room.

She stopped in surprise. Her room was dark, but there was no doubt it was coming from here. Rosemary turned on the light. Everything was just as she'd left it but for the record spinning on the turntable, the hands clapping in rhythm, Guy Mitchell's clean, clear voice, the back-up singer's *ahhhh-ah-ah* rising in the chorus, the ship's horn blasting . . .

Rosemary stumbled to the record player, grabbing the stylus. Her skin prickled with gooseflesh; the smell of Shalimar was so strong it stung her nostrils—had she sprayed on so much before she'd left?

She lifted the record from the turntable, counting the seconds as she did so, forcing calm, pushing away her fear and pretending nothing was out of the ordinary, nothing wrong, everything as it should be, but her hands trembled as she put the record away; she felt the warning they'd meant her to feel, the threat—they'd wanted her to know they were here. The only thing she didn't know was why.

Chapter 38

On Friday, the girls bounced into class just as Rosemary laid out the dittoes on each table. Barbara Trask immediately picked one up and pressed it to her nose. "Oh, they're not fresh!"

Maisie and Sandra came inside just as the bell rang.

"Where's Miss Karlstad?" Rosemary asked.

"In the vice principal's office." Maisie smirked as she said it.

Immediately Rosemary thought of their marked wrists. Maisie's and Sandra's were still covered, but Jean was always pulling at hers, always fussing.

Rosemary tried to speak casually. "What did she do this time?"

"She skipped second period," Maisie informed her.

Sandra put her fingers to her lips to mime smoking.

Skipping class, caught smoking . . . Not the *F*. Jean would be assigned chore duty for the week, and that would be it.

Maisie twisted the pseudobracelet about her wrist, and every girl who saw her do it did the same. Rosemary's skin crawled. She turned to the blackboard, where she'd written:

How to Judge the Becomingness of Garments:

Colors, Lines, Textures

Blonde, Brunette, Redhead

Style: Athletic, Ingenue, etc.

"Are we talking about fashion today?" Maisie asked hopefully.

"What's et cetera?" Sandra asked. "Let me guess, vamp, slut—"

The other girls laughed.

The classroom door opened. Jean rushed in, breathless and grinning, skirt hiked up, socks rolled down, the first buttons of her blouse unbuttoned. She waved a note at Rosemary. "I was in the office! I have a note!"

Rosemary took it, said automatically, "Miss Karlstad, your uniform," and opened the note to read *Please excuse Miss Karlstad for tardiness to fourth period. B. Frances.*

Jean hastily straightened her skirt as she slid into her seat beside Sandra. "I am *madly* in love!"

Sandra rolled her eyes, and Maisie whispered something back to Jean, too low for Rosemary to hear.

Rosemary crumpled the note. "Miss Karlstad, eyes on the blackboard, please."

"Why does it matter if our garments are becoming?" asked Sandra.

"What do you mean? It matters if we're going to get married," Lizzie said. "Though I suppose you don't much care about that, given the way you dress . . ."

Sandra half rose from her chair.

"Miss Wilson," Rosemary warned.

Sandra settled back.

"I already know how to look attractive." Jean rested her chin in her hands. "What I need to know is: How do you know when a man is interested? I mean, really know?"

Sandra gave her an incredulous look. "Are you kidding?"

"I mean, doesn't it . . . isn't it . . . obvious?" Maryanne Brown whispered the last word, and Rosemary remembered that she'd been the one to reveal the gonorrhea conversation that earned Rosemary her first warning from Stella.

"Wait . . . ," Lizzie Etheridge said hesitantly. "I don't—"

"Have you ever even kissed a boy?" Maryanne sneered.

"Miss Brown, that's enough," Rosemary warned.

"Their thing gets hard." Maryanne made a jackknifing motion with her arm. "It jumps up every time they get excited."

"That's a boy," Jean said disdainfully. "They have no control. What about a man?"

"It's in his eyes." Sandra's voice softened. "Remember how Marlon Brando looked at Eva Marie Saint? Like he both hated and loved her at the same time?"

Every girl in the room sighed.

"Like the way Gregory Peck looks at Audrey Hepburn in *Roman Holiday*," Lizzie Etheridge crooned.

"The kind of look that says that no matter where you are or where you go, it would be nothing without that person beside you." Maisie stared off dreamily into space.

They all went silent, wondering whom she spoke about, or imagining their own crush, until Jean breathed, "Yes. Yes, a look like that. So . . . you just know? Is that right, Miss Chivers?"

There was something disquieting in the way Jean watched Rosemary so carefully; Jean who had just come from Bobby's office. *"I am* madly *in love!"*

That danger again. Rosemary tried to tell herself it was nothing. She'd already known Jean had a crush on Bobby, but now that look . . . it sent a shiver down her spine. She remembered Jean's soft and wicked satisfaction at Lizzie Etheridge, and she knew now what these girls were capable of. But Jean could not possibly know about Rosemary's relationship with Bobby. She could not. They'd kept it so quiet. If Jean found out . . . Rosemary did not want to think about what might happen then.

They all watched Rosemary, waiting for her answer. "Yes. You just know. Now, let's talk about fashion, shall we?"

~

Jean was assigned a week on office duty, running notes and errands for Stella, Lois, and Bobby. Gloria joked about it in the staff room.

"Someone needs to sew that girl's blouse shut. Every time I turn around she's unbuttoned it again."

"She's got eyes for Bobby," Pearl Hoskins teased as she stirred sugar into her coffee. "He'd better be careful with that one. If I had to guess, I'd say she skipped class on purpose. Just to be 'punished.'"

"She wears too much perfume. Has anyone else noticed that?" Quincy turned to Rosemary. "I thought you were supposed to confiscate it."

"We have," she told him. "We do a weekly search. She's not wearing it in my class."

"They have ways of getting new stuff," Alicia said. "They're clever little sneaks. They may be running out to Frederick & Nelson in the middle of the night, for all we know."

"I tell you, that girl stinks of perfume every time I see her," Quincy insisted.

Rosemary wondered if Maisie managed to sneak in some of her Jean Naté. Or . . . her Shalimar had disappeared once before, what was to keep them from taking it again? Or borrowing it when they wanted?

"What I want to know is who started this new headband bracelet fad," Pearl said.

"Maisie Neal." Alicia's expression darkened. "She started wearing it and they all fell in line like little acolytes. She'd lead them off a cliff somewhere if she could."

Rosemary suddenly remembered Martin McCree's comment so many months ago about not wanting to be one of *those* teachers. *"Ask Alicia."* But she had. And had not been told the whole truth. Not by Alicia or the girls—Rosemary was sure of that now.

The table went quiet. Pearl studied her nails. Gloria took a hasty sip of coffee.

Only Quincy, as new as Rosemary, looked puzzled by Alicia's sudden and obvious tension.

Alicia stabbed out her cigarette viciously and rose. "If you'll excuse me, I've got a class to teach."

Chapter 39

The huge bouquet of pink roses was delivered in the middle of fourth period, to the delight and awe of all the girls. Rosemary herself was stunned when one of the students brought them to her classroom.

Rosemary put them on her desk, and the class rushed to huddle around them.

"They smell so heavenly!" one of them said.

"So sweet!" said another.

"Who sent them?" Jean's voice held an edge Rosemary did not mistake.

"They're exquisite," Maisie said. "They almost don't look real."

The slow consideration in her words, in the way she did not look at Rosemary as she spoke, only added to Rosemary's discomfort.

"You've never said anything about a boyfriend." Sandra probed through the greenery until she found a small card tucked amid the leaves and dethorned stems. She plucked it out.

"A secret admirer, maybe?" Maisie glanced at the card in Sandra's hand, then to Rosemary. Her dark eyes were curiously and eerily blank.

"Does this have anything to do with what you do on Sundays?" Jean stroked a petal with a single finger, gingerly, as if she were afraid it might burn. "We see you leave, but never where you go."

Maisie turned to Sandra and Jean. "She doesn't keep secrets from us. She always tells us everything."

"I don't know whom they could be from." Rosemary kept her voice light, but she felt cornered and compromised. Bobby had agreed to her wish to keep things secret. She didn't think he would have sent these.

"Should I open it?" Sandra waved the card in the air challengingly.

Open it. Don't open it. Rosemary took a deep breath. "Go ahead."

"Really?" Sandra's blue eyes widened. "You mean you really don't know?"

"I have no idea," Rosemary said.

Sandra glanced at Maisie, who nodded. Sandra opened the card. She read it quickly, and grinned. "Oh. They're from your dad."

Rosemary stared, baffled. "From whom?"

"Your dad." Was it relief in Sandra's voice? Or disappointment? *"Dear Rosie, Happy Valentine's Day. No more fear. Love, Dad."*

"Oh." Struggling to hide her relief, Rosemary took the card from Sandra and read it as if imprinting the words on her retinas would make her believe in them more truly. Dad's message was eclipsed by the oddity of his sending roses for Valentine's Day. Though when she was a girl, he always bought her a box of Brown & Haley's candy, a large box for her mother, a small one for her. She'd forgotten that, and it had been a long time since he'd done anything like this.

She put the card on her desk. "Let's get back to our sewing machines, shall we? Barbara, where are your pinking shears?"

"What does he mean, 'No more fear'?" Maisie asked.

"It's a private joke." Rosemary felt tight and a little weak, as if she'd just escaped from peril, and yet—what peril had there been? Bobby sending flowers? She glanced at Jean, still stroking that rose petal. Slowly and deliberately now, contemplatively.

After class was over and the girls swarmed out, Rosemary sat at her desk and stared at those roses until she was lost in their glowing pink.

In the hallway of the main building, she ran into Bobby, who stopped her with a low-voiced "I heard you got roses."

"From my dad."

"Your dad?" His expression lightened. "Oh."

They were near the front door and there was no one about; it was still the middle of fifth period, Rosemary's planning hour. "Yes. Do I detect a hint of jealousy, Mr. Frances?"

"Maybe. For a minute," he admitted with an embarrassed grin. "I would have sent something, but . . ."

"I appreciate your restraint."

He leaned closer. His voice went quieter. "I was surprised you did. And to leave it out in the open like that. I have to wonder what you were thinking, Miss Chivers." A tease, flirtation. He was pleased.

Rosemary had no idea what he was talking about.

It was a moment before he seemed to realize that. "You mean it wasn't you?"

"I didn't send you anything," she said.

"But . . ." How puzzled he looked. "It smelled of Shalimar, and the card itself . . . who else could it have been?"

Rosemary's dread returned. "Maybe I should take a look?"

She followed him to his office. He closed the door firmly and shoved aside a file on his cluttered desk to reveal an envelope. Written on the front in capped block letters was BOBBY. Soberly, he handed it to Rosemary. The fragrance of Shalimar wafted from it so strongly that she was surprised she hadn't smelled it when she entered the room.

He cocked a heavy brow, *You see?* "Open it."

Slowly, she drew it out. It was a cartoon drawing of a Kewpie Tarzan peering down from a tree, and Kewpie Jane in a leopard skin holding a club standing below, the words: *Are You Gonna Be My Valentine?* and a border of red hearts all the way around. There was no signature, just a hand-drawn heart in blue pen.

The conversation at the Dog House about *Tarzan and the She-Devil*. Of course he had thought it was from her. She would have believed the same. It was impossible. Coincidental. The perfect card for one of them to have given the other.

Rosemary met his eyes.

Bobby's mouth tightened. "I didn't tell anyone about that conversation. Did you?"

"No. No."

"You're not lying to me? You didn't send this? It was in the middle of my desk when I got here this morning."

"I didn't send it."

"The whole room smelled like you."

"I didn't put it there," she insisted. "I wouldn't have."

He asked, "Who else would do this?"

The answer was obvious, but Rosemary did not want to say it. One of the girls. A particular girl. "Jean Karlstad," she said quietly. "Though all the girls are in love with you."

Bobby made a sound of dismay. "Jean. I thought I smelled it on her. God knows I'd recognize it anywhere. I thought the girls weren't allowed to have perfume."

"They aren't."

"Then where is she getting it?"

"I don't know," she lied. She handed the valentine back to him.

"What the hell am I supposed to do about this?"

"Be less handsome?" she suggested. "Less charming? Maybe don't smile so much?"

"I'm serious, Rosemary. I should talk to her—"

"Maybe let me do that," she said.

He considered her. "What would you say?"

"That you're far too old for her, for one thing. And also . . . I don't know. I'll think of something."

He seemed relieved that she'd offered. He let the card fall and came around the desk to pull her close. "I suppose you could tell her my interest lies elsewhere."

Rosemary ran her fingers up his shirtfront, beneath his tie. "I don't know if that would help. Girls are very competitive, you know."

He nuzzled the tender spot beneath her ear. "Tell her it's you. Then she'll know there's no competition."

"You shouldn't do that here."

"No one's watching."

"The window—"

The knock on the door surprised them both. Rosemary sprang away so fast and hard that she hit her hip against the edge of the desk. Bobby ran a reflexive hand over his hair, smoothing what she hadn't yet touched. "Yes?"

The door opened. Jean poked her head inside. "Reporting for duty, Mr.—Miss Chivers?"

Rosemary straightened, pressing a hand to her now throbbing hip. "How perfect. We were just discussing you, Miss Karlstad. Might I have a word?"

Jean frowned. "Oh, but I'm on office duty."

"I'm sure Mr. Frances can release you for a few minutes."

Jean's gaze swept them both; her mouth set mulishly. "But I—"

Rosemary took the girl's arm. Now, suddenly, so close, Rosemary smelled Shalimar on Jean. It was unmistakable. She hadn't been wearing it in class, Rosemary was sure, and there hadn't been time for Jean to go to Rosemary's room.

"Come with me." She hauled Jean to the door; the girl's reluctance was clear.

Once they were out in the hall, Jean tried to pull loose. "You don't understand, Miss Chivers. I don't want to talk right now."

"I understand enough," Rosemary said quietly. "You sent him a valentine?"

Jean stiffened. "He told you?"

"He's twice your age, and the vice principal." Rosemary led the way outside onto the front stoop. The day was drizzly and gray and cold and neither of them wore coats, but for now this was the most private place. She pulled Jean into the shelter of the overhanging roof. "What were you thinking?"

Rosemary expected contrition, guilt, embarrassment. What she got instead was challenge. Dark, wide eyes staring back at her, unflinching. "He looks right at my mouth. I know he wants to kiss me."

Rosemary worked to keep her expression even. "You. Are. Seventeen. Where did you get the perfume? From my room?"

Jean shrugged.

"You girls must stop sneaking in there. I respect your privacy. You need to respect mine. It has to stop. I won't report you, but—"

"You're jealous." Jean's smile was sly.

"Why would I be jealous?"

"I saw you in there with him just now."

Too observant. Rosemary protested, "We're coworkers. Friends—"

"You didn't look like just friends."

"He's the vice principal. He's my boss." Rosemary heard her defensiveness. How had this turned so suddenly, so neatly?

"You're gone every Sunday. Are you with him?"

"I think this conversation has deteriorated. We should get back inside."

"You said you didn't have a boyfriend," Jean continued relentlessly. "Were you *lying* to us, Miss Chivers?"

"Of course not." This was Jean, her lovely Jean. *Maybe my daughter.* "I don't have a boyfriend. Mr. Frances is just a friend."

"Good. Because I'd hate to think you would lie." Jean tugged the headband down her arm, revealing the scar on her wrist. "We trust you, Miss Chivers. If we were to find out that we couldn't . . . it would be bad. Very, very bad."

~

That night, when Rosemary went to her room, she again heard music. Again, it was "The Roving Kind."

Warily, she pulled open the door and turned on the light. There was no one there, as she expected, but the record was spinning, the sleeve abandoned on her bed, the quilt wrinkled as if someone had been sitting there. The drizzle from earlier had turned to rain; it dashed against the window.

The clapping. The background singer's *ahhh-ah-a*. Then again. And again. *A-a-a-a-a-a*. A skip. The record had never skipped before. Rosemary frowned and went to the turntable. The needle jerked. *A-a-a-a-a-a-a-a* . . .

She lifted the stylus and turned off the turntable and picked off the single, holding it up, angling to see.

A long, deep scratch across the black vinyl glinted in the light.

Chapter 40

When Rosemary checked, it was obvious that the bottle of Shalimar had been siphoned. She asked Tom Gear to change the lock on her door, but her room no longer felt like it belonged to her. The slightest noise had Rosemary jumping. She'd somehow lost control and she wasn't sure how or how to regain it. The girls smiled as they always did. They came to meetings as they always did. Yet she felt a danger she couldn't see or touch.

Friday afternoon, the entire school gathered by the orchard. Today was the coldest it had been on a Seattle February day for years; surely there would have been better days to watch Martin McCree plant the ceremonial class shrub—one for every year Mercer Rocks had been operating. Rosemary had coiled her hair into a French twist, and Maisie, Sandra, and Jean had surprised her by styling their hair in the same fashion. Once it would have been meant as a compliment, now Rosemary wasn't sure. She hoped no one else noticed it.

Her girls were nearly identical in their gray coats and school berets, though each wore a different expression of miserable. Sandra blew on her hands and Maisie looked bored. Jean watched the school building avidly. There was no doubt whom she watched for. The administrative staff was not yet here, which meant: Bobby.

The other waiting girls fidgeted, yawned, and shivered. Alicia called to her class to keep order. Quincy led his in chanting French conjugations.

"How long do we have to wait?" Maisie asked. "It's freezing."

"I'll check." Rosemary was halfway to the greenhouse when Martin came out with a leafy shrub and a shovel, and Stella and Lois and Bobby arrived.

Stella clapped and smiled broadly. "Such a lovely day for a planting, isn't it, girls?" She reached for her hat, which threatened to fly off her head at a sudden gust of wind.

Bobby came over beside Rosemary, close enough that she felt his warmth. "Did they do that on purpose?" he whispered.

"Do what?"

"Your Flowers. Same hairstyle."

She sighed. Naturally he would be the one to notice. "I had nothing to do with it."

"Ah. It looks better on you."

"They just need to practice." She tried to understate it. "And Jean's hair is too short." When she glanced toward Jean, she saw the girl was staring at them, and Rosemary didn't mistake the hurt in her eyes.

"You're standing too close," she murmured.

He pretended not to hear.

Martin planted the shrub. Stella Bullard and Lois Vance jumped with gusto into the school song:

"Honesty and charity and goodness most of all.
Oh, Mercer Rocks, we ask of thee
Lead us to morality
Show us paths to de-cen-cy.

Good grades, good ethics, we agree, are worth striving for.
Oh, Mercer Rocks, we call to thee,

Help us to be error-free,
Fill us all with sanc-ti-ty.

Let us show to all the world
All the best of womanhood
Hurrah, Mercer Rocks!"

Some girls—mostly the younger ones—joined in desultorily until they realized that none of the older girls were singing, and faded off until only Stella and Lois sang the rousing final chorus. Rosemary didn't know the song and couldn't have sung it anyway, as aware as she was of Jean's burning gaze.

Stella announced, "Class of '55, may your laurel grow beautiful and strong!"

Rosemary clapped along with the other teachers and staff. The ceremony was over. Everyone dispersed.

Bobby lingered, touching her elbow to hold her back. "Too much Shalimar in my office today. It's distracting."

Rosemary groaned.

"Also there was a baby atomic-bomb test today in the Nevada desert. I can't stop thinking about it."

Those shadows were in his eyes again. Without thinking, Rosemary put her hand on his arm. "Oh, Bobby."

"I could use some wine and my favorite nondate."

She smiled. "I wish it was Sunday."

"You can't sneak away?" he asked, half joking. "Meet me on the roof or something?"

"Along with all the other girls sneaking out to smoke? I doubt that would get me fired or anything."

"I'd lobby on your behalf."

"Ummm, I don't think that would help if we were caught together," she teased. "But my mom used to volunteer for the civil defense committee. I have plans for building a bomb shelter in your backyard if you want them. It might make you feel better."

"Honestly I'm not sure even a bomb shelter would survive."

"My God, don't tell that to my students. Especially Sandra Wilson. She'll have nightmares."

"Don't tell me what?" Sandra was suddenly right there, at Rosemary's elbow. "What else am I going to have nightmares about? You know today they tried to blow up Las Vegas?"

Rosemary grimaced. "How on earth did you find out about the test?"

"Mrs. Dennis had the radio on while Barb was on kitchen duty this morning. She told me."

"Las Vegas barely heard it," Bobby told her. "They didn't even know it happened."

"That's what they say, anyway. Don't believe everything you hear, Mr. Frances." Sandra verged on rude, challenging.

He smiled thinly. "Believe me, I don't."

Sandra laughed—that bitter, caustic laugh Rosemary knew too well. "Can I talk to you, Miss Chivers?"

Rosemary said, "Of course," but Sandra's manner unsettled her.

Bobby said, "I'll see you later."

Rosemary realized only she and Sandra were left.

"So," Sandra said, looking after Bobby as he walked away. "You're just friends."

This again. Rosemary hesitated. For a moment she considered telling the truth, but what was the truth? She and Bobby weren't a couple. What was between them was casual; she'd made that clear, and to say anything else . . . She was an unmarried woman, a teacher having a casual, *sexual* relationship with the vice principal. If anyone found out, they would condemn her. She would lose her job. Her girls would only understand that she'd lied to them. Jean would be hurt. The other two would be furious, and what they would think of her, what her daughter would think of her . . . no, she could not bear that.

"He's my boss," she said.

"He likes you."

"He's very charming. He's like that with everyone. One shouldn't mistake it for affection."

Sandra's gaze riveted to hers. "You mean Jean shouldn't."

"Mr. Frances is very much older than Jean."

"But she's in love with him," Sandra insisted.

"She's seventeen."

"You can't be in love at seventeen?" Sandra's gaze was direct, very blue, very intent, and suddenly Rosemary thought of David and how big that love had seemed, their child that might be standing in front of her now, and the fact that she had not loved anyone like that since.

Rosemary sighed. "No, I'm not saying that."

Sandra softened. "We're worried about you, Miss Chivers. Maisie and Jean think we might be wrong about you. I hope we're not."

"You're not."

Sandra smiled, but there was no reassurance in it. Instead it was vaguely . . . sinister.

Sinister? No, this was Sandra. But before Rosemary could decide what else it was, Sandra was off, back to the dorm, and Rosemary thought suddenly of a baby bomb blowing up a Nevada desert, and a city only a short distance away that claimed to have heard nothing at all.

Chapter 41

She turned lazily in Bobby's arms, stretching against the warmth of his body, and looked up to see him gazing thoughtfully down at her.

"What?" she murmured.

"I wish you could stay the night. But then . . . I suppose it's probably a good thing that you don't."

"A good thing? I'm not sure I like the sound of that."

"I only meant I'd keep you awake."

She pressed her mouth to his bare chest. "That's okay with me."

"Not that way. I mean"—a pause, as if he wasn't sure whether he wanted to say the words—"when you told me Sandra Wilson had nightmares, I understood."

She looked up at him, feeling the coming of a revelation she was not sure she was ready to hear. "Everyone has nightmares."

"Yeah, but . . ." Another pause. "Mine are more than nightmares really. They can be . . . loud."

She propped herself up on her elbows. "Loud? You mean you talk in your sleep?"

"I mean I scream."

"You scream?"

"I guess it can be upsetting," he said wryly.

Rosemary sat up, pulling the blankets around her. "Do you have them a lot?"

A small shrug. "Often enough."

"What are these nightmares?"

"Oh, you know, the war."

"You don't want to tell me."

He winced. "It's not that. I don't like to think about them. I try not to."

"This explains it, then," she said.

"Explains what?"

"Why you're not married. Alicia wondered."

"Alicia did."

"Um-hmm," she teased. "And Pearl too. And Gloria."

He laughed lightly. "You think screaming in the dead of night makes me ineligible?"

She smiled back at him. "Are you telling me differently?"

He shook his head. "Well, I almost was. Married. I had a fiancée when I joined the army. We went together in high school and we were going to be married after college. I was mad for her, but then . . . Pearl Harbor. I was going to be drafted anyway, so there didn't seem much point in waiting around for that, and she promised to wait for me—"

It was more than Rosemary expected him to divulge, and it raised a little alarm. "It's all right. You don't have to tell me any of this."

"—and so I went. We'd . . . well, neither of us was a virgin when I left, I'll just say that. We wrote each other constantly. Or at least, she wrote me constantly. I thought about her all the time, but . . . well, war, and . . . I . . . well, I was busy . . ." He made a sound of disgust. "When I finally got back . . ." His gaze went distant, that gaze she'd seen before, where he was somewhere else, inside another emotion. "When I got back, we went right to a hotel, and I was happy to see her, and we were going to get married. All those months and months, and that's what I was coming back to. There was no doubt of it. I had no doubt. But then, there we were, and she was . . . she was just the same. She hadn't changed at all. She started talking about houses and curtains and dining room furniture, and I was waking up at night thinking there were—" He closed his eyes and shook his head, shaking the image, whatever it was, away.

When he opened his eyes again, his expression was somber, wounded. "Anyway, I started having pains in my chest. They got worse when she talked about marriage, and I just couldn't . . ." He ran his hand distractedly through his hair that she had already mussed earlier, making it worse. "Anyway, she decided the guy she worked with at the insurance office suited her better, and to tell the truth, I was relieved."

Rosemary did not know what to say.

"There was another woman a few years ago—"

"I don't need your whole romantic history," she said.

He ignored her. "She was a widow. We were together for six months or so. She wanted to get married. I didn't."

"Chest pains again?" Rosemary tried to make light of it.

His smile was tight. "No. But that's it. That's the whole list."

Rosemary laughed, though there was nothing funny about what he was saying, and she was afraid of why he was saying it and what he might expect in return. "I don't believe you."

"Why not?"

"Because"—a gesture, a wave—"you don't look like a man women ignore."

"I'm not talking about casual dating, Rosemary. There's been plenty of that."

"Like us, you mean," she tried.

He didn't look away. "Is that really what we're doing?"

She felt him waiting. She knew what he wanted her to say. The question was a simple one. She should have had a simple answer. And she did, that was the hell of it. The truth . . . the truth, if she wanted to say it, which she did not, she didn't even want to face it, was that there had not been a man since David who had meant anything to her. Had there even been anyone she'd slept with more than twice? If there had, she could not remember.

But she could not say it. She had tried not to think about what this was, or why she was doing it, or what she wanted from Bobby. If it had entered her mind at all before now, if she had allowed it to land even for a minute, she'd decided she would answer the question later, after she found her daughter. But she had known this moment was coming. She had been afraid of it, afraid of the expression she'd seen sometimes on his face—*You just know*—and what he would demand of her and what she feared to give back because it had been such a disaster before. She didn't know if she knew how to have a relationship beyond her compulsions.

She ran her hand down his chest, lower. "Whatever this is, I like it very much."

He caught her hand, stopping her. "Answer me. Is this all you want from me? Just sex? You don't feel anything more?"

She struggled to marshal her thoughts, finally whispering, "I don't know. I . . . I've got things I need to resolve. My own nightmares, I guess."

He was quiet. Then, "Is there someone else?"

She twisted to look at him. "There's no one else, Bobby. No other man."

"Then I don't understand."

"Things . . ." *Just tell him.* But the words caught in her throat and she could not get past them. She had not spoken of her life to anyone but her father, and even then it was barely referenced, memories neither of them wanted to revisit. It was as if that day at White Shield, when they'd said, *"We'll never speak of it again,"* she had signed another kind of contract, one that made her mute. "I have obligations. I need . . . I just need time, okay?"

He met her gaze, and she felt him considering, weighing, wondering. She didn't want him to push; she wasn't ready and she was afraid of what she might say if he did, what she might do, and she was relieved when he finally nodded and curled a strand of her hair around his finger and brought it to his lips. "Okay," he said.

But they dressed in near silence, and on the way back to the school, he said almost nothing, and she wondered if he had second thoughts. He drove past their usual dropping-off spot—distracted, she decided—and into the circular front drive, pulling to a stop right before the entrance. She said with a lump in her throat, "I understand if you don't want . . . if you think I'm too . . ."

He put the car in park and turned to her.

Rosemary glanced at the school, the glass-fronted doors, the windows.

He leaned forward and pulled her into his arms and kissed her hard and thoroughly, right there parked in the school driveway, in open view of anyone who might be watching.

When he finally drew away he stared at her, waiting for her reaction. But that kiss had rocked her and shoved every thought from her head.

He smiled as if he'd won something. "Good night. Sleep well."

She was unsteady as she went into the school, pausing to listen to the roar of the Plymouth engine as he left, uncertain whether to be furious with him for what he'd just done or relieved that he hadn't ended their affair or frightened that he hadn't. She was a mess of confusion as she climbed the stairs.

The dormitory floor was mostly quiet, the girls readying for bed, but when Rosemary reached the landing, someone was already there. Sandra, turning from the window overlooking the front. She looked like a ghost in her school nightgown, her hair a mass of shadow, and the overhead light threw her eyes into glittering darkness and put sharp angles on her face.

Rosemary stopped, surprised. "Oh, hello."

"I was waiting for you," Sandra said.

"Really?" The strange and distant look on Sandra's face confused Rosemary further; her heart began to race. "Why?"

"I wanted to know if I could listen to that Almanac Singers record, but I've decided I don't want to anymore."

Rosemary's confusion grew. "Of course you can. But not tonight. Maybe tomorrow we can—"

"Does Mr. Frances like 'protest' songs too?" Sandra's face was expressionless.

She had seen everything. After the assurances Rosemary had made only the other day. *"We're just friends."* It shouldn't matter. None of it should matter.

But she knew it did.

"I—I don't know," she said.

Sandra said, "Liar." Starkly. Coldly. Brutally. She pushed past Rosemary and walked away.

Chapter 42

The next morning Alicia waylaid Rosemary as she came into the staff room. "Did you see it?"

Rosemary poured a cup of coffee. "See what?"

"It destroyed his whole windshield." Alicia puffed on her cigarette with rabid excitement. "It wasn't even that big a rock, but they must have thrown it hard."

"I have no idea what you're talking about, Alicia."

"Bobby's car. Someone threw a rock through his windshield this morning right after he got here. He won't be able to drive it until it's fixed."

Rosemary froze. "Did anyone see who did it?"

"No one. Bobby heard it, though, and so did Lois. They both went running, but they didn't see anything. What do you think?" Alicia asked the question as if she'd been waiting to all morning.

The vision of Sandra's face last night wavered before Rosemary. *"Liar."* "I don't have any idea."

"No?" Alicia's voice sharpened. "You don't think it might be Jean Karlstad?"

"Jean Karlstad? Why would it be her?" Rosemary spoke with what she hoped was guilelessness.

Alicia drew heavily on the cigarette. "Given how close you are, I thought she might have come to you with a tearful story of unrequited love. Or to say that she'd done something that she was 'so sorry for'?"

"What are you getting at, Alicia?" Rosemary tried to sound outraged.

"Or maybe it wasn't Jean. It might have been any of your 'Flowers,' trying to get his attention."

"Don't be ridiculous." The defense was habit; Rosemary no longer believed it ridiculous at all.

"Oh, for God's sake, stop defending them, Rosemary. You're the one they listen to. You need to do something."

"The way you did last year?" Rosemary snapped. "What really happened that night the boathouse burned, Alicia?"

Alicia expression tightened. "This has nothing to do with that."

"Am I interrupting something?" Pearl Hoskins asked from the doorway.

Rosemary and Alicia went quiet. Then Alicia said, "I was just telling Rosemary about Bobby's car."

"Terrible. Stella's going to question everyone," Pearl said. "But I think it's only vandals. Probably those same hooligans who chalked up the drive last year."

"You're probably right," Alicia answered, but her glance slid knowingly to Rosemary.

Rosemary couldn't get out of the staff room quickly enough. She went outside to look at Bobby's car, and yes, the windshield was as destroyed as Alicia said. A hole the size of a baseball just over the steering wheel, cracks webbing out from it, spreading crazily across the glass.

Last night. The way he'd pulled her close. That passionate kiss Sandra had seen.

"Liar."

The bell rang; in a daze Rosemary made her way to her classroom. She had no idea what she would say to Bobby. *I'm sorry? It's my fault? I know who threw a rock through your windshield and why?* How could she turn Sandra in for certain punishment—if Sandra had indeed done it, and not Jean, as Alicia supposed? What about Maisie? Alicia was right; it could be any of them.

More importantly, how to do what Alicia had said and stop this before it got worse? She remembered Sandra's face last night. *"Liar."* Rosemary feared that whatever influence she'd had with them was gone. What remained?

Tell them who you are. But Rosemary was more afraid to do that than ever. None of them knew they were adopted. They might not even believe her. She remembered the only time they'd discussed adoption. *"No one wants to be, do they?" "How could you just give it away? How could you not want it?" "I would die if I knew my mother didn't want me, if she just gave me up . . ."* It was not discussed in polite company. Everyone pretended it did not exist.

She would throw each of their families into turmoil. And to what end? Would it make any difference at all? Or would it just make them angrier? Would it just make them more . . . dangerous?

No, she couldn't tell them. She couldn't trust them, and she couldn't take the chance that it would make everything worse, not until she knew which of them was hers for sure. But whatever else she did, Alicia was right. Rosemary had to rein them in. Despite her fears, she had no choice but to explain her relationship with Bobby. After all, Sandra had seen that kiss. There was no denying it. Rosemary had to take the chance that telling them the truth about him might make things worse. Maybe she could explain it well enough that it did not. In any case, another lie would definitely be a very bad idea. Bobby had forced her hand. It made her uncomfortable, but she would explain why she wanted to keep it secret. They might be angry or jealous, but in the end, she would make them understand.

She barely remembered the rest of the day. Her entire self bent toward fourth period, her class, her girls. When the time finally arrived, her heart was in her throat and a headache clawed at her temples. But there they were, the three of them, regarding her with semihostile stares and barely listening, doodling and passing notes so blatantly they were daring her to scold them.

But she didn't. She taught the class. When the bell rang, and they were leaving, she said sharply, "Miss Neal, Miss Wilson, Miss Karlstad—a word."

They came to her reluctantly. It was obvious Sandra had told them about last night. Jean's mouth was tight, and she would not meet Rosemary's gaze. Maisie was so cold she might have been made of marble. Sandra crossed her arms belligerently.

"Will this take long?" Maisie asked. "I have things to do."

Rosemary said, "I want you all to meet me in the greenhouse tonight after dinner."

They exchanged glances.

"We can't," Maisie said.

"Please," Rosemary said, embarrassed when the word broke. "Please. I need to talk to you."

Jean looked up. "You mean you'd like to tell us another lie?"

"I'm not going to lie," Rosemary said. "I promise."

"Come on, we're going to be late." Sandra pushed Jean out the door, and they were gone without saying that they would be there, but Rosemary hoped.

~

Rosemary left the dining room early, nervous. She went outside, surprised to see that Bobby's car was still parked—but then, with the windshield like that how could he drive it? She was turning to go back when he stepped from the school.

She felt strangely awkward, shy, guilty, and hoped that he could not see it. Fortunately, he was distracted by his car.

"Look at it." He waved toward it hopelessly. "Whoever did it did a good job of it."

"It's awful," she agreed. "Alicia said you heard it?"

"About fifteen minutes after I arrived this morning." He had the rock in his hand. He held it out to show her; it was the size of his palm.

"But you saw no one."

He shook his head. "Neither did Lois. I've spent all day trying to figure out who might have done it."

She ignored her needling guilt. "What will you do?"

"I don't have any enemies that I know." He turned to her. "Have you heard any rumors? Anyone who might be unhappy with me?"

She wished she could tell him the truth, all of it, but it stretched back so far, and by now dinner would be over. The girls would be waiting. She could not linger.

"I'm sorry," she said. "I have to go. I have a meeting."

"With whom?"

"It doesn't matter. I have to go." She turned toward the door. Bobby grabbed her arm lightly, and she tugged away. "I can't be late. They're already angry."

"Who's angry?"

"Bobby, I have to go. Really."

"Is it your girls? Rosemary's Flowers? I'm right." There was no triumph in his voice. "You're meeting those girls. After Stella warned you."

"You don't understand—"

"You're right, I don't. You told her you would break up the club. But you didn't, did you? God, this explains so much . . ."

"I don't know what you mean," Rosemary said stiffly.

"How often do you meet with them? What do you meet about?"

Such probing questions. They were in front of the school; anyone could see or hear. She remembered suddenly that he knew John Karlstad, that Bobby reported to the board—on whose account did he ask these questions? His own or theirs?

She didn't like her suspicions or the guilt she felt at them. "I'm not having this discussion with you here."

"You won't have it with me anywhere," he pointed out. "What is between you and those girls, Rosemary?"

Rosemary said, "I have to go."

She was relieved when he did not try to stop her this time, when he said nothing more. She had to restrain the urge to run, half expecting him to follow. He didn't, and she hurried to the greenhouse.

The glass walls were unseeing and dark. She knew before she opened the door that the girls weren't there. She switched on the light, blinking against the sudden glare, the shadows taking on dimension, the hanging plants swaying in the currents of her motion. Silent. No radio blasting. No voices.

Rosemary told herself they were late, that they would come, but she knew those were only more lies. The silence exacerbated the emptiness and made her think of her argument with Bobby and highlighted the girls' rejection, so she turned on the radio. Then she turned it off again because she couldn't bear the love songs, for all the same reasons.

She waited. When it became obvious no one was coming and the evening gave way to darkness and she knew Mrs. Sackett would be wondering where she was, Rosemary left. Already past lights out; the dormitory was still. She went upstairs, glad that Mrs. Sackett was in her room too. Rosemary would offer an excuse tomorrow.

Her door was ajar; the new lock had been no deterrent. As she went into her room, her foot struck something on the floor, pebbles or gravel; it scattered. Rosemary turned on the light and glanced down.

Smashed on the floor, broken and twisted and mangled, rhinestones loose and falling from their settings in a rainbow of pink and blue and yellow, were her mother's brooches, which had been wrapped and hidden in her drawer since she'd retrieved them from Stella.

Rosemary's flowers.

The Girls

It is freezing, and the moonlight gleams bright as a layer of ice over the deep dark of Lake Washington. Maisie blows out cigarette smoke in a careful *O*; she has been practicing this all winter and smiles when Sandy chokes on a gulp of rum and after coughing says, "When did you learn to do that?" and passes Maisie the bottle.

"In France," she says casually.

"You were never in France," Sandy says.

The wind whistles through the Rocks, a raspy, creepy sound. Maisie shivers and drinks again. She is already drunk enough that she no longer feels the cold. She gulps the last and throws the bottle into the lake. From higher on the bank, half hidden in salal and fern, Jean giggles and shifts her feet and sings, "Sh-Boom," and Samson joins in deeper harmony. Maisie frowns. He should not be here. Not here, not a witness. This is not for him tonight, and she doesn't like the way he distracts Jean from what should be a serious and somber reckoning.

A purge.

The smell of Shalimar eclipses everything else, the cigarette smoke, the water. They are fully doused in it. It took almost all of what Sandy managed to siphon from the bottle in Miss Chivers's room. The scent Maisie once loved is sickening now; she can hardly wait to get it off her skin. But once this is done, it will all be over.

"It's time," she says.

The damp breeze molds her slip to her body. She waits impatiently for Jean, who leaves Samson to scramble her way down the stairs, unfettered breasts bouncing, nipples hard against the thin nylon of the slip she wears.

"Where's the other bottle, Sandy?" Maisie puffs the cigarette into a glowing ember.

~

The rocky shore is hard against Sandy's butt with only her slip between it and the ground. She reaches behind her for the other bottle of rum, wrenches off the cap, and sucks down enough rum to be numb to the scent of Shalimar.

Sandy brings the rum to Jean, holding the bottle to Jean's mouth until Jean gulps and pulls away choking and laughing; Sandy can hardly keep Jean's face in focus; it is soft and rippling and glowing.

Then Maisie says, "Now," and takes Jean's arm and pulls her toward the water.

Sandy turns away from them both to look at Samson, who is still sitting on the bank. He stares at Jean with a kind of hunger that makes Sandy's stomach jump; she feels hot and restless and afraid. She does not look away from him when she hears Jean's gasp behind her, only a few feet away, nor does she turn when Jean mews like a small hurt kitten. She keeps her gaze on Samson, who frowns and narrows his eyes as if he's trying to see beyond her.

Samson says, "What are you guys doing?"

Sandy says, "Nothing to do with you. You weren't invited."

"Jean invited me," he says, sounding hurt.

Maisie says impatiently, "Now it's your turn, Sandy."

Sandy turns to her friends, who seem shining and ghostly on the beach. She wonders if her hand would go through them if she reached out. "You do it first."

Maisie sighs. "All right."

"It hurts worse than I thought," Jean complains.

"Come here and I'll make it feel better," Samson calls to Jean from the bank. Jean ignores him.

"I want to do Maisie," Jean says. "Since she did me."

Maisie smiles as if it's *meaningful*, and Sandy wants to laugh because it's just Jean flirting the way she always does, and Maisie, who thinks she can't be manipulated, is just as helpless at Jean's smile as Samson. Sandy abandons the rum and goes to the bank beside Samson and she says nothing when he asks again what they're doing. She has, in a sense, forgotten he is there. She is thinking about Miss Chivers, that look on her face when Sandy caught her straight out in a lie, and the noise in Sandy's head is so loud right now the whole world is fractured. She wants more of the rum.

She hears Maisie's sharp intake of breath. "That's enough!" and then Maisie and Jean race giggling into the lake, plunging in and yelping at the cold and the pain.

Maisie calls out, "Sandy, you bitch! Get down here!" and then, "I can still smell it, can't you? Damn! I can still smell it!" and Sandy is astonished that Maisie believed it would be so easy to be rid of Miss Chivers that she thought a stupid ritual could do it.

~

Jean stares at Maisie, who scrubs at her body so furiously that Jean forgets the throbbing of her wrist. "What are you doing?"

"Getting rid of that bitch," Maisie says. "You do it too. That's the whole point. Remember?"

Jean bobs up and down in the water, dousing herself because that's what Maisie wants, but she's more worried about Sandy and Samson whispering up on the bank—what are they talking about? What is he telling her? The desperation and fear Jean has been struggling to keep at bay rushes back.

"Sandy! Get down here!" Jean shouts.

The water is starting to feel cold now. Jean wants out but she waits for Sandy, who comes down the stairs and runs headlong into the water, splashing them as she does, half screaming at the shock of it, and then plunging beneath. When Sandy resurfaces, gasping, Jean can't keep from asking, "What were you whispering to Samson about?"

Sandy teases, "That's for me to know and you to find out."

Jean tells herself she doesn't care. She doesn't love Sam and she doesn't want to be with Sam and she knows he's watching her from the bank and suddenly she can't breathe. She stumbles from the lake. The air, cold as it is, is warmer than the water, but Jean is shivering hard as she wraps herself in one of the towels they took from the bathroom. Sandy is right behind her and Maisie behind Sandy.

Samson hisses, "Someone's coming!"

Sandy slides into the shadows of the salal.

"It's no one. It's too late," Maisie says, but then, "Crap!" and she dodges along the bank, hiding behind the bushes that shelter the far end of the cove, leaving Jean standing in the open on the beach, the white of her towel too bright in the moonlight. Samson quiets. Jean stands paralyzed, bracing herself for punishment as whoever it is rounds the corner, and when she sees who it is, she nearly melts with relief.

Mr. Frances.

Why he is here so late Jean doesn't know and doesn't care. When he sees her, he stops short, obviously profoundly surprised. Jean is so drunk it is all she can do to keep from wavering. But her desperation eases in his presence. He is so gorgeous. She wants him so much. He could make all her problems go away. She forgets Samson and Sandy and Maisie.

"Miss Karlstad?"

Jean sees the way his gaze sweeps her, and she lets the towel fall, knowing what he will see, the translucent wet slip plastered to her curves. "Why, Mr. Frances! What are you doing here so late? Were you looking for me?"

"I was going for a walk and I thought I heard noises. Shouldn't you be in bed?"

She giggles. "Are you offering?"

Jean no longer feels anything but an intense and fervent desire to press against Mr. Frances, to kiss him. As she approaches him, she sways her hips in that way that had Mr. Langdon practically on his knees that day in the den, and smiles in her most inviting way.

~

From the bushes where she hides with Sam, Sandy watches as Mr. Frances says, "You're freezing. What the hell were you doing? Swimming?" and takes off his coat to wrap it around Jean as he takes her back down the path, toward the school.

Samson whispers furiously, "But she's mine! He can't touch her!"

~

Maisie shivers where she stands, knee-deep in the lake, watching from her hiding place, wretched and confused, not knowing whether to be jealous or accommodating, whether to stop this thing or let it happen because she wishes for Jean to be happy.

~

Jean always gets what she wants.

Chapter 43

Rosemary had a restless night plagued with nightmares. When she woke in the morning, it was with the strangest notion that overnight everything had changed. The pain in her head seemed to confirm the feeling. She'd had headaches like this before, sometimes around her period, always on the third of July, as if her body meant to remind her of the day's special meaning, but she hadn't had one since her mother had died.

It took all her concentration to get out of bed. No sudden moves. The world wavered; nothing had solid edges. She had to teach today. She had to see her girls. She had to explain. She dressed carefully. She got as far as the hallway before she had to race to the bathroom to vomit. After which she felt marginally better, or would, if the sun would stop blasting through the windows and searing her corneas.

When she got to the staff room, she nearly fell into a chair. Pearl Hoskins gave her a concerned look.

"Are you all right, Rosemary? You look terrible. Bobby, does she look well to you?"

Rosemary had not seen Bobby come in, but suddenly there he was. His dark eyes narrowed as he pulled up a chair.

"You're not all right."

"It's just a headache. I get them sometimes."

"You should be in bed." He spoke as if there'd been no argument last night, no tension between them, and she wanted to be relieved, but she felt too battered to trust the truth of anything.

"I can't. I have class—"

"Can you get Rita?" he asked Pearl.

"I don't need the nurse," Rosemary protested. "And I have a class."

"Please. I think you'd better," Bobby told Pearl.

Rosemary closed her eyes. "I wish you wouldn't make a fuss. I'll be fine."

"You look like you can't even get out of that chair." He lowered his voice. "You were fine when you ran off last night. Did something happen after that?"

"No."

"Your meeting?"

"They didn't show. They're angry with me." She remembered the broken brooches and wanted to cry.

He said nothing, and she opened her eyes again to see his expression, which she couldn't interpret, mostly because she was too busy trying to keep the world steady.

"What?" she asked.

"Why are they angry?"

She didn't want him to see her thoughts but she couldn't keep them straight anyway, though it didn't seem strange to think that Bobby might be able to unscramble them. "You're looking at me funny."

"Your eyes are crossing." He glanced impatiently toward the door. "What's taking so long?"

"It doesn't matter what Rita says. I'm not going to bed. I have to—"

There wasn't time for more, because Pearl came back with Rita Everett in tow, and Bobby moved out of the way so that the petite, dark-haired nurse could look her over.

"You look quite ill, Miss Chivers." The nurse put her hand to Rosemary's forehead. "I do think you should be in bed."

"It's just a headache." She threw a glance at Bobby, which spun the world, and put her hand to her eyes. "It's a few days before my—"

"Ah," Rita said. "That seems to be endemic this morning."

Bobby cleared his throat.

Rosemary said, "I'll be fine. I have a class."

"I'll take over your class for you," Bobby said.

Pearl said, "He can have them read an assignment. There's a textbook, isn't there?"

"No." Rosemary tried to think. "I mean, yes, but . . . it's a bad one. I—"

"I know the book she means." Bobby smiled wryly. "I'll think of something."

"You see? For goodness' sake, Rosemary, listen to Rita. Go to bed. Bobby will handle things."

"I'd put you in the infirmary, but it's full this morning," Rita said.

"Full?" Pearl asked.

"I'll hand out Midol and in an hour I'll have a bed or two," Rita assured her. "In the meantime, Miss Chivers, I'll bring some aspirin for you."

"I have some," Rosemary said.

"Will you be okay in your room?"

"I'll make sure she gets there," Bobby told the nurse.

Rosemary surrendered. When Bobby helped her from the chair, she let him. But something came into her head then, Rita's words about the premenstrual outbreak in the infirmary, along with something else she couldn't grab hold of, something she knew without knowing . . .

"Rita? What girls are in the infirmary this morning?"

"Right now? Miss James is there for a fever. And Miss Wilson and Miss Neal."

Rosemary felt Bobby tense beside her. She said, "Not Miss Karlstad? The three of them are usually together."

"Oh, yes, she was there earlier, but she felt better so I let her go. Those girls are so close."

Rosemary's head throbbed. She tightened her grip on Bobby's arm.

When they got into the hall, he said, "What's going on, Rosemary?"

"I have no idea." She heard the fear in her voice and knew he must hear it too.

Chapter 44

Rosemary spent the next day in bed as well, but by the following morning the worst was over. By the time she got up, washed, and dressed, she'd lost the morning classes, but she thought she could teach the afternoon. Fourth period, especially. She wondered if her girls had asked about her, if they had been worried, or if their anger had swept all else away. She was afraid to know the answer. Today, anyway, she would find out.

From her window, she saw students clad in their gray coats and green berets gathering by the fireplaces for the usual after-lunch gossip and socializing before class began again. Rosemary should hurry if she meant to catch Bobby and take over. But then she saw Jean join the girls. Jean, who was not wearing a beret, and whose blond pageboy glimmered golden in the sun. Rosemary paused, arrested by the sight.

Everything in her seemed to lurch toward the girl, that bright blond hair. Rosemary searched for the other two, but oddly, they weren't there. Jean's trill of a laugh seemed to reach her even through distance and window glass; was that because they were connected, as Dad had said, entangled?

Then she saw Bobby walking toward the fireplaces in his Brooks Brothers suit, no coat and no hat, heading toward the gymnasium building for class. Her class. Rosemary's fourth period. She was too late. She saw the way Jean started toward him; Rosemary expected him to make a gesture of greeting and keep walking.

Instead he went to the group of girls and spoke to them, and Rosemary watched as they laughed at whatever he'd said and left. All but Jean. When the girls were gone, Bobby said something to Jean and she stepped up to him and adjusted his tie, and he did not step back or push aside her hands. He let her.

Rosemary saw his lips move. Again, she heard Jean laugh. Bobby smiled. Then they walked back to the building.

It was nothing. A casual moment. It was not so intimate as it looked. Rosemary was mistaking it.

But she could not make herself believe it.

~

She waited until classes were over and then she went to Bobby's office. Before she could reach for the door, it opened, and Jean stepped out.

"Oh! Oh, good, Jean, you're just who I wanted to see. I—"

"Good afternoon, Miss Chivers." Jean's smile took Rosemary's words. It was that sly, sideways smile that made Rosemary shiver, and Jean's usually warm brown eyes were blankly cold.

"I'd like to talk to you," Rosemary managed.

"I'm already late." Jean turned back to the office, smiled, and waved gaily. "Thank you, Mr. Frances!"

She left Rosemary with a freezing stare and did not hold the door, so Rosemary had to grab it before it closed in her face.

Bobby's perturbed expression changed to relief when he saw her, but he was obviously distracted. "You're up!" His smile faded quickly to wariness. "Better?"

"What was Jean Karlstad doing here?"

"Asking about a class." He avoided her gaze.

"What class?"

"Yours." He riffled through papers.

"Oh." Rosemary frowned. "How did that go?"

"I think all right. Mostly we watched that film on living in a shelter."

"They've already seen it. Weeks ago."

"They said they hadn't." Bobby cracked a half smile. "But I guess they would say that."

"We're past the atomic unit. Well into cooking now. You should have been teaching them to bake brownies."

"I can't cook."

"I'll tell you a secret: there's a mix." The tease fell limply between them. As casually as she could, she said, "Jean didn't . . . she didn't say anything to you about . . . about me, or . . . or us or the other night?"

"The other night?" He seemed confused, but she saw the moment he understood what she meant. "You mean she saw us?"

"No. No. Not at all—"

"Then I don't know what you're talking about." He became impatient. "Anyway, what does it matter if she did?"

"Because you know she has a crush on you."

Now he looked uncomfortable. "But you talked to her."

It was not an answer; there was something he wasn't saying, something he was keeping from her. "Yes, but it's not as if she can just turn her feelings off. She'll read something into everything you do, remember that. Did you get your car fixed?"

"Yes. Why?" His gaze sharpened. "Wait—are you . . . do you think that rock had something to do with Jean Karlstad?"

"No, no. It's only that I just remembered it."

"What's going on, Rosemary?"

She should never have mentioned the car. "Nothing."

"Nothing. I see. You said that the girls were angry with you."

"I'm managing it."

"Is that why they asked to be transferred from your class?"

The shock of it . . . for a moment she thought she'd misheard him. "What?"

"I've put them in Pearl's fourth period."

"But . . . Can they do that?"

"Not usually. But Stella approved it this morning. She thought there was no point in denying their request when this was clearly better for everyone. I agreed."

"Oh. Oh, I—I see." And she did. She should have known the moment she saw the ruined brooches. They were done with her.

"What happened?" Bobby asked.

She didn't know what to say. She felt embarrassed and unsettled, and she needed a moment to think about this, alone. "I suppose I'd better let you get back to work."

"Rosemary—"

"Really, I need to go."

He exhaled heavily. "Maybe this is best." So reasonable, so much the right thing to say.

"Yes. You're right."

"I mean it, Rosemary. Those girls are obviously a problem for you."

They were sending her a message, just as they'd done with the brooches. She had set something in motion . . . she felt it, a shifting in the air, a turn of shadow, something waiting for her. But, too, there was her own need, unassuaged, unsettled. She could not just let this go.

Chapter 45

That Sunday, Rosemary went to chapel. She sat in the back, watching her girls in a forward pew. When the service was over, she confronted them in the hall.

"Good morning," she said cheerfully.

They looked uncertainly at one another.

"What are you doing here?" Maisie asked.

"You're never here Sunday," Sandra said. "Don't you have a date?"

Rosemary said, "I thought the four of us could have a little chat."

"'A little chat'? A little chat. How nice, isn't it, girls? A chat with Miss Chivers." Maisie's voice was as mocking as her smile.

"We need to talk. I think there's been a misunderstanding."

"'A misunderstanding'?" Sandra echoed. "How could I misunderstand something I saw with my own eyes? You were kissing Mr. Frances. I don't think friends kiss like that—I mean, he looked like he might swallow you. Plus he was getting fresh. Or is that something friends do now? I'd suppose I could ask someone, but gosh . . . I don't know, whoever should I ask?"

"It used to be that we could ask you." Maisie's direct gaze was chilling too. "But now, of course . . ."

"We know we can't trust you," Jean finished.

The hall was empty. Still Rosemary lowered her voice when she asked Sandra, "You really needed to throw a rock through his windshield?"

Jean said, "That was Maisie."

Maisie smiled. "I have much better aim than Sandra."

Jean inspected her nails. "Sandy wanted to slash his tires."

"But the rock was a better idea," Sandra said.

Rosemary said, "Leave him alone."

"Oooohhh, look at her," Maisie taunted. "I think she might be angry."

"He has nothing to do with us."

Jean raised her eyes. "How cute you are when you're upset!"

The way they looked at her, such insolence, so much aggression. How familiar Rosemary was with that stance, that expression, the fury and the hurt, if not the intensity. But how to get past that to the girls she knew?

"It's me you're angry with. Fine. Be angry with me. Punish me. But at least let us talk about it. And leave Mr. Frances alone."

"What if he won't leave us alone?" Jean stepped forward, again with that creepy coy smile. "Come on, Rosemary. You didn't think you got him all to yourself, did you?" Her fingers trailed up the buttons on Rosemary's blouse, one-two-three, stopping at the top one. "Maybe he'll decide he likes someone else better. Maybe he's decided it already." Jean bounced her brows suggestively, then bopped her fingertip hard into the button, which hurt against Rosemary's sternum. "I hope you don't like him too much, because that would be too bad. Too, too bad."

Sandra laughed. "You should see your face."

"You're scared." Maisie, too, stepped close. "Why are you scared, Miss Chivers? Do we frighten you?"

"Of course not."

"Did it bother you when we transferred out of your class? It surprised you, didn't it? We thought it would." Maisie giggled. "But we needed you to take us seriously. We needed to show you."

"Show me what, exactly?"

"That we don't care about you anymore." Maisie spoke slowly, dropping each word like a stone. She raised her wrist. For the first time Rosemary noticed she did not wear the headband bracelet. Maisie twisted her arm so that Rosemary could see that instead of the scarred *F* there was an angry wound, a bubbly red brand where it used to be. A fresh burn. Whatever had caused it would have hurt worse than the making of the *F*. "See? We've erased you. We don't want you."

Jean raised her wrist as well. The same burn, pink and brutally painful-looking.

Rosemary looked at Sandra.

Sandra regarded her icily. "So leave us alone."

"Or we'll have to do something," Jean put in.

Rosemary swallowed. How absurd that she was afraid. She had thought them like her in their rage and frustration, but she had not been like this. She had never been this intense. She had never wanted to hurt anyone. She had only been restless and frustrated, and maybe that's how they had started, but now they had gone far beyond that. How or why that had happened didn't matter now. Bobby had warned her. Stella had warned her. Alicia too. Troubled girls. Reform-school girls.

Rosemary took a deep breath. "I can't do that. I care about you, and I'm sorry I wasn't honest about Mr. Frances, but I'll tell you whatever you want to know now. I'll explain why—"

"We don't care," Jean said sharply.

She pushed by roughly, and the other two followed, leaving Rosemary standing alone.

It was over. She'd lost their trust and they'd erased her and it was over. There was nothing more to fear from them. She'd lost her daughter, but at least they hadn't burned down a boathouse or hurt anyone . . .

Yet instinctively she knew that what was between them could not be undone with something as simple as broken brooches or transferring from her class. This had not ended, and there was danger here, and there was one person Rosemary knew who would understand and maybe help.

Chapter 46

She found Alicia in the gymnasium, picking up scattered birdies from the previous badminton lesson. The gym was still hot from the girls and from the weak sun intensified through the high windows, and a fine gleam of sweat glowed on Alicia's forehead. As Rosemary approached, the art teacher untied her vibrant orange scarf and opened the collar of her yellow blouse, flapping it to cool herself.

"You're not supposed to wear heels on this floor," Alicia said absently.

"I need to speak with you a moment," Rosemary told her. "It's important."

"You'll have to hurry. I need to—"

"I have to know what happened that night in the boathouse."

Alicia froze.

"I don't want lies, or half-truths, or evasions. You keep telling me I need to be careful of those girls. I need to know exactly why you say that."

"I heard they transferred out of your class."

"I'm afraid that won't be the end of it."

Alicia reached for the ends of her scarf, twining it about her fingers. "Have they threatened you?" Before Rosemary could lie, Alicia went on, "What did you do? How did you 'disappoint' them?"

Rosemary hesitated.

"You belonged to them, is that it? They wanted your complete loyalty. They expected you to go off with them and live in Paris and be their *maman* and you told them you had plans that didn't include them? Something like that?" The bitterness in Alicia's voice took Rosemary aback.

"Is that what happened with you?" Rosemary asked.

Alicia reached into the pocket of her trousers, obviously looking for a cigarette.

Rosemary offered one of hers, which Alicia took gratefully. When Rosemary lit it, Alicia glanced at the matchbook cover. "The Blue Moon? Really, Rosemary?"

"What happened?"

Alicia took a long drag, then blew out a stream of smoke, every gesture nervous. "I *was* their favorite teacher last year. In art we did a unit on the Pre-Raphaelites. It's always popular. Knights and fair maidens and the Lady of Shalott and Ophelia and all that. Very romantic, and then you throw in Rossetti and Millais and William Hunt and all their women . . . anyway, the girls were obsessed. They're very intense in case you haven't noticed."

Intense. Yes.

Alicia went on, "Like you, at first I was charmed. It's very appealing, isn't it, to be so liked? They've got their problems, but they're so damn clever, and too smart to be in this stupid school, and it's a compliment to have them hanging on your every word. Every teacher's dream"— Alicia laughed shortly; smoke erupted in stuttered clouds—"until it isn't.

"But then . . . they were so demanding. They wanted to meet outside of class and go through all my art books. They wanted to practice painting like the Pre-Raphaelites. It was fine. But none of them have any painting talent. They just liked to talk and imagine that they were Lizzie Siddall or Jane Morris. It became exhausting."

Alicia paused. One drag. Another. Her gaze distant in memory.

The story sounded familiar in its essence. The quest for knowledge, the meetings outside class, the desire for more and more. Rosemary hadn't been so special after all, had she? "The boathouse," she prompted.

Alicia sighed. "It was about this time of year. We were meeting there, and we had a kerosene lantern because if you put it on the floor it gave us light but not enough that anyone knew we were there. I was reading Hunt's autobiography to them that night, and"—Alicia spoke as if the memory were a hard one—"and they started talking about all the things they were going to do when they were out of here, and how we would be together forever, and it got . . . oh, it got so ridiculous, you know, how we would live as artists and not let anyone stop us and there was some talk of free love and I said something like it's all very well to pretend but in real life they'd never find husbands carrying on this way and this was all silly foolishness."

The gym was bright and hot, but suddenly Rosemary was in that boathouse dark with the kerosene lantern, excited talk falling into disappointment, and more than that, betrayal, because wasn't that what it was when someone who'd been playing along, someone who'd been in on the game, suddenly turned and told the truth of it? *This will never happen. This is a fantasy. You will never be what you dream.*

Just as Rosemary's mother had done. That same dash of reality, those same words flung with the same brutal, treacherous honesty. *Stop dreaming. Live in the real world.* Rosemary knew what the girls' response must have been; she'd felt it too, that reflexive *But I'm different,* the denial that such a reality could ever apply to her while at the same time reeling from the dawning, defenseless knowledge that it could, it must, it could not be otherwise.

No wonder they were so angry with Alicia. Just as Rosemary had been with her mother.

The cigarette had been smoked to its filter, but Alicia kept puffing on it, trying to drag out any last dregs when there were none to be had. Finally, Alicia pulled it from her lips and looked wryly at it. "After that, they started their taunting. You know how girls do. Calling me names, saying I was stupid, that I wasn't special. I grabbed the lantern and told them I was leaving and we wouldn't meet again. It was over. But they blocked me before I got to the door. They . . . they circled me and started pushing and shoving and doing this awful chanting and singing. It sounds so stupid, I know, but it was frightening. They backed me against the wall and said I wasn't going anywhere, and then Maisie grabbed the lantern, and we fought over it, and . . . I don't know. She grabbed it and threw it. Or maybe it dropped. That's what Maisie said. That she accidentally dropped it." Alicia shrugged. "It broke and caught fire."

It was just what Rosemary would have imagined, had she let herself, had she not been blinded by her search for her daughter and what she wanted to see.

"We were lucky to get out. That boathouse is as old as the school."

There was quiet for a moment. Rosemary said, "Why didn't you tell me this before?"

Alicia contemplated the cigarette filter as if it held the answer to a question she'd been asking a long time. "Honestly?" She laughed humorlessly. "Because I was embarrassed. And jealous too—I admit it. Absurd, isn't it? Those girls, they're so beguiling. They wrap you about before you realize it. I should have known better, and I suppose I didn't want to believe I was the only one who could be such a fool. I wanted you to be a fool too. I wish that wasn't true, but . . ." Alicia's expression was apologetic. "And I kept telling myself it wasn't what I thought, you know? But now . . . I can't stop thinking about how when those flames caught, they pushed me aside like I was nothing to get out of that place. I fell, and they closed the door to slow me down. They were halfway across the meadow by the time I got out. They said it was an accident, and I agreed because I wasn't sure, and it was easier, but . . . but if I had to bet, I'd say Maisie threw that lantern on purpose and closed the door. She meant for the boathouse to burn, and me with it."

317

Chapter 47

The next morning, Rosemary was up with the dawn. Alicia's story left a vivid impression, and Rosemary couldn't stop thinking about her own last encounter with her girls, the burn marks on their wrists, their anger. Whatever would be her version of Maisie throwing the lamp and closing the door had not yet happened, but Rosemary knew it was due, and soon, and her every thought revolved around stopping it. How to repair this rift before someone got hurt?

Rosemary went to the kitchen to grab coffee and then to the staff room, which was blessedly quiet so early. A bulletin had been posted announcing a statewide "surprise" test of the air-raid warning system scheduled for sometime in the next few days. Mercer Rocks would be treating it as a fire drill and emptying all buildings. Below the bulletin was the *Seattle Daily Times* article that showed evacuation routes and stated that civil defense would be practicing setting up refugee centers. The very thought only made Rosemary more tired. Even the coffee nauseated her.

Bobby came in a few minutes later with a bakery cinnamon roll. "You're up early."

"I had a bad night," she said. "I'm pretty sure you're not usually here at this time either."

"I guess we both had a bad night."

"Screaming?"

He picked at the cinnamon roll and glanced over his shoulder. "Is there coffee yet?"

She pushed her cup toward him. "You're welcome to mine. I don't want it."

He took hold of the handle, but he didn't drink it. He only stared down into it. "Come to my place tonight. I've been wanting to talk to you about something, and I . . . I've been putting it off."

"That doesn't sound good," Rosemary said quietly.

He didn't deny it. "Come to my place."

Her chest tightened. "I can't. You know that. I'm a housemother. I can't just leave."

"What about now? Before classes? Your room?" He looked hopeful.

"You must be joking. What would everyone think to see you going to my room? Why not your office?"

"There's not enough priva—"

The scream came from the stairs, then a thudding sound.

Bobby jerked in surprise, spilling coffee onto the table. Rosemary lurched to her feet. She heard running footsteps, the slamming of a door. She raced to the hall. Bobby was right beside her, shaking spilled coffee from his hand. They hurried where everyone else hurried—to the stairway from the second-floor dormitories.

A small crowd gathered at the bottom, girls still in nightgowns watched from the stairs.

"What is it?" Rosemary pushed her way through. When she saw what huddled there, she stopped short.

Jean, curled in the fetal position, clutching her abdomen, Sandra and Maisie hovering.

"What happened?" Rosemary asked.

Maisie said, "She fell."

Jean groaned.

"Are you hurt?" Rosemary turned to Lizzie, who stood beside her. "Go get Nurse Rita."

The girl looked at Maisie, who said, "No."

Lizzie stayed put. Rosemary moved to Jean, but before she reached her, Maisie stepped in her way.

"Don't touch her, Miss Chivers. She doesn't want you."

Sandra sat on the floor next to Jean and curled her arm protectively about Jean's shoulders.

Jean's hair fell into her wide eyes, which shone with tears. A bruise was already forming on her cheekbone. She stared at Rosemary so coldly that Rosemary took a step back.

Sandra straightened. "You'd better take her to the nurse, Mr. Frances. I don't think she can walk."

Maisie said, "You're strong enough to carry her, aren't you, Mr. Frances? Jean says you are."

They all turned to him. Stella Bullard was there now, watching them all, her frown deepening. Bobby met Rosemary's gaze; he looked helpless, stricken.

"Bobby?" Jean asked softly.

Bobby. Not Mr. Frances.

That danger again. Shivering in the air. Reluctantly, Bobby started toward Jean. Rosemary shook her head to stop him. There was something off here. Something that told her he should be nowhere near Jean now. Bobby frowned, but he obeyed her, and there was relief in his expression too; Rosemary didn't mistake it.

She said, "Let me help."

"She doesn't want you," Maisie said again.

The malice there, the calculation in Maisie's eyes when she looked at Bobby. It only strengthened Rosemary's resolve to keep him away from this. She ignored Maisie and pushed past the other girls, aware of the watching gazes, aware of Stella's judgment, too aware of Bobby's uncertainty, though he stayed put. Both Sandra and Maisie held their ground as Rosemary approached, stalwart guardians. "Move aside, girls, please."

They didn't, but she knew that would be the case. She had done this too, with her mother. A dozen stare-downs, a hundred. The roles reversed, but Rosemary felt strangely powerful within hers. She held Sandra's gaze until the girl rolled her eyes and stepped to the side, allowing Rosemary to go to Jean, where she bent down and asked quietly, "Can you stand?"

Stubbornly, Jean said, "I want Bobby to help me."

"Well, you have me," Rosemary insisted as she put her arm under Jean's and pulled her to her feet. "Come on, let's get you to the nurse."

Jean didn't protest but set her mouth. She went limp. She didn't fight, but she didn't help.

The palpable tension in the hallway eased.

"Are you hurt, Miss Karlstad?" Stella asked.

"I think I'm fine," Jean answered, and then, beneath her breath, "unfortunately."

Jean steadfastly avoided Rosemary's questioning gaze.

"Miss Chivers will take you to the nurse to check you over. Girls, out of the way now. Let them through." Stella gestured for the crowd to disperse. "Let's not be late for breakfast. Do you need help, Miss Chivers?"

"I've got her."

Rosemary led Jean down the hall, feeling Bobby stare after them. Once they turned the corner to the infirmary, out of sight of the others, Jean pulled away.

"You've ruined everything! Why did you even come here? I hate you!"

Such viciousness. Jean wrapped her arms around herself; tearful again, which made that viciousness pathetic and miserable, and Rosemary thought, *She's her own worst enemy.*

Rosemary sighed. "This is foolish and immature. I thought better of you."

Jean laughed—it was half a sob. "You think you know everything, but you don't. You don't understand anything at all."

"Jean." Rosemary put a hand on her arm. "Please. Stop this."

Jean jerked away. "What if I told you he touched me? He saw me naked and he touched me."

Rosemary moved toward her again. "Jean, enough—"

"Leave me alone." Jean backed away, moving quickly toward the infirmary. Her voice was loud. Too loud. From the open doorway of the infirmary, Rita Everett stepped out, looking concerned.

"It's all right," Rosemary started to assure the nurse.

"It's *not* all right! Just leave me alone, will you? *Leave me alone!*" Jean spun on her heel and ran to the infirmary, where Nurse Rita, frowning, put her arm around the girl and led her inside, closing the door firmly behind them, closing Rosemary out.

Chapter 48

Rosemary marched directly upstairs. She found Maisie and Sandra in front of the bathroom mirror with several other girls. The bathroom bustled with chatter and motion. It was steamy, too hot, claustrophobic.

Rosemary went to Sandra, always the easier one. "I want to talk to you."

"No," Sandra said.

"You don't have a choice."

"This is a free country." Maisie pulled a brush through her long, thick hair.

"Sadly for you, that doesn't apply to reform schools." Rosemary jerked her head to the hallway.

Sandra looked to Maisie.

"She's not going," Maisie said.

The other girls in the bathroom had gone quiet but for someone obliviously singing an off-tune "Little Things Mean a Lot" in the shower. Maisie's challenge echoed. Sandra glanced between Maisie and Rosemary as if only vaguely interested in the outcome.

Rosemary asked, "What would you prefer to spend your week doing, Miss Wilson? Yard work? Kitchen work? Bathroom duty? I can make it happen."

Sandra tensed.

Maisie said, "Don't, Sandy."

"Two weeks, maybe," Rosemary said. "Maybe one week rubbing stains out of laundry and another cleaning toilets."

"Sandy . . . ," Maisie warned.

Sandra threw back her head and sighed dramatically. "What do you want, Miss Chivers?"

Rosemary gestured toward the door. "This way, please."

Sandra followed her out sullenly while Maisie called, "Don't forget, Sandy!"

Rosemary led the way to Cheryl Fields's office across the hall. Cheryl raised her eyebrows but stepped out and closed the door behind her, leaving them alone. Sandra crossed her arms and stared blankly at Rosemary.

"What doesn't she want you to forget?" Rosemary asked.

Sandra only cocked her head insolently.

"All right. What was all that about with Jean just now?"

Sandra shrugged. "She fell down the stairs."

"I meant with Mr. Frances. What was all that?"

"I don't know."

"I think you do."

Silence.

"What are you girls playing at?"

Silence.

Rosemary brought her gaze level to Sandra's. "I'll ask again: What are you girls playing at?"

Sandra stared back, but the look in her eyes changed from blank insolence to something both taunting and secretive. It filled Rosemary with edgy panic. As if Sandra knew it, she smiled, and spun, opening the door, obviously meaning to walk out and leave Rosemary without answers, with nothing. Rosemary grabbed Sandra's arm to stop her. Sandra yanked; Rosemary's hand slid down the girl's arm, to her wrist, locking on, and Sandra twisted back, her eyes huge, her face bony and suddenly a flash of *something* caught Rosemary off guard. Her grip loosened on Sandra's wrist, which turned in Rosemary's hand, her scar beneath Rosemary's thumb, and Rosemary realized with surprise that there was no bumpy lump of a burn there, but an *F*.

"You didn't . . . you didn't erase it like the others," she said.

Thanks to Rosemary's surprise, Sandra jerked away easily. She cupped her other hand around her wrist, as if trying to hide it. "What of it? I don't like burns."

There was something there, something Rosemary didn't understand, the *F* remaining on Sandra's wrist and the weird flash that had so rattled Rosemary. She felt off balance and at the same time more in control than ever.

"What's going on, Sandra?" she asked. "Tell me the truth."

Sandra rubbed her wrist as if trying to rub off the feel of Rosemary. "That's funny coming from you."

"Whatever you girls are doing is dangerous. Trust me."

"Trust you?" Sandra laughed shortly, then her voice became fierce. "I thought you were different. I thought you belonged to us, but you didn't, did you? You were never on our side, not really. You let them put us in isolation and then Mr. Frances and you—" She broke off in a sudden burst of emotion, a caught breath, or sob, but when Rosemary moved toward her, she lurched away. Sandra opened her mouth to say something else.

And then suddenly Maisie appeared in the doorway, and Sandra's mouth snapped closed and whatever she had been about to say was gone and the vulnerability that had been in her expression was gone too. Rosemary felt the change with a bitter and hopeless frustration that only grew worse when Maisie took Sandra's arm, claiming her, and Sandra settled into herself again. Whatever it was Rosemary had seen disappeared. Rosemary would have thought she'd imagined it if not for how shaken it left her.

Maisie pulled Sandra from the doorway. "If you have questions about Jean, Miss Chivers, maybe you should ask Mr. Frances." Her full mouth curled in a sneer. "I don't suppose he's told you about her, has he? I wonder if he'll tell you the truth." Her face was almost luminous with triumph as she led Sandra into the hall, where Maisie paused, a final stab. "I wish I could be there to see your face when he does."

She pulled an unresisting, silent Sandra with her. Rosemary let them go.

Chapter 49

With Maisie's words, Rosemary suddenly understood the game. It was Bobby. They meant to hurt her by hurting Bobby. All the other teachers knew about Jean's crush on him. *"She has eyes for Bobby."* Jean had finagled office duty to be near him. Shalimar. This morning, calling him by name . . . Rosemary's uneasiness. *"He saw me naked and he touched me . . ."* They were going to take their revenge on Rosemary by destroying Bobby if they could.

He was gone that afternoon; she could not talk to him. "Meetings," Irene said, and Rosemary remembered whom those meetings would be with. The board. Would John Karlstad be there by phone or otherwise? When she called Bobby's house that night, there was no answer.

"I wonder if he'll tell you the truth." Oh, how well they'd set it up. How blind she'd been.

There was no chance to see him the next morning either. He was not in his office. Irene said she believed he was in the building somewhere with Tom Gear, but Rosemary couldn't wait or look for him; classes began and she had to go to her classroom.

She'd been teaching ten minutes when the bell for the statewide test drill rang over the intercom. Rosemary was already nervous; she jumped so hard some of her students laughed. Her heart still raced as she ordered the girls to evacuate.

They joined the other classes in the meadow. Out of habit, she looked for her girls. Maisie was easy to find, that dark head and her confident bearing, though this morning she seemed glum and restless, as if she'd inherited Sandra's inability to stay still. There was Sandra too, sitting on the bench of a picnic table, swinging her leg, studying the ground, her hair falling forward to hide her face. Again Rosemary had the sense of something . . . off. Something wrong.

She ignored a sudden press of dread and glanced around for Jean, but just then Stella and Lois Vance and Bobby—who looked worn and tired and disheveled—came into the meadow, and Rosemary forgot Maisie and Sandra in the quick urge to race over and pull Bobby aside. Impossible. Every eye had turned to him and Stella and Lois, but at least he was here; Rosemary could talk to him after the drill.

"Girls," Stella announced. "Today is a statewide practice drill for the Emergency Warning System. A mythical nuclear bomb exploded over the Bremerton Naval Shipyard approximately"—she checked her watch—"seven minutes ago. May I commend you all on your rapid evacuation! If this were a real emergency, buses would be arriving to take you all from the city. Mrs. Vance and Mr. Frances will be taking roll call to make sure all students are present, and then we will return to class."

Stella went back to the school, teetering on her heels in her march over the meadow. Lois rested her clipboard on her hip and looked over the crowd. Bobby pulled a list from his coat pocket and began to call the roll, the rote names, the rote return, *Jane Bestler? Here! Elizabeth Chad? Here! Lizzie Etheridge? Here!* . . . on and on, so that Rosemary mostly stopped listening as she waited impatiently to talk to him, and then suddenly she was aware of a change in tone, a rising vexation, and then, concern. She realized Bobby was calling for Jean, and he'd called more than once.

"Jean Karlstad?" he called again, searching the crowd. "Miss Karlstad?"

No answer.

Rosemary glanced toward Maisie, who stared off at the trees bordering the lake, her expression tight and hard.

"Jean Karlstad!"

Bobby looked to Rosemary. She shrugged.

"Does anyone know where Miss Karlstad is?" Lois called.

The dread Rosemary felt earlier returned, worse now. She went to Sandra, who was closest.

"Where is she?" she asked. "Where's Jean?"

Sandra looked up through her hair, which covered one eye. The other was curiously blank. "How should I know?"

"The last I checked, you and she and Maisie were inseparable."

"We don't have class together now." Sandra looked down.

"When did you see her last?"

"Am I her keeper?" Sandra jerked to her feet and strode off.

"Has anyone seen Miss Karlstad this morning?" Bobby asked.

"I haven't seen her since last night," Lizzie Etheridge volunteered.

"Me neither," said another girl.

Sarah Waller said, "Wasn't she in the dining hall for breakfast?"

"Was she, Miss Neal?" Lois Vance asked Maisie, who stared straight at Lois and said, "I don't know, Mrs. Vance."

"You don't know?" Rosemary asked in disbelief. "How can you not know? You have breakfast with her every morning."

"I missed breakfast today." Another straight stare.

"Is anyone else missing?" Bobby asked.

Lois frowned. "Where's Sandra Wilson?"

"She was just here," said Lizzie. "I mean—right here."

"I saw her walking back to the main building," someone else said.

In obvious exasperation and worry, Bobby said, "Everyone back to class! Tom and Martin, if you could see me, please."

Something was terribly wrong; Rosemary knew it. She tried to catch Bobby's eye as she gathered her class, but Tom and Martin were already moving in, and his attention had turned to them.

~

When Rosemary heard the siren less than an hour later, she told herself it had nothing to do with Jean's disappearance.

The class quieted, and then went eerily silent when the siren stopped. Then came another siren, and another. All growing loud as they approached, all stopping abruptly.

"What's happened?" one of the girls asked, wide-eyed, frightened. "Is it about Jean?"

Another said hesitantly, "I think it's just part of the emergency drill? Isn't it, Miss Chivers?"

The intercom buzzed. "All students are instructed to stay in their classrooms." Lois Vance sounded shaken. "I repeat, students are not to leave their classrooms at this time. Teachers, please await further instructions."

Lunch was brought to the room, plates of sandwiches and apples, already warm bottles of milk. Few ate. Finally, around two, Lois asked everyone to report to the dining hall. By then, Rosemary was frightened. In the dining hall, Stella Bullard and Lois Vance talked with an unfashionably suited man wearing a gray felt porkpie hat. Lois looked as if she'd been crying, and Stella's expression was racked. The police lights outside refracted off the glass in the doors and the hall walls.

Bobby talked urgently with Quincy as classes entered. Bobby's hair was ruffled as if he'd run his hand through it many times, the shadows beneath his eyes pronounced as bruises, his full mouth set in a tight line. He didn't look at Rosemary as she settled her students, who murmured worriedly among themselves. The air in the hall was grim and fraught, as if the building's spirit had infected everyone. No one spoke above a whisper.

Rosemary went back to Stella and Lois and the man with the porkpie hat.

Stella introduced Rosemary to Detective Prine. "Miss Chivers is a home-economics teacher here."

"What's happened?" Rosemary asked.

"There's been . . . so horrible . . . one of the girls . . ." Stella pressed her lips tightly together as if trying to hold back emotion. "One of the girls is dead."

"Dead? What do you mean, dead? Who? What happened?"

"Martin found her in the boathouse."

Rosemary's heart plummeted. Boathouse. Suddenly, she was seeing stars. "No. No, no, no."

Stella took her arm. "I think you should sit down, Rosemary—"

She could barely speak through her panic. "Who . . . who is it?"

"Rosemary—"

Rosemary yanked her arm away. She was barely aware of the detective, of Lois, who faded into the background, pale faces, lights flashing. Rosemary's voice was too loud in her own ears. "Who is it?"

Stella took a deep breath. "Jean. Jean Karlstad."

Chapter 50

Rosemary sat in the staff room with the others. The girls were being questioned separately by other detectives, in other rooms. Smoke from Alicia's cigarettes and Andrew Covington's pipe swirled in the sun churning through the closed windows. They'd gone through one urn of coffee already and were working on the second.

Rumors played tag through the halls. Jean had been stabbed. She'd been shot. Strangled. She'd slit her wrists, she'd been meeting a lover, she'd been drinking and dancing, she'd had on lipstick . . . No one knew what was true except that Martin had found her in the boathouse, which was currently swarming with police officers.

And so here they were, waiting, and all Rosemary could think was that Jean was dead.

Jean. Beautiful Jean. A hundred images swirled in Rosemary's head, the last few days, Jean creepily coy, Jean at the bottom of the stairs, Jean tearful and angry.

No one spoke. The sound of breathing . . . it was so loud, really unbearably loud. Rosemary ground her thumb into the table, glanced up to see Alicia looking at her. Alicia's expression . . . sad, sympathetic, worried for her . . . Rosemary looked away.

The door opened; they all straightened as if they were connected. Stella came in, along with the detective and another police officer and

Bobby looking gray and frazzled and sloppy—he hadn't fixed his hair. He was in his shirtsleeves, his tie loosened. His gaze found her and then flicked away. He closed the door and then came around to the back of the room, where she was with Alicia and Quincy. He sat with them and pulled a pack of cigarettes from his pocket.

Rosemary put out her hand. Wordlessly he gave her one. It shook between her fingers as she brought it to her mouth. She drew on it before Bobby touched her elbow and with a thin smile gave her a light.

"Well," Stella began from the front. "As you all know, there's been a terrible tragedy." She inhaled deeply. "Detective Prine and his men will be questioning you separately, but for now . . . Miss Karlstad's father has been notified and is on his way. Fortunately he was home in Olympia. We will be taking a break from instruction for the rest of the week. Parents are currently being informed. If they would like to take their girls home, they may. Those who stay will of course be watched carefully over the next days. I will be talking with each of you about your individual responsibilities. The live-in staff especially."

Rosemary pulled hard on the cigarette.

"Now, I believe the detective wishes to say a few words."

Detective Prine was no longer wearing his hat, and his balding head gleamed in the overhead light. The detective stood and gazed out over them, slow and measuring. Rosemary felt his eyes land on her; she glanced away and tried to still her trembling, the shaking cigarette.

"The girl was found by the groundskeeper at approximately noon in the boathouse. She had bled to death."

A general murmur of sound. *Bled to death.* Someone whispered, *"Suicide."* The word took up space; it had weight and force. Suddenly Jean's voice was in Rosemary's ear. *"You've ruined everything!"* *"It's not all right!"* Rosemary shook so hard she dropped the cigarette. Alicia grabbed it from the floor and stubbed it out into an ashtray. Bobby placed his hand on Rosemary's back, warm and comforting.

"The body has been taken to the coroner, who will do an autopsy to determine the cause," Prine informed them. "Beyond that, we have no other comment on her death."

Andrew Covington raised his hand. "Excuse me, Detective, but—should we be worried?"

"Worried?" the detective asked.

"Was it . . . murder?"

"At this time, we are not ruling anything out. It's early yet in the investigation. We're asking that anyone who knows anything about Miss Karlstad—her habits, her friendships, whether she was seeing anyone . . . anything like that—come forward. Any information at all might be helpful."

Bobby's fingers curled against Rosemary's back.

"Thank you," Detective Prine went on. "We'll be calling on you one at a time for questioning. Miss Chivers—we'd like to start with you, please."

Rosemary sat motionless until Bobby nudged her, and then she looked over her shoulder at him, noting again how bad he looked, how sad he was.

He whispered, "Go on."

She rose, feeling the slipping away of his hand in a sudden chill. She followed the detective to Stella's office, where she sat and looked idly out at police activity in the front drive. Some of the neighbors had gathered on the sidewalk to watch—what? The spinning lights?

"Are you all right, Miss Chivers?"

She looked at him. "Am I expected to be all right, Detective?"

"I understand that you were close to the dead girl."

"To Jean. Yes. Yes, though we'd had a falling-out."

"Over what?"

"Have you spoken to Maisie and Sandra?"

Detective Prine looked down at his notebook. "Maisie—?"

"Neal. Sandra Wilson."

A moment while he looked. "They were close friends, I take it?"

"What did they say?"

He gave her an inscrutable look.

"I only mean that if Jean was in a state, they would know."

"You wouldn't?"

Rosemary's vision blurred. "No. Not anymore."

"Why is that, Miss Chivers?"

She couldn't say. Didn't want to say. It didn't matter anyway, did it? How strange it would sound to this detective to say, *They were angry with me.* She could not account for it herself, and if she tried, well, how could she explain that they belonged to her in ways she had told no one—or at least, one of them did, and because of that, she'd embraced them all. Too tight. Too close.

"We had an argument."

Detective Prine made a note. "About what?"

"Do you have a cigarette, Detective?"

"I'm sorry. I don't smoke."

"Oh. We had a disagreement. You know how it is, Detective, between teachers and students."

"I don't, I'm afraid. Never been a teacher. What was the disagreement about?"

"Umm. She snuck into my room and stole my perfume." It was the only thing she could think of that implicated no one else. No matter that it was a lie.

"Ah." He jotted a note. "Miss Everett said she saw Miss Karlstad screaming at you in the hallway outside the infirmary. This was"—a quick check—"yesterday? Do you recall what Miss Karlstad said then?"

"I'm afraid I don't."

"Really?"

She tried to steady her racing heart. "The girls scream all kinds of things all the time, Detective. This is a reform school."

"Maybe this will refresh your memory. She told you to leave her alone, according to Miss Everett."

"Oh. That could very well be."

"She had fallen down the stairs that morning and you helped her to the infirmary, I understand."

"Yes."

Detective Prine eyed her. "She didn't want you to take her there."

Rosemary tried to smile. "She was still annoyed with me."

"Mrs. Bullard said she'd warned you about your relationship with Miss Karlstad."

Of course. Rosemary should have expected it.

"What was the nature of that warning?"

"Stella felt I was getting too close. She asked me to step back. I did."

"'Too close.' What do you think she meant by that?" The menace was there, the danger in his question.

"Um . . . well, these girls are troubled. They . . . seem to pick a favorite teacher every year. This year it was me, and I . . . I admit I was flattered." How stupid it sounded. How impossible to describe. Thank God no one knew what really went on in their secret meetings. Or about the *F*s the girls had carved upon their wrists, now thankfully obliterated. But for Sandra's. *Why not? Please, God, no one ask about that.*

Rosemary could not keep still. "I'd given them gifts for Christmas, you see—nothing much, some old brooches of my mother's, but it was against school policy."

"They? Not just Miss Karlstad?"

Rosemary cursed inwardly. "Miss Neal and Miss Wilson. The three were inseparable."

Another jotted note. "Anything else?"

"Not that I'm aware."

"Are you sad that Miss Karlstad is dead, Miss Chivers?"

He blurred before her. "How can you even ask that? She . . . she was . . . special to me. I cared for her very much. Yes, I'm sad. I'm heartbroken."

"Just a few more questions, Miss Chivers."

Something pressed into her hand. A handkerchief smelling of the oakiness of fading Aqua Velva. She wiped at her tears, and as he came again into focus she noted how intensely he watched her.

"Was Jean Karlstad seeing anyone romantically?"

"Romantically?" Her voice caught. "She's in a girls' school. Are you asking me if she's involved with another student?"

The detective looked shocked. "Goodness, no! I mean with a man. Or a boy. What do you know about Miss Karlstad's relationship with the McCree boy?"

"There isn't one that I know about. He's fifteen. You know how seventeen-year-old girls feel about fifteen-year-old boys, I assume?"

A slight wince. She'd hit a sensitive spot.

"I think they spoke occasionally, but beyond that . . ." Rosemary pressed her trembling hands to her thighs.

Detective Prine nodded and made a note. "Yes, I see. Below the notice of a girl like Miss Karlstad, I imagine. What is your relationship with Mr. Frances?"

Rosemary was not expecting that. "What does that have to do with Jean?"

"Answer the question, please."

"We're coworkers. And friends."

"Does he confide in you?"

"Detective, I'm unsure what this—"

"Every little bit of information may be important, Miss Chivers," he said patiently. "Does he confide in you? Has he ever spoken to you about Miss Karlstad?"

Rosemary's sense of danger intensified. "He agreed with Stella that I was getting too involved with all the girls, not just Jean." Close enough to the truth.

"On the day Miss Karlstad fell down the stairs, she asked for Mr. Frances to help her to the infirmary, didn't she?"

"Yes, but that—that was only because she had a crush on him. In that, she was hardly alone."

"What do you mean?"

"He's a handsome man in a girls' school. Nearly every student here swoons over him."

"Do you think he had an interest in Miss Karlstad himself?"

Oh, what they had done. The perilous game they'd played.

"No, Detective," she said firmly—maybe too much so, she realized, when she saw how sharply he looked at her. "I don't think Bobby had any interest in her. And I certainly don't think he had anything to do with her death, if that's what you're implying."

The detective considered her, then nodded. "I'm going to ask you not to leave the state until we're done with our investigation, Miss Chivers. Just a few more days. In case we have more questions."

"Of course."

She handed him back his handkerchief, and then she left with as great a carelessness as she could muster, though what she wanted to do was run.

Chapter 51

An officer met her in the hallway to take her back to the staff room. On the way, they passed a tall, stooped blond man with fair hair and a harried manner heading toward Stella's office. He looked so like Jean that Rosemary stopped in surprise.

The same wide forehead and high cheekbones, the same large, wide-set eyes. It could only be John Karlstad. That Jean was his daughter was no doubt.

Jean was not the one.

The knowledge brought no relief. It was not irrelevant but it was too late to bring anything but an abiding, gnawing grief and a deeper sense of things lost that could never be recovered.

The staff room was choked with smoke. In the haze, only a few remained like ghosts. Rosemary had been with the detective for much longer than she'd realized. Pearl Hoskins was still there, and she gave Rosemary such a baleful stare that she stepped back.

"Such an abomination," Pearl said in a low and vehement voice. "How could it be? One of our girls? You were supposed to teach them."

Rosemary frowned. "What are you talking about, Pearl?"

"It was an abortion." Pearl nearly spat the word. "What happened to the Karlstad girl."

The word was a slap. "What? Where did you hear that?"

"Didn't the detective tell you?"

"No." Why hadn't he? Rosemary's mind spun. This was why Detective Prine had asked if Jean had a romantic relationship *"with a man or a boy."* The questions about Sam McCree and Bobby. Jean had been pregnant. Rosemary remembered how gray Bobby had looked this morning. Almost sick. She remembered him saying there was something he needed to talk to her about. But no, of course not. It was the girls. It was their game to involve him. *An abortion.*

"Mr. Karlstad is in a state. Weren't you to teach them family planning in your class?"

Rosemary barely heard her. "I don't believe it."

"Well, it's true." Pearl took three sips of coffee in quick succession. "She tried to abort a child and bled to death. My God, it's not just tragic, it's murder. That poor baby—"

"Please," Rosemary managed.

"Such a sin."

"Don't, Pearl, please."

"It's against the law, and a waste on top of it. She could have had it adopted—"

"Stop!" Rosemary's voice thundered louder than she'd intended.

Pearl snapped her mouth shut.

Rosemary had to force out the words. "We don't know the circumstances."

"John Karlstad doesn't care about the circumstances. He wants the father found and punished. He says whoever the father is pushed Jean to get rid of the baby. He wants him prosecuted."

"Can he . . . can he do that?"

"Don't you remember who he is? He can do whatever he wants. He's on the House Un-American Activities Committee, for heaven's sake."

"It's not illegal to get a girl pregnant." Rosemary was barely aware of speaking. "Nor is it particularly un-American."

"No, but it is immoral, and that is un-American," Pearl noted.

An attempted abortion.

"What was she doing, having . . . relations at this age? Isn't the proper way to do things part of your curriculum?"

"The proper way?" Rosemary tried to understand.

"You know, dating, becoming engaged, abstaining until marriage . . ." Pearl waved her hand airily.

Rosemary laughed.

Pearl looked offended. "That is the curriculum. I'm not mistaken about that. That's why we're here, to train these girls to be good wives and mothers so the Reds don't win—"

"Shut up." Rosemary spoke calmly, slowly, to be sure that Pearl heard.

The English teacher stared at her. "What?"

"I told you to shut up. This is a tragedy, and the reason is bullshit like that curriculum."

Rosemary walked out, ignoring Pearl's stunned expression. *Jean.* Jean, who'd worried that she liked boys too much. Jean, who longed for her mother's pearls. Suddenly, Rosemary was crying, sobbing in the middle of the hall, and she hurried blindly to the stairs, stumbling down; the roar and rushing of the washing machines in the laundry room filled her ears, muffling her own sobs as she cried in the basement.

Finally, exhausted, she stared blindly at the ceiling.

If what Pearl had said was true, if Jean was in enough trouble to attempt an abortion, why hadn't she come to Rosemary? Rosemary would have helped; all three girls had to know that. She'd told them everything—

She froze, putting her hand to the wall to steady herself.

She'd told them what an abortion was. She'd told them what was done the same way she'd given them information about birth control and gonorrhea and homosexuality. Suddenly she saw Jean's fall down the stairs in a different, deliberate light. *"I'm fine. Unfortunately."* Jean had been trying to miscarry, and when that didn't work . . . when that didn't work, she knew what else to do, because Rosemary had given them the information. She believed they should know, but she'd also believed they trusted her, that if they needed something like this, they would come to her . . . She had never imagined what might happen if they stopped trusting her and needed something like this and had nowhere else to turn.

But that's exactly what had happened. They had stopped trusting her, and that was her fault too.

Her own history, the weight of her own silence, the admission she still could not bring herself to say out loud: *I had a daughter. I gave her up, and I have been angry at myself for that every day since and told myself I wasn't. They told me to forget, to go on, and I thought I had.*

I thought I had.

But she hadn't. Dad was right. She was afraid of being hurt again and had not found a way to be unafraid, and this was the result. Of all her lies, the ones she had told herself were the most costly. Don't get involved. Don't care so much, and yet she'd been doing both things. She'd been unable to admit that she was getting too involved in their lives, or to be honest with herself or them about Bobby. Rosemary had not been able to tell the truths that mattered, and everyone knew she was lying, and so Jean had not come to her with this and had died alone on that boathouse floor, just as Rosemary had been alone that long-ago night, surrounded by other women but alone, the devil mask cutting off her vision and the smell of cardboard and the vinyl seat pressed against her cheek, freezing, so damn cold, and then the porch and the song she could not bear to listen to even now. "Goody Goody," what a stupid song, what a vindictive song, the lights flashing, the voices, so cold and so frightened and she could not bear to think of Jean so afraid, so alone . . .

But—

She wouldn't have been alone, would she? Those three did nothing without each other. They would not only know the father of Jean's baby, but they would know what happened, and if what happened was what Rosemary suspected, they would be drowning in their own guilt and grief—and fear too.

That was something she could not leave them alone with. She had taken them to this point; she would help them through the rest, whatever it might be. It was time to find the truth.

Chapter 52

The clock ticked the minutes; Rosemary heard Mrs. Sackett groan in the room next door, the creak of a mattress.

Rosemary waited until the noises quieted. She put on a robe over her pajamas and went barefoot down the stairs. She waited what seemed like forever until Cheryl Fields turned from her book to grab a bottle of Coke from behind her. Rosemary hurried past, breathing a sigh of relief when she made it unseen. The light from the bathroom lent a dim glow until she reached the turn of the hall, and then there was only the lambent light from the high window at the end.

Jean's door was locked, and the sight of it was a visceral punch. Most of Jean's things had been boxed up and taken to the police station. Rosemary turned purposefully away, trying to banish both grief and guilt.

Which one should she try first? Maisie or Sandra? Sandra. Quietly, she crossed the hall to tap on Sandra's door. There was no answer.

She tried the knob. It opened easily to reveal a room torn apart. An unmade bed, clothes strewn everywhere, books thrown about, papers torn into shreds. It stank of Shalimar. Besides herself, only Jean had ever worn it. What did it mean to smell it so heavily in Sandra's room?

Rosemary would think about that later. What mattered now was that there was no sign of Sandra.

Rosemary must be missing something. In this mess it would be easy to overlook a fallen body, another body . . . her heart dropped. But no, it was just mess. She backed away, uncertain. Raise an alarm? After Jean . . . Rosemary turned to the room across the hall. The girls were connected. What one knew they all knew.

She tapped on Maisie's door. Nothing. This time Rosemary was not surprised when she opened the door to see no one. Maisie's room wasn't a wreck, but it, too, smelled of Shalimar, though only the ghost of the scent, and maybe only because it was still so strong in Rosemary's nostrils.

Where the hell were they? The bathroom had been quiet. The kitchen, the basement . . . there was the greenhouse. No one could get in the boathouse now.

From the corner of her eye, she caught a flicker of light from the window.

There it was again, the flashlight beam. There, then gone, snapped up by the darkness created by the budding oaks. It had to be them. Rosemary grabbed Maisie's rubber boots by the door. They were too small. She found Sandra's in her room. They fit, though tightly. Rosemary had a key to the back stair, but she didn't need it; the door was unlocked, the lock jammed by a piece of cardboard. Unnoticeable unless you looked closely. This was how they'd been escaping.

She raced down the stairs and out, pulling her robe tighter against the chilly night. The meadow was dark, the willow a big, bunchy shadow, the fireplaces and picnic tables looming in the darkness. Just before the path between the oaks an owl hooted, a rush of wings through the boughs overhead. Rosemary flinched and slowed, trying to be quiet. Though her eyes had accustomed to the dark, she couldn't see much on the path before her.

Then, as she neared the stone stairs, she heard them. Whisperings. A voice—a male voice.

Rosemary halted, surprised and confused, afraid. Who was that? She crept closer, keeping to the foliage of the lakeshore.

Another voice—Maisie, and then the clink of something, glass against rock, a splash, then a murmur and a slew of splashes, a cascade of pebbles thrown into the water.

A few feet closer, now with her heart in her throat, fearing what she might find.

Sandra's voice now: "Hand it over."

"It's almost gone." Maisie.

"Damn. I should have brought two."

"That wouldn't be enough either. Nothing will ever be enough." Maisie's voice cracked on tears.

The male voice, a murmur Rosemary could not make out.

"How can you say that?" Sandra asked, slurring. Something splashed hard into the water.

"Shut up!" Maisie cried. "I can't stand it!"

"I didn't mean it that way." The male voice, louder now, distinct. "You know that's not what I meant."

"What was that?" Sandra asked. The slide of feet on rocks. "Did anyone hear that?"

"Hear what?" Maisie asked.

"There was a sound."

"You're just jumpy."

"Why shouldn't I be?"

"No one's coming. No one cares." Maisie's voice once again caught on a sob. "No one cares but us."

Another murmur.

Sandra said, "No."

"Don't tell me you're changing your mind."

A pause. "She can burn in hell."

There was no doubt in Rosemary's mind of whom Sandra was speaking. When Maisie said, "Wait, I hear it now," Rosemary summoned her courage and took the last few steps to the stone stairs.

Maisie and Sandra huddled together on the fallen log. A flashlight, half hidden against the log, cast a beam of light across the gravelly shore, where, sitting cross-legged, was Samson McCree.

And Rosemary understood it all when she saw them staring up at her, empty eyes in their pale faces in the starlit darkness.

Maisie lurched to her feet, dislodging the flashlight so it rolled and came to a stop against the edge of the stair, casting an eerie light onto the water, out at the Rocks. "What are you doing here?" Her voice was sharp with fear.

Rosemary looked at Samson. "You were the father."

"Don't blame him," Maisie said.

"I'm not blaming anyone," Rosemary said.

"It's your fault! If not for you, it would never have happened."

The calm that came over Rosemary seemed surreal, as if she were watching from the Rocks, witnessing. "Why didn't you tell me?"

Samson rose. He looked terrified.

Maisie's eyes glimmered in the reflected light. Samson looked ready to race into the night. Sandra . . . Sandra . . . watching her so carefully, waiting . . . waiting for what? So promising. So merciless. Young but not young enough. That strange middle land where the world wanted her innocent at the same time it expected her to bear the consequence of every decision she made, no matter how harsh.

"What happened?" Rosemary asked softly.

The girls wouldn't look at her. Samson faced her with a brave and nervous fear that made her feel like a monster. "No one meant for it. No one knew what to do."

"You should have come to me," Rosemary said. "I would have helped you find a way—"

"Shut up!" Sandra nearly screamed the words.

"It wasn't anyone's fault." Sam stumbled over the words in his haste to get them out.

"Go, Sam," Maisie ordered, and then, when he hesitated, she screamed, "Go!"

The boy threw a glance at Rosemary, and then he raced into the darkness, leaving Rosemary alone with the two girls. Rosemary had never felt a silence so painful, so loaded with anger and blame and hostility—no, that wasn't true, she had. She'd just never been on the receiving end of it. She thought of her mother at White Shield Home, that expression Rosemary had seen as cold and patient irritation, which she understood now had been sorrow and pain.

The realization shook her; she had so much more in common with her mother than she'd thought.

"Perhaps you should tell me everything," Rosemary said calmly.

"Perhaps you should go to hell," Maisie said.

"Start with Samson. Was he there last night? I'm right that he's the father of Jean's baby?"

Both girls regarded her sullenly. Then Maisie said, "We don't owe you an explanation." She started up the steps.

Rosemary blocked her. "Sit down. Both of you." To her surprise, they did. "Was Jean alone when she died?"

It was a question calculated to shock them out of whatever story they were planning to tell.

Sandra gasped. "No! How could you think we would do that?"

Maisie turned to her furiously. "My God, Sandy! Why don't you just tell her everything!"

"It would be best if you did." Rosemary worked to keep her voice even. "If you want me to help you."

"You've helped us enough, don't you think?" Maisie said bitterly.

The words fell into the Rocks' eerie whistling. A chill swept Rosemary that had nothing to do with the breezy night.

Sandra said dully, "Jean told us her dad would have kittens if he found out she was pregnant and that he would destroy Samson if he ever found out who he was. Sam had nothing to do with last night. He wasn't there and he didn't know we were going to do it."

Maisie said, "The stairs didn't work. We didn't know the right kind of poison—"

"I told you the stairs and poison were dangerous and the wrong way to do it. I *told* you it needed a doctor or a midwife. I would have helped you. Why didn't you come to me?"

Maisie laughed shortly, her anger erupting. "*Why didn't we?!* What would you have done except tell Mrs. Bullard, and then Jean would disappear into some unwed-mothers home and Samson would be in trouble too. We know how that goes. You're just like all the others. Pretending to care. Pretending we *matter* to you. You didn't help us with anything. Not with Jean's field duty, not with isolation, nothing! You lied to our faces about Mr. Frances and you didn't care about Jean's feelings. You ruined everything."

Rosemary flinched, her own guilt overwhelming. "But to do this . . ."

"You said it happens more than we know. And we thought it would be fine! We thought because we loved her and because she was ours and we did everything we could to keep her safe, but the bleeding wouldn't stop—" Sandra broke on a sob.

Their grief, their guilt, their fear . . . it was in their faces and their voices and it wound about the eroded desolation of the Rocks like a fog, and Rosemary knew then that she would do whatever she could to help them, whatever it cost her. One of them was hers, but that wasn't the only reason. She'd given them the information that led to Jean's death, but that wasn't the reason either. In the end, the reason was simply that she loved them, and she needed them to live the lives they wanted, and not to be punished at seventeen for a decision they'd felt they had no choice but to make.

"I'll take care of this," Rosemary said grimly.

Maisie snorted a laugh. "You sure will, Miss Chivers."

But Rosemary didn't hear.

Chapter 53

She dressed in her best suit, the light brown flannel she'd interviewed in all those months ago, nylons and her favorite slingback heels that Sandra had vomited over on her arrival, but which Rosemary had cleaned—so many uses for her home-ec degree. She put her hair in a French twist, smoked a cigarette, and opened her door—

To see Bobby standing on the other side, raising his hand to knock.

She glanced around, checking for Mrs. Sackett. "Did anyone see you come up?"

"I don't know." He was distracted, flustered, and he looked awful, exhausted, his eyes shadowed. "Can I come in?"

"Are you crazy?"

"I think so. Please, Rosemary. Talk to me."

She had been on her way to Detective Prine, but Rosemary ushered Bobby in quickly and shut the door. "What is it?"

"Did the detective ask you yesterday about me? About me and Jean Karlstad?"

"He asked if I thought there was anything between you. I told him no. That she had a crush on you but so did everyone else. I didn't say anything about the valentine."

He looked at her as if he was trying to decide how to say something and ran his hand nervously through his hair. "A few weeks ago, maybe longer, I was here, working late. I was"—a pause—"not sleeping, thinking about you . . . I didn't want to go home. I decided to walk down to the lake, have a smoke. I heard noise. Laughing, singing. It was pretty obvious some girls had snuck out and were down at the lake. I thought about just letting it be." A short, wry laugh. "I wish now I had."

Rosemary didn't ask who it was. She already knew.

"When I got there, it was only Jean Karlstad. She'd been swimming. Cold as hell, and she was drunk too. She only had on her slip, and she was shivering, and . . . what was I supposed to do?"

"What did you do?" Rosemary asked quietly.

A bleak look. "I gave her my coat. I took her back to the dorm. She was all over me. Hanging on my arm, leaning on me. At one point she fell and I had to pick her up. As I said, she was very drunk. Then, at the door, she . . . kissed me."

Rosemary had never seen him so wretched. "And?"

"And what? Isn't that enough?"

"Did you kiss her back?"

"No. I pushed her away. That was it. I left her there. She said she could get in. But . . ." He rubbed his eyes as if to rub out the memory. "But she's been threatening me with it since. Threatening to go to her father . . . a scandal . . . I've been wanting to tell you, but I was afraid . . ."

"Afraid of what?"

He met her gaze. "Afraid you wouldn't believe me. She was one of your girls."

So many mistakes she'd made.

"I don't know how he knew, but Prine asked me about it."

"That's because she told Maisie and Sandra. They were probably at the lake that night with her, even if you didn't see them. I'm so sorry, Bobby."

Bobby frowned. "You're sorry?"

"This is my fault. You're only involved because I did something stupid. It's me they meant to punish. They wanted to hurt me by destroying someone I care about."

"Do you?" His voice was so soft she barely heard him. "Care about me, I mean?"

The truth at last. "Yes. Yes, very much. You warned me, and I didn't listen. My dad said something about how once two particles are together, they can't really be separated. One reacts to the other, no matter how far apart they are. He had a name for it . . . I don't know how to explain it, but . . . he told me something like this would happen with her. He told me not to get involved. He told me that at the start, but I did exactly what he told me not to do. Everyone told me, but I wanted . . . I wanted . . ."

She felt Bobby waiting, but he didn't ask.

"A long time ago—years ago—I made a terrible mistake." For a moment, she didn't think she'd said the words out loud, then, when she realized she had, she was horrified—or was it relief? It was hard to tell the difference. She finished lamely. "It was . . . it was all because of that."

She realized that none of what she'd said would make sense to him, but he didn't ask for an explanation. Nor did he say, *We've all made terrible mistakes*, or *Maybe you should forgive yourself*, or any of those stupid platitudes, and he had more reason than most. He'd been in the war, after all. She did not want to imagine the things he'd done, the things that gave him nightmares or chest pains, the things that had kept him from marrying the woman he'd dreamed of marrying. And because he did not say those things, because he only looked at her with those vulnerable eyes, she thought, *Maybe. Maybe he won't despise me if I tell him.*

But she didn't tell him then—it wasn't the time, and the habit of silence was still too strong to so simply speak—and he didn't press, and finally she said, "Jean's dead, and I can't ever make this right."

After that, what else was there to say? It was true; neither of them could deny it. Then she was in his arms, her face pressed against his chest, the cigarette smoke and spicy aftershave scent of him.

She held him close. He whispered against her hair, "Don't do it, Rosemary."

"Don't do what?" she murmured.

"Whatever it is you're thinking."

She pulled away slightly and looked up at him. "My mom used to sing this rhyme to me. I used to hate it. 'Rosemary, quite contrary, how does your garden grow?'"

Bobby tilted his head with a puzzled little smile. "Why did she sing that?"

"Because I never did what anyone told me to do, but always just the opposite. It was her way of telling me that I would reap what I sowed, but I was too busy breaking things to listen. I hung around socialists because my parents hated it. I studied home ec when I really wanted to study organic chemistry because my mom wanted me to be a scientist or a mathematician, and I simply . . . refused to make her happy."

"Just like all kids," Bobby said.

"Maybe. Or maybe I just wanted to throw everything up in the air and see where it would land. I don't know, Bobby. I was restless. I hated being a child. I understand these girls, and . . . I'm starting to understand how my mom must have felt when she had to deal with me. So helpless. All you can do is try to save them from themselves, but they'll find a way to turn that against you too if they want." She took a deep breath. "I was on my way to talk to the detective when you got here."

He tightened his arms around her. "No."

"I need to do this, Bobby. Believe me, it will help you too. They suspect you."

"I don't want your help." He lowered his voice, but it didn't lose its urgency. "I don't need your help. If what you mean to do is take the blame for Jean's death, I'm telling you not to do it. You did nothing."

"I did," she told him. "I gave them information. I didn't stick to the curriculum. What happened to Jean—it's my fault, and I mean to tell Prine that." She tried to pull away.

He didn't release her. "That's not what killed her. You weren't there. Were you?"

Rosemary paused. "No."

"You strayed from the curriculum, that's all. That's all you'll tell him, right?"

Rosemary remembered those panicked faces in the darkness by the lake. How afraid they'd been. How much she wanted for them. She pulled away from Bobby and went to the door.

Bobby said, "I'm coming with you."

She gave him a grateful smile.

Police were everywhere. The dormitories were locked down, classes canceled. Parents picked up the girls who'd been released, and the school was emptying quickly. Detective Prine had made Stella's office his headquarters. Just outside, Bobby stopped her.

"Are you sure about this?" he asked.

Rosemary nodded.

Detective Prine was in the anteroom, as was his lieutenant, drinking coffee and laughing with a flirty Irene. They looked up in surprise as Rosemary and Bobby came inside.

"Detective, I've come to turn myself in," Rosemary announced.

The man choked on his coffee.

Bobby exhaled in exasperation. "For God's sake, Rosemary."

Detective Prine recovered quickly. "Just to be clear . . . we're investigating a murder. Is that what you're turning yourself in for?"

"Rosemary," Bobby protested.

"I am," Rosemary said firmly.

The detective looked from her to Bobby, then nodded. "All right, Miss Chivers. We'll need to take you into the station."

The bright overcast sky lightened the room through the window. Through it, Rosemary saw the cars parked in the drive, the narrow front lawn, the neighborhood beyond the school through the budding tree branches shifting in the slight breeze. The radiator clinked. It was warm. Hot, in fact. Rosemary was sweating now through her blouse and suit coat.

Bobby said, "Not without a lawyer."

"Just a few questions first," the detective said. "But if you'd like one . . ."

"Absolutely," Bobby put in.

Detective Prine looked directly at Rosemary, who nodded.

"Lieutenant, if you would . . ." Detective Prine motioned to his fellow officer, who reached for the handcuffs hanging from his belt. Irene, watching silently, gasped.

Bobby threw the man an irritated glance. "Yes, she certainly looks violent."

"I don't think those are necessary, Lieutenant," Detective Prine said testily. Then, to Bobby, "But she has just turned herself in for the death of a young girl."

That silenced them all. Suddenly the nerves Rosemary had managed to contain rushed at her in a battering wave, and it felt like a dream. If not for the bright window, the solid wood floor beneath her feet, Rosemary might have thought it was.

To Bobby, she said, "Would you call my father, please? His number is in my file."

Bobby nodded.

Rosemary said, "All right. I'm ready."

Detective Prine and the lieutenant led her out of Stella's anteroom and to the car out front, which was not marked, thank God. She could not bear the thought of the girls watching her being driven away in a police car. From the back seat, Rosemary numbly watched the passing city. When they reached the station, she was hardly aware that time had passed, that she'd traversed any space. She was frightened; she could admit that now. Without Bobby's steadying presence, she was very frightened. But this was her choice. This would remove suspicion from Bobby. It would save young Samson. Most importantly, it would save Sandra and Maisie.

The detective and the officer ushered her into the building and through a hallway into an empty room that held only a table and some wooden chairs.

"Would you like some coffee, Miss Chivers?" Detective Prine asked. "Or a cigarette?"

He seemed to exist in a haze; she tried to focus. "Coffee, please. Black."

He motioned to someone outside the door, and they waited in silence until a young man in shirtsleeves brought her a stained mug with steaming coffee, which she only stared into.

The detective picked up his pen and bent over his notebook. "Can you tell me where you were the night Miss Karlstad died?"

"I believe I asked for a lawyer."

"Were you with her?"

Sorrow swept her again.

Detective Prine tried again. "Were you with her, Miss Chivers?"

She tapped the edge of the coffee cup. She closed her eyes.

"Just tell me what happened. Who performed the abortion? Was it you?"

Rosemary felt the blood leave her face.

"You knew how to do it, didn't you?"

"A lawyer. Please."

"Who was the father of Miss Karlstad's baby?"

She saw Samson McCree staring at her in the darkness in defiance and fear. Heard again his father's tacit plea. *"He's going to college. He knows better than to mess with these girls." "Jean said her father would destroy Samson . . . He wasn't there."* "I don't know."

"No?"

Rosemary said nothing.

Detective Prine looked at his notebook and cleared his throat. "Sources put Bobby Frances with Miss Karlstad on several occasions. She was often seen coming from his office. There was an incident where someone threw a rock through his car windshield—do you know of this?"

Here it was. One of the reasons she was here. She didn't want or need a lawyer to remove suspicion from Bobby. He was innocent of everything. "He's the vice principal. His office is where students normally meet with him. And yes, I knew about the rock."

"The rumor was that Miss Karlstad threw it in a lovers' quarrel."

"That's not true." Rosemary could not hide her indignation.

The detective's gaze sharpened. "I see. How would you know that, Miss Chivers?"

Rosemary sighed. "I know because I was the one having an affair with Bobby. He wasn't . . . having sex . . . with Jean Karlstad. Believe me, he wasn't interested in anyone else, and he surely didn't have the time. Frankly, he couldn't have had the energy either."

If Prine was shocked, he made no sign. She heard the scribbling in his notebook. "I see. No one at the school seems to know of this affair."

"No. I wanted it kept secret. He obliged."

"He received a Valentine's Day card drenched with perfume. The secretary spoke of it. Everyone thought it was from a student."

Rosemary nodded. "I did that. It was my perfume. Shalimar."

"A strange thing to do if you wanted it kept secret."

"Have you ever had a passionate affair, Detective?"

He squirmed.

Rosemary tried a sly smile. "Let's just say it kept things alive."

"People—including the secretary—assumed it was the Karlstad girl who sent it. I understand she, too, wore—what was it? Shalimar?"

"She stole it from me, and the bottle was confiscated long before that. Trust me, Detective. I sent the card."

"I see. Why did you want this relationship kept secret?"

How complicated things became suddenly. Everything wound together, all her reasons and motivations, everything trailing back to the girls, the girls, her daughter. Again, Rosemary felt the crushing weight of shame. "I thought it would cause problems."

"Problems how?"

"With everything. With the school. The girls. The world." She laughed shortly, trying to deflect. "I'm a single woman, Detective. A teacher. Surely you know what I mean."

"Your reputation," he said.

"You get an A."

"You say you thought the girls would have problems with it. Do you mean the club? Rosemary's Flowers?"

"It wasn't a club."

"Why did you think they would have problems?"

She gave the answer he wanted to hear. "They're impressionable girls. I didn't want them to think worse of me."

"I see. Do you know who threw the rock through his windshield?"

"No. I assumed it was some sort of prank. You know this is a reform school."

"Hmmm." He made a note. "What kinds of things did you talk about in this club?"

She said nothing. This was no longer about Bobby.

"You taught them how to play the guitar, didn't you?"

Of all the things she'd taught them, that seemed the least important. Still, she was surprised he knew, surprised into admitting, "Yes."

"What songs did you teach them?"

She had no idea where he was leading. It seemed best to remain silent, though surely "This Land Is Your Land" seemed harmless enough.

"One of them—Miss Wilson, I believe, says you taught them union songs. That you own several records of communist music. The Weavers. The Almanac Singers."

The reference to Sandra caught her off guard, the revelation that Sandra had told them this.

Detective Prine's eyes narrowed as if he'd found a weakness. "What else did you teach them? Communism? Socialism?"

The urge to defend herself was overwhelming. "No, of course not."

The detective flipped through his notes. "What do you know about the Young People's Socialist League?"

"Are you joking?"

"About 1936? You were associated with a gang of young people—among them David Tapper, who was a leader in the Seattle chapter. Did you know there's a Rosemary Chivers on the membership list? Not you, perhaps? Or perhaps you've conveniently forgotten?"

Until then, she had somehow thought . . . what had she thought? That she would do this and it would end? That it would all be all right somehow? That she would survive it?

"We have informants that put you with the Federal Theatre Project at that time. Does the Seattle Repertory Playhouse sound familiar? The Negro unit?"

Now she was frankly terrified. She remembered her fear that her name might come up at the Canwell hearings six years ago and her relief when it had not. But she should have known. She and David and their compatriots had not bothered to hide anything then; they'd been proud of their views, of their compassion, of their hopes to better the world. She would have been easy enough to uncover if one cared to look, and no doubt Prine and his people had been investigating her since the moment Jean was found.

"Tapper went to Spain, didn't he? Fought for the Republicans. Broke the law to join the Abraham Lincoln brigade?"

The detective was very skilled. It took all Rosemary's will to keep her lips pressed tightly together.

Detective Prine sighed. "Did Mercer Rocks School know of your associations when they hired you? Did they know you lied when you took that loyalty oath?"

"I would like a lawyer, Detective," she insisted.

"Both Miss Wilson and Miss Neal say you taught them about abortions and unsavory sexual practices. You taught them how to get an abortion. You taught them how to prevent pregnancy so they could practice promiscuous sex."

She stared at him silently, challenging. They sat there like that for some minutes. It felt an eternity.

Finally, the detective rose with another heavy sigh. He said, "Abortion is illegal, Miss Chivers."

Somehow Rosemary had thought Maisie and Sandra would keep those secrets. Now, she remembered what she should have from the start, Maisie's answer when Rosemary had said, *"I'll take care of this."* *"You sure will, Miss Chivers."*

Her relationship with those girls was over, she understood finally. Whomever was her daughter, Rosemary had ruined any chance of knowing the girl in that way. She'd told her father at the start that she didn't expect to. Now she knew she'd been hoping otherwise.

Detective Prine said nothing. He went out the door, shutting it behind him. Rosemary heard the thunk of a heavy lock, and footsteps in the hall that paused outside the door. A guard.

The room was windowless. The overhead lights were too bright. Someone had carved a shallow *XO* into the table. The oppressive silence grated on her, but she worked not to show it, nor to show the tangle of her thoughts, David and the past and the present roiling. Bobby saying, *"Don't do it."* She wondered what her father would say when Bobby called, but mostly . . . mostly she thought of Maisie and Sandra and Jean, and how had things gone so very, very wrong?

She had no idea how long she sat there. It seemed forever before the lock thunked again, and the door opened. No Detective Prine this time, but two officers, one of whom said, "Your lawyer is here to see you, Miss Chivers."

She'd gripped the coffee cup so hard and for so long that her hands had fallen asleep, though she hadn't taken a single sip. She shook them to bring back feeling. A man she'd never seen before came in, tall, distinguished and expensive-looking, with a full head of well-manicured gray hair.

"Miss Chivers, I'm Mark Stanley. Your father called me." He sat across the table from her, exhaled heavily, and said, "So tell me, how in the hell did you get mixed up with John Karlstad?"

Rosemary burst into tears.

Chapter 54

The jail in the County-City Building was only a few years old, but it stank of industrial cleaner and sweat and urine. Rosemary spent an uncomfortable night huddled on an uncomfortable cot in a group cell also inhabited by a woman who did not stop muttering, two prostitutes playing cards, and another woman thrashing and moaning in the throes of withdrawal. The clang of metal doors from down the hall and guards barking orders and women shouting back only exacerbated the biting tension of her own fear, not just of the jail, but of her future. Mark Stanley had been matter-of-fact. Rosemary had been charged with manslaughter and attempted abortion. She was facing at least five years in prison for the abortion charge alone. Manslaughter could get her another twenty.

"The information you gave those girls was unsanctioned curriculum," Mr. Stanley said. "You were hardly teaching them to be good American wives and mothers. They will testify against you."

She thought she'd reconciled herself to this, but her disappointment said she hadn't managed to banish the hope that she might be wrong. "Are you sure?"

The lawyer shrugged. "They've been interviewed by the police. I haven't seen the discovery yet, but I understand they were very cooperative. Unless you can cast doubt on their veracity . . ."

He waited. She knew what he was waiting for. The truth as she knew it. The story of what really happened.

Rosemary thought of Maisie's challenge and the way she'd clutched Jean's pillow close. She thought of Sandra's anger and bitterness. The two of them at the Rocks and their grief and the way they'd looked for someone to blame.

"The gardener—what's his name—ah, here it is, McCree—confirms you were meeting with Miss Karlstad and the other girls in the greenhouse, which of course corresponds to the girls' stories that you insisted upon teaching them rather unsavory things—abortion and birth control and such."

Finally Mr. Stanley had folded up his papers. "We'll talk more when we see exactly what they have. There will be a bail hearing tomorrow. I'm assuming they'll let you out unless Karlstad pulls some strings, which is not unlikely. Don't worry, Miss Chivers. There is still some decency in the world. It will depend on the judge. I'm not sure who's on the calendar in the morning. If you pray, I'd do so."

The night was long and loud and very dark.

~

They came for her the next day. Police officers led her to the courtroom. Mr. Stanley was already there, as were her father and a few reporters who began scribbling eagerly in their notebooks when she appeared. She didn't know whether to be relieved or discouraged to see no one from the school. Not Stella Bullard or Lois. Not the girls, but she hadn't expected them.

Not Bobby.

She didn't know how to feel about that, or what it meant, but Rosemary was reassured by her father's smile and her lawyer's whisper that Karlstad wasn't there. "Thank your lucky stars for that."

Rosemary sweated as the charges rang in her ears, seeming to refer to someone else, each one both hers and not hers, and when Mr. Stanley rose to speak, his words were only a buzz in her ears; she had to ask him later what he'd said, what anyone had said, the arguing back and forth, and then it was over, and Mr. Stanley was leaning down with a smile to say, "You'll be out by this afternoon," and she could only stare blankly and say, "What?"

"As soon as your father arranges it," he said. "Five thousand. I was expecting ten. Didn't you hear him?"

Rosemary shook her head.

"For now, stay away from schools and places where young people congregate," he said. "You're not to go within five hundred yards of Mercer Rocks. Otherwise you'll be back in a jail cell. I'll go over the terms with you later."

Rosemary nodded, but those words, too, flowed over and around her without landing.

~

Dad picked her up later that afternoon from the jail. He drove as if it were any other day, and Rosemary had just opened her mouth to say, *Dad, I'm so sorry,* when he said, "Is it true, Rosie? Did you do what they're saying?"

It was a complicated answer. "I did enough."

"The abortion—"

"Dad, please. I cared very much for her, and I'm"—she choked on the word—"devastated."

A long silence. The news rattled on the radio. He turned it off, which was a relief. Then he said, "I wish you'd talked to me."

"I did. I tried."

"You're lucky you haven't put McCarthy himself on your heels, though Karlstad is bad enough."

"I was just trying to get to know them."

"By teaching them stuff like that?" He sounded appalled.

"I wish someone had taught it to me," she snapped back. "I wish I'd known any of it."

Dad sighed. "Oh, Rosie . . ."

"They wanted to know and one of them is my daughter and I thought it would help me find out which one. It was all I could think to do, Dad. I couldn't find anything in what Mom left behind, and I went through *everything*."

"Not everything. There were still a few boxes. Those sewing patterns, and the textbooks. I put them in your room."

Rosemary frowned. "I did go through the sewing patterns, and the textbooks are yours."

He shook his head. "No. They were your mom's."

"But they're all science and math books."

"Your mom was studying on her own whenever she could. They were hers."

Rosemary stared at him. It should not have been so surprising. After all, Mom had always said she'd wanted Rosemary to have the opportunities she'd never had, and there were all those conversations between Mom and Dad, full of scientific words, but Rosemary still found it a shock. She'd been so blind about so many things when it came to her mother. "I didn't know that."

"She liked learning." Dad smiled wistfully. "She was quite a woman, your mother, and she had a fine mind. You know, you take after her in so many ways."

For the first time in Rosemary's life, it didn't seem an insult.

~

When they got home, she went to her bedroom, where Dad had put the boxes. She ignored the sewing patterns and knelt next to the old textbooks. *Atomic Spectra and Atomic Structure, An Introductory Course in College Physics, General Biology* . . . Another piece to the puzzle of her mother that fell into place, that explained the ceaseless gazing into the void of the backyard—not resentment as Rosemary had thought, or not *only* resentment, but depression also, and yearning. Did things like that pass through the blood? Was that Rosemary's real inheritance from her mother, and was it something Rosemary had passed to her daughter too? *"Do you ever feel like the world is too small for you? Like everyone wants to put you in such a little box and you just can't breathe there?"*

Her mother had understood her better than she'd known. Rosemary drew her finger across the spines, stopping when she reached *Experiments in Organic Chemistry*. Gooseflesh prickled her skin. Instinctively Rosemary reached for the book, pulling it from the box. The cover was loose; it waggled at her touch, and when she opened it, a faded brown envelope with a string closure fell onto her lap.

And she knew. She just knew, without knowing how she knew or why she knew it, that this was what she'd been looking for.

It was too late, she told herself. Whatever was in this envelope, it was too late for it. Just as seeing Jean's face in John Karlstad's told Rosemary that he was Jean's father was too late. Both Maisie and Sandra hated her. They had borne witness against her, they would testify.

In the end, did Rosemary even really want to know which of the girls was hers? She didn't think she could face watching her daughter speak against her at trial. Better to be ignorant still, to instead hold close those moments when she belonged to them. Maybe that could be enough.

She stared at the envelope. Yes, for now it could. The day had been long, and she wanted to sink onto her bed and sleep and not think about anything. Not the wretched night or the stressful day, not the future trial or whatever else might lie ahead. Not the girls and their complications and pain that she'd made worse.

But when she rose to shove the envelope into her dresser drawer, she instead found herself pausing, taking hold of the string closure, uncoiling it. When it hung loose, she paused again, one last chance to stop, to put it away, to not look. Then again, maybe there was nothing to see here. Nothing to know.

Yet her pulse raced; she felt that *knowing*, an answer waiting here for her to find, and she opened the envelope and pulled out a small stack of pictures.

Her premonition strengthened and coiled more tightly. There were about a dozen black-and-white photographs, some bent and discolored, some square and some tiny, some on thick paper and some glossy and some with pinked edges. Some fell upside down; there was writing on the back—her mother's handwriting, faded ink. *Uncle Don, Grandpa and Grandma Bettis, Cousin Paul 1919.*

Rosemary leafed through them. *Me and Uncle Don, 1906.* Mom as a girl, in a pinafore, smiling next to a rustic farm fence with a tall man in cuffed trousers leaning over her with a pail in his hand. Another picture of Mom and a disembodied arm clutching her shoulder, the other half torn away. On the back:

The name scratched through. She remembered Aunt Pat saying something about Mom's mother remarrying and wondered if this arm belonged to him.

Rosemary turned over another photograph. Another little girl in pigtails with a face like her mother's. *Sister Pansy 1910–1918 died of Flu.* 1918. Mom had come to Seattle late that year, according to Dad. Because of this? A new stepfather, a dead sister with the name of a flower. Mom had given her daughter a flower name too. *Rosemary.*

The story began to coalesce. Slowly Rosemary turned over the next. Uncle Don again, and another photo of the Bettis grandparents, and then an old card, not a photo but a daguerreotype—

Rosemary stopped.

It was a picture of Sandra. But then . . . no, of course it wasn't. It was sepia, and the girl wore a nineteenth-century gown, and she was not smiling. The forehead was too wide, the jaw more square, something different about the nose, but . . . in all other ways, it was Sandra. An adolescent girl with wispy curling hair that Rosemary recognized even though it wasn't loose but escaping from a chignon, and those big eyes—blue, maybe?—stared into the camera, challenging, a dare, *Look at me.*

That look. Rosemary knew that look.

Her heart pounded. She turned over the photo. On the back was written *Grandmother Elizabeth Erickson 1857.* Rosemary's great-grandmother.

Sandra.

Sandra was her daughter.

With Rosemary's exhilaration came grief because whom could she tell? What did it matter? Sandra would testify against her. Sandra did not know she was adopted and did not want to know it. Sandra might not have erased that *F*, but maybe it was only as she'd said, that she hated burns. Sandra wanted nothing to do with Rosemary, and why should she? Rosemary had already upended the girl's life. The only thing left was to make sure it was not upended more.

It was over. She'd had all she would ever have. It was more than she deserved.

Chapter 55

Rosemary's nights were tormented by dreams of Jean's ghost and Sandra's white face demanding justice and Maisie's sly smile. Rosemary heard the watery slurp and whistle of the Rocks, not just in her dreams but in her waking hours, sneaking up on her in the gurgling of coffee percolating or the hissing shower or the whine of Dad's drill when he worked in the garage. She was on edge and jumpy and she did not recognize her own wan face in the mirror.

Two days after she arrived home came the delivery of a dozen red roses in a vase, with a card—*I miss you. Bobby.* That was all. She hadn't heard from him since.

"From your vice principal?" Dad had asked.

"It's just a thank-you."

"Red roses? No, maybe yellow roses for that."

"You're an expert on flowers now?"

"What's the thank-you for?"

"For telling the police something they didn't want to hear."

Her father had frowned. "What was that?"

"That we were dating. They wanted to believe something unsavory was between him and Jean, and I told them the truth. She had a crush on him, but he had a crush on me."

"Looks to me like he still does."

"I think it's over, Dad. He's gone through hell because of me."

Dad said, "You never know."

She'd put the flowers on the kitchen table, but she tucked away the card in the drawer in the nightstand. She meant to call Bobby to thank him, to ask how everything was, and what he would do now that the school was closed, but Mark Stanley told her not to.

"He may be testifying against you, Rosemary. It wouldn't look good."

That shocked her. "Testifying against me? Why?"

"He can't put you with him the night of Miss Karlstad's death, and if they question him, he'll have no choice but to say that he found your relationship with them concerning and that he warned you to keep your distance. I would not call him as a defense witness, even if he's on your side."

It was all closing in. Everything she cared about gone once more. Everything falling away. No one to blame but herself. She remembered how Bobby had looked that day when Jean had fallen down the stairs and reached out for him. *"Bobby."* That stricken expression. How he'd so quickly obeyed her gesture to stay where he was. He'd known then how much trouble he was in—her fault—and Rosemary wondered if maybe the roses were a goodbye.

The school had shipped her things to the house, but not before the police had gone through them, noting each record in her collection— they'd tagged certain ones as if they'd wanted her to know they found them of special interest. The Almanac Singers and the Weavers and every 45 or album that might have had any connection to unions or social protest, and suddenly she was remembering trying to teach Jean how to play the guitar, singing "This Land Is Your Land" in the green- house and the smell of the dirt and compost and the rain so loud against the glass. It had been the day Rosemary had given them her mother's pins because Jean had a trust fund and yearned for her mother's pearls, and Rosemary had wanted to imprint herself on Jean too and now could not forget the way Jean had pressed her hand to her heart, *"I'll think of you every time I look at it, and all the things you've taught me."*

All the things she'd taught them. Rosemary wondered what she would have done had Jean come to her and asked her for help. A girl not her daughter, but maybe her daughter, because she hadn't known then. Would she have done what Maisie and Sandra had said she would do? Tell Stella, inform Jean's father, let them send her to someplace like White Shield?

Or would Rosemary have given the girl money and helped her find a doctor to perform the illegal abortion she wanted?

It was a deeply troubling thought. Either choice troubling. Neither of them hers to make.

That was the mistake, believing otherwise.

~

Whether it was a nightmare or a premonition, Rosemary couldn't say. She woke in the middle of the night sweating and feverish, her hair clinging to the back of her neck, the taste of fear in her mouth. She went to the window and stared at the cold moon illuminating the backyard so it looked alien and barren and thought inexplicably of Sandra and her dream of a nuclear blast and racing to shelter only to find her skin peeling away, everything too late, already gone, already done, and the ache in Rosemary's chest was too deep to breathe. She smoked a cigarette and went back to bed.

The phone rang early the next morning. Her father's spoon clanked loudly as he stirred boiling water into his Maxwell House, and Rosemary pushed down the lever on the toaster with too much force. Lately the telephone only brought bad news. Witnesses offering more and more examples of Rosemary's errant behavior, deep dives into her past by both police and news reporters, Mercer Rocks closing possibly for good and the press attributing it to the hiring of socialist teachers . . .

It did not stop ringing, and Rosemary went to answer it. It was, as she feared, Mark Stanley.

"There's been a development," he said the moment she answered. "I need you and your father in my office immediately."

"Am I going back to jail?" she asked.

A pause. "Not exactly. It's the strangest thing, but it looks like the state is dropping charges against you."

Rosemary stilled. "I'm sorry, it sounded like you said they're dropping charges."

"Apparently the most important witness has said her testimony was a lie. One of the girls."

Rosemary's heart beat wildly in her ears. "Which one?"

"Miss Wilson. Sandra Wilson. Do you know why she might have done that?"

"No." Rosemary could not force her voice above a whisper. "I have no idea."

~

"The prosecutor is not happy," Mark Stanley said from behind the expanse of his polished walnut desk. "But there's not much he can do if she says both she and Maisie Neal lied. Miss Wilson won't testify against you, and Miss Neal's parents have now refused to make her available. The girls are their main witnesses. They'll both be lucky if they're not charged with making false accusations, though somehow I think their parents will end up smoothing things over. The prosecutor seemed resigned when he saw their last names, which tells me they won't be pursuing it."

Rich and consequential families.

"What did Miss Wilson say?" Rosemary asked.

Stanley consulted his notes. "That they were angry with you because you refused to help them evade punishment and because Miss Karlstad was jealous that you were dating Mr. Frances, and so they made up this story about you. They knew nothing about Miss Karlstad's abortion. She went off on her own."

Rosemary thought of that night at the Rocks. Their horror and grief and fear. That night was the truth, she knew. Sandra's *"No! How can you think that!"* to Rosemary's question about whether Jean had been alone. Her agonized description of the bleeding they could not stop.

Sandra had lied. Why? To help Rosemary? To save her?

She hesitated to think it. She hesitated to think Sandra felt anything for her at all.

But there had been that strangeness that woke Rosemary the previous night. What had that been? Dad would say entanglement. Maybe it was.

Maybe.

Mark Stanley cleared his throat. "All they have is your confession, but as I pointed out to them, you didn't really confess to anything except teaching the girls what you thought they should know. That's not a crime, despite what McCarthy and his ilk might want to say about it. They have no physical evidence that you were at the scene."

Dad said, "That all seems good news, so why don't you look happy?"

The lawyer exhaled. "Although the state declines to press charges, John Karlstad is very upset. In fact, he's threatening a civil suit."

"For what?" Rosemary demanded.

"Wrongful death."

Rosemary's father made a sound of disgust.

"It's not as if he doesn't have grounds for it," Stanley said. "He's claiming that in teaching against the board's curriculum, you gave the girls information that led to Jean's death, and there's plenty of evidence for that, and plenty of witnesses. The gardener, the other teachers, the warnings you received from the principal—all in your disciplinary record."

Rosemary glanced at her father, who sighed.

Mr. Stanley tapped his fingers on the desk. "Karlstad also wants you examined by the House Un-American Activities Committee when they return to Seattle for hearings next month."

"I'm not a communist."

"You're an agitator, though, wouldn't you say?"

"I'm a high school teacher!"

"That's how the Reds get in," Dad reminded her. "Teachers indoctrinating students."

Rosemary glared at her father. "Dad, you know very well I'm not a communist."

"Yes, I do," he said firmly. "But that's what everyone said about the professors at the university when the Canwell Committee was Redhunting in Seattle six years ago, and it's no better now, is it? Back then they investigated all of us. Me included."

"You?" Another surprise. He'd never once mentioned it, and Dad was so anticommunist Rosemary had never suspected he'd been under investigation then. She wondered if her past had something to do with that too. How much trouble had she inadvertently put him through? It was something for them to talk about—sometime, but not now.

Stanley glanced between them and then said to her, "The committee is nothing to dismiss, Miss Chivers, and Karlstad is on it. If he wants you interviewed, you'll be interviewed. I can't say we'd win a wrongful death lawsuit, though I'll be honest, even if we did, given your socialist past and the things you taught these girls . . . well, it would be devastating for you."

The office was freezing, though the sun shone brightly through the window.

"What are you saying?" Dad asked quietly. "Is there a way to settle this?"

Stanley paused. "Apparently there was someone close to the board who convinced Karlstad not to drag the school through the mud with you. He's agreed to a compromise. I'm not sure you'll like it, but in the spirit of a good compromise, no one leaves happy."

He tapped a slim sheaf of papers that Rosemary noted on his desk for the first time. "It all goes away if you sign this."

"What is that?" Rosemary asked warily.

"A contract stating that you'll give up teaching, and not take any job that allows you regular influence over young women. Your name will be added to a federal list of communist sympathizers and remanded to the FBI. This will of course guarantee your compliance."

Rosemary said quietly, "If my name's on that list, I won't even be able to get a job at a drive-in."

"That's the idea."

"And if I don't sign?"

Stanley said, "One thing you might consider as well: if Karlstad moves forward with his suit, he will drag the school with him, as the board fears. We'll have no choice but to bring in girls to testify on your behalf. Perhaps Miss Wilson, who did you the favor of changing her testimony. In case that matters to you."

Sandra.

"You're very lucky to get this offer. You're lucky to be a woman, Rosemary. It's not as if you need to work. I understand you have a"— Stanley glanced at her father and then cleared his throat—"Well. You're an attractive woman. You'll be married one day. You'll have children. You'll put this all behind you and go on to have a happy and fulfilling life as a wife and mother."

That tight little box, shrinking around her. Rosemary could fight, yes . . . but she would lose in one way or another. The only other option was to tell the truth, but that was no option. That was the most impossible thing of all. Sometimes there was no choice.

She'd wanted to save her daughter. In return, Sandra had saved her. She could not now turn around and destroy Sandra's life or Maisie's or Samson's. They were so young. So much ahead of them, and who was to say the truth would change anything? It was her responsibility, and the truth was complicated and nothing good could come of telling it.

"Okay." She could hardly hear her own voice. "I'll sign."

"Good." The lawyer pushed the papers over to her, along with a pen.

"It's for the best, Rosie," Dad said.

Again, papers to sign. Again, a surrender. Again, the words bouncing in her head. *You can have the life you're meant to have and you'll never have to talk about any of this again . . ."*

The only difference was that this time, it was her decision.

Chapter 56

"Rosie!" Dad called from the patio door. "You've got a visitor."

Rosemary glanced up from pouring birdseed into the feeder. Her father was grinning; she understood why the moment she saw the figure behind him and Bobby stepped onto the patio. He was dressed casually, an open-necked shirt that revealed his throat, and he wore relief like a new suit—he radiated, though his smile was hesitant when he approached her. The day was warm for early May; Rosemary had not expected visitors, and in her dungarees and short-sleeved blouse had not dressed for one, but she was strangely not surprised to see Bobby.

"Hello," she said.

Dad withdrew into the kitchen, closing the door to allow them privacy—or at least what privacy could be accorded in a backyard in a neighborhood like Wallingford. From the near distance came the sound of children playing, the steady bang, bang, bang of someone building something, the hum of a lawnmower. All so residential, all so normal. All so American.

Bobby said, "I didn't know if you'd want to see me."

"I know you couldn't call. And they warned me not to talk to you. But I got the flowers. They were beautiful. Thank you."

There was that quiet expression, so vulnerable, waiting.

"You're the one who convinced John Karlstad not to sue me."

"I did what I could."

"You know him better than you said."

"Not really. But he cares about appearances, and he likes being seen with a war hero."

"Now *that* you never told me."

Bobby made a disparaging face. "There's nothing heroic about it. I was running for my life and trying to keep Ron on his feet long enough to get back to our unit."

"Ron? The guy with the feral dog?"

He nodded grimly. "Before the dog."

"Ah." She felt vulnerable herself now. "I can't imagine it's a good idea for a war hero to be seen with a known communist."

He glanced about, then said in a low voice, "You told me you liked protest songs. You said you used to hang out with socialists, not that you'd *been* one. I couldn't do much to change Karlstad's mind when he learned that. It was the only deal he would make."

"I guess neither of us told the whole truth, did we?" She attempted a smile. "I lived with them for a while. One of them was . . . I loved him. The things you do as a kid never leave you, I guess." It was truer than he could possibly know. "Go ahead, you can run away. I won't be offended."

"I don't think I will."

"Seriously, Bobby, this isn't a joke. An association with me will hurt you."

"I think I might be in this for the long haul."

"Bobby, you don't know anything about me—"

"I know enough." His voice was firm, that brown gaze dark and intense. "You don't have to save everyone, Rosemary, and I don't need saving from you. I'm old enough to decide the risks I want to take."

She thought she'd been prepared for him to walk away. She was startled at how glad she was when he didn't. She stared down at the bag of birdseed: millet, sunflower seeds, cracked corn . . . listing every seed in her head. She looked up to find him watching her carefully.

"What now? What will you do?" he asked.

"I don't know. Short of running away to join a circus—do you think circuses check the FBI list of known communists?"

He chuckled. "I'm sure there must be easier things than the trapeze. You said you always liked organic chemistry. I don't know, maybe there's something in that."

How odd, how unexpected, to find that little box creaking open. Impulsively, she said, "Go for a ride with me?"

He looked surprised, but he said, "Sure. Where are we going?"

"You'll see." She led him back into the house. "Dad, I need your car."

"Mine's just out front," Bobby offered.

She shook her head. "Not for this."

Her father motioned to the counter. "Keys are right there."

"We won't be gone long." She threw the keys to Bobby. "You can drive."

As they got into the Buick, she gave him the address. "It's in Laurelhurst."

One of the wealthiest neighborhoods in Seattle.

"Oh-kaay." He started the car. "This is strange."

"No stranger than anything else about me, I imagine."

He laughed softly. "I guess that's true."

As he drove, Rosemary's heart was in her throat. "Have you heard anything? About . . ." She wasn't sure she could have said more had she tried.

He understood. "Maisie Neal's parents have taken her to Paris for a long-overdue reunion. I talked to Sandra's mom and dad. She's doing better, but they're considering taking her away for a while too. They're good people. Concerned. They want to do what's best for her."

It was a relief to hear. Sandra wasn't unhappy, just dissatisfied. Rosemary's daughter indeed.

A long silence. Then Bobby said, "That night . . ."

"I didn't know Jean was pregnant, and I didn't know what she meant to do."

He took a deep breath. "Okay."

"That's all?" she asked in surprise.

"I've decided it doesn't matter. It's over. If there's more you want to tell me, I'll listen. If you need me to. If you don't, that's fine too."

It was a measure of kindness and faith Rosemary had never thought to want.

The address was not far away, and traffic was light. The radio was on, news droning, and Rosemary reached over to change the dial to KJR. She turned it down low, and she and Bobby fell into a comfortable silence, but with every block closer, Rosemary's nerves ratcheted.

Finally, Bobby said, "Here we are," and parked the car. He leaned to peer through her window at the house across the street—on Lake Washington, of course. A large brick Tudor with leaded windows and manicured gardens and a rock-wall border. Pink, yellow, and apricot roses bloomed all along the drive. Ivy climbed one wall. Rosemary could never have given her daughter a home like this, nothing like this. Golden light shone from the windows into the growing evening. It looked peaceful. One never knew what went on in other people's houses, of course, and obviously it was no perfect home, but . . . good people.

Bobby asked, "Whose house is this? Why are we here?"

The words lodged hard—they did not even make it to Rosemary's throat, but sat in her chest, unyielding. She could not say them, the habit of silence was too hard. Then, the shadow of someone in an upstairs window, and Rosemary tensed, unbearable to hope so much, to want so much. The shadow crossed the room, suddenly there was music, the radio turned on, "Cherry Pink and Apple Blossom White," matching the song playing in the car. KJR, of course. The trumpet blasted into the evening. The shadow resolved itself in the light—a girl—so familiar, began to dance.

Rosemary opened her purse and took out the daguerreotype. Wordlessly she handed it to Bobby.

He glanced at it, brow furrowing. "Why do you have a picture of Sandra Wilson—wait—this isn't Sandra."

"It's my great-grandmother." Rosemary could not raise her voice above a whisper.

Bobby met her gaze. "So . . . Sandra's related to you?"

"She's my—" She couldn't say it. She tried again. "When I was seventeen, I—"

Bobby waited. She saw when it dawned on him, when he knew.

"She's your daughter," he said.

His words released the impossible binding in her chest; Rosemary gasped—she'd been holding her breath, it burst now, shattering. She could only nod.

Bobby said, "This is the obligation you had to resolve."

Again, she nodded.

"Does she know it?" he asked.

"No," she managed. "And she won't. Unless one day she wants to."

He looked down again at the picture, then up to the window, Sandra spinning, throwing out her arms, dancing as if her motions could not be contained. He said, "She'll forgive you eventually."

"Maybe. But I'm not hoping for that. She's got too much of me in her. I don't need her to forgive me. I just need her to . . . to live her life the way she wants. To be what she wants. As long as I know she's doing that, I'll be fine."

"How will you know? You don't mean to . . ."

"No. I'll leave her alone now that I know her. And . . . I'll just know." As Dad had said. Once connected, always connected. Something else she had in common with her mother. She would just know.

The song changed. "Rock around the Clock" now. Sandra's hips jerked, shoulders shaking, hair flipping.

"Her father used to dance like that. Full out, like he couldn't contain himself." Rosemary should have seen it from the beginning. Sandra unable to keep still. Always listening to music, always swaying, feet tapping. David in her every motion.

"The socialist boyfriend? Do you want to talk about him?"

"Not today." Rosemary's smile was wistful. "But someday, yes."

Bobby smiled back.

She took his hand, weaving her fingers through his. "Do you mind if we just stay here for a bit? Just a few minutes?"

"As long as you want," he told her.

And so Rosemary sat and watched Sandra dance.

AUTHOR'S NOTE

Seattle, Washington, in the 1950s, according to many sources, was a big city with a provincial feel. As a port town, with large army and navy bases close by, a shipbuilding industry, and of course, Boeing, Seattle was still a very industrial city, and earlier in the century had a reputation for radicalism. Given that Washington State held many potential targets for the Soviets during the Cold War—not just Boeing and the military bases and shipyards, but also Grand Coulee Dam and Hanford Engineer Works (part of the Manhattan Project)—it was also thought to harbor a great many communist spies and fronts.

At the time of this novel, while resistance toward McCarthyism and Red-baiting was growing, the House Un-American Activities Committee (HUAC) was still actively holding hearings in Seattle, and witnesses were busy naming hundreds of people as members of the Communist Party. While few lost their jobs thanks to these hearings, many found themselves shunned by their friends and colleagues, and the communist watch list kept by the FBI was a fact and a weapon.

The Canwell Committee in Washington State predates both McCarthy in the Senate and HUAC by a few years. In 1947, the Washington State Legislature created its own un-American activities committee (the Joint Legislative Fact-Finding Committee on Un-American Activities) and made Republican Albert Canwell its head. The University of Washington, the Washington Pension Union, and the Seattle Repertory Playhouse (where David Tapper works when Rosemary meets him) were some of the groups and organizations the Canwell Committee investigated. Among the victims were six University of Washington professors. Of those, three lost their jobs and never taught again. The Seattle Repertory Playhouse was forced out of business.

The Federal Theatre Project began in 1935 under the auspices of the Works Progress Administration as a way to reemploy those who worked in theater during the Great Depression. It produced plays, sponsored contests for playwrights, began a children's theater, founded variety companies that toured the Civilian Conservation Corps camps, and produced public-service "living newspapers." The Negro unit was the most successful of the Seattle units. Florence and Burton James, who founded the Negro Repertory Company in 1936 and who ran the Seattle Repertory Playhouse (thought to be a Communist front) were notably progressively liberal and suspected of holding subversive views. Their experience with the Canwell Committee in 1948 effectively destroyed them. The Federal Theatre Project fell to the political anti–New Deal battle-ax in Congress after only four years.

In 1948, Alfred Kinsey published *Sexual Behavior in the Human Male*. At 804 pages, the book was huge, and expensive at more than six dollars a copy. Still it was a bestseller, and a revelation for most Americans. It was generally referred to as "The Kinsey Report." *Sexual Behavior in the Human Female*, published in 1953, was perhaps even more of a shock to the average American.

The use of "practice babies" in home-economics classes is real. While I don't know if Central Washington College of Education (now Central Washington University) employed this practice, it was the perfect plot point, and I added baby Mary to the very real A Child in the Home class at Central. Beyond that little fiction, the details of the practice baby are as true as I could make them given my research.

Mercer Rocks School for Wayward Girls is based on a real school and a real location. Martha Washington School for Girls was a juvenile girls' residential school where delinquents who were wards of King County were held under court order. It was run by various entities, including the Washington school system, until it was sold to the city of Seattle in 1972. The following year it was transferred to the parks department, and the location became a favorite hangout for vandals until the buildings were destroyed in 1989. The site on south Lake Washington became a small park. The willow tree is still there, and the only grove of Garry oak trees in Seattle is also there. The park was indeed known by Indigenous people as Taboo Container, and it is said to be haunted and is listed as one of Seattle's "liminal spaces." It's a beautiful location, though the Mercer Rocks themselves are a figment of my imagination.

The theory of entanglement is of course integral to quantum physics. It was also the inspiration for this book—in a way. Just before the pandemic, I read an article in an older (2015) issue of *Science News* about new research that showed that women carried genetic material in their bodies, not just from their parents but from their children—even children that they didn't carry to full term. During pregnancy, cells slip back and forth between mother and child in a process called fetal-maternal microchimerism, and some of these cells remain in the mother even after the child is gone. They've found this DNA in women's brains decades later. What this means is that mothers are chimeras—they hold in their bodies bits of their mothers and their children. Walt Whitman was on track when he said, "I contain multitudes."

While scientists have not yet determined exactly why this is so, or what the purpose may be, my own brain leaped to the fact that in my family, my mother and sisters and I, as well as my daughters, share a weird feyness—I can think of my mom and the next thing I know she's calling me. Or I'll have a dream about my sister and something significant has happened to her. If we all have cells from each other in our bodies, doesn't it make sense that we are "entangled"? The idea would not leave me alone, and I began thinking of adoption, and women who are separated from their children, and from there, the idea for *A Dangerous Education* came slowly and painfully into shape.

Finally . . . a few small things. While many think of "Fleet Week" as having come into being in Seattle with the first Seafair celebration in the 1950s, it was indeed an event in the 1930s, as evidenced by many articles, photographs, and headlines in the *Seattle Daily Times* of that period.

Details in the timing of real events may have been changed to better serve the plot, such as the citywide evacuation drill that took place on May 20, 1955. I've moved the date to slightly earlier in the spring to coincide with Jean's circumstances in my novel.

Research is of course a necessary part of every historical novel, and this one is no exception. While I explore and fact-check the times and places of the story as diligently and thoroughly as I can, some things are bound to escape my attention. Any errors are my own.

ACKNOWLEDGMENTS

Writing any book is both a labor of love and a true physical and mental labor, and *A Dangerous Education* was no different. Settling on the right story to tell when my baseline idea was "Spooky action at a distance, DNA, and Seattle in the 1950s—and maybe a girls' school?" was no easy thing, and I owe my agent, Danielle Egan-Miller, and her associates Ellie Roth Imbody and Mariana Fisher—and Scott Miller too!— at Browne & Miller huge thanks for their brainstorming ability and patience as they persevered through many, many synopses and Zoom calls, as well as my thanks for shepherding this book through editorial and sales and production and everything else.

As always, thanks must go to my critique partner lo these many years, Kristin Hannah, for everything, and to my husband, Kany Levine, who truly went above and beyond the call of duty on this one. I'm afraid to tell him that he's bought himself a permanent position in my pantheon of first-draft readers now—he kept me sane and reassured me more times than I can say. A shout-out to Donna Smith, who both gave me the idea for the boathouse scene and talked me through many panicked moments. The best thing we ever did was reconnect, Donna.

Thank you to my editors: Heather Lazare, who once again proved herself invaluable—truly she has a gift for understanding what I'm trying to do and helping me get there, and her ideas make the book better at the same time. I always feel such relief and gratitude when the book is in her hands. Jodi Warshaw, who has been a wonderful champion as well as a smart and honest one. I have treasured her insight and ideas, and I'm going to miss her. Thanks also must go to Danielle Marshall and Chris Werner, who took on *A Dangerous Education* and have put it through its paces. I am so very grateful for your efforts and your enthusiasm.

To Jen Bentham, the best production manager around, to the copy-editors, cover and interior designers, proofreaders, marketing and sales department, and everyone else at Lake Union Publishing who have been involved in getting this book out into the world, thank you. I'm always so impressed with the detail and effort you put into your jobs, and I could not be more pleased with the work you've done on this book.

To my daughters, Maggie and Cleo, to Kany, and to my family, who have listened to me moan about this book for months and months, thanks for putting up with me, and for your advice and unconditional love, and to my friends, who have dealt with my moments of uncertainty, depression, and annoying and often unjustified confidence . . . well, I don't envy any of you. But thank you just the same. You know I love you.

ABOUT THE AUTHOR

Photo © 2012 C. M. C. Levine

Megan Chance is the critically acclaimed, award-winning author of more than twenty novels, including *A Splendid Ruin*, *Bone River*, and *An Inconvenient Wife*. She and her husband live in the Pacific Northwest, with their two grown daughters nearby. For more information, visit www.meganchance.com.